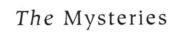

The Mysteries

The
Mysteries

ROBERT McGILL

M&S

National Library of Canada Cataloguing in Publication

McGill, Robert, 1976–
The mysteries / Robert McGill.

ISBN 0-7710-5521-8

I. Title.

PS8625.G54M98 2004   C813'.6   C2004-902795-6

We acknowledge the financial support of the Government of Canada
through the Book Publishing Industry Development Program and that
of the Government of Ontario through the Ontario Media
Development Corporation's Ontario Book Initiative. We further
acknowledge the support of the Canada Council for the Arts and the
Ontario Arts Council for our publishing program.

Typeset in Sabon by M&S, Toronto
Printed and bound in Canada

This book is printed on acid-free paper that is
100% ancient forest friendly (100% post-consumer recycled).

McClelland & Stewart Ltd.
The Canadian Publishers
481 University Avenue
Toronto, Ontario
M5G 2E9
www.mcclelland.com

1 2 3 4 5   08 07 06 05 04

For S. S.

"Here are the voices presently shall sound
In due succession. First, the world's outcry
Around the rush and ripple of any fact
Fallen stonewise, plumb on the smooth face of things;
The world's guess, as it crowds the bank o' the pool,
At what were figure and substance, by their splash:
Then, by vibrations in the general mind,
At depth of deed already out of reach."

– Robert Browning, *The Ring and the Book*

"What? it feels nervous and strange to be coming here
again after all these years?"

– Stephen Leacock, *Sunshine Sketches of a Little Town*

CONTENTS

✦ *You call me Robert. It gives our relationship a formality I dislike – I who want to be known by you intimately, without borders. Can two people ever understand each other that well? You'd be the one to know, with the time you spend in courtrooms, prying for truth. You've heard the revelations that come in taxis and prison cells after the verdict has been given, the stories a judge and jury never hear. There are things I could tell you myself as we drive this road together, but we have an agreement. No more confessions. Lately I've been admitting all my faults to you, and you're sick of hearing them. When we left the city a few hours ago the sun was already low on the horizon, as though it belonged to a world one slot over from our own, and we talked about the weather forecast, the pre-Christmas traffic. Now we travel silently through darkness, the highway north revealing itself through the windshield a few feet at a time.*

Ahead there's a man standing on the snowy shoulder, waiting – the first human figure we've seen in more than an hour. A sympathy for him rises in me unexpectedly, but the feeling has already passed when without warning you slow to a stop on the asphalt and ask me to unlock the door. What are you thinking? There have been articles in the newspaper about hitchhikers on this highway, good-Samaritan tourists whose bodies are never found. Would you do this if you were on your own? Have you done this in the past, even – stopped for young men on roadsides? It wouldn't be so different from the way you met me. I understood your motivation then; there are the contracts people sign in offices and there are the ones they make at night when they're lonely. But this evening we're together and I want to go on with you, only you.

"Where are you heading?" you ask the man as he throws a small, battered duffle bag into the car and follows it through the door. When he looks up to reply, his expression turns to one of horror.

"I didn't know it was you –," he begins, but his eyes narrow and he seems to realize something. He glances quickly from you to me, then settles back in the seat. "Sorry. Never mind."

"What is it?" you ask.

"Nothing. I thought you were somebody else. An old friend."

You chuckle and shake your head, but the man still watches you in the rear-view mirror. He's tall, young, and long-haired with a grey denim jacket, a red scarf. The type of man you might find attractive. He slides to the middle of the back seat to give himself more room, or perhaps to be closer to you, and I wonder if he really did make a mistake. But if he knows you, why should he hide it?

When he says he's going to Mooney's Dump, you smile and say we're going there too. You add that they changed the name of the town a few years ago. Nowadays they call the place Sunshine. It's to attract tourists. They had a vote. You laugh, but the man just nods as if this is something he's known and forgotten. Then he frowns at me, and I realize I've been staring over my shoulder for too long. Hastily I turn toward the front of the car. No one speaks. There's only the road and the awareness of this stranger behind us, my stomach twisting into knots. I can see your eyes straying peri-odically to the mirror, and it's impossible to know whether you're watching him, whether he looks back. I'm timid and jealous, hurt by this unforeseen invasion, betrayed – betrayed by you, because the invasion is one you invited – while you drive onwards, lost in your own thoughts.

"Yes, Sunshine's a beautiful place," you say after a few minutes, as though the three of us are in the middle of a conversation. "Have you been up that way before?" The man murmurs a yes. "I

2

bought a cottage there last month, right on the bay," you tell him. "Turns out the mayor lives in the house next door." Without bothering to explain that you're a lawyer, you say the connection has brought you a new case, defending the town council against land claims made by the Native people on the reserve nearby. There are disputes over a map, accusations of boundaries redrawn. "These things should have been settled decades ago," you say. "Sunshine has two thousand people. A little town like that should be able to live in peace."

This is the first I've heard of land claims or a mayor. I thought we were going to Sunshine for a weekend together, but now I remember the briefcase in the trunk and wonder.

"The Indians are on a roll," you continue. "They've already taken over the local quarry. It was the mayor who owned it too. He'd put millions into the business. Can you imagine?"

"Maybe the land really belongs to them," says the hitchhiker.

"Sure, hundreds of years ago," you reply casually, not seeming to notice the anger in his comment. "But it was handed over in a treaty. People can't just turn back the clock."

The man behind us coughs. My face feels hot.

"What's the reserve like?" I ask, wanting to change the subject. An argument between strangers is as unappealing to me now as the possibility of a covert acquaintance between the two of you.

"I'm sorry – this is my friend Robert," you say to the hitchhiker, ignoring my question. You haven't even told him your own name yet. Perhaps you don't need to. "Robert's never been to Sunshine, so I'm going to show him around."

"Lucky man," says the stranger, and I can't tell whether he's mocking you, me, or the town.

Your friend. Is that what I am? Perhaps next you'll tell him you're married. Or maybe you're going to seduce him in front of me. For now you just explain that the history of small places has become a hobby of yours in the last couple of years. You've been up to Sunshine a few times, you've visited its library and read about the town's earliest settlers. Loggers, you say, whose descendants are

3

still in the area. There are probably people up there who know less about themselves than you do.

"You'd have a lot to teach them," agrees the stranger, but an irony lingers in his voice. Blithely you agree and go on, explaining that there are things an outsider notices about a place that locals usually ignore. As you offer facts and dates to him, I close my eyes and try to sleep, supposing myself too much of a city boy to be interested in country matters. But my mind is busy reconfiguring its picture of you. I took you for just another urban dweller, not someone with a passion for farms and harbour towns. It's impossible to harmonize the historian with the gentle, hungry lover I've met other nights. When you tell the hitchhiker about your love of the land, I can't quite believe you, and I wonder what other reasons you could have for returning to Sunshine so often.

Eventually sleep takes me in anxious, uncomfortable fits, and then the hitchhiker's rough-throated voice startles me awake. I keep my eyes closed and listen as he says a friend has told him there's going to be a celebration tonight near Sunshine. He wants to know if you've been invited.

"Not that I know of," you reply, with an edge of annoyance. "What's this celebration, again?"

"I'm sorry," he says, but his tone isn't apologetic. "I was sure you'd have heard about it." He explains that today's the winter solstice, and that at a wildlife park a few miles outside of the town hundreds of people will be gathering to greet the new season.

"Oh, is there a wildlife park?" you say, as if this is the most surprising thing in the world. The hitchhiker tells you the place is owned by a man who moved up from the city a few years ago and has caused a stir with his interest in pagan rituals. You're probably wondering how much this stranger really knows about Sunshine, whether you've been talking to someone more familiar with the town than you. All your authority has vanished; it almost makes me happy.

"The party sounds like a good time," you say. "Maybe we should go." I feel your hand touch my thigh. "Hey, are you awake?"

I keep my face turned and try to ignore the pressure of your fingers. All day I've been hurrying toward an evening in Sunshine with you, eager to be shut up in the cottage together. It's cruel to suggest taking that away from me now.

In a sly and whispering voice that implies a secret being shared, you tell the hitchhiker I'm sleeping. You say that perhaps if he's going to the party, you could drop him off and have a look. The silence that follows and then the indecipherable sounds of movement make me desperate to open my eyes. There are gestures being offered, glances shared in the mirror, I'm sure of it. If I were quick now, I could catch you and him in some horrible act of conspiracy. But instead I straighten in the seat, groan, pretend to wake up slowly from a deep slumber.

"Guess what?" you say. "We're going to a party."

I try to act surprised, but it's too much. I'm not ready to play along, after all.

"I know," I mutter. "I wasn't sleeping."

You say nothing more, and I realize I've changed in your eyes, simply in the wake of that little comment. You thought you'd been told all my faults; now you know that in addition to everything else I'm capable of deception. I press my forehead against the cold, wet window, and as I follow the passage of snowbound fields, the weave of cedar rails, the cattle huddled and steaming in corners, I wonder what this means for us.

Soon sulphur lamps begin to line the highway.

"We're almost there," you say quietly, tenderly, and I don't know whether you're speaking to me or him. I want the cottage and a hot bath, your hands on me. Please, I think. Drop him off here at the roadside. We don't need parties and strangers tonight.

A row of houses appears, then another, and finally the road descends through a rock-cut into the town itself: a few hundred roofs reflecting the moonlight, hemmed in by cedar forest and limestone escarpment on three sides, the frozen gape of a long, narrow bay on the fourth, the highway bisecting it all like the needle of a compass and climbing again through rock at the north end.

"*Blink and you'll miss it*," you say, although you don't bother looking yourself, and I watch, transfixed, as the stores scroll by. After so many miles of isolated farms, the buildings seem incredible, not just plain Victorian brick, but marble towers and gilt palaces that have waited centuries to be discovered. The hitchhiker slides across the seat to stare, then slides back, fidgeting like a fugitive who has returned by accident to the scene of his crime.

Without slowing, you urge the car up the hill north out of Sunshine. In a voice that starts deep but breaks after a few words, the hitchhiker directs you to the next turnoff. It's a county road with a heavy accumulation of slush that grabs at the tires. A few minutes later, parked vehicles begin to appear on the shoulders. The stranger extends an arm between us and points to a long lane that disappears into the woods. His hand is trembling.

You pull over and we get out of the car, stepping carefully on to the slippery ground. We walk down the lane three abreast with you in the middle, as close to the stranger as you are to me, and you reach over to adjust his scarf, then laugh as though you've just done something very daring. Might you really know each other? Against all plausibility I wonder if there's some plot between the two of you to abandon me, to drive to the cottage together or back to the city. The hitchhiker seems to grow uneasy as we move farther from the road; his eyes dart ahead, and then he glances over his shoulder. A moment later you lean over and kiss me on the cheek.

"I've forgotten my hat," you say. I can still feel the moistness of your lips cooling on my skin. "Wait here, I'll be back in a second."

I'm left with the stranger. He stands slightly hunched, kicks at the ground, and brings up gravel from beneath the packed snow.

"What an idiot," he says, once you're too far away to hear.

"What do you mean?" I ask, shocked and delighted. I want you to be an idiot, at least in his eyes. I want him to speak more words of disdain.

"All that stuff about the land claims and turning back the clock —"

"Oh," I say, to stop him. I tell him you're not as bad as that, most of the time.

"How do you know?" he says. "How long have you been together? A week? Two?"

My cheeks burn. It's been a month of weekends, but I don't correct him.

"Tourists," he says with contempt. "A couple of visits to a place and they think they own it." A second later the sound of the car door closing comes from the road, and the hitchhiker starts.

"What are you so nervous about?" I ask him, more bluntly than I intend, but he only looks at me; his mind is on something else. Then he sets his duffle bag on the ground and unzips it, reaches in with both hands.

"Listen, I've changed my mind," he says as he searches through his belongings. "I'm not going to the party after all."

"What will you do, then?" I ask. There are no other houses in sight.

"I know a place a couple of miles down the road. Don't worry about me. Look, you're definitely going?" I nod, although I'm not sure. So far it's you who's made the decisions. "Then could you do me a favour? I was supposed to give this to someone. I've owed it to her for a while now." From the bag he produces a small note-book, its yellow cover stained in the centre, a rubber band holding the pages together. "If you run into a woman named Alice Pederson, can you give it to her?"

I shake my head. Didn't he say there would be hundreds of people? I can't promise anything. But before I can protest, he hands me the yellow book. It's clear from his expression: this is to be a secret between me and him, something I can't share with you. I weigh the book in my hand, unwilling to speak, afraid I might reveal my guilty excitement at this sudden intimacy.

"You and your friend should enjoy the party," he says. "From what my friend told me, it's going to be an entertaining night." There's a smile on his face now, as though the book has been a burden that he's glad to be rid of.

In the first seconds after he disappears, I stare at the abandoned notebook, then turn to peer into the darkness and see the lights of Sunshine far away. From somewhere in the trees come voices, laughing, shouting, singing. A fire flickers through the cedars. I slide the book into my jacket pocket, and a moment later you're back from the car, reaching for my hand. I tell you the stranger has gone, that we're on our own. The book lies stiff against my side as we tread down the long lane toward the wildlife park, and I wonder how to start this search for Alice Pederson.

RELATIONS

L et's begin with Susan. When she was a girl, she used to lie in bed waiting for the angels to visit. This was during the longest, coldest nights in Ithaca, after the trudge home from school along sidewalks almost subterranean with their high banks of snow, after the three girls bickered during dinner and made their mother eat her day's ration of patience, after *The Andy Griffith Show* and homework, after her father lurched through a familiar bedtime story, after the lights went out. Winter felt like years of silence, the snow muffling the landscape so that if Susan listened, she could hear the low, fugal voices of her parents downstairs and, once they were asleep, the feathering of her own breath against the pillow. She kept her body perfectly still, anxious for the sound of angels approaching. When she could finally discern the gentle buzz of their wings in the distance, she lifted herself to the window, scratched away frozen condensation, and strained to see the flickering light of their bodies moving across the fields. They slid smoothly through her range of vision, their golden glow doubling on the pale skin of the land until they dipped over the brink of Potter's Hill and disappeared. It seemed like they always came from the north, and Susan decided that somewhere up there must be their home. Even once she was a teenager who had no time for the whine of snowmobiles interrupting her sleep, she harboured a secret conviction that angels came from Canada. Then in the summer of her thirty-first year she moved to that country. Driving with Marge and Daniel toward Mooney's Dump, watching the stream of stumpy cedars and the burnt lawns of ramshackle bungalows, the old fantasy nudged her from a place deep in her memory, and she laughed at herself.

That was fifteen years ago. Now she was alone in the new apartment, pacing the kitchen with the pot roast in the oven and the vacuuming still to be done, while Marge was a ferryman once more, driving with her child to bring back someone from a foreign land. But this time the child was Zeljka, and it was Daniel who was arriving in Sunshine. All morning in the apartment the little girl had been so impatient that keeping still was a physical impossibility. She'd be no better in the front seat, Susan thought, and it would serve Marge right; she'd spent days talking the kid into a frenzy. *Daniel is coming, Daniel will be here on Saturday from England* – Daniel, Daniel, all day long until his name seemed to signify anything absent and expected. By the end of it, Zeljka was doing somersaults whenever Daniel was mentioned. You could only get that excited about someone you had never met.

In the apartment above, cranky, lonely Mr. Aligarry shuffled around his living room. Gabe and Beatrice next door were watching their television at full blast as usual, and for once it was almost a relief. Without its interference Susan would have been on the alert for voices down in the foyer, footfalls on stairs. The acoustics in Sunshine Apartments didn't allow for privacy. When she'd moved here with Marge and Zeljka in the spring, she believed that apartment buildings were like prisons, each cell isolated from the rest, the presence of other inmates assumed but never felt. It was nothing like that at all. People's lives were always in your ears, intruding when least desired, day or night, so that strangers who'd never introduced themselves were known as intimately as lovers through their night-time noises, their bathroom groans. They probably knew her and Marge just as well in turn, but she didn't like to think about that. The two of them were good, at least. They didn't raise a fuss over endless blaring commercials, just as Gabe and Beatrice never said anything about creaking bedsprings or late-night giggles. But Zeljka – how to explain privacy to a six-year-old? Already there'd been complaints. Sometimes Susan wished they were back in the old house outside of town, but then she reminded herself that selling the place had paid for the lawyer who'd won her and Marge their daughter.

A knock at the door sent her heart thumping to escape her body. It was far too early. As she went to answer she abandoned the schedule she'd prepared: the hour for cleaning, the half-hour for cooking, the hour of searching for the emotional equilibrium that would let her speak civilly with Daniel. Oh well, she thought as she placed her hand on the knob, Marge can play umpire if things get out of control.

But it wasn't them at all. It was Bobby Boone, the landlord, come to measure the floors. He leaned heavily on the door frame, still puffing from climbing the stairs, his face pitted and red in the cheeks but increasingly pale toward his hairless crown, like a pimple about to burst. Susan frowned, remembering for the first time his phone call the day before when he'd announced he'd be stopping by.

"So Danny's coming home today," he said, stepping across the threshold and grinning as though he was in on some dirty secret. "It's been two years, eh? You must be excited."

"Eighteen months," murmured Susan. "How did you hear?" She had a sudden dread that it had been in the paper, that everyone was talking. But he pointed to the painted banner on the door: *Welcome Home Daniel*. Susan had written out the letters in pencil for Zeljka to trace, and she considered it a personal reminder as much as anything else. *Note to self: Welcome home Daniel.*

"When you expecting him?" Bobby Boone wanted to know.

"Any minute," she said. "Marge and Zeljka are picking him up from the shuttle."

"Sunshine expects big things from that boy," Boone proclaimed, and Susan stifled a snort. She disliked people who presumed to speak on behalf of the whole town, even if they were the mayor. "I suppose he'll be after my job soon enough, won't he?"

"Daniel doesn't have the money to be a landlord," she replied. Boone's face darkened.

"I meant the mayoralty," he said.

She shrugged and thought to herself that Daniel didn't have the money to become mayor either. Then again, maybe he did. Who knew? Boone was waiting for her to say something else, but she stayed quiet and he cleared his throat.

"I should get around to those floors," he said. He patted the pockets of his coveralls until he found his measuring tape, then lingered by the doorway, examining the walls. She wondered what was wrong. Of course, she realized, he wanted her to help him. He was waiting for her to offer.

"Don't let me get in your way," she said. "I'll be in the kitchen."

She left him without another word. Bobby Boone was one of those people who was neither an enemy nor a friend. In a town the size of Sunshine it took effort to retain such distance. The best you could do was stay off the streets, keep the shopping down to once a week, nod without replying whenever the gossip began. Even then you ended up more implicated than you wanted. She and the mayor hadn't been in the same room more than half a dozen times, but Boone still probably had a whole unwritten dossier on her and Marge by now. Susan could only imagine the juicier bits in a file like that one.

There had never been a ceremony of any sort for Marge and her; there weren't even explanations to friends. "You don't do things like that," said Marge. "Not here." The long, bankrupting legal battles to adopt Zeljka the previous spring were fought in Toronto. The most public event Susan and Marge ever staged in Sunshine was a trip together to the town's only lawyer, Solomon DeWitt, when they changed their wills, years after they should have. They put it off and put it off, until finally Daniel turned eighteen and

Marge had to go in anyhow. The amendments regarding each other seemed an adjunct to the other business. Only in bits and pieces did Susan and Marge begin to confirm implicitly what everyone already knew. When Marge said to people, "We've just changed Susan's room into a study," it was next door to confession. Susan had never slept there except when they fought, and on those nights it didn't feel like her room at all.

She found nothing to do in the kitchen and walked into the living room, where Bobby Boone was bent down by the television with the measuring tape distended the full length of the wall. He touched a button, and there was a long metallic slurp as the yellow strip wriggled home.

"Listen, about Danny," Boone began, standing up and brushing off his overalls, even though he'd only been kneeling on carpet. "He's not going to be, uh" – he seemed to be searching for the diplomatic word – "living with you, is he? That is to say, indefinitely-like?"

"No, he's just visiting."

"Because I warned you before, Susan, this is a two-person apartment. Between you and Marge and that cute little girl, you already have one too many. I did you a favour just by agreeing to three, remember?"

"I remember."

"Well, you don't want to push it. Danny is a good boy, no doubt about it, a smart boy, and we're all proud of him. But there've got to be rules."

"Don't worry, he's just visiting for a few –," but she couldn't finish the sentence because she didn't know. "He's just visiting."

Bobby nodded again, unconvinced. They caught each other's eyes full-on for the first time, and she saw her own frustration reflected back at her, the look of a person behind the civil sheen who was as tired by the ritual of politeness as she was. It was hard being decent. If they were another species they'd probably just commence butting heads or clawing at each other.

"Why don't you go do the bedrooms," she said. "I'll bring some tea."

As she filled the kettle her thoughts drifted to the map of Ontario in her mind, and she tried to imagine where the van might be on the highway as it brought Daniel home from the Toronto airport. Sunshine was the gateway to a dead-end peninsula fifty miles long that petered out just above the forty-fifth parallel, not really north itself but as north as southern Ontario went, a hangnail of rock and forest dangling from everything that mattered. To visit you needed your own car, or you took the shuttle service to Owen Sound and had a mother pick you up, as Daniel did. Right about now he'd be watching as office buildings shrank and warehouse compounds began to disappear while the shuttle van started its climb out of the hot concrete sprawl into the shadowy woods atop the Niagara Escarpment. He was due in Owen Sound at six o'clock.

Susan carried the tea to the bedroom and watched Boone crouch along the walls with his measuring tape, getting the size of things. He moved in a way that was almost childlike, whistling disjointedly through his teeth. He enjoys this, she thought. He has a wife and five children at home, he has the whole town in his back pocket, he can probably tell a joke better and drink a beer faster than anyone else in Sunshine, but he's happiest here, on his own, working peaceably with his hands. If only men could be kept busy measuring floors, the world might be a nicer place.

"I tell you, these new carpets are going to cost me a pretty penny," he said, looking up.

"Well, it's very kind of you."

"And there's no guarantee they'll even work. Honestly, Susan, if you wanted quiet you should've stayed in the country. Sound isn't light. You can't just shut it out."

"I still think it might be easier to change apartments," she said, but he didn't seem to register her comment. He was probably busy regretting his decision to let them into a seniors' building with a child. If she had any guts, she'd tell him how they didn't even like the apartment, how they'd only rented it because it was all they could afford.

"What colour do you think the carpet should be?" he asked.

"I don't know – something dark," she said. She almost added "something to hide the dirt" but caught herself in time. He'd think they never cleaned; but then, he probably thought that already. No doubt he'd decided that if a woman didn't have time for men, she must not have time for housework either.

"What about beige?" he asked. "I think beige might be good."

"No, it wouldn't work with the walls. You need something darker."

"You're sure about the beige?" he persisted. Somewhere along the line he'd probably been given some free beige carpet. For a moment she considered going along with it to earn his gratitude.

"Beige definitely wouldn't work," she said. His shoulders slumped.

"Well, we'll see," he replied. "I'll have to ask the other tenants and make a democratic decision. There's no pleasing everyone, you know. And they don't always have a full selection of colours." She nodded sympathetically. The tray with the tea was still in her hands.

"Tell me," said Boone, "Sunshine hasn't heard much of Danny since he left. How's he been keeping himself?"

"Oh, fine," she said. "Busy studying."

Boone chuckled. "He says that on the phone, but he'll probably show up here with some English girl on his arm. That's how it goes, isn't it?"

"I guess."

"Sure, sure, I remember what it was like at that age." He drew a deep breath and put his measuring tape in his pocket. "It's a shame Danny has to come home now . . . with things the way they are."

"What do you mean?" Susan asked, tensing. Boone was watching her. Hurriedly she turned from him, set the tea tray on the bookshelf next to her, and began to shuffle a stack of magazines.

"I'm just thinking how the town's all worked up," he said. "About Alice Pederson."

"Oh, of course," she said. "Of course." He was testing her, she could feel it, and she wondered how much he already knew.

"You going to the funeral tomorrow?" he asked. "It'll be standing room only, I bet. No journalists, though. Apparently the only news worth reporting was that they found her." He said this in a tone of disappointment. "After all that uncertainty it's a relief more than anything else, isn't it?"

"Not for Stoddart Fremlin," Susan said. She was glad they were no longer talking about Daniel.

"No, not for Frem," Boone agreed. "Who'd have guessed he was that kind of man."

"But he hasn't been found guilty yet," Susan said tentatively, as though she were asking a question. Dr. Fremlin had only been arrested the previous day.

"No. It doesn't look good, though." Boone's eyes had lost their workman's humour altogether. "A terrible business. And Alice's poor husband, that coloured fellow, what's his name –?"

"Mike," she said, despite herself, and he nodded.

"Yes, a terrible business." Then he took a step toward her and peered at her face inquisitively. "Say, Susan, are you flirting with me?"

"Pardon?" she cried.

"You keep winking," he said. "Is there something in your eye?"

"No, no," she said, putting a hand to her lid and feeling the twitch of the lashes against her fingers. It had been happening too often lately, not just in the apartment, but out on the streets, at work. Soon they'd be calling her One-Eyed Susan behind her back. "The doctor says it's just stress."

Boone nodded and laughed as though this was the punchline to a joke, then started for the door.

"Well if you're all right, I think I should be going." He patted the little notebook in which he'd been scribbling numbers.

"Oh, but you didn't touch your tea," she exclaimed, too loudly, with an overblown regret that revealed the pleasure underneath. She wanted to be alone; she didn't want Boone here when Daniel arrived.

"Ah, well, it's a bit too warm for tea today," said Boone, playing along. She flashed him a smile of real delight and showed him out. "You keep a clean place, Susan," he said as she closed the door between them. "I'm grateful for it."

She didn't really hear him. A married woman, she was saying to herself for the thousandth time. What was Daniel thinking?

"I was a married woman once, too, you know," Marge had replied a few nights earlier when Susan said it out loud.

"You don't need to remind me. And so what if you were?"

"I'm saying married women aren't always happy. Marriage is not always in their best interests. You should know that. When did you become so respectful of heterosexual institutions, anyway?" Marge was good with the fancy phrases. Susan had her share of education too, but somehow when they talked together a degree in speech therapy didn't measure up to a doctorate in literature. Or maybe it was just the difference in age: Marge had an extra nine years of arguing behind her. Susan sighed. Her forty-sixth birthday was a few days away, but that had been forgotten with Daniel's phone call yesterday.

It was quarter to five and already her insides were beginning to burn. When she went to lie down on the couch, though, she found the living room in subtle disarray – Boone had moved furniture to get at the walls – so she set about putting things in their place. The work should have been distracting, but amid the tidying of papers and the scrubbing of surfaces, thoughts of Daniel flurried like unsettled dust.

Two days ago Marge had sent him an e-mail. It wasn't unusual in any way; there were no accusations, no pleas, only a dutiful mother's summary of local hearsay, the kind she sent to Cambridge every few weeks or so with the vague hope that eventually he might write back. The news about the body was thrown in with everything else. *Some divers found bones off Cavalry Point. There's a forensics team up from Toronto to do tests, but everyone thinks it's Alice Pederson. They're saying she probably fell through the ice.* Neither Marge nor Susan expected a response, so yesterday when Susan answered the phone she didn't realize it was him until he asked to speak with his mother. She only noticed the utter cheerlessness of his voice.

After half an hour, Marge got off the line and repeated what he'd said about Alice and him. Susan shook her head.

"Look, honey, he couldn't have. We would have known. Are you sure he's not making it up? People do, you know, when someone dies. They want to think they had a closer relationship than they really did." But apparently Daniel had offered details to prove it was true.

"What's he going to do now?" Marge asked. "He can't tell anyone. Can you imagine how it would look? People will think he left because he had something to hide. Oh God, he should have told the police right away."

"He didn't know until yesterday she was dead," Susan pointed out.

"No. But she was missing. And he left the day after she disappeared."

"It does seem a little –"

"Don't say it," snapped Marge. "It's ridiculous even to think it."

"But you said it yourself: he knew she was missing! How could he go? How could he stay away all that time?"

"Please. Please let's not talk about it now."

Susan shook her head. Not speaking about things was always Marge's solution.

"Sweetie, I love him too," Susan insisted. "But he's human. Strange things happen. He's barely spoken to us in the last two years." When Marge said he was coming home in twenty-four hours, Susan wanted to know for how long, and Marge only shrugged wearily.

In the process of cleaning up after Bobby Boone, Susan began to see the apartment as Daniel was going to, for the first time, expecting the space and light of the house he had grown up in, not this

18

dark, plain cavern with its jumble of furniture meant for larger rooms, its boxes of toys for a little girl whom he'd never met and who was suddenly to be accepted as his sister. Susan started to tidy the apartment all over again. She vacuumed the trim along the floors, she pushed a mop into the corners of the ceiling. By the time she finished it was six o'clock. They were at Strikersville in her mind, fifteen minutes distant, when they arrived for real. It was all quick and implausible: a key in the door, and then all three hurrying through at once as though there was a man with a gun behind them.

"What do you know? The shuttle was early," said Marge. She spoke like it was an everyday occurrence for the shuttle to be early with Daniel aboard. Susan almost didn't rush over and grab him.

"We're so glad you're home," she whispered loudly, her cheek pressed against his short whiskers, as red as the familiar curls on his head. Those are new, she thought, and realized they were probably only the first of many changes to be noticed. He stood there unmoving with a bag in each hand.

"Hi, Susan," he said. "Where do I dump all this stuff?"

She helped them carry in the rest of his luggage, and once the entranceway was filled, Marge ordered them to leave everything there and rest.

"I'm not tired," said Daniel.

"Well I am," said Marge, sinking into the couch. "And it would exhaust me to watch you. Get yourself a beer." Zeljka still stood by the door, tugging on her ponytail and staring at Daniel, but a second later an invisible switch was thrown and she rushed madly around the living room, yelling some incomprehensible song.

"Go ahead, tire yourself out, kiddo," said Marge. "Woo-ee, woo-ee, that's it." She coughed and kicked off her shoes on the second attempt. Sometimes Susan thought Marge was too old to be a mother again.

Susan hesitated before heading back to the kitchen. She noticed Daniel was watching Zeljka now, frowning, as though the girl was an uninvited guest who might steal the ashtrays at any moment.

He looked at the ashtrays with suspicion too; Marge had sworn she'd finished with cigarettes for good. It was never going to work with the four of them in this tiny place. Not with Daniel here. How many times through the years had she overheard him complaining to Marge? "She's not my father." "Susan doesn't understand me." But then, she'd never heard "I hate her." Never "I wish she would go home."

He started toward the couch, but Marge told him to take off his shoes first. They were black, the same colour as his shirt and trousers, his knee-length coat. The Daniel she knew would have been in primary colours, jeans. This one looked more like a Jesuit priest.

"I don't like this place," he said, after he put his shoes by the door and returned to survey the living room. "It's too hot. It's for old people. Next thing you know, you'll be headed to Fort Lauderdale in the winter. You only retired last year."

Marge eased into her slippers and said nothing. Zeljka was doing laps of the small round dinner table they'd dragged from the kitchen earlier in the day.

"Hey, Chelka," Daniel said. She didn't even look up.

"I told you, it's Zeljka," said Marge. "Like *je* in French."

"Zeljka," he tried again. "Hey, Zeljka, come over here." Zeljka fell to the ground dramatically, flopped on her back, and began to wave her arms up and down along the floor. "What, did I get it wrong again?" he asked.

"She's shy, don't take it personally," said Susan.

"She wasn't shy in the car on the way here," Daniel muttered. "I couldn't hear myself think."

"She's been dying to meet you," Susan went on. "She wouldn't leave us alone until we promised you'd sleep in her room with her. And you know, it makes sense. She's up watching the tube by six-thirty and you'd never get any peace if you slept in the living room. We borrowed a mattress for you." She knew she was blathering, but she couldn't help it. Anything to avoid direct contact, anything that could trace as wide a circle as possible around Alice Pederson.

They'd agreed to wait and hear his side of the story, not to make hasty conclusions. But now that he was finally standing before them, his side of the story was the last thing Susan wanted to hear. She found herself searching desperately for the sort of questions that discouraged stories.

For the moment, at least, they were safe. By the time Zeljka had broken out of her mania, Gabe and Beatrice next door were at it hammer and tongs, and their shouting, normally unbearable, was a welcome distraction. Zeljka pressed a yellow plastic cup against the wall and used it to listen, cocking one hip and studying the floor as though there were subtitles spelled in the carpet to supplement what she heard. She'd stripped down to her camouflage panties and nothing else.

"You never cooked a decent casserole in your life," said Zeljka, in a voice that was an impressive reproduction.

"Doesn't that girl have any shame?" asked Daniel. "She's almost as loud as they are."

"She's only six," retorted Susan.

"She's six and a half," said Daniel. He was confident about Zeljka's statistics because they were all he had of her. Everything he knew had come in e-mails from Marge.

"Six, six and a half, she still doesn't know any better, and that's fine," Susan insisted.

"You wouldn't know a decent lasagne if it bit you on the arm," said Zeljka.

"And what about the camouflage?" Daniel wanted to know. "I thought you were a pacifist, Mom."

"Camouflage is cool right now," Marge replied. "What can you do against coolness? I fought those battles once with you already, buddy, remember?"

Daniel grimaced, then got up and trundled down the narrow hallway with his bags. Susan and Marge moved to the kitchen, where Susan rummaged through a drawer for the turkey baster while Marge gathered spoons and coffee mugs. They spoke in whispers.

"He's thinner, did you notice?"

"Taller too, I think."

"Could that be right? Can you grow in your twenties?"

"Maybe it's us. We've shrunk."

They laughed quietly together. Now that they were alone Susan could relax, and she felt a compulsion to plan. With plans you could approach things directly. She wanted to speculate on his tone, anticipate conversation, assign questions. I'll ask him about his classes, you ask him if he knows Stoddart Fremlin is in jail on murder charges. You ask him how he got mixed up with a married, thirty-six-year-old woman, and I'll ask him about the warm beer and bangers. Or the reverse, even. She was willing to support any strategy that would fix everything. But Marge would never ask any questions. When it came to certain subjects, she was the most amazing coward.

"Go tell him to set the table," she said to Susan. "This isn't a hotel."

"You tell him."

"I'm busy," Marge replied, pointing to the sink full of dishes in front of her. Susan reached over, dipped two fingers into the water, and splashed suds on to Marge's skirt.

"Why you little –" But she was smiling, and she placed a soft, wet hand on Susan's cheek. The soap was still collecting on the ridge of her jaw as she walked down the hallway toward Zeljka's room. Daniel didn't seem to notice her lean into the door.

It was true, his face was different. You could see the cheekbones; the crease in his forehead was deeper when he frowned. He sat there on Zeljka's tiny bed examining each wall in turn like a bewildered giant in a room abruptly reduced to human proportions. Susan tapped on the door frame until he looked up.

"How is Cambridge?"

"Fine."

They were both enraptured by a bare patch of carpet. She didn't know what else to ask him.

"Zeljka's great, isn't she?" she said finally.

"Sure," he replied, without much enthusiasm. "She looks a bit like her mother."

Susan nodded slowly. Jelena had died not long after Daniel went to England; he'd only met her a few times before that in the summers when she'd been vacationing in the cottage down the road, and he hadn't come back for her funeral.

"Well," Susan said. "Dinner's ready." When he returned to the kitchen he was annoyed by the discovery that it wasn't and he was just supposed to set the table.

"You're always watching the television," said Zeljka, her ear still pressed against the cup on the living-room wall. Marge grunted approvingly.

"Beatrice is right," she told Daniel. "Gabe watches three or four hours a day, and all without his hearing aid, so we end up listening to the soap operas along with him." But this information didn't seem to interest Daniel. He was too busy staring at Zeljka again.

"You shouldn't let her do that," he declared. "It's not polite. And what if they say something nasty? You want her to repeat it?"

"Daniel, you've been here five minutes already –," began Susan, advancing toward him, but Marge shooed her back. They'd vowed to be better with him this time, more understanding, more compassionate. Well, so much for vows. She wanted to tell him that Alice Pederson's funeral was the next day.

"I wish I never married you," said Zeljka.

"All right, Zed, sweetheart, that's enough," said Marge wearily. "Nobody wants to hear what they're saying." But Zeljka didn't move and neither did Marge; she just stayed hunched over the kitchen counter, chopping parsley. The blouse she was wearing, carefully chosen this morning, looked grimy and wrinkled.

Daniel grabbed a fistful of dinner knives and left the kitchen. When Susan followed, she found him placing them around the table in the living room so slowly that she couldn't tell if he was being meticulous or lazy. She bent to lay the bread basket in the centre and felt him move beside her to speak, his voice low and uneven in her ear.

"Is she okay? I mean, is there something wrong?"

"Your mother? She's fine. Really. Why?"

"You'd tell me, wouldn't you?" he insisted. "If there was a problem?"

"What do you mean?"

"She looks old. Frail." He sounded like he might weep.

"Nothing's changed, Daniel. She's two years older. You're different at fifty-five than you are at fifty-three, that's all."

He stepped back to look at her, and she knew her eye was winking again, even though she was trying hard to keep it open. He took in her brown corduroys, striped vest, the frizzed brown hair over her shoulders with its unruly bolts of grey.

"You look just the same," he murmured. Then, slowly, he raised his hand to her face and pressed a finger against the skin beside her winking eye. She froze, disconcerted.

The twitching stopped. It seemed to surprise him as much as it did her, and she saw on his face the sheepish beginnings of a smile. When the eye began to wink again a second later, though, his expression faltered. He drew away his hand and went back to the kitchen without a word. She followed, wanting to get there first, to tell Marge what had happened, but it was too late; he was already standing over his mother's shoulder, scowling and muttering as before.

"I can't eat those, you know," he said, pointing to the carrots and potatoes as Marge spooned them from around the roast into their own dish. "I told you in the car, I'm a vegetarian now."

"So you're a vegetarian," Marge replied. "These are vegetables." She said the word *vegetarian* like it was a disease.

"You cooked them with the meat," he insisted.

"That's how I always cook them."

"Don't you see –?" He shook his head in disgust. "You're unbelievable. You really are!"

"Hey, keep your voice down," hissed Marge through clenched teeth. "The walls are thin. You want everybody in the building to hear you?"

"Who cares if they do?" Daniel yelled. "Let's call a town council meeting about it. Let's see what everyone thinks."

"Yes, talk louder, Daniel," said Susan. "Everybody should hear the whole story, don't you agree?"

His eyes dropped and he didn't say anything.

"No, everyone should not hear the whole story," said Marge. "At least not until after dinner." She had the carving knife in her hand and was pointing it at Daniel, then seemed to realize what she was doing and set it down quickly on the counter. Susan glanced into the living room, where Zeljka was still listening through her cup. She wondered what Beatrice and Gabe had to say that could possibly be so interesting.

There was a soft knock on the door, but no one appeared eager to answer it. Marge had busied herself in rinsing off the potatoes, and Daniel was watching her intently. Susan frowned, certain of what was ahead. Marge was thinking that she would clean a few and Daniel would eat them, but you couldn't simply wash the meat-juice out of potatoes once they'd been cooked in it. Marge was wasting her time and her food, and it was just like her to do it without asking him. Soon enough she'd offer them to him and he'd refuse, she'd act like she'd been rebuked for doing the most considerate thing you could imagine, and both of them would sulk for the rest of the meal.

Susan took a deep breath and went to answer the door. On the other side was a woman in a pink dressing gown, her eyes barely even with Susan's chest, her silver hair radiant under the hallway lights.

"Oh, hello, Beatrice," Susan said. "Marge, it's Beatrice from next door." The woman was so small and fragile that Susan didn't think to stop her when she marched across the threshold, past the kitchen, into the living room where Zeljka was listening through her cup.

"Where has that wife of mine gone?" Zeljka said, her eyes fixed on the ground.

"You goddamn parrot," whispered Beatrice. "You monster."

"Come back, please," said Zeljka. It wasn't until after she said this that she realized she'd been spoken to. She turned her head slightly, as if her ear were stuck to the plastic, still listening but straining to make contact with the reality of her own home. She saw Beatrice looking down on her, and Susan could tell that half of Zeljka's brain, the important half that makes decisions and moves the mouth, remained intent on what it heard through the wall.

"I love you, Beatrice," said Zeljka, and before Susan could grab hold of her, Beatrice's hand came down without mercy across Zeljka's cheek. Not long after, in the middle of the crying and yelling, Mr. Aligarry upstairs started to bang on the floor with a broom handle, as though he was tired of being a polite neighbour and for the first time in his life was doing something about all that racket.

PILLAR OF THE COMMUNITY

The first search party was just Mike on his own in the dark, once he'd put the kids to bed and Alice's mother had arrived to mind them. It was the second day of winter, twenty-one hours after Alice should have returned from the celebration at the henge. He'd already alerted the Mooney's Dump police and phoned family members to ask if she'd been in touch. No, nothing wrong exactly, he said each time. Let me know right away if you hear from her. Then he drove to Cam Usher's wildlife park, walked the perimeter of the outer fence and surveyed the adjacent field while unseen creatures growled and cackled from their cages. A packed trail led to the centre of the field and the henge itself, a circle of rocks he'd never seen before but knew well enough from Alice's diagrams. He kicked one of them before stumbling into the bush. Rain clouds had descended on the peninsula the night before, but in the morning a northeasterly wind had skated over the bay to freeze everything again. Now there was a thick shell of ice on the earth that made walking difficult, and each step he took punched loudly into the soft snow beneath. The world sounded like a busy place as long as he kept moving.

Alice's mother had driven up from Walkerton within an hour of hearing from him. She was a small, thin woman who never looked at Mike directly when they spoke, her head continually bobbing and turning, reminding him of a bird at a feeder. When she arrived, their hug was cool, dutiful; they knew well enough their feelings about one another. She'd mellowed to him somewhat in the years since the separation from her husband, but Alice seemed to keep her updated on their difficulties, financial or otherwise, in long weekly conversations on the phone, so that it still felt as though a portion of Mrs. Mooney's judgment was always held in reserve. Who knew what stories she was telling herself now? *Believe the best of me*, he wanted to protest, even as she held him stiffly.

"Was it another fight?" she said. "The way you two go at it, I wouldn't be –"

"It's just some misunderstanding," he replied. With no sign of Alice all day and the sun setting, he'd stopped preparing a diatribe to inflict on her when she turned up. Even though he was used to her absences, the hours spent at Usher's henge without telling him in advance, she'd never been gone overnight before, and already the stoic adult calmness he'd cultivated to soothe Oliver and Nel had been betrayed by the hysterics of his imagination. Perhaps it was her father, he thought. Maybe he's taken her away from me. The old bigot's probably been wanting to do that for years.

As he stomped through the icebound swamp near the wildlife park, his mind went from one horrific possibility to another, and the slide show only paused when a cedar branch caught his jacket, as if to remind him of something. He looked up and realized he didn't know where he was. What was he thinking? There wasn't any reason to suspect that Alice had entered the swamp in the first place. Perhaps she was just angry with him, staying at a friend's and refusing to call.

A few minutes later he found a trail of footprints that looked like his own, and he followed them until they came back on themselves. Icy water sloshed in his boots. The trees seemed to multiply; the world became interminable. He stopped and called Alice's name, but the landscape smothered his voice. She wouldn't hear his cries as human; she'd take them for a distant animal howling, if she heard anything at all. Everywhere was stillness. The moon, bright and fully dilated, had tangled itself in the branches over-head. He had a sudden, overwhelming urge to sleep, and he lay down on his back, stared at a sky so crowded with stars that they might have been snowflakes preparing for descent.

"*O holy night –*"

But it felt hollow, and he broke off. What had made him want to sing that? The carol was one he and the children were supposed to perform tomorrow night at the United Church, after fawning appeals from the school's music teacher. "Oliver and Nel are won-derful, and I've heard about your voice," she'd said, leaving him to wonder who could have told her. Not the children, surely. Perhaps it was only a hypothesis being tested about black men's singing. "We'll call you the Pederson Family Trio," the teacher had exclaimed, sounding delighted by her own idea. He'd said yes reluctantly, telling the teacher that Alice would have to agree. Later, when he found out about the five hundred dollars Alice had withdrawn from their savings account, the concert had been for-gotten. It was the last conversation they'd had before she left for the party at Cam Usher's to unveil his henge. A fight. Alice yelling and walking out, leaving Mike to brood at being left behind, even though earlier he'd happily volunteered to watch the kids, prefer-ring a warm house to frozen feet and pointless conversations with strangers. After a few minutes he'd gone to Nel's bedroom and found the children sitting silently. *Mommy's not angry with you,* he told them. *We're just having a disagreement. Things will be better tomorrow.* They'd heard such reassurances before, but a novelty awaited them: tomorrow arrived and Alice did not come with it.

Lying in the swamp, he realized how inadequately he'd dressed; his hands were bare and numb, his jeans soaked. In a few minutes the denim would be stiff as sheet metal. He got to his feet and started in a direction where the snow was unmarked by tracks, not particularly caring if he ended up pinned under a boulder or shredded by bears. A fantasy overtook him in which Alice returned with her head bandaged and the searchers meant for her were sent out for him instead. He was almost ready to lie down again and call to them when he saw the lights of Cam Usher's farmhouse. He wasn't more than a quarter of a mile from where he'd started. With his arms spread for balance he walked back along the untrustworthy road and down the lane to the wildlife park's lot, wary of ice, his eyes on the ditch. Cam Usher was waiting for him next to the car.

"I'm sorry this has happened," Usher said. The night and the hood of the man's parka made his face almost invisible. "I spent all day phoning people, but no news."

Mike told him he was grateful for his help. "It's not your fault," he found himself saying, and felt foolish. Of course it wasn't Usher's fault. But then, it was this man's party from which she'd disappeared. It was because of Usher that she'd attended in the first place. Mike stared at his feet and said he needed to get home to the children.

They didn't perform at the United Church on Christmas Eve. He put off calling the music teacher, first hoping that Alice would appear in time, then assuming the woman would hear what had happened from other sources. She'd know he was traumatized, preoccupied, could not possibly be asked to remember something as minor as a church performance when his wife was missing. But his negligence ate at him, and finally he called her Christmas Eve morning, apologizing profusely, expecting her to interrupt with an expression of understanding. Instead it sounded like he had a dead connection.

"Hello?" he said in the middle of one of his own sentences.

"I'm still here," her voice replied.

"Well again, I'm so sorry. It would just be too much for Nel and Olly right now –"

"We won't be able to find anyone else on such short notice," the voice said slowly, as though broaching a negotiation. "It leaves a gap in the program."

Mike didn't know what to say. He was suddenly terrified that she was going to try to talk him into it.

"I'm sure you'll figure out something," he said quickly, and hung up.

That evening he and Alice's mother and the children chewed on delivered pizza, and although he should have been thinking about Alice, going over her last words to him or searching the house for clues, he found himself wondering about the music teacher. Could she really be that indifferent? Perhaps it had to do with Alice's disappearance. Perhaps there were already rumours. He knew of people who'd be glad to talk along those lines. Alice wasn't only the town dentist, she was a Mooney. Her ancestors had founded the town after Elijah Mooney bilked the Natives of their peninsula on behalf of the Queen. The mayor, Bobby Boone, was the son of a Mooney, and the water south of the Pedersons' house was still called Mooney's Bay, even if the town itself was probably going to change its name from Mooney's Dump to Sunshine after the referendum. Alice said she was outside of the family's politics, but Mike was certain other people thought differently. They weren't happy that she'd married a man from the city, an African Canadian – although he doubted they would use that term. A man with a university degree who didn't work but just looked after the children. Rumours of a novel published long ago, a career abandoned. The sort of man to be suspected at a time like this.

Nel and Oliver weren't interested in their pizza. Nel was explaining something to her grandmother, her voice cautious and muted. Oliver had picked off all the pepperoni from his slice and left them stacked at the side of his plate like chips to cash in at the end of the night. When he left his seat and came over to give Mike a hug, the gesture was almost too precious for Mike to accept, until Oliver asked if this meant that Christmas was going to be cancelled. Mike sighed to himself, relieved. Oliver was worried about his mother, of course, and even concerned for his father, which was touching, but at four years old he had a little self-regard in the matter too. Thank God. Mike reassured him that no one was cancelling Christmas, but that it might have to be put on hold for a few days this year.

Once the children were in bed Mrs. Mooney hovered around the kitchen longer than necessary, making her birdfeeding movements, then browsed his record collection in the living room. One hand propped itself against her tiny waist, the other fluttered over dust-sleeves. It was clear that she wanted to talk.

"What's on your mind?" he asked, feeling brave for making the first move. He knew what it was, of course. She wanted to go over the why, the how. Alice's car was still in the driveway, her clothes still in the bedroom drawers and closet. But there was the five hundred dollars gone from the bank. When he'd mentioned it to the police they'd asked for details and he couldn't tell them anything more. They'd wanted to know about the car, and he explained that Judy Sutter had given Alice a ride to the party, that according to Judy, Alice had told her she'd find a lift back with someone else. People had seen Alice walking down Cam Usher's lane toward the road after midnight, but no one knew anything about where she was going. Nobody admitted to giving her a ride. It was because of the five hundred dollars that Mike had to organize his own search party; the police were determined not to be hasty if they were dealing merely with a runaway.

"It isn't like her," said her mother. "She didn't leave any note? You weren't fighting?"

"No, not really," he muttered, thinking of the last argument. "Just little things. It's a stressful time of year."

"What things?" she said accusingly.

There were dozens of them, he thought. Money, work, no time together. All normal enough, all heartbreaking when he recalled them now. As grounds for desertion they were each implausible and likely. He looked at Alice's mother and shrugged.

"It's not like her," she repeated. "There must be something else you're not remembering."

He let her leave it at that, but he wanted to say, Who are you to know what Alice is like? You didn't think it was like her to marry me. You didn't think it was like her to stop speaking to you either, back when you were sticking by that old racist.

He remembered a river. They were both still in university; it was Alice's first summer not living in Mooney's Dump. To be with him she'd repudiated her parents and her home, consigned herself to the heat of the city, a cramped apartment, his chain-smoking friends with their endless conversations about art. The kayaking trip was his idea, a way to satisfy her fierce love of nature, a chance to get away without returning to the peninsula.

"We could go right to Mooney's Dump from here if we had to," she said on the first morning. "A hundred miles downriver and across Georgian Bay. It's all one body of water, you know." They were sharing a boat, singing an old Indian canoe song she'd taught him line by line. He lost himself in the rhythm of it, dazzled by the moving water, the flashing paddles, the muscles of Alice's shoulders in front of him, until he realized he was singing alone. Alice had stopped paddling; she was trailing her fingers in the river with her head bent low. When she told him what was wrong, he steered them to shore and they held each other on the smooth rock.

"They're from a different generation," he whispered, repeating arguments he still didn't quite believe himself. "Don't worry, they'll come around eventually." He brushed her hair from her forehead and smiled at her until she smiled back. "Who could push away a daughter as beautiful as you?"

CHRISTMAS MORNING the children woke him before dawn to beg that he go downstairs with them. He'd already told them no presents would be opened until their mother returned, and he sent them out of the room, lay there listening to their voices in the hall. It had been a long night with little sleep, and he had no desire to leave the bed, but after a few minutes they returned, wanting breakfast, so he got up and dressed. The meal was such a sombre affair that eventually he relented and let them tear into their stockings, while the boxes under the tree were left in their gift-wrap.

"We'll leave those for when Mommy gets back," he told them from his slouch on the sofa. Mrs. Mooney sat in a chair across the room, watching stonily. Then Nel came over to him, crying, and he gathered her in his arms clumsily – she was eight now. Oliver stood by the tree and stared at the presents.

"Those are for when Mommy gets back," Nel shouted at him, still sniffling.

After lunch Mike drove out along the township road again, past the airfield, past the cemetery, until he reached Cam Usher's place. Dozens of people had turned up to begin searching, despite it being Christmas Day. Most of them he recognized as Mooney relatives or patients from the dental clinic; the rest seemed to be friends of Usher's: the organic farmers, artisans, and environmental activists Alice had told him about. They lived in the country, taught their children at home, and seldom shopped in Mooney's Dump. Around town they were rumoured to practise witchcraft and Druidism under Usher's guidance.

The two groups kept separate from each other in the parking lot, Usher's friends watching silently as the others gathered around Mike to offer awkward words of sympathy, express their concern, tell him how proud of his wife they'd been at the opening ceremony for the henge. Usually he relied on Alice to make the small talk with these people. Now he was asking them how they were, commenting on the weather, dragging out conversations as though speech alone might solve everything. Faces began to blur together; the lot began to take on a sense of unreality. He wasn't sure what he was trying to prove. That he was a capable and caring husband, maybe. That she hadn't disappeared because of him.

"Good to see you," he heard himself saying, again and again.

Each day that week they scoured a different area – the shore of the frozen bay, the bottom and then the top of the escarpment to the north – while he sat at home surrounded by cellphones and walkie-talkies, watching over the kids even as he co-ordinated movements and gathered updates from people like Usher. It's his fault that she's gone, Mike repeated to himself as he waited for news. If not for the man's henge, Mike and Alice might not have fought in the first place. Mike wouldn't be calling the First Nations band, requesting permission to enter their reserve. He wouldn't be asking all the people he'd ever met in Mooney's Dump to help. Day by day the numbers grew, until it seemed like half the peninsula was tramping through the wilderness. Reporters and camera crews assembled at the end of Usher's lane, eager to make Alice's face famous across the country. It seemed inevitable that she'd be found, her ankle broken, perhaps, her body frostbitten, but alive. I'm like the general of an army, Mike told himself, on the brink of victory. He refused to shed any tears.

When the police finally got involved, Mike was called into the station and the chief, Harry Midgard, asked him in a detached, official tone where he'd been the night Alice went missing. It was as though the two men didn't know one another, as though Harry had just been trucked in from playing some city cop on television. Confused, Mike repeated what he'd said when he first reported the disappearance, that he was at home with the children so that Alice could attend the party. No, they didn't get a sitter. They'd talked about it but Mike was feeling tired. "And you were going to rest by looking after the kids?" Harry asked. Mike nodded. Was that implausible? Kids weren't so tough if you were used to them. "What about after they went to bed?" Harry wanted to know. Mike frowned. What about it? He'd watched the news and fallen asleep. No, there were no telephone calls. No, he did not wait up. He was a heavy sleeper, so in the morning he assumed that she'd come in late and risen early, as she often did. He didn't realize anything was wrong until the clinic called wondering where she was. She'd scheduled extra hours that week because the clinic was brand new and there were bills to be paid. He wanted to tell Harry how it was a good building, with plenty of natural light and bright, warm walls, how when Alice first showed the place to him she'd beamed with pride. But all Harry wanted to know was whether they'd been having any arguments. He asked to talk with the children. "Don't you believe me?" Mike bellowed. Of course, said Harry. We just need to ask a few questions, for the record.

As Harry led him out of the office, he reminded Mike not to expect too much from the investigation. He said there were hundreds of people from the henge party to interview, not all of them in Mooney's Dump – some had even come up from the States for the night – and it could take a while. They'd be in touch if they found out anything. Harry's tone was polite and congenial, but on the way home Mike wondered if the man had already begun talking with people, if some from the search parties ended their days at the police station, telling Harry what they'd seen. *The guy doesn't even help with the search. He just sits in his kitchen drinking coffee like he doesn't care.*

It was Harry who told him that they'd managed to solve the mystery of the missing five hundred dollars. Cam Usher had heard the gossip about money, and he'd come forward to explain that Alice had donated it to help finish building his henge. Mike was outraged but not surprised, after all the hours she'd spent working on the thing, those days when she wasn't at the clinic, with a husband and two children at home. He thought of Usher's efforts in organizing the searches and had to push away suspicions that he didn't have the energy to deal with. When a reporter asked him about Alice's fidelity he stopped talking to the media.

But then, the media had virtually stopped talking to him as well. No evidence had come to light, the police were stymied, and by the middle of January the only newspaper still carrying the story was the *Mooney's Dump Beacon*. In February, after the referendum on the town's name, it changed to the *Sunshine Beacon* and mention of Alice was dropped altogether, as though people were eager to abandon her along with Mooney's Dump. The only reports left were the whispers he heard on street corners: . . . *voodoo and orgies at Usher's. Only a fool would have let her go . . . Or, occasionally: . . . a good-for-nothing, never had a real job. No wonder she ran away . . .*

SOMETIMES, LYING AWAKE at night, he heard the floorboards creak in the spare room next door where Alice's mother slept, listened to her racked breathing. By day, though, her only emotion seemed to be contempt. She made it clear that she no longer wanted to be sharing a house with him.

"What will you do about Nel and Oliver once I'm gone?" she said. "You can't raise two children all by yourself. You'll need to find help."

"Like who? Your ex-husband?" he retorted. Mike's own parents had died several years ago, and as for Alice's father, Nel and Oliver had never met the man. If Mike could help it, they never would. "Listen, I'll be fine," he told her. "I've always looked after the kids, remember? Even before Alice disappeared."

"What does that mean?" she exclaimed. "Are you saying she's a bad mother?"

"No," he said quietly.

"Because you'd have a lot of nerve, blaming her, when you're sitting around this house and she's been kidnapped, or murdered, or –"

"She's not dead!" he cried.

The words seemed to fluster her. She stopped making her bird-feeding movements and reached to push a strand of hair from her forehead.

"Well of course she isn't," she said flatly. "I wasn't suggesting otherwise."

Unlike her daughter, Mrs. Mooney left in stages. First she took a room in a bed and breakfast nearby; a week later she returned to Walkerton, driving up once a week to look after Oliver and Nel while Mike went into the clinic and tried to keep things going. At first the hygienists worked on their own, and then dentists from

Owen Sound came in on a rota. Harry Midgard only ever called to say there'd been no developments, no sign of Alice anywhere. He began to hint that Mike might be better off selling the practice, moving someplace else. But where? Mike wondered. He couldn't just leave. The new building hadn't been paid for, and the children couldn't simply be taken out of school. They were upset enough already. Each night he read to them, devised games and stories to distract them, but often he ended up cuddling and consoling, telling them that everything would be fine, that Mommy would be back soon. After a few months this ritual of consolation began to fall away, and strangely they didn't seem to notice its absence, though Mike offered no new account of their mother's whereabouts to take its place. It seemed impossible that Alice could have done anything – run off, be murdered, commit suicide – and left so little trace.

He started to scan the classifieds for jobs, only to discover there was little demand for stay-at-home husbands and failed novelists. Then, one night, he went from closet to closet in the house until he found the box he was looking for. Inside was a stack of handwritten pages, no more than a hundred in all. He skimmed over them, admiring the carefully constructed phrases, the confidence of the voice. It was good writing, he thought – he'd worried it wouldn't be – but he didn't feel any relief. The words weren't familiar to him any more. Whatever mind had devised them, it wasn't his. In the intervening years some aspect of himself had warped, deadened. Now there was nothing in him waiting to be said, only a dull, inarticulate desire for things to change. When he came to the place where the manuscript ended, with its last sentence incomplete, he had no idea what possibly might happen next. But then, he hadn't known five years ago either. He'd spent months living with that sentence, trying to decide where to take it, before finally he'd consigned it to the box and a high, dark shelf. At the time he'd told Alice that it didn't matter. "Writing was something to distract me before you and the kids came along," he'd said. "I don't need it now."

He dreamed of summer evenings, camping trips, and sex. In the mornings he awoke with the melody of "O Holy Night" swelling in his head and the empty bed beside him a little more familiar than it had been the day before.

IT TOOK A YEAR before the money ran out completely. By then he couldn't remember the last phone call he'd had from Harry Midgard. Still, when he signed the papers to sell the clinic, he wondered how he'd explain himself to Alice when she returned.

Once the new owner had moved in, Mike stopped by to pick up some chairs from the waiting room and the man insisted that furniture had been included in the sale price. Mike stormed out, then drove back the next day, the contract beside him covered in yellow highlighter circles, his line of reasoning scrupulously rehearsed. But somehow he still managed to lose the argument. He left with his fingers digging into his palms and had to stop at the door to compose himself. He tried to think about what was happening to him, and he wondered whether he'd lost the ability to feel the normal human range of emotions. Anger, elation, jealousy, grief – they'd all merged. This wasn't the right way to live.

As he walked toward the car he saw two sandy-haired boys sitting on the curb across the street as though they'd been waiting for him to come out. He couldn't place them, but they didn't look much older than Nel. Perhaps they were friends of hers from school, or maybe they'd simply been Alice's patients and knew he was the husband of their missing dentist. They seemed troubled.

"Hello, gentlemen," Mike said. The boys stood up and brushed off their shorts, staring at him but not saying anything. He went to the car and unlocked the door, planning to drive off, then reconsidered and began to cross over to them. "It's all right, you know –" But they bolted down the street, their heads turning to see if he was in pursuit.

"Your wife's a goner," one of them shouted, still running. "Somebody raped her and dumped the body."

"She was a bitch. Everybody says she deserved it."

They cut across a lawn and disappeared between two houses.

Little bastards. They'd want him to chase after them, want him to respond. Then they could wait for him to break down in the middle of berating them. Sometimes it was hard not to think of children as evil. But boys were mimics; they were probably just repeating what they'd already heard. He wanted to find the careless parents and visit the sins of the children upon them. He wanted to smash someone in the face.

Usher, he thought, despite himself, before he forced his thoughts back to financial matters. Usher would be the one to rape her.

The life insurance company wasn't any help. When sixteen months had passed he sat down to apply for a return on her policy, rushing through the form as though his hand could work independently of his brain, but they sent back a note saying sorry, the claim was invalid without proof of death. A person had to be missing for seven years. He hired a private detective, and when the man discovered nothing, the insurance company agreed to send their own investigator, Bronwen Ferry, up from Toronto on Mike's tab.

"Don't worry," she told him the first day. "We'll get to the bottom of things." It turned out Bronwen was a Mooney's Dump girl like Alice. She had brown hair, a fuller body. She said she was staying at her parents' farm next to the airfield while she looked into the case. He had a perplexing sense that he'd seen her somewhere before, but he knew better than to speak a line like that out loud.

"It can't be safe for them to give the company a human face like this," he told her instead, and she smiled.

"Don't get the wrong impression," she replied. "I'm tough."

"I can tell."

Every few nights she came by the house to report on what she'd learned. He was grateful to her for it, but there was seldom much to relate, and even when she did share one of her hunches, she refused to throw around names, so he had to read between the lines if he wanted to discern what she was really suggesting. That was how he found out for sure about Alice and Cam Usher. "You're not listening to me," Bronwen protested. "I never said I believed it really happened." But Mike waved his hand dismissively, remembering all the times Alice had left for some environmental protest or gone to work at the henge. He used to joke about her disappearing down the rabbit hole again.

"It was Usher, then," he said to Bronwen. It was more a question than a declaration. "She wouldn't leave me for him, and he killed her." It still unnerved him to speak as though she might be dead. He waited for Bronwen to reassure him, but she only murmured "Possibly" in a tone that indicated it wasn't very possible at all.

"Mike, if you go on like this you'll end up suspecting everyone in Sunshine."

"So what?" he replied. "They all suspect me. Half of them won't even say hello any more. Sometimes I hate this place, I really do."

"Sure," she said. Her eyes were blue, so peculiar and bright a shade that you'd think they were plugged into something. "But maybe it's not the town you hate right now."

"I thought you were an insurance investigator, not a psychologist."

"Well? Am I wrong?"

Mike took a deep breath, puffed it out like smoke.

"She was unfaithful. How can I not be angry?"

"But in your heart, you still love her."

He raised his eyebrows. It sounded as if she was accusing him.

"Well, my heart is stupid," he replied. She laughed gently. It was a nice laugh.

AFTER EIGHTEEN MONTHS, bones were all they found. Not a body. Alice had long ago dissolved in the bellies of fishes. By now she was a dorsal fin, a tadpole, a cluster of reeds. A pair of divers from Ohio discovered what was left, a few hundred yards from the shore near Usher's henge. They weren't even searching for her, but for some steamer that had disappeared in a gale more than a century ago. It was early in July, a heat wave was scorching the peninsula, and Mike found himself soothed by the thought of being down there with her, resting in the depths of Mooney's Bay, anchored by the weight of all that water.

Immediately there was a debate over jurisdiction between the Sunshine police and the police at the Ojibwa reserve. The Natives claimed the water was First Nations territory, and every day Harry Midgard explained the dispute to Mike in great detail, as though it was significant. Mike only shook his head and asked what had been discovered. When a court order was acquired and the body transferred from the reserve to Sunshine, Harry didn't ask him to identify it; he said it was "too far gone." Even before the dental records provided confirmation, though, Harry offered up her gold wedding band as proof. Mike tried leaving it on the bureau in their bedroom, but then, on an impulse, he ended up taking the thing and squeezing it down his little finger. It barely fit. When the imagined scenes of her and Cam Usher played in his mind, he thought of throwing the band into a gutter somewhere for the town bum to find – but the bum was Archie Boone, another member of the Mooney clan. Mike felt an ill-defined, inexorable spite for the Mooneys nowadays and refused to give them anything more.

At first Oliver clung to his father's side when Mike explained what had happened. After a bout of sobbing, though, the boy went to his room and began to play calmly with his fire truck, as though the tears had been a necessary ritual. Nel was less easy to deal with.

"I knew it all along," she declared with hate in her eyes. "I knew you were lying. I knew she was dead the whole time." Mike thought he understood what was behind it; her teacher had called several times. Apparently there were classmates at school who'd been no more sensitive with her than they'd been with Mike outside the clinic.

For the rest of Sunshine, the news of the body was like a key in the door. Within hours, a man from Strikersville turned up at the Sunshine police station to say that on his way home from the party he'd seen a car parked near the water. Someone else confirmed it was Stoddart Fremlin's car. When Harry Midgard told Mike two days later that the town librarian could recall seeing it slow down to pick up someone a little after midnight, he couldn't believe it. "She just remembers it now?" he shouted. "What the hell?" Harry raised his hands as though in surrender and said this was how it happened sometimes. It was probably a dead end anyhow. But the next morning they brought in Stoddart Fremlin for questioning and they didn't let him go. They told Mike they wanted to do more tests on the remains.

"When can I bury her?" Mike demanded.

"How are the kids?" Harry said in reply. "You know, you've been a great father to them, everyone knows that."

Mike ignored him. "Is all the testing really necessary?" he insisted, and Harry looked at him with suspicion.

"I'm a little concerned about you," Harry told him. "Don't you care how she died? What about justice?" Mike nodded wearily.

Harry said they could rule out nothing: suicide, murder, misadventure. The last one was an insurance word but the most romantic. The wheel of lethal possibilities spun until they blended together in a white haze that left Mike with migraines. When they were at their worst, the same scenarios kept seeping through the fissures of pain. He imagined packing up the car without telling anyone, driving off by himself, leaving Sunshine forever. There must be some circus, some freak show he could join. *Come one, come all. See the Incredible Grieving Cuckold.*

After things with Harry had soured, Mike was left to talk with Crommelynck, the new constable. Crommelynck told him there was still some controversy over marks on the bones; they were waiting on experts from the States. If he could just be patient, Crommelynck said. Mike heard other words under the surface of the man's admonition. *She's already been gone all this time. What's the hurry now?* There were hints that if the funeral was so important, for the time being it might be better to bury an empty coffin.

"I will not wait any longer," said Mike. "The children need closure on this. My son doesn't understand it when his father says

43

Mommy is gone, but he knows what a gravestone means. The community needs an ending too. Every day someone asks me when the funeral will be. They don't ask about an empty coffin. I'm not going to bury an empty coffin." With a week gone since the discovery and the July heat unbearable, he ranted at Crommelynck until the man admitted they were done, at least for now, and drew up the necessary papers.

The morning of the funeral, Harry Midgard showed up on the doorstep with a court order. They were taking the bones after all. Alice's mother was staying at the house for the weekend, and without explaining his destination Mike told her he'd be back soon. Then he tailed the police car to the funeral home, where he pleaded with the coroner. Mike's voice was faltering now. The night before, after tucking in the children, he'd pulled out the old photo albums, bent on purging himself of tears in private, and the effort had wrenched his vocal cords. Now his throat ached and he felt nothing but rage as he listened to the coroner tell him that the day's ceremony would have to proceed without the body.

Mike lingered in the cold basement of the funeral home to watch Harry and the coroner carry down the metal packing case that would be used to transport Alice's remains. He left when they lifted the lid from the coffin, afraid of what might happen if someone fumbled and he had to witness a large grey bone, her clavicle or thigh, clatter on the tiles. As he walked to his car in the hot sunlight he thought of them handling her, and he wanted to run back and kill them both.

When he returned to the house, Nel was sitting alone at the kitchen table in her dark blue dress and there were screams coming from one of the bedrooms. He took the stairs three at a time, but it was only a tantrum. Oliver had refused to put on his suit, and Alice's mother was trying to slip his hand into the arm of the jacket.

"I don't want to go, I don't want to go," Oliver yelled in between sobs. Mrs. Mooney looked at Mike and shrugged.

"He's been like this ever since you left," she said. Mike could tell she was spent. "He has to come, of course." Mike nodded.

Once she left the room, he took her place beside Oliver on the bed.

"What's the matter?" he asked, and waited. "If you tell me, maybe we can do something about it." There was no response.

He knew what Alice would do; she'd promise to bring out her telescope. Nel and Oliver were in its thrall whenever she set it up on the patio. Mike liked to watch from inside as they solemnly obeyed her instructions to be careful, to take turns. When they finished, they'd tell him what they'd seen. Pluto, Mars. The Sea of Tranquillity. But then, the telescope was the reason she'd become involved with Usher's henge; it was all because of her damn preoccupation with the alignment of the stars.

No, there wasn't time for telescopes now. He'd had enough. Without another word, he grabbed Oliver and started to wrestle him into his clothes. He'd never done this to one of his children before. He'd vowed never to do so. There was almost always time to strategize, to plead, to coax. Other parents seemed amazed by such tactics when he practised them in public, as though his forbearance was somehow offensive. He wondered what they'd think now if they could see him grabbing legs, ramming them into pant-holes, straightening stubborn elbows to slide them though sleeves.

"You can cry all you want, but you're going," he said at the end of it, wincing at the rawness of his throat, and left Oliver to scream in the room while he went downstairs to the phone.

"Who are you calling?" asked Alice's mother.

"I don't know," he said. "Someone to look after Oliver." He punched a few buttons, waited, hung up, and pressed the receiver to his forehead. He'd thought Bronwen might be able to do it, but the line was busy. In the background, Mrs. Mooney was asking him how Oliver would feel later on if he didn't go. Her voice was aggressive, almost shrill.

"You heard him," Mike said impatiently. "He doesn't want to."

Then his mother-in-law did something that surprised him. She stepped forward and laid her head against his chest. Confused, he put his hands around her. Every few seconds her body shuddered gently, as though a motor inside her was trying to start.

"Do you want to lie down until we go?" he said. "I can get the kids into the car –"

"No, I'm all right," she said, pulling a tissue from her pocket and turning her face from him. "You have enough to handle, you've made that clear enough. You don't need me falling apart too. I'm a good grandmother, don't worry."

"Of course you are," he said. "Whoever said you weren't?"

"No, don't bother about me," she went on. "I'm strong. My brother died when I was eight, and my mother the year I married. I don't need you coddling me."

He'd been about to reassure her, make an empty remark about the need to hang in there, carry on, but he stopped himself.

"I – I don't know what to say. If you feel I haven't been sympathetic –"

"No, forget it, Mike. Forget it." When she turned back to him, her expression was just as stone-faced as always. Look at her, he thought. She's the one who does nothing but criticize, who makes it seem as though she's invulnerable to grief. Well, I won't start feeling guilty now.

He went to the phone and called Susan Sutherland, whose daughter Zeljka had been in Oliver's kindergarten class. It was a long shot – they'd probably be going to the funeral with Marge – but perhaps she'd hired a sitter who could watch Oliver too. When Susan said hello, his throat was so sore that he had to repeat himself twice before she understood who was talking to her.

"We're in luck," he told Alice's mother after he'd hung up. "I found somebody." Then he went upstairs to tell Oliver the good news.

SUSAN AND MARGE both answered the door once he arrived. Oliver had fallen asleep in the car, so Mike was carrying him, and he passed him over to their waiting arms as though delivering a parcel. He could hear another person moving around somewhere deeper in the apartment.

46

"I didn't know you had guests," he said, wincing at his own rasp. He wondered if he'd make it to the end of his eulogy before he lost his voice altogether.

"Oh no, that's Daniel," Marge said. "He's home visiting. He'll stay back to watch Olly and Zed."

"Listen, Mike," began Susan. At the bottom of his vision her hand reached for Marge's. "In case we don't get to say it later –"

"It's okay," he replied quickly. He had enough experience with condolences now that he tended to pre-empt people and put in their mouths the words that he could most easily bear to hear: Yes, it's unspeakable, yes, we're still coming to grips. The children have been real troopers. "We all miss her," he said on this occasion. "People have said such kind things. The other day Oliver asked me if Mommy really was a pillow of the community." He put on a practised smile, and they laughed dutifully before saying goodbye.

At the church he had only a few minutes to talk with the minister before people began to arrive. They filled the pews, the balcony, even the folding chairs in front where he sat with Nel, Alice's mother, and countless other Mooneys who knew him as little as he knew them. With so much of Sunshine gathered in one place, the pale uniformity of their skin was apparent to him in a way it seldom else was any more, and he found himself wondering about Alice's father. Mrs. Mooney hadn't mentioned whether he was going to attend. Even though the man lived in town, he hadn't spoken to Mike or Alice in fifteen years, and it would be surreal to see him now. He was her father, though. Of course he'd be here, if not to grieve, then at least to hold Mike accountable for what had happened.

A few minutes into the minister's sermon, Alice's mother put her hand on Mike's shoulder and pointed toward the back row. He's come, after all, Mike thought, but when he turned to see, there was no sign of the man. Then he saw what Mrs. Mooney had observed: Daniel Barrie, sitting at the back of the church with Marge and Susan on either side of him like prison guards, and Oliver and Zeljka next to them.

"Should I bring Oliver up here with us?" Mrs. Mooney whispered.

"No, let them be," Mike croaked. He glanced at the glass of water on the lectern at the front.

"People will talk," she whispered. "They'll say it's wrong for him not to sit with family."

People are already talking, he thought.

When the sermon ended they sang "Onward, Christian Soldiers," and after that it was Mike's turn to address the mourners. He'd agreed to do so believing that if he didn't make some claim on her, the town would swallow her completely and clench its jaws before he could follow. He'd been the one to lose her – they all knew that, and they hated him for it – but now he had to make them appreciate that there was nothing more he could do. The police, the insurance company, the investigators, the bank, the lawyers . . . They'd made her something else. She was the dozens of dotted lines that he lay his signature upon. He walked to the front holding a carefully written page in front of him.

When he started to speak, nothing came out. His mouth stalled on the first round vowel, pushing silent air. He stopped to try again. A murmur began in the pews. He coughed, took a drink of water, and when he brought the glass from his mouth he could see concern in people's faces. They thought he was breaking down, but he'd just lost his voice. It wasn't surprising after the past few days, the late nights, the telephone calls and arguments. It was unacceptable for people to think he was a victim. This was not an expression of grief, he wanted to yell. This was the exhaustion of grief by life.

"My wife's not in this coffin," he whispered, pointing. The community had been tricked, this whole event was a sham and they needed to know, but already Alice's mother was standing, walking over to lead him back to his chair, saying things in his ear. She was crying; what was she crying about? He didn't want to sit down with her, she couldn't make him. To refuse his seat would appear outrageous, though. It would be out of proportion. It would just confirm what they already thought of him. For the rest of the week they'd talk about how he'd fallen apart, after all those months of trying to hide the cracks. Grudgingly he took his seat again and listened to the minister lead them in prayer.

A few of the mourners who'd stood at the back were milling around outside, smoking and talking quietly, when they carried out the casket. Mike had insisted on being a pallbearer, and he was so much taller than the rest of them that if there'd been anything in it they might have heard the slide of bones. The coffin was ridiculously light, and he had an impulse to take it in both hands and carry it over his head like a canoe. I don't need any of them, he thought. I could walk to the cemetery with it all by myself. Then he noticed Cam Usher there in a group of men to the side, wearing a preposterous brown suit from the seventies, and was outraged.

As he got into the lead car, Marge came up holding Oliver's hand.

"I hope it's all right," she said. "He changed his mind at the last minute." Mike nodded and gestured for Oliver to join him, then took him in his lap and held him tight.

At the interment they planted a tree for her. The minister had cautioned him that it wouldn't be allowed to stay. It was against the cemetery's regulations, and besides, the hospital was planting one for her in a ceremony the following week. Mike shrugged with apparent indifference, ready to snap, and replied that it was in the will. They'd plant it, and if there were problems he'd deal with them. Then he went home and slept into the evening, awaking to sweaty sheets and the metronomic shriek of Nel on the rusty swing in the backyard. Downstairs Alice's mother and Oliver were scribbling in a colouring book. There was nothing out of the ordinary. Mike remembered from his boyhood the funerals of relatives, with the constant rush of visitors at the house and the kitchen overflowing with food. All of that had failed to materialize here.

The event hadn't celebrated a life or brought people together in their grief; it felt more like the signing of a treaty, sober and pointless, after a war of attrition had been lost.

SUMMER IN SUNSHINE was the season of anxious profit. The town had begun to awaken in April: the last luminescent patches of snow deserted the shade, the ice heaved out of the bays, and northbound cars grew more frequent on the highway with their loads of tourists seeking country peace. Now, with most of July gone, there already seemed to be an uneasy communal apprehension of the season's end. Mike thought such an atmosphere explained his compulsion to visit the cemetery and check if Alice's tree was still there, even though it was only a week after the funeral. He arranged for a sitter, then drove into town, where there were no empty parking spaces along the whole stretch of storefronts. He drove up and down twice, cursing. Finally he double-parked, ran into the florist's, and demanded a dozen lilies. When he walked out, Daniel Barrie was holding the door open, red-faced and awkward, as if embarrassed to have seen him.

Sick of humanity, he decided not to take the paved route out to the cemetery, but followed the checkerboard of concession roads that cut stubbornly through hills and maple stands. With the thrum of the engine, "O Holy Night" began to play in his head. The song hadn't come to him in a while, but it still woke him sometimes in the mornings, and it was an old, resented friend. He whispered the words now, testing the strength of his voice, letting them fill his head the way he wished the sound of them could fill the car. *O night divine! O night! O holy night!* The world burned away by one stark, radiant noun.

"Maybe you like it because it appeals to lonely people," Bronwen had said when he mentioned the song's recurrence. "It tells you there's a comforting presence, even at night when things seem worst."

"I'm not lonely, though," he'd replied. "Alice is always around."

"Jesus, Mike," she'd said. "At some point you need to let go of her."

"I want to look forward, believe me. But this town, it won't let me forget."

The cemetery was at the end of a long gravel track that snaked along the top of the escarpment before descending into a slough between the cliffs and the bay. With the window open he could smell pockets of swamp-gas hanging in the air. The land farther on was strewn with glacial debris, but there was soil for farming and burial. He parked by the low stone wall that marked the edge of the cemetery and walked toward the gate.

It hadn't rained in over a week, and the vegetation outside the walls was tinged with brown, but inside the cemetery the lawn was a vibrant green. As he walked up the hill toward the place at the back where Alice's tree stood, he thought again about the cemetery's prohibition against such plantings. He was sure that Alice would have known about it, and her request made him suspect that she'd been hoping for him to circumvent the rules. But then, she'd been thirty-six, an age when nobody really thought they were going to die. Even the discovery of her will had been a surprise: he'd found it at the bottom of a drawer in her dresser. It was one of the ones you could buy at a drugstore for twenty dollars, no doubt completed by Alice on a lark, just for the satisfaction of apportioning all her possessions, fantasizing about how things might be after she was gone. Everybody did that. When she wrote the will, she'd probably imagined exactly this situation, Mike climbing the hill with his stoic face, bent into the gusting wind.

Ahead of him, in the place where he thought that Alice should be, there was a surge of orange. If it were October he would have thought it a garbage bag, the kind with a jack-o'-lantern face that you filled with leaves, caught here after blowing across the fields. He wasn't expecting an animal of any sort. When he realized what it was, he looked right and left, hoping for some sign of human control over what was happening. Cam Usher's wildlife park wasn't far from here. The animal must have escaped. There was no other way to account for a tiger in this place.

It lay on the grass with its head turned toward the bay, its eyes almost closed, the fur around the edges of its face rippling. The tiger was as large as a man – bigger, even – and it had been obscured by monuments as Mike approached, so that now he was less than thirty feet away, motionless, his heart berserk. He didn't know what to do and tried to remember, but there was nothing to recall. With bears you made a lot of noise, except for one of them – grizzly, brown? – when it was better to curl up in a ball. No one ever said what to do with tigers. He knew how these things went: whatever choice he made would be the wrong one.

In the end he decided to retreat the way he'd come. Slowly he edged backwards, watching for the tiger's eyes to shift toward him. His feet got the better of him and moved more rapidly, more loudly than he would have liked, but he was thankful at least that he could keep his body from turning to run. He'd made it almost halfway down the hill when he backed into a low grave-marker and fell, the lilies in his hand scattering across the grass.

He lurched upright, first kneeling, then standing, to find the tiger was gone. He spun in a full circle but saw no sign. It might have vanished over the crest of the hill, or it might be somewhere in the forest, watching. He tried to continue as before, but the strategy of a patient retreat to the car seemed less appealing now. Should he run? That might just encourage it to attack. He looked around for shelter and saw nothing plausible, which was a relief. There wasn't much to commend the idea of sitting somewhere, not just out of sight but out of seeing, waiting for anything to happen. Think, he told himself. Think clearly. Either the thing is gone or it's still here and it knows you're here too. Animals have better senses than we do. There's no point trying to hide, but perhaps you could frighten it with noise.

The first note lodged itself somewhere down in his lungs. He'd forgotten that his voice was gone. He tried again, lower this time, but it was no use; the best he could manage was a faint wheezing, like something wounded. That would just encourage the damn thing.

By the time he saw it charging out of the woods he could do nothing except be amazed at how little noise it made. Adrenalin was quick, too, fast enough to paralyze him with chemical overload just as the tiger reached him. His scream died in his chest and he presented the creature with an enormous reedy yawn the moment before it swerved. He turned, bracing for another charge, only to see a dozen crows climbing the air on frantic wings, and a blur of muscular colour slashing into them. Mike watched it leap and snare one of them with a paw as if it were catching a baseball. In seconds the bird was nothing but a mess of feathers on the lawn and the tiger was moving again, away from him. Mike felt strangely abandoned, as though he had wooed and been passed over.

The tiger went in the other direction, toward the west. It travelled with such fluidity that he imagined in a different place it would blend with the environment and he'd easily lose it. But now, no matter how discreet its progress, there was always a contrast between the fiery body and the surrounding cedars, the loud green grass. Its exposure made it less fearsome than vulnerable. Only now in the cloud-filtered light of the closing sun did it have some semblance of belonging. The way it moved – not ambling, slinking, slouching, lumbering, or gliding, but somehow all of those things. It cleared the cemetery fence without touching the top of the stone wall, without even an increase in pace. He stayed there watching, and a few minutes later it was there again in the distance.

On the drive back to the house he thought of pulling into Cam Usher's place to tell him what had happened, but he didn't feel up to maintaining the pretence of civility, so he stayed on the shore road. He'd make the call from home. Sails hung flaccid on the boats cruising Mooney's Bay, and mast lights were starting to wink. The tiger still padded through his mind, and he tried to see some meaning in its appearance. But that was foolish. It was just an animal, no matter how exotic or unlikely.

He arrived at the house to find the sitter's jeep gone and another car in the drive: Bronwen Ferry's beaten red hatchback. Its appearance in the evenings was growing more frequent and soothing these days. She stood waiting in the kitchen for him, the children playing nearby and apparently indifferent to the substitute.

"I told Christie she could go home. I hope you don't mind me taking over until you got here."

"No, of course not," Mike whispered, remembering his voice was still weak. "I'm glad to see you." Nel ran up wanting to play outside, and Mike shook his head.

"It's getting dark," he rasped. "And I don't think you two should play outside for the next little while."

Bronwen looked at him, concerned.

"What's up?"

"Something I saw near Cam Usher's," he said, still watching Nel. "I'll tell you later." He didn't want her or Oliver to hear anything about tigers or they'd be compelled to sneak outside for a glimpse. They knew tigers as something friendly and cute. A child didn't see a tiger in the same way a tiger saw a child. When Nel realized he wasn't going to change his mind she returned to the living room and he whispered the story to Bronwen.

"It must have been from Usher's park," she agreed. There was a moment of awkward silence. "Listen, I don't know if you want to hear this now, but that reminds me of why I came," she said.

"Why? Did you find out something more about him?" So she'd come on business, after all. He tried to steel himself by imagining what revelation could possibly be worse than what he already knew.

"No," said Bronwen. "But tell me something first. A couple of years ago, did Alice ever mention getting a speeding ticket near Orangeville?" Mike shook his head. "Then I have some news. It's about Daniel Barrie."

54

He moved to the coffee machine with its half-empty pot, wincing at the double-clink of the gold rings on glass as he wrapped his fingers around the handle. It suddenly occurred to him that he'd forgotten to check whether Alice's tree in the cemetery was still standing.

"Tell me," he whispered, talking to the wall.

MORELS

"Honestly, the guy is a coward." According to Esther's watch it was ten past two in the morning, but the fluorescent lights above her blanched the darkness so that the hour seemed meaningless. She was counting money at the Sunshine Variety and talking at the same time. "There he is at the back of the line to pay, right, and I'm not expecting it, he's supposed to be in England. He's studying the newspaper rack pretty hard, so he must have spotted me at the last moment and got trapped. When it's his turn, he hands me the milk carton without looking up like he's ready to walk straight out the door."

"You're not counting and talking at the same time, are you?" Stump's head appeared from the grocery aisle. "For Christ's sake, Esther, you're the reason I get an earful from the accountant every month."

"Sixty-five, seventy, seventy-five," she bellowed, slapping down bills. Stump grumbled and went back to checking the bread. He was always careful not to end up with spoiled stock, but sometimes it still happened. When customers pointed it out, he put on his most apologetic voice, and after they left he aimed at Esther all the words he'd wanted to use with them, with his ex-wife, with God, it seemed.

"So what did you say to him?" he asked from behind the shelves, his body elongated by the convex security mirror in the corner.

"One-eighty-five, one-ninety, one-ninety-five."

"All right, wise guy, I get the point," he snapped. She grinned at having won. "Come on, what did you say?"

"I said hello. And then he was stuck. There wasn't anyone else in line, so we had all day. Poor guy. At Cambridge he probably had his butler buy the milk." Stump snorted. "Finally he said, 'Esther Fremlin, what do you know!' and asked me how long I've been working here."

"He mention your dad?"

"No, he was trying hard to avoid it. Two-ninety. Two ninety-five. But at the end he said he hoped everything would turn out okay for me."

"What did he mean by that?" asked Stump. She shrugged. "Esther? I asked you, what did he mean?"

"And I shrugged!"

"Oh." He peeked around the corner. "Did you lock up?"

"Sure," she said to appease him, and he disappeared again. He insisted on shutting down promptly at two, but she liked to stay open until she left. It was nice, the look of gratitude you got when someone arrived expecting you to be closed. And there were cool breezes through the door. She and Stump could never agree on the temperature at the Variety. "I'm burning up in here," she'd say, but Stump kept the thermostat pegged at seventy. With the heat from the radiator hitting the cold air from the chest freezers, tiny weather systems swirled into being and swept down the aisles.

"You're having hot flashes," he'd chortle.

"Don't be stupid. That's only with old ladies."

"I know. I just said it for a laugh."

"So who's laughing?"

But today she'd seen Daniel Barrie and arguments over the temperature were forgotten.

"Tell me again," Stump said. "How come you were friends with him? Teachers' kids, right?" She nodded. Stump had been raised in Owen Sound and knew next to nothing about Sunshine, so half the time she felt more like his tour guide than his girlfriend.

"Daniel's mom was the English teacher at our high school, my mom was History," she said. "We sort of grew up together."

"It must have been weird for you, going to your mom's school. What was she like in class?"

"I don't know," Esther replied. "By the time I got to Grade Nine she'd already left town."

She heard him shuffle some loaves of bread and wasn't surprised. Silence was usually what Stump settled for when he wanted to be compassionate.

"What about Daniel's mom?" he said finally.

"Oh, Marge was cool. She knew how to say the F-word in the classroom and get away with it. She had these asymmetrical earrings that came down to her shoulders, and she dressed in black. You'll always do fine with kids if you wear asymmetrical earrings and say the F-word at the right time."

Esther yawned and started rolling coins. She hadn't been sleeping well lately. Most of her nights were spent sitting up in bed, listening to Stump snore, or curled up on the sofa in the living room, smoking one cigarette after another and thinking about where her father had ended up. It was too much to deal with on her own. I miss Alice, she thought. I miss our talks at the clinic. They'd be even better now that I'm with Stump – plenty of material there. Before it was mostly her who spoke, worrying about Mike or the kids, and me feeling like I had nothing to offer but my sympathy. But I'm a woman now, Alice. I live with someone and cook for him and let him make love to me. You'd have liked Stump if I'd introduced you, I think. But I met him the night you disappeared. I wish the timing was different. I wish you were here to see how much I've changed.

The door bleeped and a couple of men sauntered in, wanting to buy firewood. They were both in their twenties, bearded and ball-capped and raging drunk, probably right out of the Confederation Hotel and headed to the beach for a bonfire. One of them was tall with a cocky grin on his face. The other was barely five feet, all gristle and bone. He looked like some parts had been left out when they built him.

Esther told them they didn't have firewood. "Some folks sell it along the highway," she suggested, hoping that would send them off. Then they noticed the money on the counter.

"Did you make that all on your own today?" the tall one said. "That's a lot of cash for a little girl like you."

"It's after two, we're closed," said pudgy old Stump, coming around the corner in his blue work shirt and tie. They both turned as though to leave, but they regained their composure when they realized how small he was.

"The door was open," the tall one answered defiantly. The short one hadn't said a word yet. He was staring at her with fish-eyes.

"Stump, get these guys out of here, they're creepy," said Esther.

"Come on, Stump, you heard what she said," said the tall one. "Get us out of here."

Stump grimaced. "You can leave on your own. Like I said, we're closed." He walked behind the counter and pointed to the back. "You see that up there?" Esther didn't think they were going to bother to look, but the tall one did. The short one just kept staring at her. She was going to scream. "You try anything, you'll be doing it on tape," said Stump. He picked up the telephone. "I'm calling the police."

The short one still didn't blink. The tall one scowled, glanced again at the security camera, then broke into his grin again.

"Buddy, we were just kidding around. Don't go crazy on us. You're the one who's open after two. We were worried about you. Hey, can you prove you even work here?"

"Hello, this is the Sunshine Variety," said Stump into the phone. "We have a couple of strangers here who refuse to leave the premises."

"You're nuts," muttered the tall one, and they walked out.

Neither Stump nor Esther said anything for a long time. After a while he went to the door and locked it. Then he disappeared into the back room and returned with cigarettes for the shelves behind the counter. She was putting the last of the money into the deposit bag when he started to chuckle.

"Didn't I tell you about that security camera? It just paid for itself." The camera cost forty-five dollars at the electronics store in Owen Sound. It was hollow plastic and not even plugged into anything. She looked at it briefly, then started to load the register with a new roll of receipt paper.

"So what do you think of that?" he said. "I tell you, I'm sick of taking people's crap. This is my store, and I'm not going to be threatened in it." She didn't reply. "You're the one who's always saying I kiss up to the customers. How about it?"

"They weren't customers."

He let it sit for a while before he turned on her.

"Why are you acting like I did something wrong? I did exactly what I was supposed to do. That's why we have things like police and security cameras. And here you are, looking at me with that face. God damn it, you piss me off, you know that?" There were dark patches under his armpits surrounded by rings of salt. "What did you want me to do? Should I have grabbed them by the collars? I bet that would've made you happy. You wanted me to get into a fight with both of those drunks at once, when they could have been carrying knives or guns for all you know. Well no thanks, Esther. I'm not an idiot."

She closed the lid over the receipt paper and banged it tight against the register.

Just wait until later, she told herself. He talks like a big man now, but watch what happens when we get home. He thinks he's pretty smart, pulling one over on me, hiding that rifle under our bed. Well

I know it's there, Stump, and I'm going to give you a piece of my mind about it. You probably feel all macho buying a gun, but you're a spineless little shrimp and you know damn well that I'm not going to let you keep that thing, not while I'm living there.

And what are you doing with a rifle anyway?

THE PREVIOUS WEEK her father had been arrested for Alice's murder and she'd been the last one in town to know. Working at the store all day, she'd wondered what was going on. The regular customers seemed withdrawn, and they avoided conversation; there was just the quick exchange of bills and coins. Only when Stump told her after closing that night did she understand what all the quiet had been about.

"How long have you known?" she'd asked him. Just a couple of hours, he said, but she was furious that he hadn't come to the store right away. "He's in jail for killing Alice and you let me keep working like that?" She thought back to their afternoon together before her shift: Stump watching television, completely silent for once and not all over her. He'd probably known then too.

"The man's my father, for God's sake," she shouted. "Come on, drive me to the police station."

"It's too late tonight," he said. "Tomorrow. Besides, I didn't even think you'd want to see him. The way you talk about him –"

"That stuff doesn't matter now," she said.

But she wasn't sure.

Her father was displeased with her. As he saw it, apparently, her adult life had been one bad decision after another. First, going to community college in Belleville rather than university. Never mind what her grades had been like; every time they talked, he reminded her that she'd condemned herself to a life among the great unwashed. Then there was her return to Mooney's Dump once she'd graduated.

"This place chokes the life out of you," he'd said when she told him she was coming back. "Look what it did to your mother."

According to the story the two of them got by with, it was the town that had driven her out.

"If Mooney's Dump is so rotten, why are you still here?" she wanted to know.

"I'm not, half the time. I travel. I get away." She knew he was thinking about the glory days with his washed-up hockey team and Rocket DeWitt, his washed-up star.

"You stopped coaching five years ago," she exclaimed. "When was the last time you went to a tournament? Rocket doesn't even play any more. He works at the gas station, remember?"

He didn't reply. Rocket was someone they never talked about.

"The point is," he said after a while, "that you don't have any responsibilities here, Esther. You're free to make something of yourself."

He was right about the town at least. Success was a foreign word in Sunshine, something that happened to people you never met, in places you never saw. It was all well and good that the world had room for successful people, but the size of the world could be frightening too. It was tempting to shrink it by coming home, settling down in a comfortable house with a comfortable person like Stump. Her father didn't approve. He'd hired her as a secretary at his dental clinic, but then she'd decided to stay with the job two years ago when he retired and Alice took over. In his eyes it was a betrayal for her not to leave with him, and he wasn't any happier when she started to work at the Variety. The news about moving in with Stump at the start of the summer had been the last straw.

"Your employer? A convenience-store owner? What kind of security is that? Eleven years older? Not even a proposal? You're twenty-four, you're still a girl. You'll end up pregnant and abandoned. Don't come back here, that's all I'm saying. There won't be any sympathy from me. I'm telling you right now. You used to be such a sensible child. I don't know you any more. You've changed."

Well, she thought, that's what people do, don't they? She hadn't talked to him since. It had been almost three weeks, and Stump was all for maintaining the silence.

"I love you, pumpkin, but your dad is a bit strange. Everybody knows that. It was a miracle you turned out like you did. I think it might be good to have some distance from him, see him for what he is."

"And what's that?" she asked. But he didn't answer.

The morning after Stump told her about the arrest, she walked to the police station. Her father wasn't there. They said he'd been moved to Owen Sound, where there were cells for long-term detention. She went to the Variety, demanded the pickup truck, and took the back roads where she could speed as much as she wanted. But at the city limits she slowed to a crawl. Either he'd be indifferent to her coming or he'd be desperate for her. Whichever it was, a visit might not be the best thing. She didn't want to do him any favours.

When she entered the courthouse, part of her hoped there were no visitors allowed, but the clerk just smiled and asked her to wait. Then he led her to a small room. No bars, no glass partition with little microphones, just two folding metal chairs and a table. Her father came in accompanied by a police officer, but without any handcuffs or a prison uniform. They didn't speak until the officer had left and closed the door.

"It's pretty relaxed around here, isn't it?" she said.

"A real spa," he agreed.

"I didn't mean it like that," she said, and he nodded tiredly. "Look, do you want to talk? Are you happy to see me?" She regretted how anxious she sounded.

"Of course I am," he replied, his face blank.

He told her there was nothing to worry about. The evidence was non-existent, the witness unreliable. He'd hired Solomon DeWitt, and Solomon was convinced the charges would be dropped within the week.

"But what really happened?" she asked. "That's all I want to know."

He shrugged and said it was a bit of a problem. He'd had too much to drink at Cam Usher's party, and there was a gap in his memory between the time he arrived and the next morning when he woke up in bed. He couldn't remember a thing. Certainly nothing about Alice. He'd told them the same story two years ago when they were investigating the disappearance, and back then Harry Midgard had just nodded understandingly. Now they refused to believe him.

"Alice and I were just business partners," he said. "And that was over by the time she disappeared. I barely knew her. Where's the motive?"

Esther couldn't answer. She was wondering the same thing.

"I'll talk to Solomon and get it all sorted out," she said. Everything he'd told her had already been reported in the Owen Sound newspaper that morning, but she felt better hearing it from him in person. He asked her to bring some clothing, check the mail at the house. Sure she would, she said. Of course. She got up to hug him. Here he was in jail, on charges neither of them had even mentioned out loud, and they were making up. His whispered request for her to stay a bit longer almost made her weep. She thought he might prefer small talk, so she searched her brains for something interesting, but he didn't give her any time. He wanted to know if she'd seen Rocket.

"Solomon is worried about him," he explained. "Apparently he's left town and not told anybody."

At a time like this, her father must have better things to worry about than his lawyer's son.

"I thought you and Rocket didn't talk much any more," she said. It was a subject her father had never discussed with her, and she only knew it through her own guesswork. He opened his mouth as though to deny it, but after a moment he nodded.

"I hoped if he heard the news, he might –" He took in a breath. "Ah well."

"If I bump into him, I'll let him know."

"Let him know what?" asked her father sharply.

"That you want to see him."

"No. Don't tell him that. It doesn't matter anyway. I'll be out in a couple of days."

But a week had gone by and he was still there, the Owen Sound newspaper more confident of his guilt with every new edition. There were quotes from old patients, people whose teeth he'd fixed for decades, about how he was resentful when Alice took over the clinic. No one came forward to defend him against the charges; it seemed they'd all be happy to see him die in jail. And now Stump was saying everybody thought he was strange. What was that supposed to mean? Every day she finished reading the latest article with a heavy gut, longing to phone the reporters and tell them her father was not a bad man. But she never did. She couldn't bring herself to make a single call.

Because what if she was wrong?

Rocket hadn't returned either, and people were saying all sorts of things about him too. Like how come he'd disappeared just after the body was discovered? They didn't know him like she did, though. At school he used to swear and get in fights, sure, but he never bullied people, never goaded and humiliated like most of them. There was the time Phil Whitehead pinned Beth Connors on the cafeteria table and pretended to do it to her, and everybody just sat there watching until Rocket came in and decked him. After that Esther had almost nodded whenever they called her Rocket's girlfriend. They figured it would make sense, considering all the time he spent at her house. But she ignored him whenever he was there, knowing that he'd come to be with his coach, not with her. Her father was so intent on making him the best hockey player in the country. He used to say Rocket would show the world how Indians could be superstars. Well, look where all that work had got them now.

When Daniel Barrie had appeared at the Variety earlier in the day, looking so forlorn and nervous, she'd almost said, "I guess you heard about my dad." Then they could have talked about things, and she wouldn't have had to feel so alone. No, no, Daniel would have said, your father could never kill anyone. And she'd have laughed and said of course not, especially not Alice, not my friend. And Esther and Daniel would have started to feel close again, like they did in high school.

But instead she let him wriggle.

"Why it's Daniel Barrie. I thought you were in England on some big scholarship."

"I was, I was. Back for now, though."

"Well everybody sure will be glad to see you."

"I don't know about that."

"Oh, they were all real proud of you. You should've read the newspaper articles."

"My mother sent them to me. They were nice."

He glanced up at her, and suddenly she was conscious of her clothing, the yogourt stain on her shirt. She crossed her arms over it and was about to smile at him when he asked if she knew where Rocket was. He wasn't even interested in her, after all.

Daniel Barrie, the amazing genius at school, the biggest coward on earth. No job, no friends except for Rocket. And who could find that red hair of his attractive? If he was so smart, he should know that he'd never be happy in a place like Sunshine. Why didn't he go back to England and leave her alone?

IT WAS CLOSE to three when she and Stump finally left the Variety, the world outside dark and yellow under the sulphur lights. She wanted to be the one who took the garbage to the bin behind the building tonight, in case Archie Boone was rooting around back there, but Stump gripped the green bag so tightly that it looked like he was on a mission to deliver it. She let him go without a protest, hoping that Archie wouldn't be there after all. Archie didn't care much for people. Usually when she came upon him sorting through the trash he turned like a frightened animal, then went back to his work once he realized it was her. He knew by now that she put the best of the old food at the top of the bag for him.

Stump would probably raise a holy racket if he found a bum going through his garbage, but tonight he came back without saying anything, so it must have been all right.

There were no cars or people down the entire length of Manitou Street. It had been a blistering day and even now the air held a memory of heat. This was her favourite Sunshine, the town in summer late at night, stripped of people and warm enough to wander in comfort. When she locked up on her own, she left the pickup in the lot and walked to the bank with the bag of money against her belly, tucked under her shirt with her hands holding it. Stump would freak out if he knew, but it felt safe enough. After she slipped the bag into the night-box, she toured the perimeter of the street grid. The houses looked different, so dark and quiet. She passed the Sutters' or the Farrells' without quite believing they were really inside. And if she ever passed by someone, the rest of the walk back to the Variety was spent in contemplation of what had brought them on to the street. Her own meditations seemed embarrassingly transparent – nowadays everyone must know she was thinking about her father – while the minds of others were a mystery. When she saw Marge Barrie, Esther wondered whether she was lonely or there'd been a fight. If it was Dr. Easterbrook, maybe someone had died in his care. She wanted to call out to him and ask, as though it were an obligation to confess when you were caught on the street after midnight, but she never uttered a word.

"So tell me more about Daniel Barrie," Stump said from behind the wheel, but then he stopped beside the bank and she was saved from having to answer. She got out, slid the bag through the slot at the side of the building, then ran back like she'd stolen money rather than deposited it. He put the pickup in gear and started into the questions again. "Daniel Barrie. You never said why you don't get along with him."

"I thought you knew why. He's a coward. Always won prizes for his grades, but put him in the woods by himself and he'd jump at his own shadow. It's pathetic."

"Hey, you don't think he had anything to do with Alice, do you?"

Esther cringed. "Where'd you get that idea?"

"I mean, weren't they having an affair?"

"That's the stupidest thing I've ever heard," she replied. "Alice and Daniel didn't even know each other. Why? What are people saying?"

"Nothing," he said. "Never mind."

Esther shook her head in wonder. Alice would never waste her time with a wimp like Daniel Barrie. It wasn't right for rumours like that to spread. But then, look what they were saying about Bronwen Ferry and Mike.

Wherever you are, Alice, she thought, you should know that your family's all right. It was heartbreaking to see how choked up Mike got at the funeral. He hasn't given up on you; he has a woman trying to find out what happened. He still brings the kids into the Variety once in a while, and I want to tell him all the good things you used to say about him, but I worry that he's angry with me. He might think that my father killed you.

My father couldn't have done it, Alice. He has to be telling the truth about not remembering. He does drink too much sometimes, but he'd never hurt anybody. You know that, don't you? You'd say the same thing if you were alive.

You should see me lately, when it's five o'clock in the morning and I don't know what to do. I start to imagine leaving, just like you did when things were bad. I used to think you were serious about it. When you disappeared, I even told the police what you'd said. But now I know you never meant it, because I've tried leaving too, and no matter how many reasons there are to go, by the time the sun comes up there's always some excuse not to pack. Maybe all these fantasies are just a way to cope with staying in the same place.

THEY CAME to the town's only stoplight. Esther knew she shouldn't let Stump get away with his claim about Alice and

Daniel, but for some reason she couldn't bring herself to press him any further, and she let him change the subject.

"Listen, you ever been to the reserve, Esther?"

"No, I never got out that way."

"It's near the airfield, right?"

"Are you crazy? It's ten miles farther than the airfield. You've got to go right past the cemetery and the wildlife park. Why?"

"Just curious."

She gave a low, irritated growl.

"This doesn't have anything to do with Rocket, does it?" she asked.

"What, you mean Rocket DeWitt?" Stump wasn't very good at faking ignorance.

"You know any other Rockets? Of course I mean him."

"Why would I want to know about Rocket DeWitt?"

"I don't know, but you're asking about the reserve."

"He doesn't live on the reserve."

"No, but his dad grew up there before he went off to law school."

"Well look, this doesn't have anything to do with Rocket. A few of the guys from the Veterans Club were talking about going hunting out there, that's all."

"It's all scrubland, Stump. There's nothing to hunt. They wouldn't have given it to the Indians if there was." Stump shrugged. "Besides, it's private property."

"So?"

"So you think they want white men with guns coming onto their land?"

"Well, the guys were talking like Solomon might take them."

"You're not thinking of going, are you, Stump?"

"I don't know, I wasn't invited."

"But if you were –"

"Why shouldn't I?"

"You don't even own a gun," she said. She watched him closely.

"That's true," he agreed quietly, and turned off the main street.

Stump's house was a square bungalow with white aluminum siding. He'd purchased it the previous year after buying the Variety and moving to Sunshine, and he said that at the end of this summer they'd be able to afford something better. Her father's house, Victorian and huge, cast a long shadow from the top of the hill at the other end of town. Stump fumbled trying to put the key in the door, his right hand holding a plastic bag.

"Let me take that," she said, but he shook his head and began grunting at the lock again. Sometimes his stubbornness annoyed her, but tonight it was just funny as he wrestled with the door and the bag like a dog trying to play with two toys at once.

"What you got in there?" she asked cheerfully.

"None of your business," he said, then turned the knob to go inside.

The lights were on – her fault, she realized, but he didn't say anything. Instead he went straight into the bedroom without taking off his shoes and returned a couple of minutes later, empty-handed, heading for the kitchen. He frowned at her as he passed. She was still standing at the door.

"You waiting for an invitation?" he said. "Come in already."

"I thought you wanted to hear more about Daniel Barrie. About why he's such a coward."

"Sure, but tell it inside, okay?"

She took a deep breath. Stump's attention was a slippery fish, all right. He wouldn't even notice if she didn't mention Daniel again tonight. For some reason, though, she wanted to tell him more, even if there were bits she'd have to edit out.

For instance, she wasn't going to tell him that once, when she and Daniel were five, they played doctor in the spare bedroom upstairs. In later years they almost never talked about it, even when her mother was gone and her father was away with the hockey team every weekend, leaving her alone in the house and free to invite Daniel over for long conversations during which the two of them always seemed to gravitate upstairs again. Stump wouldn't want to know about that either, even though there'd never been any sex – or at least, not sex as Stump thought of it. She wondered whether Daniel remembered. He used to tell her everything, because he knew she was good at keeping secrets. The first time he'd confessed his anxieties about Marge and Susan to her, he'd been twelve. Officially the two women were best friends, but Daniel knew well enough that they slept in the same bed.

"Don't you wish you had a father?" Esther had asked. She couldn't imagine not having a father. Daniel said that Susan was practically one, but Esther didn't believe him. She wondered if he even knew what a father was.

Stump was banging around the kitchen, opening and slamming cupboard doors.

"What are you looking for, at this time of night?" she asked.

"Nothing."

"It doesn't sound like nothing."

"Well, it's nothing."

"Then why don't you stop looking for nothing and sit beside me? I'm not going to tell you about Daniel Barrie with all that noise." She stood up to see what he was doing and noticed the candles on the kitchen table. Why did he need candles? Stump saw where she was staring and hurried over to drag her toward the sofa with him.

"What's going on with those candles?" she demanded. But he was busy kissing her neck. "Stump, you're acting weird." He looked up like it was a shock for her to be speaking.

"What's – so – weird – about – this?" he asked, punctuating each word with a kiss. He was sliding past her tank top to her shoulder now.

"Nothing, I guess." Once his lips were at her collarbone, she knew she might as well give up on her story.

"Why don't we go to the bedroom?" he suggested, kissing her chin.

"Okay," she said, and stood up promptly. He froze on the couch with his lips still puckered. "What? What is it?"

"Never mind," he said, sullen. "I'll be there in a second." Sometimes she didn't understand him at all. As she went down the hallway she reflected that the house was a mess, and that when they moved she'd make sure they started off on the right foot: lots of shelves, lots of containers. Everything in its place.

The television in the bedroom was on, the sound turned down. That wasn't her fault, but Stump would probably yell at her all the same. She wondered if he was still sulking on the couch, or if he'd gone back to messing around with those candles. Was there supposed to be a storm tonight? She took off her clothes, folded them carefully, set them on the chair next to the bed, and crawled under the covers. Then she realized what was on the television. She chuckled.

"Hey, Stump," she called. "Come here, this is incredible." She searched for the remote control, found it with her feet, turned up the volume. Her eyes were fixed on the screen when Stump entered the room.

"Can you believe they're showing this? What channel is it, anyway?" She turned, and Stump was standing there naked, a lit candle in each hand.

"Hello, my love," he said.

She pretended not to notice him.

"Look at this, Stump. Who would have thought?" Then she realized it wasn't a channel at all. It was a video. "Wait a second. What's going on?"

He was placing the candles on the bedside table. He flicked off the overhead light and slipped in beside her.

"Good Lord, is this supposed to be romantic?"

"It's not porn," he said. "It's one of those ones where you follow along. It's instructional."

"Oh God," she said and sat up, stiff, her eyes unfocused on the shimmering images. She stabbed at the remote control until the television went black. Then he tried to kiss her again.

"Don't, Stump. Just – don't." She withdrew to the edge of the bed, pulling the comforter around herself.

"Look, Esther. I just saw it in the store, I thought it might be, you know, sexy. People rent it all the time."

"Well, we're not like those perverts."

"They're not perverts. Dr. Easterbrook took it out the other week. He said it was good."

"Pervert."

"All right, I'm sorry. Things have been tough, I was just trying to help. I didn't mean to upset you." His hand made a tentative foray across to her side of the bed. "Do you forgive me?" Fingers touched her knee. "Is everything okay?" They slid upwards slowly, like eager snails.

"My father's in jail, Stump. What do you think?" The fingers paused on her thigh. "I'm not in the mood. Is that a problem?"

"No," said Stump, unconvincingly. Esther rolled away from him, pretending to hear only the words, not the tone.

"Good night, then," she said, and closed her eyes.

THE REAL STORY about Daniel Barrie would reveal her as a liar. She'd told Stump that she'd never visited the Indian reserve, but it wasn't true. She'd gone once. Inexplicably, her father had invited her along with him and Rocket on one of their expeditions. She'd asked to bring Daniel too, and her father agreed without any of his usual nasty comments. He didn't like Daniel, because Daniel had never played hockey.

"I feel sorry for people like Marge and Susan who live in places full of ignorance," her father said. "But what they've got against hockey is beyond me. Not letting that boy play – it's snobbery. Bad for the reputation of all the professionals in town for them to act like their son is better than the rest, no matter how well he's doing in school. That's one thing you'll never be, Esther, is a snob." To be sure of this, her father had enrolled her in the softball team and the Girl Guides.

They went to the reserve to look for morels. On the way there, her father and Rocket sat in the front seat while she and Daniel rode in the back. Daniel's hand rested close to her leg on the uphol-stery, palm down like he was covering something. All three of them were fifteen, but no one would have guessed Rocket and Daniel to be the same age, much less friends with one another. Rocket was more than six feet tall and people said he'd already done it with Sandy Williamson at a party on Beaker's Beach. In comparison Daniel was still a kid; he was shorter and skinnier than Esther and only in the last few months had he lost the baby fat from his cheeks. For her own part Esther felt about eleven. Daniel's proximity had produced a surprising giddiness in her, and it was annoying. Such a sensation had never surfaced during all those hours alone with him, but somehow it was different now that they were together by daylight in the public space of her father's car.

As for her father, he was making the trip difficult. Usually he had a habit, developed over the mouths of patients, of talking at length without expecting a response, but for some reason today he was full of interest in Daniel. He directed question after question at him, while Esther sat silent and burning with rage.

"You play any sports, Danny?" Daniel had dropped "Danny" along with the baby fat, but her father had forgotten or didn't care. Daniel replied tersely that he didn't play anything right now, but that he might try out for the badminton team in the fall. There was a moment's silence. Esther knew what her father thought of badminton.

"And how's Mrs. Heimway doing? You liking her class?" Mrs. Heimway was the new history teacher, the one who'd replaced Esther's mother.

"She's all right, I guess."

"Is she running the same field trips Judith did?"

"I don't know. You don't do field trips in Grade Ten."

"Judith knew local history through and through," her father continued. "I was a little worried when they hired an outsider. Do you think it's made a difference?"

"I guess, a bit –"

"Dad, leave the guy alone," exclaimed Esther. "Daniel's not on trial."

They'd already passed the airport and the cemetery, and now they were driving through rolling, rocky country, the wide road almost clear of vehicles. Occasionally a pickup truck passed in the opposite direction. She strained to see if they carried Indians, but the sun was in her eyes and she saw only hazy silhouettes that could have been anyone.

Although the reserve had always occupied a place in her consciousness, it was as invisible to her as the far side of the moon. Some of her classmates lived there, but she'd never thought to ask them what it was like. They dressed and talked like everyone else, so the only time she really thought of the reserve was during Native Awareness days at school, when it turned out that Elliot Keeshahno could play drums and Lindsay Pedoniquig danced. Then Esther recalled the things that adults had said about the place and found dusty fantasies of rural squalor: shanties built out of corrugated tin, stripped-down cars on concrete blocks, feral dogs. She'd heard the stories: *They'll get drunk at a friend's place and walk home, lie down right in the middle of the road, and sleep it off.* Hugh Ellison's dad claimed you couldn't finish a beer at the Confederation Hotel without a couple of them walking in.

"Here we go, folks, into hostile territory," her father announced as they passed the sign that proclaimed the boundary of the reserve. "Don't be frightened, we've got an insider on our team." And he put his hand on Rocket's shoulder. Esther's face tingled with hot blood. She knew what was coming, and she was already embarrassed for Rocket. Somehow Mr. Ellison's Injun jokes were easier to bear than her father's lectures on the injustices done to Native people. *They were a noble race before we came. It was Europeans who turned them into welfare cases.* She wanted to explain to him how at school Rocket didn't hang out much with Native kids, how people didn't even think of him as an Indian, despite the fact that he was Solomon DeWitt's son.

You are entering a First Nations Reserve, the boundary sign read. And then one word: *Baushkidauwung.*

"What's that mean?" her father asked.

Rocket shrugged. "It's the name of the place."

"But what's it mean?"

"I don't speak Ojibwa," said Rocket derisively.

"No, no. Of course you don't. This isn't exactly your home, is it?"

Rocket didn't reply. If it were just him and Daniel, she knew, he'd be the one talking, telling them about some book he'd just read and what he thought of it, and then Daniel would pipe up to disagree somehow. She'd heard them carrying on like that together in the cafeteria. But with his coach, Rocket was a different person. Esther wondered what kind of discipline her father kept up in the locker room, and whether it was making Rocket quiet now. It disturbed and thrilled her to think her father could have such power over someone else her age.

"We've come here on trips before," her father said. "You remember those times?" She didn't, but then she realized he wasn't talking to her or Daniel. Rocket slumped in his seat, as if he was aware of this too, and embarrassed to be the object of attention. For a moment she caught her father's eye in the rear-view mirror, and she thought she detected an uneasiness in his expression. A second later he was looking at Daniel. "You'd have liked those hikes, Danny. One time we found an amazing cave along the coast. It would be great to go back there someday."

Daniel just nodded. Esther studied his face, thinking of the conversations she'd been having with him recently. Last night, for the first time since it happened, he'd talked about playing doctor as children. She'd giggled and laughed, as though she hadn't thought of it in years.

They crested a hill to find a majestic sprawling cape hundreds of feet below them. Storm clouds lurked far out over the lake, almost black, but they only emphasized the brilliance of the land, which blazed with the sun's light. Waves crashed on the shore from three sides, and the water seemed like wrinkled tinfoil stretched to the horizon. In the middle of the cape Esther could see a cluster of buildings around a crossroad. She looked at Rocket, who was taking in the landscape too. But he had family out here, she thought; surely he'd seen it all before.

"Don't let anybody ever tell you these people got second-rate property," said her father, turning to Rocket. "This is the jewel of the peninsula." Then he pointed to an outcropping on the escarpment. "See that?" he said. "There's a legend that a warrior fell in love with a princess from an enemy tribe, and when their families protested, the two of them jumped off that point."

Rocket murmured something, and her father asked him to repeat it.

"I said, nobody around here believes that. It's for the tourists."

"Yes, of course," said her father hastily. "But it's still a legend. Legends don't have to be true."

The road slid down the escarpment and Esther's father made a show of putting the car into neutral to see how far they would coast. They swept toward the village Esther had seen from the top, the engine quiet and the wind whipping through the open windows. Along the way there were a few houses set back from the road, small buildings that looked precarious perched on bare shale, but neat and respectable, like anything in Mooney's Dump. No children in tatters, no broken beer bottles. In the distance Esther could make out the stubborn stone tower of a church.

They didn't make it as far as the village. In the middle of a wood Esther's father pulled to the shoulder.

"End of the road for us," he said. "All you pirates, let's go. Nature's bounty awaits. There are morels out there to be had, I can smell them." His voice was urgent, his movements jerkier than usual. If she didn't know better, she would have thought he was drunk.

"Are you sure this is the right spot?" asked Rocket.

"Oh, I've been here before. I remember a place when I see it."

"He always says that on trips and we always get lost," Rocket muttered.

"Yeah, Dad, you have no sense of direction," Esther joined in, but she felt odd once she'd said it. It was completely beyond her whether her father had any sense of direction or not.

"Maybe we should ask permission first," said Daniel. It was the first time he had spoken without being prompted.

"No one around to ask," said her father gruffly. "Let's get going."

"What about the village?" Esther suggested.

"We're only after morels," Dr. Fremlin declared. "We're not stealing cattle."

They retrieved some baskets from the trunk and started into the woods together, her father leading the way, Esther and the boys at a shy distance, not even speaking with one another. When they were a few minutes from the road, her father stopped.

"I suppose you two will want some time to yourselves," he said.

She realized he was talking to her and Rocket. This was a surprise. He'd never said anything about the two of them – and what was more, she'd never said anything either. She didn't know how to respond. Rocket looked just as bewildered and embarrassed as she felt, while Daniel's face was tinged with some other emotion.

"That's all right, Frem, we can stay with you," said Rocket. "I don't even know what a morel looks like."

"Sure you do. Remember, we found some last year around Umbrella Lake. They're brown ovals, like mushrooms but bigger. I think we'll have a better chance if we spread out."

"What if we get lost?" Esther asked, finding her voice.

"You won't. There's field on three sides of this forest, and the road on the other. It isn't more than a square mile." He seemed impatient. "Look, you two don't have to go together. It was just an idea."

"And what about Daniel?" asked Rocket. "Maybe he doesn't want to split up." They all turned to him. He stood there looking uncomfortable, as though searching for the answer that would make them all happy.

"Ah, don't worry about me –"

"We'll split up too," said her father confidently. "We should all go different ways, really. I just thought you might want some company, Esther."

She shrugged.

"I can manage on my own." And she started to walk off in a random direction. "I'll see you guys back at the car. Don't step on any snakes."

She didn't look back. Trying to put her and Rocket together was thoughtless, cruel. No doubt her father just saw two people of the same age who were both in his life, so he'd decided to play matchmaker. Because Rocket was a nice guy and a hockey star, he figured Esther would naturally fall for him. And poor Rocket – her father probably hadn't even thought about his feelings. Didn't he know there were girls clamouring for Rocket's attention? Beautiful girls, smart girls, and not just ones from Mooney's Dump either.

She was still furious when she heard her name being called a few minutes later. It was Daniel. He was running through the undergrowth and jumping over fallen branches to catch up.

"I thought you might want some company after all," he said, panting, as he reached her.

She didn't say anything, she only kissed him. It was their first real kiss – the first one not disguised by the pretence of careless experimentation, by blathering suggestions, and, afterwards, a careful, detached discussion of each other's technique. Her fingers were on his stomach and pulling up his shirt before she'd even taken a breath. He was topless by the time he seemed to realize what she was doing.

"Your dad –," he whispered, but he was already dragging her sleeves from her arms, tugging at the bra.

"You ever been outside with no clothes on?" she asked, and he shook his head, then bent and moved his clumsy mouth along her skin, his hands stiff at his sides as though he could only focus on one thing at a time. She slid her fingers into his feathery red hair and pulled a lock of it tight in her fist. They were standing on their clothes, and gently, even as he touched her, she guided him off them so that the fabric wouldn't be ground into the loamy forest floor. When he pulled away she thought it was to lie down, and she bent her knees to join him, but instead he stood. His eyes were locked behind her. She turned and saw two women watching them.

They were about twenty yards away, with no discernible expression on their faces. Both had long, black hair. One of them had hers in a bun, and she wore a plain black T-shirt and jeans. The taller one was wearing a summer-weight dress, her hair flowing freely around it, almost to her waist.

Daniel grabbed frantically for underwear, shirt, socks.

"Come on, let's go," he whispered. When she turned back he was already running, their clothes bundled in his arms. What was he doing?

"Daniel!" she shouted, but he didn't stop. Her legs refused to follow. She watched until he disappeared, then looked back to the women. They hadn't moved either. She managed to step behind a tree trunk that was thick enough to cover most of her body.

"Don't come any closer," she said.

"Why, you think we're going to hurt you?" said the one in the dress. They seemed concerned, and Esther felt foolish for what she'd said.

"Are you all right?" asked the one in jeans. "He's your boyfriend, is he? He didn't drag you out here?"

"Everything's fine," Esther said, mortified and amazed at what was being implied.

"Sure it is," said the other woman. There was a smile on her face now. "She look fine to you, Lil?"

"Fine? Hell, she's wearing a tree." Both of them laughed.

"Your friend Daniel's a little skittish," said Lil. "Don't take this personally, but I suspect you could do better than that. You think so, Evie?"

"I don't know. He runs pretty fast," said Evie, and they laughed again. "Speak of the devil – here he comes."

Esther turned to see Daniel walking toward them. He was dressed now, and her clothes were in his hands, neatly folded.

You jerk, she thought. You rat. Go back, run away again.

"Hey, mister, you forget something?" said Lil. "Evie, he looks different, doesn't he? I can't put my finger on it . . ."

"Shut up, or we'll frighten him off."

He held out Esther's clothes to her, eyes averted, and she grabbed them from him. Everyone was silent as she dressed, Daniel keeping his back to her and the women watching him with disdain.

"Sorry to disturb your walk," Esther said when she was finished. Evie smiled sympathetically at her, while Lil continued to glare at Daniel. Then Esther headed off in the direction of the car, with Daniel following a step behind her.

"Why didn't you run with me?" he asked once they were out of sight. "We could have got away."

She whirled to face him.

"God damn it. You left without me, Daniel!"

He stopped walking, his mouth open in surprise. There were bits of leaves still stuck to his shirt.

"I'm sorry," he said quietly. "I was scared."

"What's to be scared of?" she shouted. "They were a couple of old women."

"I didn't know that," he said. "I thought they were men." These last words were barely audible.

"You thought they were men."

"It happened so fast, I didn't –"

"You thought they were men, so you left me naked in the forest, alone with them?"

"I mean, I wasn't sure," he began, and she started off again. "Hey, I came back, didn't I?"

She was beginning to say something over her shoulder, not even knowing what it was going to be, when a voice came booming through the forest.

"You two! Look what we found – morels!"

She broke into a run and headed in the direction of her father's cry until she came upon him and Rocket hunched over the ground behind an old rotten log. At their feet was a ring of brownish, egg-shaped heads hanging from pale stalks as though in shame. Daniel jogged up behind her, panting, but she kept her eyes fixed squarely on the morels. Her father demonstrated how to pick them, and with barely a word spoken they filled two baskets.

"Can we look for more?" asked Daniel in a cheerful, maddening tone when they were done.

"Not today," replied her father sharply. His joy at the discovery of the morels had somehow turned to apprehension, and he scanned the forest with darting eyes. "This might be private property. Let's just take these and go."

A FEW WEEKS AGO she'd seen one of the women again in the Sunshine Variety. Lil, the woman with the hair down to her waist. It was even longer now, practically at her knees, and an incredible lustrous white. The woman greeted Esther as she would any stranger, paid for her lemonade, and headed for the door. It felt like a chance lost. Esther wanted to call out, to tell her anything that would make her stay a little longer, but instead Lil stopped unprompted at the threshold and turned.

"What's that red-haired Daniel doing nowadays?" she said.

So she remembered, after all. Even his name. Esther grinned, then struggled for a reply. The truth was, she didn't know the answer. In the end she shrugged, and Lil nodded, seeming to understand, before she walked out. Esther should have said more; she should have followed her to the parking lot and asked her about Evie, but there was another customer, a man waiting to pay for his chocolate bar, so she stayed behind the till and served him.

Lying in bed now, Esther turned things over in her mind. She didn't believe that Daniel and Alice could have been together. How did these rumours get started? Alice, you would have told me, she thought. You'd never have kept that a secret from me. I was always loyal to you, wasn't I? I wouldn't have been jealous. But you know, if you really were having an affair with him, I don't think I could stay quiet about it now. I'd have to tell Solomon DeWitt, the police. Because it might help to free my dad. And I don't care what happens to Daniel. Really I don't. He hasn't even been able to look me in the eye for the last ten years.

She felt Stump shift on the mattress toward her.

"Esther," he said. "Are you still awake?"

"What is it, Stump?" She glanced at the alarm clock on the bureau.

"I just remembered Daniel Barrie. You were going to tell me more about him, weren't you?" He said it gently, almost pleadingly, and she smiled. He wanted to make amends, and to him that meant letting her talk, listening to her story. She realized, though, that it wasn't one she wanted to tell him. Maybe she never had. At first she'd thought it would reveal something about Daniel, but now, Daniel didn't seem so important to the memory any more. Rocket and her father were the ones bothering her instead, sitting in the front of the car together, talking privately while she was ignored, forgotten.

"Look, never mind about Daniel," she said to Stump. "It's too late for stories. Blow out those candles, would you?"

She rolled over to him, expecting a protest, but he was yawning, his back arched, his arms and legs straight out like a cat. Stump was harmless, really, once fatigue set in. You just had to be patient sometimes. He was so tired that when she put her hand on his hip he only pulled her closer. They lay motionless until his breathing started to stretch and deepen. Then she reclaimed her arm to curl up on her own side, alone. His sleeping patterns hadn't changed lately; only hers. She wondered how long you could keep going on three hours a night before you keeled over for good.

She wanted there to be an end. Her father freed, Alice's killer apprehended. It was too hard trying to see people's thoughts, suspecting everybody all the time. God was the one, not her, to keep track of good and evil, to make sure people got their due. It would never be sorted out on earth, at least not in this town. Not in this room, when she slept every night with a rifle beneath the bed. Was it for hunting? she wondered. Did Stump really want to prove he was a man by shooting animals with the mayor and Harry Midgard? Or perhaps it was for security. Maybe he'd decided that guns were needed as protection in Sunshine these days. But how could that be? He'd told her he wanted to raise his children here.

She was desperate for sleep, but when she squeezed her eyes shut, she found a familiar image waiting underneath the lids: Alice's face, staring from behind her surgical mask. Esther was sickened by what she felt for her now. Anger. Anger at a dead person, for having died, and for taking her secrets with her.

Sometimes, though, she found herself believing that Alice wasn't dead at all. She was just relaxing on a tropical beach somewhere, reading mailed copies of the *Beacon* for reports on the investigation. Laughing at everybody. But if that was true, Alice was the one missing out, right? Because Sunshine really was a beautiful place in the summer.

✦ Someone has gone to a lot of trouble. All along the lane that leads to the celebration, there are torches on wooden poles plunged into the snow. The first person we meet brandishes one of them like a lance as he runs past, not acknowledging our presence, just whooping and crowing while he makes his way toward the line of cars and the frozen bay. It seems that you and I are the only witnesses to this spectacle.

"What a nut," you say, and I laugh, glad we're by ourselves again. The hitchhiker hasn't reappeared, and we don't speak of him. The only vestige of his existence is the stained yellow notebook in my pocket.

At the end of the lane there's a parking lot packed with vehicles. A trail of cardboard arrows begins at the farmhouse beyond it, pointing the way along a well-trampled path, but the voices and music coming from behind the building make directions needless. Rounding the corner, we find hundreds of people gathered in a dark field. There are guitars playing, dancers, snowballs flying, an enormous bonfire that shoots sparks high into the night. One woman has brought a set of bongos.

"Look," you say. On the other side of the field, bodies glide across the surface of the earth. "How would you like to go skating?"

I shake my head, not wanting to tell you that I don't skate, that I didn't even realize they were skaters.

"Well then, why don't we split up?" you say quickly. "I'll meet you back here in an hour or so if we don't run into each other before that."

I nod, stunned. You smile and reach over to hold my hand, but I don't take it.

"What is it? What's wrong?"

I'm not sure where to begin. After bringing me all this way, you're going to abandon me. I can't believe it.

"We haven't even looked around," I mumble.

You turn your head dramatically from side to side, taking in the breadth of the field.

"A bonfire and a bunch of people drinking," you say. "What else is there?" But you can tell this approach isn't going to work, and your voice softens. "We'll have the whole weekend together, I promise. I just want to skate, that's all."

How easily you move from sarcasm to consolation. I don't know why you even bother, when you seem so certain that my approval isn't needed, when you're so confident about the legitimacy of your desires. Giving rides to strangers, coming to this place, deserting me; what next? What will I let you get away with? You seem to know the answer better than I do. But I'm tired of surrendering, nodding, keeping my suspicions to myself.

"That hitchhiker we picked up – you'd met him before, hadn't you?"

You frown, apparently as unprepared for the question as I am in asking it.

"What? That's completely absurd. I'd never set eyes on him."

"You set eyes on him often enough in the car." Why disguise my jealousy any longer? You don't need to be protected.

"When did you become so paranoid?" you demand.

We're not really having this conversation, I tell myself. It's a dream. People like us don't share these sorts of thoughts. We let each other guess what we're thinking. To speak some things aloud would be unbearable.

"You knew about this party too," I say, despite myself. "You wanted to come here the whole time."

"What are you talking about?" you exclaim. But there's a belligerence in your response that tells me I'm right. You've been

hiding something from me all along; you're afraid of its coming out now. "Look, I'm sorry we picked up that guy, since he seems to have bothered you so much. If you think I was even a bit interested in him, you're crazy. I was just trying to be a good person. And I'm sorry about the skating, I already told you that." You didn't, I want to say. You never actually apologized. "But if you're so worked up, maybe it would be better for us to be by ourselves for a while, after all."

I don't reply.

"What do you think?" You reach for my hand again. "We can find each other when we've cooled off a bit."

I let you squeeze my fingers, not squeezing back. With a reluctant shrug you release them, my arm falls to my side, and you walk off toward the distant outdoor rink.

I shouldn't have allowed you to go like that. Now if I want a confrontation I'll have to be the one who gives chase – you're waiting for me to do that, no doubt – but I'm still too proud and wounded. It's after eleven, and even if we were to come back together and make up somehow, the night would practically be over by the time we arrived at your cottage. Everything is ruined.

Forget about it, I think. Find a distraction.

Looking around the field, taking my time to distinguish the various groups and points of light, I see nothing. But then, to the north, a series of shapes begins to resolve out of the darkness: tall, solid forms jutting straight up from the ground. It's a set of stones, formidable and carefully arranged.

At first a trick of perspective makes them look like a line of parallel grey teeth. As I move closer, I recognize the circular geometry: twelve slabs, head-height, ringed around a central stone that is taller than the rest, with a smaller stone just off-centre. I thought this sort of thing existed only in ancient times, exotic places. It deserves protective barriers, interpretive signs, but the people here are talking to each other as though oblivious of its existence. Only a few children are enchanted, darting between the rocks, trying to scale them. I walk around the structure, excited, taking it in. Here *is something to discover, to tell you about and show you. You'll be angry with yourself for not having seen it first, for rushing off to that stupid rink, for leaving me.*

When I've examined every stone, every detail, I wander across the field to a high chain-link fence where another group of people has bunched. They're peering through it, shouting and pointing. Drawing near, I can make out movement on the far side. Two enormous eyes stare at me from the darkness, then disappear. Some large, unidentifiable beast, pacing back and forth. A girl is pawing at the ground, digging through snow in search of grass to offer it, while the man next to her sloshes beer from his bottle through the fence and laughs.

I want to ask what kind of animal it is, but now every voice has stopped and heads are turning toward the house. More people have appeared by the porch – thirty or more adults and a few children, close together, some holding placards and others wearing sandwich boards. At an unseen signal, they begin to march in single file, meandering slowly through the crowd.

STOP DANCING ON GRAVES, reads one of their signs. Everyone is silent, both the protesters – if that is what they are – and the people who watch them. The new arrivals keep their eyes on the person ahead of them in line, never looking at the bodies they pass on either side, even though sometimes they're so close as to brush against clothing. When they approach the fence, I see they've painted their faces to look like skulls. Another sign reads, RESPECT THE DEAD.

"They shouldn't be here," mutters the tall man beside me from underneath his wide-brimmed hat.

"Who are these people?" I whisper.

"First Nations," he replies. In a low voice he explains about the reserve a few miles from here. The band claims this land was once a burial ground, that it should be returned to them. The case has been in the courts for several months.

I ask if the protesters are right about the burial ground, and the man says he hopes they aren't. I remember your conversation in the car with the hitchhiker. People can't just turn back the clock, you said. A little town like that should be able to live in peace.

"Why do you hope the protesters are wrong?" I ask the man.

He turns and tilts the brim of his hat from his face to look at me, as though he wants to be sure that I can be trusted with what he's about to say.

"Because I own this place."

I'm not sure how to reply. We watch the marchers' procession until they arrive where they began and the line squashes into a cluster again. Many of the partygoers are hanging their heads or looking into the trees, anxious for the interruption to be over. From somewhere near the bonfire a man's voice rings out.

"Go home!" it shouts.

The protesters look at each other. A few break into weary smiles. One of the women in front takes a step forward and stares in the direction of the voice.

"Buddy, this is it," she replies. "This is home."

Soon the protesters disappear down the path toward the lane. No one is willing to move, until the bongos start up again and the spell is broken.

"Tell me, have you been here before?" the man beside me asks. He seems intent on my answer, and I shake my head. "But you know what's going on?" I say yes, remembering the hitchhiker's story about the celebration of the winter solstice. When I introduce myself the man shakes my hand without giving his own name in return and offers to show me around the henge. I feel like I've passed a test.

As we walk over together, he points out the thin moat clogged with ice and cattails that surrounds the stones. All proper henges have one, he says. Next he gestures to the tall rock in the middle and identifies it as the North Star stone. During the day its shadow indicates the season. The nearby acolyte is the pointer stone. There's a deep gouge in the top of it, and he says that if I sight the top of the North Star stone through it I'll see the pole star beyond, hanging static in the heavens.

He tells me about the process of cutting the rock, of ensuring the correct alignments, but I've stopped paying attention. I've remembered the notebook in my pocket, and I'm wondering about Alice Pederson.

It might be some kind of trick. I think of you out there skating on the rink and imagine the hitchhiker using me to play some kind of game with you. I should open the book here and now, see what it reveals, end the conjecture for good.

But it's preposterous, I realize; you couldn't have known that man. Why would the two of you go through the ritual of meeting on the highway, the pretence of anonymity? No, there must be something else going on, perhaps something even more extraordinary. Maybe undercover police officers have been instructed to apprehend the person who hands Alice Pederson a yellow book tonight. Or maybe there's no Alice Pederson at all. Her name might be the code word that will introduce me to some agent hidden in the crowd. Could it be just a coincidence that the first person to speak with me is the lynchpin of the whole event?

Suddenly I'm uncomfortable in the man's presence. Cutting him short, I thank him for the tour and move off into the crowd as though I've just spotted old friends. I look from person to person, watching for someone to return my gaze. Anybody here could be the right or wrong one to approach; there might be only one key figure to locate, or the whole town might be involved.

I turn to make sure the owner hasn't followed me, then realize I'm being foolish. It's too tempting to indulge in fantasies here, where I'm responsible to nobody and every face is a riddle to be guessed at. The thought of conspiracy is just something to keep me from having to break the ice and talk with strangers, from facing you again. The prospect of finding Alice Pederson has only made it easier to focus on one person, to pretend the rest don't matter. My hand slides down my jacket and presses on the flat surface of the notebook in my pocket.

Perhaps I should go to the rink and find you. I could tell you about the hitchhiker and the book; you'd know what to do. Then we could put the arguing behind us and find this Alice Pederson together.

As I try to decide, I make my way to the chain-link fence again. The little girl who was digging in the snow is still crouched by the barrier, alone, watching whatever animal is on the other side.

Seeing her gives me an idea. Never mind you, I think. I can do this on my own.

"Excuse me," I say to her, almost under my breath, not knowing why I should be so cautious. She's only a little girl. There's no chance of embarrassment, of ridicule. "Do you know where Alice Pederson is?"

She looks at me with unblinking eyes and says nothing. For an instant I think she's about to scream. Then I'm certain that she's going to answer in a calm voice, saying of course she knows Alice, she can take me to her right away.

Instead she stands up slowly, still watching me. I put out my hand a few inches to reassure her. A second later she turns and runs into the crowd.

INVENTING THE WHEEL

Every time Bronwen drove up the lane to her parents' farm-house, her father was sitting on the porch, his mouth clenched around an unlit pipe, waiting to ask a favour of her. It had been like that for over a month now, ever since she'd come back to stay with them in Sunshine during her investigation. She worried that this ritual of his betrayed an essential, lifelong loneliness in him, but what bothered her more was the speed with which their encounters had become routine. Each evening the return home seemed less strange, the house more familiar and expected, as it had been in her childhood.

"Bronny, can you head over to the airfield and move some of the cows?" her father asked her tonight. She nodded resignedly. After so many weeks of such requests, her patience was wearing thin. Today was slightly different, though: it was the first day of the Civic Holiday weekend, with all three of her brothers in Sunshine to visit, and she was in no hurry to rejoin the Ferry family dramas any sooner than necessary.

"Dr. Fremlin wants to take off and they're in the middle of the runway," her father added, as though it were an afterthought. She didn't register what he'd said at first; then, after she'd asked him to repeat the name, she told him he must be mistaken. But apparently he'd heard it over the radio: Stoddart Fremlin was out on bail. And now he was half a mile from them, staring at their cattle.

"Don't know what they're doing on the runway," her father mused.

"It's a rally," Bronwen speculated. "They're protesting against the old bugger." Her father took no notice. Long ago he'd told her bedtime stories about talking elephants, Martians, and magic spells, but when it came to cows he was all business. She sighed and got into the hatchback again, then drove along the rutted lane that ran through the southwest pasture to the airfield. The car wasn't meant for this sort of terrain, and each time the undercarriage grated against the earth she muttered a few words about her father, as if it weren't her own choice to take the shortcut instead of the paved road. Besides, as he liked to point out, it was her fault for buying a city car. Her father didn't have much time for cities. He was born in Toronto and claimed the place had left a bad taste ever since. In all the time Bronwen had lived there, her parents had never visited.

She steered the hatchback along the service road next to the runway and spotted Stoddart Fremlin at the far end of it, standing by his four-seater with his arms folded across his chest. He didn't wave, not even when she pulled up beside him, and she wondered if he'd heard she was in town to investigate the Alice Pederson case. But if he knew that, he must also understand that she wasn't after him. In fact, ever since the discovery of the body and his subsequent arrest a month ago, her insurance company had been urging her to prove him innocent. Then there'd still be a possibility that Alice had committed suicide, and they could continue to deny Mike his claim. If there was any justice in the world, Fremlin would be paying part of Bronwen's salary; he'd be welcoming her with joy. At the moment, though, he didn't seem to appreciate what a great friend he had before him.

When she'd heard of his arrest, her biggest surprise had been that he was even still alive. The dentist she remembered from her youth was an old man with an old man's demeanour, and she'd long ago packed him off to her mental crematorium. But as she looked at him now, she realized that the sharp nose and bushy eyebrows were just the same as thirty years ago. It was impossible, of course, but then she'd noticed that people didn't always stay the same in her memory. Sometimes she aged them, perhaps to prepare for meeting them again, or maybe because she couldn't allow herself to be older than authority figures from childhood. It was a shock to think that the Dr. Fremlin she'd known, with his grandfatherly beard and sour, antiseptic musk, had been younger than she was today. It was even more shocking that the man standing before her had been charged with murder. But then, it seemed like everything shocked her now. The fact that Fremlin was out on bail, for instance. Given the nature of the charge against him, she would have thought they'd never let him loose.

"Your cattle are ruining my evening, little girl," he said after she stepped out of the car. Apparently it didn't matter that she was forty-one and greying; he was just as confidently condescending as when she'd been twelve. It was odd to hear that tone again. What she remembered as playful and wry now suggested irony, contempt. Perhaps she'd committed a crime in growing older.

"Did you try moving them?" she asked, glancing over her shoulder at the Herefords, which were loitering in the middle of the runway, heads raised and alert, bellowing like an unholy choir. She'd tried to set her voice at the same level of detachment as Fremlin's, hoping that she was joining a game and that matching him would call his bluff. But he just seemed annoyed.

"I'm a senior citizen," he said. "I thought I should leave it to the experts."

Bronwen said nothing more, only turned and walked toward the Herefords. The sun was setting directly behind the herd, and even when she squinted she could only apprehend dark shapes with blinding outlines, as though the light had set their shaggy maroon backs on fire. She couldn't remember the exact number of head – was it twenty-four or twenty-five? – but she knew there were supposed to be three calves, and she counted two. "Get out of here," she said, lightly pressing her hand against a random haunch, and at once they all galloped off the tarmac to the grass. She returned to the place on the runway where Fremlin was waiting.

"There you go," she announced. "Twenty years of expert training put into action." Fremlin didn't seem to find it amusing. He was already climbing into the cockpit of his plane. "Must be nice to get away from all your worries for a while," she said, but he wasn't listening.

"Those cows aren't going to walk across again as I'm taking off, are they?" he asked.

"No, they're smart," she said. "They don't want to end up dead any more than we do."

"You know, I always opposed renting the airfield to a farmer," he informed her. "Damn dangerous business. The federal government would never allow it if they heard." An edge of threat in his voice.

The conversation was frustrating. There was supposed to be animosity between detectives and suspects, everybody knew that, but this was turning into a political debate. She'd just spent the day trying to stir up leads on where Rocket DeWitt had gone, and now here was the man who'd been Rocket's hockey coach and mentor, who probably knew Rocket better than anyone, so where were her piercing questions? Where were his cryptic replies? At this moment Fremlin might be preparing to skip bail and fly out of Sunshine, out of the country entirely, but instead of stopping him she only stood there mutely as he closed the door, gestured across the field, and told her he'd seen a dead calf lying in the grass.

She stayed to watch him taxi down the runway, hit the throttle, and roar into the air. These days not more than half a dozen planes used the airfield regularly, and Fremlin's was as big as any of them, even though the strip had been built to accommodate the jumbo jets that passed overhead. Sunshine was on the route of a major transcontinental airway, and vapour trails constantly threaded the sky above the town, but no one ever landed. Planes that took off from the field always ended up back where they started. She pictured Fremlin skimming the clouds, peering down at Sunshine like God, and wondered if the place looked any better from the air. Maybe seen from up there it might actually make some sense.

Things had been simpler when she was a girl. Growing up in Mooney's Dump, she'd considered her parents to be at the centre of the community – the centre of the world, even – and all the happenings in town fit together in terms of them. She supposed every child saw things the same way. Eventually she'd learned that to anyone else's eyes the two of them were peripheral at best, just a couple of people who'd fled the city for rural peace and quiet. Now, in the weeks since she'd been staying at their house, the imagined web of relationships from her childhood had returned, but it was Alice Pederson who occupied the centre, and Bronwen's job was to see everybody, everything in terms of her death. As she watched Fremlin's plane ascending, it felt natural, almost a compulsion, to go over his motives and opportunities one more time.

Jealousy was always a good place to begin. Stoddart Fremlin belonged to a generation of dentists that had begun to practise before the advent of malpractice suits, back in the days when they could chisel and gut people's mouths like quarrymen cutting rock. People called him the Jawbreaker. There were rumours of a scandal in England long ago that had precipitated his flight to Canada and Mooney's Dump, where the locals welcomed him unquestioningly, grateful, it seemed, that any dentist would choose to set up shop there. As Bronwen's mother claimed to remember, people were relieved when he stayed in town after his wife left him, even happier when he started coaching hockey and turned out to be good at it. But she also said that by the time Alice Pederson finished her training and announced her intention to return to her birthplace, dozens of residents with botched fillings had quietly changed allegiance to dentists in Owen Sound. They greeted Alice's arrival with thinly concealed pleasure, and the old man must have known how they felt. Even as he took Alice under his wing, he must have sensed he was being supplanted.

Or else the motive could have been money. When Fremlin had retired, he must have handed everything to Alice, including the accounting books, and if his ineptitude extended to finance, who knew what deceptions had been executed there? Overcharging patients, defrauding insurance companies: Bronwen herself had investigated several doctors on those grounds. Or falsified dental records, even. Maybe Alice had discovered them and confronted him. Whatever it was, the police hadn't found anything.

And of course there was the possibility of an affair: illicit, passionate, and fatal. At one time Bronwen would have thought it outlandish for a woman of thirty-six years to sleep with a man of sixty, but now it didn't seem so difficult to imagine. She tried to see Fremlin as Alice might have, searched for some attractiveness in the pursed lips, the creased forehead, the sharp bearded chin. There was nothing, only a cold arrogance. She thought of the way Fremlin had told her so casually about the dead calf.

When his plane was no more than a speck in the sky, she crossed the runway and began to walk in the direction he'd pointed. The first days of August had yet to bring relief from the previous month's drought, and the short, dry grass made it easy to spot the carcass. As she approached it, her first thought was that a plane had hit the thing. She saw a panicked pilot, a placid animal, the grind of a propeller into hair and muscle, the wrench of bolts and twisting of struts, the stricken bellow and the choked scream of the engine. Never mind how it could have gone unreported, or how the calf ended up so far from the runway. Bronwen suspected this tendency to fantasize made her a bad investigator. The fat, lizard-eyed supervisor at the insurance company liked to remind her of this frequently. *Facts, sugar. That's all the judges want from us, so that's all we want from you.*

She looked over the carcass with an eye for facts and grudgingly granted Fremlin some respect for his powers of observation. Many people wouldn't have known it was a calf, in that state. Something had stripped it almost clean of flesh; only the skeleton and pieces of the head were left. Hardly the work of an airplane. Then, on her way back to the farmhouse, she thought about Mike Pederson's encounter in the cemetery and a completely different possibility sprang to mind. A telephone call to Cam Usher was in order.

When she told her father what she'd seen, he thought she was exaggerating. He had to drive out in the pickup to see for himself.

"Even the bones crunched through," he announced when he returned. "What do you suppose could have done that?" Bronwen would have answered him, but the question was addressed to his wife, as though there weren't eight other people at the dinner table as well, waiting for him to sit down so they could begin the meal. The youngest son, Jay, and his wife, Lucy, had put themselves between their two children, Cody and Tyler, to keep them from fighting, but still the boys fidgeted and threw bits of paper napkin at each other when they thought no one was looking. Bronwen's oldest brother, Seth, and his new girlfriend, Kathy, were opposite them, while Hamish and Bronwen, the two siblings unencumbered by lovers, sat kitty-corner to one another at the far end.

"A mysterious death, eh?" said Jay. "Sounds like a job for Miss Marple." He glanced at Bronwen slyly, then looked to Hamish and Seth in expectation of their laughter. Neither of them had taken up his new nickname for their sister, but Tyler and Cody liked it, even though they didn't get the reference. Cody was four and pronounced it "Miss Marble."

"Never mind, Jay," said her mother. "Bronny has better things to do than worry about cows. How is your investigation going, honey?"

Bronwen gritted her teeth.

"I've been trying to find Rocket DeWitt," she told them obligingly. "Like half the town is."

"Oh no, maybe he's the next victim," said Seth with mock fear.

"I doubt it," she said flatly. "The pickup truck's gone from his driveway and the house is locked tight."

"He's the murderer, then," said Jay. "It's obvious."

"Maybe," murmured Bronwen. But where was the motivation? No, she'd been over the possibilities often enough in her head.

More speculation was pointless. The only way to learn anything would be to talk with Rocket himself.

"The guy you should be watching is that Cam Usher," said Seth. "Have you heard about him? Some people at the drugstore today were saying he's into voodoo." Bronwen didn't reply. She'd already spoken with Usher, but she didn't feel like going into that meeting now.

"So much intrigue for such a small place," exclaimed Kathy. She'd lived in Vancouver all her life and apparently thought towns like Sunshine belonged in storybooks. Seth rolled his eyes.

"It's not intrigue, it's just a mess," said Bronwen. Kathy nodded deferentially and went back to eating her peas one at a time. In the silence that followed, Bronwen held out a weak hope that the night's interrogation was at an end. Then Jay spoke up.

"You going over to debrief Othello again this evening, Bronny?" he asked.

"Jay, that's awful," her mother said, blushing.

"Come on, Mom, it's been how long since she had a boyfriend? If I was Bronny, I'd be over at Pederson's place every night too."

Nobody spoke; they all thought Jay had gone too far, she could see it in their eyes, and they were waiting for her to react. Well, she thought, she wouldn't give them the satisfaction.

"Mike's a good guy," she replied coolly. "I don't mind saying it, I like him a lot."

"I bet you do," said Jay, without much conviction. He'd seen the others' faces.

"I wish I had more to tell the poor man, but there's nothing," Bronwen continued. Poor man, she repeated to herself. That was how she really saw him. It should have been different; crime movies were full of tall, dark, handsome men like Mike. But then, in movies the detective didn't have to look after the man's children while he wept in the bathroom.

"I'm sure everything will work out in the end," said Seth, as though to put a cap on the conversation. Usually he was the first one to offer Old Maid jokes, so she knew he wasn't trying to spare her feelings. More likely he was afraid Kathy would open her mouth again and embarrass them both. He must have sensed his parents' distress at her presence, when they were so obviously eager that the weekend be a time to pull the family together. Jay and Lucy were to be feted for producing a proper nuclear family, while Cody and Tyler were to be spoiled rotten no matter how loudly they bickered (in her mind Bronwen had named them Codeine and Tylenol, and thought they were spoiled enough). Hamish, the live-at-home, would be pressured into coming out of his trailer for once, and Bronwen, at forty-one years a spinster and her mother's sorrow, would provide the nightly entertainment with stories from her investigation. It was a neat and tidy plan, but Seth was ruining it. He was supposed to be recovering from his early divorce ("They should have stuck it out at least two years," said her father. "Even movie stars last that long"), not introducing a stranger.

"Can you believe it?" her mother had whispered to Bronwen the previous night. "That woman is almost as old as I am."

Privately Bronwen was not a fan of Kathy either, but for some reason she found herself eager to defend the woman against her mother.

"Kathy's only in her fifties," she'd said. "Seth will be too, in a few years. I admire them. It must be tough, starting out with someone new. They have to learn everything over again."

"Nonsense," her mother had muttered. "It's reinventing the wheel."

"Come on, Mom. If Dad died wouldn't you get a boyfriend?"

"Don't even talk like that. It's disgusting."

Bronwen could only shake her head. When she was growing up, she'd listened to endless mealtime sermons on women's rights and sexual liberation, yet somehow her mother still considered mating a practice that was supposed to be for life. It was a nice idea as fairy tales went, but what did it mean for a man like Mike Pederson, alone and not even forty? What was he supposed to do?

She'd first met him ten years ago, when she'd returned home for Christmas and didn't yet know that Alice Mooney had married. He was just a lanky, good-looking man in the supermarket, his head shaved to the skin. Bronwen shouldn't have been staring, but she couldn't help it; she'd never seen a black person in Mooney's Dump before. Other people were watching too. Their eyes followed him along the aisles, and she admired him for his apparent obliviousness to it all. He was hunched over his cart, guiding it with his elbows, frowning as though deep in thought. She wanted him to notice her, to see her smiling, not suspicious and frightened like the rest, but he was too intent on whatever preoccupied him. When she got into the cashier's lineup behind him, he didn't even glance at her until she spoke.

"Hey, you come here often?" she said. She was thirty and bold. He looked at her, saw the expression on her face, and grinned.

"Sure, I shop here all the time. Why do you ask?" He surveyed the store with a smirk. "Are you saying I seem out of place?" The other customers were peering intently in every direction but theirs. They both laughed. Then the cashier made a throat-clearing noise and dutifully Mike finished unloading his cart. Bronwen watched the movement of his hands, wondering what her parents would say if she invited him to dinner, until she realized there was a wedding ring on his finger.

"Oh," she said out loud, despite herself. He turned in response, and she had to tell him to never mind, it was nothing. After that she waited silently for him to go, her eyes down, with a guilty feeling that she'd done something wrong.

"That's the one Alice Mooney married," her mother told her when Bronwen returned to the farmhouse and mentioned the man she'd encountered. "Her parents are furious. But apparently he's published a novel." She said it as though that were compensation for something.

When Bronwen had met him again six weeks ago, he showed no sign of remembering her. After all that time it wasn't a surprise, and she didn't remind him. As they discussed the investigation, though, she realized that some things hadn't changed: his head was still shaved, the wedding ring was on his finger, and no doubt customers still looked at him apprehensively in the shops. But now the sin of marrying Alice Mooney was forgotten; the suspicion of people in Sunshine was that he'd gone and killed her too.

ONCE DINNER was finished, Hamish said quietly that he might go out to his trailer and work. Bronwen knitted her brow, embarrassed for him; he was asking to be excused from the table like a little boy. Her mother nodded and waved him away.

"What's he working on?" asked Kathy blithely. It seemed Seth hadn't briefed her very well.

"He's an inventor," her mother replied. "He's developing a broccoli rack." Kathy stared without responding and Bronwen's mother had to explain. "It's for roasting broccoli evenly in the oven. He's got little prongs in a circle. You impale the florets individually and then the whole thing spins due to the heat or something. It's all very complex." Kathy said she'd never thought about roasting broccoli before. "Well, it might not turn out," Bronwen's mother admitted matter-of-factly. "But he's always having good ideas. He doesn't just do broccoli."

Bronwen knew this was said only for Kathy's benefit; usually her mother was less enthusiastic about Hamish's inventing. Sure enough, once she was alone with Bronwen and Bronwen's father in the kitchen she took a different tack. "He's thirty-nine and no job," she complained. "And no education either."

"But he's smarter than the rest of us put together," Bronwen's father replied. "And he practically runs the farm by himself now."

"It's not good, him spending so much time alone in that trailer," her mother insisted.

"What, you'd rather he hung out with you two every night?" asked Bronwen. She could say these things now that she didn't live here permanently, but she had to be careful, since she was sensitive as to how she was spending her own nights lately. It was too hard to fraternize at the Confederation Hotel when everyone in town was a suspect, and her friends from high school had long ago moved away. Some evenings she visited Mike, sure, but that was strictly business. The rest of the time she stayed at home and spent long hours with her parents at the dinner table.

"Of course it's not good for Hamish to be around us all the time," her mother agreed. "It wouldn't do for him to be a mama's boy." Too late, thought Bronwen. "But that trailer – have you seen it? Have you smelled it?"

"Why, what's it smell like?" asked Jay, who had wandered into the kitchen.

Their mother looked Jay and then Bronwen in the eye, tried to say something, stopped. She leaned closer.

"It smells like" – she swallowed – "saliva."

Jay and Bronwen stared at each other, then wrinkled their noses and burst out laughing.

Their mother couldn't stop attributing sin to Hamish now that he'd found religion. The family's continuum of belief had always run from Bronwen's atheism to her father's hazy sense of a higher power, with uncertainty the well-populated median, but recently Hamish had begun to spend much of his week in the small Catholic church on the hill in town, telling the priest who-knew-what. The very idea of him talking to anyone at length was shocking. Apart from the occasional disquisition on famous inventors, Hamish kept to himself.

"He spent five hours at that church last Wednesday!" exclaimed their father, who was usually unmoved by any manner of family crisis. "What could he possibly have to confess that could take five hours to tell?"

"An affair?" guessed Bronwen.

"But he never goes out," their mother protested. She was looking around the kitchen as though to make sure that Kathy wasn't eavesdropping from one of the cupboards.

"Maybe it's bestiality," suggested Jay. "With the cows."

"Good God, where do you get such ideas?" their mother cried. "I mean, really." Their father just glared at him.

"Torturing them, then," guessed Jay, enjoying his train of thought. "Vivisection."

"Don't be ridiculous," said their father angrily.

"Maybe he's not confessing at all," said Bronwen. "Maybe he has a relationship with the priest."

"All right, that's it, never mind," insisted their father.

"No, he's too old to be abused," said Jay to Bronwen.

"Nobody's too old to be abused," she replied.

Their father scowled even more. "This conversation is finished." He looked frustrated, and she wondered if he was disappointed by the fact that they were too old to take behind the house with his belt.

That wasn't the end of it, she knew. They'd talk about Hamish all night if they could. It was easy to make fun of him, simpler than bringing up Seth's divorce or Jay's chronic depression. She felt sorry for Hamish, but still she was relieved that for once it wasn't her life under the microscope. Her family had all sorts of good ideas for her: she should drop the investigator's job and go back to journalism; she should join a fitness club to meet men. No doubt they swapped other such plans behind her back. She tried to ignore her family's good ideas. She focused on her job, became passionate about house fires, thefts, and, in the last few weeks, what the lizard at the office called "unexplained death." She put her nose to the ground and hunted after humble facts, letting her life be held together by other people's catastrophes. She tried to stay objective and detached, and most of the time she pulled it off, but here in Sunshine, detachment was not an easy thing to have.

BRONWEN REMEMBERED Alice vaguely from high school; a bright girl, three years younger than herself, always busy with the student council, the debating team, and half a dozen other activities, one of the people you felt certain wasn't going to get stuck in Mooney's Dump. The news about her returning to take over Fremlin's dental practice had been a surprise, even though Bronwen realized that not everyone was as eager to leave the town behind as she'd been. There was an inertia here; children grew up and built houses next door to their parents. When she'd heard about Alice's disappearance a year and a half ago, it had only seemed to confirm a long-held belief: Don't go back, or the place will get you eventually. And now she'd ended up here herself, investigating Alice's death, consoling the lanky, good-looking man she'd met a decade ago in the supermarket. She hadn't wanted this case. With Mike's wife dead and the town against him, she'd known it would be dangerous in all sorts of ways to spend time with him. But when he'd arranged with the company to hire one of its investigators, the lizard had insisted that she be the one to go. You know those people inside out, he'd said. You have connections.

In the middle of June she'd packed a suitcase, driven up from Toronto, and dropped off her things at her parents' house before meeting with Mike and making some initial inquiries. He related to her the events leading up to the henge party, the last argument he'd had with Alice, his misgivings about the time she'd been spending at Cam Usher's. Next there was a talk with Harry Midgard. At that point Alice was still a missing person, and the police seemed to have given up hope of finding her. Harry took an hour explaining to Bronwen all the dead ends in the investigation. "Murder. Suicide. Abduction," he said. "Or just a runaway. Who knows? We can't even tell what kind of case we've got." At the end of it he shook her hand and wished her luck.

On her second day in town she'd driven out to the Moonstone Wildlife Park. Too much time had passed since the solstice party for there to be any evidence still lying around, but it seemed like the right place to start, and besides, she had one important question that she wanted to ask Cam Usher. The gap-toothed teenager who sat in the booth at the entrance to the parking lot didn't know where Usher was, and he insisted that if Bronwen wanted to look for him inside the grounds she'd have to pay. She started into an argument, then decided it wasn't worth it and handed over ten dollars.

Her mother had mentioned rumours that the wildlife park was losing money and that Usher would have to sell the place, but that day it was crowded with tourists. The animals' pens were tidy, spacious, well kept, set on either side of a footpath that wound around at least five acres. The loop began with ponies and turkeys, which didn't quite fit her conception of "wildlife," but the children walking among them didn't seem to mind. Then on to an ostrich pecking at dust, a crotchety llama, some ordinary white-tailed deer asleep under an awning, and miniature ones with corkscrew antlers drinking from a trough. In one cage there was a brown bear heaving on the ground with its rump in the air, flies circling. "Is it hurt?" a little girl asked her mother. Finally the pen for the tiger, but when Bronwen looked she saw nothing. At last she spotted it in the dappled light under some pine trees in the corner, sprawled just like a housecat, its tail waving to her. She waved back, in spite of herself.

The loop ended without a glimpse of Cam Usher, so the teenager in the booth pointed her toward a century farmhouse not unlike her parents'. As she approached it, Usher greeted her on the veranda. Though it was well into the morning, he was wearing a bathrobe and holding a mug of coffee in one hand.

"Bronwen, hello, come in," he said with a familiarity that confused her. As far as she knew, they'd never met before. "People have been talking about you; they thought you might turn up here sometime." So much for the element of surprise, she thought, and wondered who'd been talking. According to what some residents of Sunshine had told her, Usher attracted a close-knit coterie of people who were rarely seen in town, gathering instead at the farmhouse to take part in witchcraft and fertility rites. Public events like the party at the henge seemed only to strengthen the group's association with debauchery and the bizarre. Bronwen looked at the man standing there in his bathrobe and thought he seemed too ordinary to be the Cam Usher who engendered so much gossip.

As she started up the stairs, there was the sound of distant thunder. She stopped to peer at the sky but couldn't see any clouds.

"That's not rain," Usher said, sounding disappointed. "They're just blasting over at the quarry on the reserve. It drives the animals crazy."

He led her into the house, down a hallway to a living room with large windows, and sat in a leather armchair with his robe so conscientiously gathered around him that she thought he might not be wearing anything underneath. Below his neck she could see an even tan and thick curls of blond hair, and the hand that held his coffee mug was missing not only a ring, but most of the ring finger. The beginning of it was bent around the handle, but then it simply ended in a smooth knob of skin. Bronwen had heard about this too; a man at the Veterans Club said the finger had been cut off on purpose, sacrificed in a rite of devil worship. She wondered if Cam had heard the myths about him in Sunshine, or if he fathomed the amount of energy people spent trying to figure him out. She'd have to count herself among them now; part of her was eager to ask him the question she'd had on her mind, but she decided to wait before making her move.

"I just took a stroll around the park," she told him. "You have a lot of land."

"Almost four hundred acres," he agreed. "But it's mostly bush and swamp."

"Must have been hard on the people searching for Alice," she said, and he nodded slowly, as though trying to determine what was being implied. She wasn't sure herself. "Why'd you buy so much property?" she asked, remembering the fields she'd seen as she'd driven here, the low cedars, the tangled brush, and deep pools of water. Good land for hiding a body. She knew the police had combed the place a dozen times, but she wanted to see what Usher would say.

"I don't like to feel boxed in," he replied, and drummed his fingers on the arm of the chair.

She told Cam she didn't really have anything to ask him. He'd given the police a good account of his relationship to Alice: she was his dentist, they shared an interest in astronomy, and when he got the idea to build a henge she'd agreed to help with the design and construction. At the party he'd seen her during the opening ceremony and then again, very briefly, before midnight when she'd said goodbye. He didn't remember exactly when she left, or with whom, but he recalled that she'd been in good spirits. Usher nodded at Bronwen's recounting of his own words. It was all true. When she didn't say anything more, he took a sip from his mug, then raised his eyebrows expectantly.

"So – did you want to look around the place or something?" he asked her.

"I wasn't planning on it. Why, do you think it would help?"

He shrugged. "Scene of the crime and all that."

"Who said it was a crime?" she asked, and he began to stumble out a response. "No, don't worry, I know what you mean." She said it in a reassuring tone, even as she tried to decide whether the slip might mean anything.

"Well, if you don't have any questions –" He made to get up, apparently hoping for her to follow, but she didn't budge and he sank back into his chair. She bit her lip, then launched into the one question she'd been waiting to ask.

"So you never had an affair with Alice?" There. She'd said it.

He frowned at her, his stare hardening.

"No," he said. "Definitely not. Like I told the police."

She left soon after, sure he was lying. There was nothing to prove it except his emphatic denial. Somehow that seemed enough.

WHEN THEY'D FOUND Alice early in July, things had changed. Until then, Bronwen's employers at the insurance company had been confident that as long as Alice was missing, there was no possibility of a payout for the woman's death, and they'd considered themselves generous in lending Bronwen to the husband. Now, with the body recovered, the lizard phoned to tell her she'd have to come back on the company payroll and put aside Mike's agenda. She was to remain in Sunshine and search for facts that pointed to suicide, not to murder.

"There were plenty of reasons for killing herself, right?" said the lizard. "Love affair? Money problems? Out-of-work husband?" Bronwen made murmurs of assent and hung up as quickly as she could.

That night when she told Mike of the new arrangement, he barely seemed to hear her. Nel and Oliver were upstairs with their grandmother, and he was sitting at the kitchen table with a catalogue for headstones lying between his hands. What would be easier on him? she wondered. To find out that Alice killed herself, or that she was killed by someone else? Somehow each possibility seemed to Bronwen more horrible than the other. She stood behind him and kneaded his shoulders while he read. It was wrong of her, she knew that; the gesture might be misinterpreted. She was already coming over far too often, even on nights when there was no business to discuss. It was too tempting to hide out here with him, just as he'd been hiding from the town in this house all these years, raising his children. No, she should go home right now. But she couldn't bring herself to leave him alone like that, staring at grave markers.

"I'll still stop by to let you know how things are going," she told him.

"Sure, sounds good," he agreed without enthusiasm, staring at the catalogue in front of him and turning the page. "There, that's a nice one," he said flatly. "Star blue granite. She'd have liked that." Bronwen looked down at the gravestone in the picture, then at the hand that rested next to it, and saw that Mike was wearing two wedding bands. One of them was familiar to her, and then there was another, smaller one on his little finger.

"Is that –?" she began, pointing to it.

"A gift," he replied, "from Harry Midgard."

The next day Stoddart Fremlin had been arrested for Alice's murder. Until that point Harry had been more or less amenable to Bronwen's presence in the station, permitting access to files and even encouraging her to talk with people whom the police had interviewed, but suddenly things changed. He ordered her not to speak with witnesses any more and not to inquire about evidence.

"Are you afraid the case against Fremlin won't stand up to scrutiny?" she asked, feeling bold, and he walked away without answering. When a coroner arrived to investigate the time and cause of death, Bronwen was instructed not to speak with him either, so the following morning, after the man had departed with the body for Toronto to do tests, she drove down as well, partly to check on her apartment and escape her parents for a night, but also because she knew there'd be a better chance of getting information out of the coroner without Harry beside him. Still, when she visited the man's office she expected him to be wary of her, and she recited her ingratiating lines of introduction with as much warmth as she could manage in such a place. It was a relief when he offered her a seat and began to ask her about her work, about where she'd grown up. Perhaps, she thought, just after he'd invited her to see what was left of Alice Pederson, it was simply her good fortune to be dealing with a man who was lonely.

"You might want to cover your nose," he said when he'd closed the laboratory door behind them and she was already fighting nausea. He moved to the examining table and drew back a white plastic sheet, gingerly, as though there were a sleeping person underneath. Mike had said there were just bones, but as the coroner laid aside the cover Bronwen realized that Mike must never have seen the remains himself, that Harry Midgard had told him euphemistic half-truths. There was more than just a skeleton: there was a human figure, emaciated and incomplete. A nightmare with human hair on it. She couldn't distinguish any skin, just a waxy, grey-white substance, like crumbling cheese. The coroner told her it was hydrolysis due to prolonged immersion. He pointed to scrapes and deep abrasions that were as black as charcoal and said they were a result of the body being pushed around by winter ice. They'd found her far out in the lake, but it was clear she'd travelled some distance before settling on the bottom. The coroner picked up a metal prod and slowly inserted it into flesh.

"Look," he said. "The uterus is still intact." His tone grave, but lurking underneath it something different, almost conspiratorial. She wanted to be out of there.

When she asked him if it could have been suicide, he didn't answer her directly. Instead he explained the various methods by which he'd calculated the date of death: proteins in the bones, amino acids, the status of blood pigment, and of course the flesh's decomposition. Deterioration in water was slow, twice as slow as air; with the near-freezing winter temperatures of Mooney's Bay, it would be virtually nil. But still, there'd been time for the body to sink, to become lodged somewhere for a long summer of decay. The coroner believed that Alice had died sometime within a month of disappearing.

"So it might not have been the first night?" Bronwen asked.

"Not necessarily."

She could have been abducted then, Bronwen thought. All that time they were looking for her, she might have been hidden away in some backwoods cabin, alive. Her mouth gagged, hands bound. Bronwen could almost feel the cords tight around her own wrists. There were holes in the roof, the floorboards rotten. A kerosene lamp burned on the table and threw a pale light on the walls. She saw a shadow pacing in the corner, nearly beyond the lamp's reach. The shadow of a man, she thought, but she wasn't sure. It wouldn't hold still long enough to be identified. And another shadow, Alice's, kneeling in the centre of the room, her head tilted down as though in prayer.

Bronwen shuddered. Even the body in front of her was easier to deal with than that. She tried to concentrate on it while the coroner spoke. He circled the table leisurely and told her he couldn't be sure about the cause of death.

"No sign of strangulation, but then, there's almost no neck. Same with these other lacerations: nothing obviously lethal, but there's too much gone for it to mean anything. No sign of any foreign substances in the body, either. No bullet holes. No broken bones."

"Then it's possible that she drowned. An accident, or –"

"It's a funny story, that one," he said. "Used to be, you could run what's known as a diatom test. In natural fresh water there are algae called diatoms. As you're drowning, your heart still beats while they penetrate the alveolar walls in the lungs, and the pulse pushes them around your body. So I can take a cell sample, spin it, and look for them under the microscope. Diatoms in the body are pretty much a guarantee that drowning was the cause of death."

"So?" she said. "What did you find?" She was still waiting to see what was funny about the story.

"The thing is, diatoms are only found in unpolluted fresh water. It used to be a reliable test for bodies of water like Mooney's Bay, but now there are all those speed boats, and sometimes sewage treatment plants dump their excess into the lake." He turned pensive. "I hope you're drinking filtered water up there."

"So there's no point to any of it," she said, ignoring the last remark.

"Well, I did the test and nothing came up, so it's inconclusive. Wishful thinking on my part even to go through with it, really."

That's all right, she thought as the coroner pulled the sheet back over the body. It was wishful thinking for me to come down here. Wishful thinking for Mike to hire an investigator. Wishful thinking for the company to assume that suicide could be proven. The case had been nothing but wishful thinking from the start.

Instead of staying in her apartment that night as she'd planned, she drove the three hours back to Sunshine and Mike's place. Then she offered him a version of what the coroner had told her, mopped clean of references to abrasions, uteruses, and her own imaginings. It wasn't a story Mike seemed to enjoy.

"I'm sorry the trip didn't turn out the way you wanted," was all he said. His voice was hoarse with laryngitis but she could still hear the bitterness in it.

"What way is that?" she asked defensively.

"I don't know. Slit wrists. A rope burn around the neck or something. Some top-notch evidence for your company." He didn't meet her gaze.

"Don't say that," she said. "It doesn't matter who's paying me, Mike. I'm not out to ruin your insurance claim. I'm after the truth, just like you. Even if they took me off the case, I wouldn't just disappear. I promise."

"I don't understand," he said, barely audible. "Why does it matter to you? You didn't even know her."

She couldn't answer him.

"I didn't know Alice," she agreed after a time. "But I know you." She stood up from the couch where'd they'd been sitting. "Mike, I'm sorry –"

He stood up next to her, put a hand on her shoulder, squeezed gently, and let his fingers lay there a while.

"Don't worry about it. We'll be all right." It was a novelty for him to be the one providing comfort, and she should have smiled, but instead she only felt even more confused. Alice's funeral had been the previous day.

THE LIZARD was getting impatient, and the news of Fremlin's arrest didn't lessen his anxiety. He wanted proof of arguments, depression, violent behaviour.

"Didn't the husband give anything away when you were working for him?" he asked.

"No," she said curtly. She wasn't interested in discussing Mike any more than necessary.

"Come on, it's not like you two shared attorney-client privilege." When she didn't reply, his voice became harsher. "If you've gotten involved with him –"

"Don't be ridiculous. Look, he said something about construction problems with her new office that upset her. Maybe that will pan out." So the next day she went into the town hall to get copies of the plans for Alice's clinic, even though she knew it was grasping at straws. She thought at least it would be a quiet afternoon of going through paperwork, but instead she got the runaround from the clerk, had to dig in her heels, and ended up speaking loudly enough for Bobby Boone, the mayor himself, to emerge and give her the runaround from the very highest level.

"Your company should pay Mike Pederson his money," Boone said. "His wife was murdered by that son of a bitch Fremlin, for God's sake. Even the police are saying so now."

"The case is flimsy," replied Bronwen. "There's no hard evidence. Just an old librarian who claims to have seen her getting into Fremlin's car at night."

"Mrs. Mason's eyesight is second to none," Boone exclaimed. "You're not saying otherwise, are you?"

"People get confused."

"Try telling that to Mrs. Mason." Boone took a deep breath that swelled his chest. "I hope you don't mind me saying this, Miss Ferry, but the problem with people in your profession is that you go around defaming innocent women like Mrs. Mason to suit your interests when you're supposed to be finding out who's really guilty."

"No," she said. "I don't mind you saying that at all." She did mind, though. People like Boone were the reason she'd never wanted to return to Sunshine. They didn't care about the truth; for them it was more important to circle the wagons and pretend everything was all right. Bobby Boone and his kind managed just fine, they were on the inside, but others like Mike were left to fend for themselves, and sooner or later they got torn to pieces. That night her sympathy for Mike in this regard slipped into anger, and she found herself grilling him like he was on trial instead of a victim. "Why did you ever come to live here? Didn't you know how it would be? It's not like you were born here; you got to make a choice."

The next day she visited the police station and convinced Harry to let her go through Alice's record, which revealed a single speeding ticket. It was dated Thursday, September 23, 1999, and had been issued in Orangeville, almost two hours' drive from Sunshine. Alice was supposed to have worked that day, yet according to the files in her office, all her afternoon appointments had been rescheduled. When Bronwen tracked down the secretary who'd been on shift, the woman vaguely recalled Alice leaving in a hurry, saying there was a family emergency. Later, the secretary said, Alice had claimed her mother was ill. But her mother lived in Walkerton, and Orangeville was nowhere close to it.

Bronwen went to the *Sunshine Beacon* and borrowed the back issues from that September. At home she spread them on the kitchen table and tried to ignore the presence of her mother, who hovered over her shoulder as she leafed through the pages. Nothing stood out.

"The biggest news was Daniel Barrie leaving for England on his scholarship," Bronwen complained.

"But he didn't," said her mother.

"What? It says in this article –"

"He missed his flight from Toronto. Left his passport and ticket at home. Maybe there's a note about it in the next week's issue –" She reached down to turn the page but Bronwen brushed away her hand and looked again at the date. Daniel had been scheduled to leave the same day Alice Pederson got her speeding ticket.

"Why didn't you tell me this before?" she cried to her mother.

"I thought everybody knew that story. They were all talking about it: the big-shot scholar making a mistake like that –"

"But this could be important, Mom!"

"Well how am I supposed to know what's important? People pass in and out of town every day, I've got better things to do than –"

"Okay, I'm sorry. Never mind." She should have left it at that, but there was one more thing she needed to find out. "Tell me, when did Daniel end up going to England, then?"

The answer was very interesting. Then, when Bronwen called Marge Barrie and asked how to reach Daniel in England, she found out he wasn't overseas any more; he'd returned to Sunshine just before the funeral.

"Curiouser and curiouser," she said to herself.

From there she'd hoped for things to resolve themselves neatly before her eyes, but the rest of July had offered little more in the way of clues. Now, standing in her parents' kitchen with the discussion about Hamish and the priest at an end, her mind returned to the case, and she found herself repeating the list of names she'd accumulated, trying to make connections. Daniel Barrie. Cam Usher with his henge. Stoddart Fremlin arrested for murder. After all this time, none of them seemed to bring her any closer to solving the riddle of Alice's death. And then there was Rocket DeWitt, Fremlin's protégé and a friend of Daniel. Even in the city she'd read about Rocket's hockey exploits; he was probably the biggest reason anyone in Ontario had heard of Sunshine. Finding him was what mattered, she decided. Even if it turned out that he knew nothing about Alice Pederson, even if Bronwen came no closer to the truth, the discovery of his whereabouts might redeem the whole investigation, for herself if not for anyone else. Then, at least, she could claim to have returned some kind of order to the town, to have lessened the uncertainty, however great it remained.

"Why don't you try the village fair?" Jay suggested. "Everybody shows up."

"Jay, the police are after Rocket too," she replied. "I hardly think he's just going to appear so easily."

"But does he know they're looking for him?" asked her mother. "Maybe he just hasn't heard."

"Around here," Bronwen snorted, "everyone hears everything."

BEFORE SUNSET the Sunshine village fair was a tame event, full of small children and short-tempered parents. By the time Bronwen arrived with Hamish, though, it was after dark, and electric lights had transformed the place into a hub of danger and energy where anyone might appear and anything could happen. On Monday the carnival company had arrived at the town's waterfront park to begin construction, bringing to Sunshine strange, gaunt people with moustaches and tattoos who were watched closely when they shopped in the downtown stores. By Thursday night the rides were still practically formless and it seemed they would never be finished in time, but once Friday afternoon came everything was ready: the Merry-Go-Round and the Bouncy Castle for toddlers, and for adults the Tilt-A-Whirl, the Scrambler. The Salt-N-Pepper Shaker turned passengers upside down and every year someone threw up at the top. The operator stood under an umbrella. At the far end of the grounds were games of chance run by the Rotary Club, in cheap plywood huts with ten-year-old paint. The carnival company had such games too, with brighter lights and bigger prizes, but children were warned that these games were dishonest. Hamish wanted to check out the target-shooting game to see if the rifle sights were skewed, and Bronwen said she'd catch up with him later.

She walked past the dunking machine, the corn roast, the bingo pavilion, and stepped across a bundle of electrical cables. Looking back on the ring of illuminated tents and plywood from only a few feet away, the whole thing seemed diminutive and surreal. She was in Sunshine again, the town quiet and dark, the bay peaceful, flecked with moonlight. She walked along the sand beach and then out the length of the dog-legging government pier. Most yacht owners preferred the community of the marina, so there were only ever one or two boats moored here. A single green light blinked at the end of the concrete promenade, and she swung around its post like a girl before heading back the way she'd come. The water appeared deep and secretive, blocking vision but amplifying sound, the inland whirl of the carnival rides and the barkers' enticements no louder than the distant buzz of fishing boats on the bay. She gasped at the unexpected swirl of a carp surfacing.

Jay had been right: everyone, it seemed, was here. Returning to the fairgrounds, she saw several men and women she'd interviewed over the past six weeks. But tonight when they greeted her, they didn't behave in the way she remembered; suspicion and nervous irritation had been replaced by a general expression of summer-evening placability. Perhaps they could sense she was after someone else tonight. There was no sign of Rocket DeWitt, though – she'd suspected there wouldn't be – and after half an hour she gave up the pretence of searching for him. Remembering her encounter with Stoddart Fremlin at the airfield before dinner, she regretted again not asking the man any questions. Perhaps he would have had an idea of where Rocket might be.

Bronwen had last seen Hamish at a concession stand near the parking lot, but the way there was blocked by a snake of people waiting to ride the Ferris wheel. When she attempted to cut through, she realized she was stepping in front of Mike and his children.

"I was hoping we might run into you," he told her when she said hello. "I'm really glad you came." She nodded cautiously. There was something in his eyes tonight, she thought, something slightly reckless and wild. "You want to try the wheel with us?" he asked, exhibiting a long string of carnival tickets. "We have extras and this is the last ride for the Pedersons tonight."

There was still no sign of Hamish so she joined them in line, ignoring the glares from the couple behind them. Nel smiled a greeting, but Oliver took no notice of Bronwen; he was busy demanding a return to the Bouncy Castle.

"It's past his bedtime," Mike said to Bronwen. "It's my fault, I got carried away."

"You don't have to apologize," she said. "I'm not the one who has to get them to sleep tonight."

Then Nel wanted to show her the stuffed elephant she'd got at the duck race, and Oliver held out the panda Daddy had won at the rifle shoot. Mike was silent, gazing up at the revolving wheel as though a stranger to his own family. She wondered if he wanted this respite from the children's attention, or if he liked having them close at hand, where their demands could provide a distraction from his own thoughts. Perhaps keeping them up past their bedtime was not so unusual now.

"When I was a teenager it was a big deal to kiss at the top of the Ferris wheel," Mike said out of the blue, still watching the ride. Bronwen felt a twinge of embarrassment. She wondered what Nel would think about her father saying such a thing, but the girl just stood there hugging her elephant. Apparently at ten years old she was still young enough not to feel shame.

Once it was their turn to mount the ramp into a waiting car, Mike counted out an arm's-length of tickets for the operator. The man looked them over and tore off a few to hand back.

"Family discount," he said. Mike looked at Bronwen with a sheepish smile, shrugged, and put them in his pocket. They stepped forward and sat down on the red sponge seat.

"But she's not family, Dad," said Nel.

"Never mind, honey," he said quickly, and glanced at the operator. "Hey, is this thing safe?"

"Hope so," the man replied, and snapped shut a thin metal bar in front of them. Bronwen pulled Oliver on to her lap.

"Can we rock it at the top?" asked Nel.

"No," said Bronwen before Mike had a chance to say anything. "Definitely not."

They ascended backwards in short spurts as the cars were filled with new passengers, and Oliver squirmed to lean over the front.

Bronwen tried to hold him back, but that only made him squirm harder.

"I want to see how far up we are," he complained.

It seemed a wholesale change of the twelve passenger cars was underway. The stop-and-go continued until they were stalled at the very top of the wheel, higher than the trees now, and all of Sunshine spread around them: the town hall, the ball diamond, the squat green recreation centre, the edges of the bay forking into darkness. She followed the line of the north shore until she saw the warning beacon of the airfield, and she counted the seconds between each revolution of its beam. Seven, just like always. For decades the light had been a slow, unwavering heartbeat for the town. In her room at home it shifted the shadows endlessly from dusk until dawn, lulling her to sleep with its regularity. It was hard to believe in a time before air travel when the light had not existed.

Once they got moving, Oliver started to moan with fright. He was screaming before they hit full speed, and when they reached the top again he began to swing his fists at her.

"Everything's fine," she shouted to Mike above the clamour of the boy's wailing, the motor, and the tinny carnival music. "I'll hold him." She wrapped her arms around Oliver, lay her cheek against the top of his head, and whispered that there was nothing to worry about.

"I told you he was too little," said Nel, and Mike nodded grimly. Every time they swung past the operator and the waiting line Bronwen could see people staring at them. It was a relief when the ride finally stopped, even though by then Oliver had calmed down.

She told Mike she had to find Hamish and asked if he'd keep an eye out, then made a full tour of the grounds before returning to discover Mike and Hamish chatting in the place she'd started from. The children were running around the men's legs, and Hamish was telling Mike the history of the Ferris wheel. He'd discovered that at some point in the centuries the Ferrises were actually Ferrys. Then the name had been corrupted. As far as Hamish was concerned, he was a blood relation of George W.G. Ferris, the inventor.

"Chicago, World's Fair, 1893," Hamish was saying. "They wanted something to beat the Eiffel Tower. The first one was two hundred and fifty feet high, four thousand tons. This is 1893 we're talking about, eh? Everybody thought old George was crazy, but the thing held together. It took twenty-four hundred people at a time. The whole population of Sunshine. Can you imagine that one?" Mike shook his head duly.

Bronwen knew Hamish could have talked for hours about George Ferris.

"Come on, let's go," she said, putting a hand on his elbow. It was Mike more than Hamish who seemed to register the words.

"Oh, are you heading home already?" he asked, and she nodded.

"I'm tired. It's been a long day."

"I don't suppose you're coming over later on, then?"

"No, not tonight," she said quickly, annoyed that Hamish was there listening, that this exchange might be reported tomorrow at the Ferry dinner table. Goodbyes were better at Mike's house, where they were said in private.

"Well, I'll see you soon," he said and stepped forward, as though to hug her. Her arms stayed at her sides. She didn't move. What was he doing? They'd never hugged before. His children were right there, watching. She looked past him to Nel and found the girl staring at her, full of hate.

"Good night," said Bronwen, and turned in the direction of the car. Hamish followed, silent, apparently too much of a coward to taunt her.

"You didn't need to tell Mike all about the Ferris wheel, you know," she said once they'd reached the parking lot. She didn't want to give Hamish a chance to say anything about the hug.

"Come on, the guy's wife died," said Hamish.

"So? That doesn't mean you should bore him to tears."

"Well, what was I supposed to talk about? Ask him how he's doing?"

"Yes," she said. "That's exactly what you should have done." She knew such extensions of empathy were beyond Hamish's social range, but she couldn't stop herself. "The man feels alone. He doesn't need people babying him. He needs compassion."

"Oh, is that what you give him when you're at his house all those nights?" It sounded half-hearted, though; Hamish didn't tease nearly as well as his brothers.

"We talk about the case, Ham, and that's it. I don't get any kick out of going there. He's all twisted up inside." Then a hand tapped her on the shoulder. It was Mike.

"Hi," he said. "Listen, could I talk to you for a second?"

She nodded, bright red in the darkness.

"Of course. Hamish, I'll be back in a couple of minutes."

"Or I can give you a ride home," offered Mike. "Hamish doesn't have to wait." When she told Hamish to go on without her, her brother shot her a knowing, self-satisfied look and said goodbye. After he'd got into his car, she walked with Mike back toward the fair grounds.

"Where are the kids?"

"We ran into the Norrises," he said. "They offered to take them for ice cream and drop them off later."

"Oh." She shifted away from him slightly. It felt like a possibility had taken human form and walked between them. "So what did you want to talk about?"

"I'm not sure," he started, then coughed. "Look, I have enough tickets left for another ride on the Ferris wheel. You up for it?" She said yes, not knowing whether she really was, and his face lit up as though the two of them were about to set off on a great adventure.

They threaded their way through the crowd and got in line. It was shorter this time, only adults, and soon they found themselves alone together in a car, their bodies a foot apart. They made the first ascent in silence, looking out separately upon the town. The ball diamond lights were being turned off now, one by one, so that every few seconds another part of the visible world disappeared. Mike sat bent over with closed eyes, his hands in his pockets and his forehead creased. Whether the thing he'd been so eager to talk about was now forgotten or tormenting him, she didn't know. Stop beating yourself up, she wanted to say. It's too soon. The funeral was only three weeks ago.

Her stomach lurched every time they passed the summit. Trying to look down, she found it odd that she couldn't see any other passengers on the wheel. Here they were, passing through each other's spaces, breathing each other's air, completely anonymous. She shivered. It would take guts to lean over the safety bar, rock the car forward and shout hello, try to make a connection.

"You cold?" Mike offered his jacket but she waved it away. They weren't sixteen any more. When he put his hand on her shoulder she almost pushed it off.

"I'm too old for you" is what she said, and he removed his hand of his own accord. For the first time, she noticed that the two wedding bands were gone from his fingers. "It wouldn't work. You'd just feel worse."

They didn't say anything for the rest of the ride, nor during the drive back home. She sat there repeating her excuses to herself, hoping that together they might add up to something approaching the truth behind her reticence. Past mistakes, professional dignity, fear. It was tempting to glance at Mike and search his face for emotions, but she made herself look straight into the night.

"I want to keep our relationship on a business level," she said as they reached her parents' lane. But when she got out of the car she gave him a kiss on the top of his smooth, shaved head, then another, very gently, on his nose.

She was halfway up the porch stairs when she realized that her father was sitting on his wicker chair, waiting.

"It's late, Dad," she muttered. "Hurry up, out with it."

"Out with what?"

"Don't you have something for me to do? Has the well gone dry again or something?"

"No, no," he said, as though he were genuinely startled by the suggestion. Could it be that he'd never detected his own habit? "I just thought you might want to know, I've figured out what got the calf."

"A tiger," she said promptly. His shoulders sunk; it seemed he'd been looking forward to surprising her.

"I guess you've heard the same things I have," he murmured. "Anyhow, a few of the local boys are holding a hunt for it on Monday. Hamish is planning to go."

Bronwen shook her head. Who had time for Alice Pederson any more, with all these other intrigues vying for attention? It seemed as though only she and Mike were left with the duty of remaining loyal to the dead woman's memory. But then Bronwen remembered Mike's smooth skin against her lips, and she wondered how loyal she had ever been.

Her father's face had taken on a puzzled expression, but he wasn't scrutinizing her; he was watching something past her, his eyes tracking across the sky.

"Hey, Bronny, would you take a look at that."

Before she could move, his face was illuminated by a bright orange light that flared across the whole house and extinguished. At the same time, a terrible din reached her ears – crashing, popping, squealing. She turned toward the airfield. There were the usual bright blue lights along the runway and then, at the far end, a streak of low flame.

"What happened? I can't see."

Her father was getting up from his chair.

"Plane," he muttered. "I saw the fuselage when it hit."

"Jesus." She suddenly remembered her encounter with Stoddart Fremlin. It had only been a few hours ago.

"Go inside and get on the phone," she said. "Fire department, ambulance, police." She waited for him to argue and say that she should be the one to call while he investigated, but she realized that the authority of a movie detective had unexpectedly crept into her voice. Her father nodded and opened the screen door. As she hurried down the steps she heard the others rushing to the front of the house, anxious to see what was at the root of all that light and noise, and her father telling them to put on some boots. The keys to his pickup truck were in the ignition, and she took the shortcut.

When she reached the airfield the flames had died, and to her eyes the runway looked normal. Then the first chunk of metal appeared in front of the truck. She turned off the engine and there was utter silence, save for the drone of invisible crickets. The cattle had been put in the barn for the night.

"Hello?" she shouted. "Is anybody out there?"

As she moved out of the headlights' glare, she began to see the shapes of white objects scattered across the dark field. A wheel, a door, a portion of the aircraft's tail. Dozens of unidentifiable metal pieces. Farther ahead was the main section of the plane, and she realized that it must have slid more than fifty yards to have left wreckage behind it for such a great distance. She called out, and when there was no response a sickening ache grew in her gut. She stepped forward with dim horror, afraid of what she might trip over.

After the litter of parts that preceded the bulk of the fuselage, she was surprised to see the body of the plane was almost undamaged. The windows had shattered, but it was still upright and otherwise intact. Perhaps the burst of flame was simply from the friction of impact, the resulting fire only burning grass, so dry and dead along the runway that it had been consumed quickly.

From beyond the fuselage she heard sounds of movement.

"Who's there?" she said.

There was no answer, but the sounds continued: the clatter of metal against metal. She moved slowly around the plane, thinking against all probability of the tiger. When she reached the far side, her chest contracted at the sight of a figure on all fours. It wasn't any animal, though. It was Stoddart Fremlin.

He looked up at her.

"Help me," he said. "Help me gather it all up."

"Dr. Fremlin, are you all right?"

"I don't want them to see what happened."

"You shouldn't be moving. You could be injured." She went up to him and put a hand on his shoulder, but he shrugged it off. He smelled of alcohol. "We shouldn't be this close to the wreckage. The fuel could ignite."

"There's no fuel," he mumbled. "Damn thing ran out of gas." He continued to slide around on his hands and knees, picking up pieces of debris and throwing them into a pile. It was difficult to tell in the darkness, but she couldn't discern any wounds – no gashes in his clothing, no contorted limbs.

"Dr. Fremlin, you were just in a plane crash. You're in shock. You need to go to the hospital." But she almost believed that he didn't.

"They'll put me back in jail," he said. "I wasn't supposed to be flying."

"Don't worry about that. The important thing is that you're all right." She heard the sound of engines and looked back to see headlights approaching from the road – her hatchback, and then the other Ferry cars behind it. "Please try not to move, Dr. Fremlin," she said. "There'll be people to help you soon." She ran to meet the approaching vehicles.

"I called the emergency numbers and then your mother took over," said her father from the hatchback as she drew near. "The whole town will be coming now."

He was right. Within fifteen minutes, it seemed like everyone had arrived. The peace of the night was replaced by the flashing lights of ambulances, police cars, and fire trucks. Esther Fremlin and her boyfriend were on the scene, and Harry Midgard was talking to them. But Stoddart Fremlin was nowhere to be found. In the interval when Bronwen had run to speak with Hamish and her father, he had vanished.

THE ARCHIVIST DREAMS
OF AN OPEN HOUSE

Wrong, wrong, wrong. It was wrong and he was bad. Call the police, that's what you were supposed to do, any moron knew that. But the fever – ohhhh, it was here again. The fever was on him and there was nothing to be done. Before he could stop himself, Archie opened the door of the pickup truck, reached in, and grabbed the rifle from those cold fingers. They held on tight, like he was wrestling with a ghost, and maybe they were going to snap right off if he pulled too hard, so he went knuckle by knuckle, rubbing and kneading until he could coax those fingers from the trigger and stock. A deer fly was crawling on his skin, now another. They bit off pieces of him, flew away, lazy. His hands were too busy to shoo them. The rest swarmed farther up, around the headrest and the ceiling, the back seat.

The rifle was his at last, and he laid it behind the front tire on the gravel, out of harm's way. Then the man's shirt, a fistful of it in his hands. Grab his belt too, and lift. Lift hard. All that gunk sealing the clothes to the upholstery. Easier if he leaned back and tugged sideways, bit by bit. A leg swung free and dangled out of the truck, a polished leather shoe on the end of it. The rest tottered on the edge of the seat; he had to hold it in a bear hug. An arm flailed over his shoulder and clapped him on the back.

He dragged the body to the side of the road, the flies following angrily, and left it for them while he cleared a space on the trailer behind his bicycle. It was going to be heavy, maybe too heavy for an old man like him. The early-morning sun was hot, the ground still slippery with dew. Better to be in bed than out here. He was crazy. Birch leaves whispered secrets, exploded into gold. Fields of sticky webs above his head, the stuff he'd pedalled through on the way here while doing his research. He dragged the man to the trailer, squeezed him in, tucked the rifle beside him, and closed the door of the truck. Back to the bicycle after that, pumping the pedals, watching for rocks on the old logging road. Home, cried the fever. Home without getting caught. Home to finish it. Already the shameful pleasure of accomplishment started to spread through him. Once it was over, he'd admit to Bobby what he had done.

A LONG TIME BEFORE, way back, when Archie moved into his parents' home on his thirtieth birthday, Mrs. Eudora Northey came over from next door wearing a lily-patterned dress that ended just below her knees.

"I know this isn't right for mourning," she told him in her singsong voice, before he could say hello. "But I thought I'd wear something to cheer you up. Here. I brought you this." Carefully she handed him the cake she'd been holding, which was made in the shape of the house. There were cookies to simulate the doors, waxed paper for the windows, and the roof was horizontal just like the original. But then, the resemblance was no surprise. The Boones' house was the only one in the modernist style for fifty miles, a novelty built by Archie's father that was more likely to be made fun of than admired, and Mrs. Northey had done well selling similar cakes to people in the neighbourhood who were throwing parties and wanted a laugh. She'd only been in the town a year, six months of it as a widow, and she didn't seem to realize it might upset anyone to do that sort of thing.

"I'm sorry for your loss," she said to him as he set the cake on the kitchen table. "I hope they put away that truck driver for good."

In the afternoon Bobby arrived with a van to remove the furniture and other items Archie didn't want. Bobby was getting the contracting business, despite what the will said. Archie, the older son by twelve minutes, had been the one who worked for their father, hammering and lugging two-by-fours, but he agreed that his brother was better at things like building permits and negotiating wages, and that he'd take the house instead.

"What about the rolltop desk and the dartboard? Did you want to keep those?" Bobby asked, barrelling down the hallway with a lamp in each hand, and Archie shook his head.

Within a few months Archie no longer had time to go to work. Bobby said nothing about his absence, and paycheques continued to arrive in the mail, so Archie remained free to do his research. Every weekday morning a different part of the town placed bins on the curb for disposal, and it was all he could do to keep up. Now, nearly thirty-five years had gone by since his parents' death, and he was certain that he'd nearly completed his project.

Mrs. Northey was very polite the first time she found him going through her garbage. At that point it had been only half a year since he'd started to patrol the streets, and his findings were still contained within one room of the house.

"Have you thrown something into my trash can by mistake, Mr. Boone?" she asked cheerfully, stepping through her front door with a purse in her hand. He looked up at her, stone-faced. The fever had him and he wasn't quite able to reply. "Take your time," she said with a comforting smile. "If it's something important and you don't find it, I'll help you when I get back." This was before the bike and trailer, when he was still loading his discoveries into a baby buggy he'd found abandoned by the town reservoir. She walked by as though it were invisible.

Once he was home and the fever had passed, he thought about what she'd said. There was no doubt that she'd heard the gossip around town, that she knew well enough what he was doing. It had all been an act to protect him, to spare him the humiliation that she believed he'd feel at being caught out.

It was true, there was shame. Shame in the middle of researching, in the fever's glory, shame that he shrugged aside. It was worst in bed, when he was trapped in the house with the darkness and all his discoveries around him. He thought of doctors then, he made resolutions to change. But the next day the streets were waiting for him and the night's decisions seemed too drastic. With his nose full of stench and his hands digging for buried treasure, shame only thumped away in the back of his skull and stirred up the fever even more. Truth be told, he'd almost not recognized Mrs. Northey at all.

A few hours after their meeting by her house, when he'd just finished sorting his day's findings and had removed the hockey helmet that he wore to protect himself during his work, she appeared on the front step with a casserole and a bottle of wine. She smelled of perfume, her hair looked as though it had come straight out of rollers, and her lips were a different shade of red than usual.

"I don't care how old you are," she said, "or how long you've lived in this town. A boy without his parents needs to be cared for." She made it sound like they were from different generations, but in fact she wasn't much older than he was. He looked down at himself and was relieved to see corduroys and a checkered work-shirt, not the overalls he'd worn during the day.

"Come in," he said, feeling as though her presence might be something he could handle, as though she wasn't his first visitor since Bobby had left in the van six months ago.

Over dinner they talked about Bobby's success with the business and the town council, about his new bride and the baby on the way. On the face of it Mrs. Northey was the one asking questions and Archie the one who answered them, but he hadn't seen his brother for weeks and it was clear that with her network of confidantes around town, she knew much more about Bobby's goings-on than he did. Still, she got him to confirm things for her, smiled when he talked, laughed at anything that seemed to be a joke. He almost felt comfortable.

When she asked about his work, he shrugged and said he was trying something different. She wanted to know more.

"I'm collecting," he said cautiously. It had been a long time since he'd thought about describing his project, to others or to himself. When he was on his own, no explanation was necessary. "Things from people's garbage."

"Oh dear," she said, and tittered. "What do you mean? Newspaper, scrap metal?"

"Everything," he replied. "Everything important."

She asked how long this had been going on, and he lifted his hands as though to say it was just a hobby. He mumbled vaguely when she asked about the precise contents of his collection, but then she requested that he show her some of what he had found. No, he thought. That wouldn't do. It might be better to satisfy her with a description after all.

He told her he didn't really collect everything, just ordinary items: bottles, clothing, furniture. Things thrown out in laziness that had some value, if scrubbed, patched, shown a little care.

"Yes," she said, nodding expectantly. "What else?"

He pushed squares of casserole around on his plate, unsure of where to begin, even less certain of where to stop. Calligraphy sets and badminton racquets seemed safe enough, but would she want to hear about colanders clogged with spaghetti? Love letters and hate letters and eviction notices? Bobby had warned him several times that they were going to get a shredder at the town hall, but they never had. If Archie went on long enough, perhaps she'd start to meditate on what he was leaving out, what his project really entailed: the wading through rotten fruit, stinking dishtowels, tampons, diapers, tangles of hair. Sometimes there were pets buried at the bottom and, if he looked hard enough, the food, the grooming supplies, the leashes and collars.

He tried to distract her by talking about the bottles of diet pills abandoned, the unsmoked cartons of cigarettes that appeared in the same bin, week after week. In the excitement of it, he found things slipping out that he never thought he'd describe. A slight, elated stutter crept into his voice as he told her of all the mistakes he'd found. Children's dental appliances, eyeglasses, even wedding rings.

"Oh, but surely you give those back," Mrs. Northey exclaimed. She seemed more delighted than appalled at the thought that he might not. He nodded. "They must be very grateful to you."

"I – I don't talk to them," he replied. "I just slide – uh, slide things through the mail slot."

"But what do people think when they see you going through their garbage?"

He shrugged. "It's only junk they don't – um, don't want," he said. But the truth was, people were strange. If they noticed you walking off with an item from their trash can, half of them were likely to yell, to give chase. It seemed that nothing was ever surrendered for good; if someone else valued the thing they'd thrown out, it became valuable again in their eyes too. But most people in Sunshine were used to Archie's presence by now, and they let him go about his business. Only the sanitation workers cursed him, as though he was competing with them and not an ally. Children weren't any better. They called him Freak, and Rat-Man.

The thought of their taunts made him suddenly ashamed. Why now, when he was never bothered by them in the middle of his work? He looked across the mess of dishware and half-eaten casserole to Mrs. Northey, so intent on listening to him, and felt a wave of suspicion. She was just here to gather information for her friends, to embarrass him, he was sure of it. He should have known.

"What – what's with all these questions?" he demanded. "Has someone – have they got you – have they put you up to this?"

"No," she said quietly. "Not at all. I'm just concerned for you."

He was about to get up, but he hesitated. She sounded hurt.

No. It was too late now, anyway. He'd said too much.

"You – I think – I think you should go now," he told her, standing. "Thank you for dinner." When he looked down, he realized that one of his hands had crept into his beard, and he didn't remove it until she was out of the house.

The morning after, she appeared again at his step, this time carrying a large cardboard box. The singsong was back in her voice when she greeted him.

"What's this?" he asked, smiling in spite of himself.

"I felt badly about last night," she replied, "and I wanted to make it up to you. These are some things from my attic. I thought you might like them for your collection."

She handed him the box and followed him into the living room, where he set it on the floor by the couch. They sat and stared at it together.

"Well, go on, open it," she urged, tugging her dress down over her legs. He lifted the lid and reached in, placed the contents one by one on the coffee table. There was a pocket watch, a map of the world, a telescope, a beret.

"They were all my husband's," she said.

He started putting them back in the box.

"They're too good – uh, too fine for me," he mumbled. "I couldn't accept them."

"But last night, I thought you said that you collect valuable items. Aren't these the sorts of things you want?"

He looked down at the collection spread across the table: things selected and saved, assigned value. They were dead and useless to him.

"You should keep them," he told her. "It's not – uh, I would – I wouldn't feel right."

Once he'd managed to convince her that she should take them back, Mrs. Northey stood up and walked to the door with the box under her arm.

"I only thought," she said once she was on the threshold, turned away from him, "that two people living alone should be able to enjoy some company. That's all I thought."

It wasn't until later, as he lay in bed with the world scoured and sorted for the day, that he wondered with a dull curiosity about those things she had brought, and what worth they might have had.

THE FEVER was a clever thing. Oh, it was so smart. It didn't turn him into a robot; it only stroked him and fondled him and whispered gently in his ear until he was ready to do anything, absolutely anything it asked. Even this. Biking down shortcuts, alleyways, fire allowances on a hot summer's morning, pulling the man in the trailer, trying to avoid being seen. There goes Esther Fremlin walking by and she isn't watching. There goes Cam Usher in his car. Everybody circling, circling, and they might as well be blinded by the sun.

At the house Archie pedalled up the driveway and parked his bicycle in the backyard, where there was a stone wall on one side, a tall wooden fence on the other. The elm tree in the corner, dead for thirty years, threw a shadow across the piles of collected things on the lawn. A few rickety boards were still nailed to the trunk, the last bits of a fort his father had built for him and Bobby. That's the place, said the fever. In front of the tree: the patch of grass he never cut, the one that grew so high in the spring, it seemed like a tiny jungle in the middle of Sunshine. A green heron was there now, stalking slowly, following the salamanders that went creeping through the shade. Never mind it, the fever whispered. Inside with you.

Entering the house was always a relief. Here everything was known, in its place; thirty-five years of the town under one roof. He wanted to stand there and let the logic behind the piles unfold with its usual magic, but the fever wouldn't let him. Go, it said. Along the narrow passageway, between the stacks in the living room, through the still air and the familiar heat. As he went, he ticked off the things on either side, knowing he could recite the location of everything he passed, every article he'd taken from Sunshine, now in piles, boxes, drawers. The broken things in the dining room: flashlights with the bulbs gone, measuring tape yanked out too far. Electric toothbrushes, toasters, calculators, kites. Then the bathroom, with its oversized paper clips, hotel notepads, coin holders, ink pads and name-stamps, crayons. The walls and ceiling of the den were covered in carpet samples, every colour and texture, perfectly placed together so that not a single inch of the drywall underneath was visible.

Keep going, Archie. Forget the basement with its six hundred shoeboxes. Forget the photographs. Oh, but he wanted to look at them again. Grey and fuzzy, sun-spotted, poorly composed, underlit, overexposed. People from Sunshine frozen on film, faces he could identify. Sometimes he thought he'd return these images to the men and women who matched them, but whenever he found a person who fit one of the pictures, he didn't have the courage to say anything. What would they think, realizing that a version of them had been living in his house for months, years?

Never mind the photographs today. Down the hallway instead, to the closed door at the end, the one he hadn't opened since the day of his parents' funeral. He didn't want to go in there now, but what he needed was inside. The knob turned smoothly in his hands, and there was only a soft squeal from the hinges when he pushed.

Dust covered everything, but that wasn't a surprise. What startled him was the absence of some things: the bedside table, the porcelain Christ on his mother's dresser. Things that still lived there in his memories. Then he realized: Bobby had taken them. The bed itself probably remained only because it was fixed in place, part of the architect's design and more an outcropping of the wall than a piece of furniture. The sheets were pulled tightly over the mattress, and Archie moved around it slowly, tempted to lie down. But the creases were too perfect to do that; his mother's work had held up all these years.

There, said the fever. In the corner.

And all at once he's in the cemetery again, his parents have just been buried, everyone else has gone back to the church for tea. He's taking off his jacket, rolling up his sleeves, fetching the spade from the trunk of his car. The teenage boy there to fill the grave is laughing.

"Sure you can do it," the boy says, lying on the grass and removing a package of cigarettes from his pocket. "But go slow: I get paid by the hour."

After Archie had finished, he'd driven back to this house and placed the spade in the bedroom as a memorial. Now he had need of it again. The fever was desperate. Hurry back, it said, or he'll be gone. The trailer is empty, someone has snatched him. Archie grabbed the spade from the corner and dashed outside.

No, it was all right. The green heron had vanished but the body was still there, and Archie began to dig in the place where the bird had hunted. Hard work, at this age, with the ground rock-solid from weeks of drought. Four feet, not six, would have to do.

When the hole was deep enough he urged the man into it using his voice and feet as well as his hands. "Come on," he grunted, shoving the body with his boot. "Get in there. It's where you should be." Once the legs had descended he took the fingers in his own and lowered the body slowly, then leaned over to look at the pale, grinning face. At one time he would have recognized it, he was sure, but somehow in death it had lost its character, become anonymous flesh.

As he returned the earth to its proper place he realized that he'd forgotten to keep the sod intact when he removed it, and he had to leave the grave covered in a grey-brown slurry of soil and grass. His shoulders ached, his back was in spasm. The fever had begun to fade, and shame was creeping in beside the satisfaction. His hand reached into his beard and pulled hard. This wasn't right, not normal. People would be angry with him. Bobby would be furious. How had he ever come to this? Dig up the body again, he told himself. Put him back in his truck. But Archie's brain was wet tinder now and the thought sputtered. He needed to sleep.

Afterwards he'd find Bobby at the baseball diamond and try to make him understand.

BY THE TIME a man began to visit Mrs. Northey on Wednesday nights in the mid-seventies, Archie's routine was nearly perfect. He never ran into her any more as he rummaged through her trash; each of them had a carefully kept schedule that prevented them from crossing the other's path. He never said anything about the rubber he found wrapped in tissue every week at the bottom of her garbage can. By this time he knew how long it took to search each street, could almost list in advance the contents of every bag. And the house had begun to fill. In the first months, he'd stored everything he found in his own bedroom, until there were boxes stacked to the ceiling, drawers were brimming, the closet was packed and only a single pathway provided access to the bed. Eventually he turned to Bobby's room, before cramming the basement and the hallway in turn. The piles were beginning to encroach on the living room when Mrs. Northey appeared at his door for the first time in a decade, sobbing into a handkerchief and wearing the same lily-patterned dress she'd worn on her first visit years before. Her legs were thicker now, and her face was pale and glossy, as if she'd been laid up in her house for the summer.

She was so upset that she didn't register his shock as she walked down the narrow hallway to the living room. No one other than Bobby had been past the entranceway for nearly four years.

"My, you've been busy," she said when she finally glanced up from her handkerchief. She sat on the couch nervously, watching the piles around her as though they might slink toward her if she looked away. She made a joke about bachelor life, threatened to break in and clean up this place one day when he was out. Archie smiled half-heartedly. His attention was held by the ruby brooch she was wearing. Its pin had come unfastened and it hung precariously from her breast.

"How have you been?" she asked.

"Fine," he said, his voice raspy from disuse. With relief he sensed that she didn't really care, that he didn't need to say anything more.

"I was seeing a man," she declared abruptly, and she glanced up, seeming to expect a reaction. "He's left me now." She didn't understand that he already knew.

"I'm sorry," he told her.

"It's nice to live in a town and not in the city," Mrs. Northey said. "People here look out for one another." It was an invitation for him to sit beside her, he thought, so he did. She pressed into his side and wept, burying her face in the sleeve of his shirt.

"Oh never mind," she said to him after a while. "Never mind any of it. Tell me about things."

She waited patiently, but he only shook his head. He didn't want to talk. What could he possibly say?

"I – I can't –"

That wasn't enough for her, and she turned her attention to the stacks surrounding them.

"Look at me, barging in here, full of my own problems. Making jokes about this house, when it's so clear that –" Her voice was gaining energy. "Archimedes, what has happened to you? Have you thought about that? Look around. This isn't right." She stopped, swallowed, frowned, as though saying it had brought up bile. She must have seen the distress on his face. "I'm sorry. I shouldn't have said that."

This is normal, he thought. This is what normal people do. They talk about things. All I am being asked to do is to talk. I can do that.

But he didn't. Instead his hands went fumbling along the couch, around her body. It was warm and rigid with surprise.

"Oh," she said. "Archie – I don't –" Her hands found his back, and they pulled him toward her until his head was against her chest, the cold eye of the ruby brooch digging into his jaw.

"Have you wanted to do this for a long time?" she whispered. He didn't say anything. The impulse had just come to him. He sat there being held, unable to move.

"I know all about the loneliness," she said. He thought of how sometimes he sat at the kitchen table, polishing things for hours, and then awoke from the trance, not even knowing where he was. Was that loneliness? He never felt regret then. It was only now, with Mrs. Northey's breasts like some foreign jelly against his face, that he felt freakish. In a few years he might not even remember how to talk.

"It was because of your parents' accident, wasn't it?" she said to him, squeezing him tighter. "That's what started these piles." When he tried to shift away, something stabbed into his cheek. The pin of the brooch had broken the skin. He turned from her and pressed at the wound with his fingers.

"Archie, you can stop all this. Tomorrow. It will be easy. We'll rent a truck and clear the whole house."

Oh no. No, no. He raised his head, the blood trickling down his thumb, and tried to fathom what she was saying.

"But – but there's no –" His heart was racing. "I couldn't. Where else would it go?"

After she left, he spent half an hour tracing over the route she'd taken through the house, checking every article within reach, certain she'd added or removed something and upset the perfect, fragile balance. It was near the end that he circled back to the couch and discovered the brooch had fallen in between the cushions, its gold clasp snapped in two.

The next afternoon when he returned from his research, the front door was wide open. There were stacks of magazines sitting on the step. His eyes darted everywhere, saw nothing. He ran into the house, his feet going numb, his head about to explode, and found her in Bobby's room. She was gazing at the wall, her whole body trembling.

"What is this?" she screamed. "What is this?"

In front of her was a display case he'd dragged home from behind the high school long ago. Since then he'd been filling it with a special collection: his record of her own life.

"I was going to clean for you," she said. "Just one of the rooms, to show you the difference." She turned back to the case, and he tried to see it as she was seeing it: the perfume bottles. The casserole dish. The rubbers. "You're disgusting," she told him. "You should be put away."

He stepped toward her, hands out.

"No, none of that," she said. "Not any more." She pushed past him and ran out of the house. When he went to gather the magazines from the step, she was standing at the edge of his lawn, brandishing the brooch in her hand.

"It's theft, you bastard," she cried. "How dare you?"

For the next week his heart pounded every time he came home, expecting the police at the door, but instead Bobby arrived to tell him that Mrs. Northey had filed a complaint with the council about the mess.

"Don't worry, she won't get anywhere with it," said Bobby. "I just thought you should know what the neighbours think. Then again, you probably know enough about them already, don't you?"

Not long after, a man appeared outside to draw a string between Archie's house and Mrs. Northey's. Later he returned with a truckload of stone and built a low wall along the property line. Archie was kept awake that night with a flickering sense of regret, but at the same time he felt comforted too. It's better this way, he told himself. Don't forget your dream. If it's ever going to come true, someone like Mrs. Northey is best kept behind her walls.

Archie's dream was that one day his project would be complete. Then he'd throw open his home, and people would come to rediscover all the discarded contents of their lives before them, varnished, mended, watered, cleaned, waiting for their owners to claim them once again. There'd be cheering and shouts of "I've found it!" echoing through the house. The inhabitants of Sunshine would realize there was nothing they ever needed to throw away, if they cared enough. They'd see their whole lives, all the town in order.

"SO SHE SAYS to me, 'Stump, what are you doing with that gun?' but I don't tell her, I just keep polishing it, right? Then she says, 'You going to shoot me with it or something?' And you know what I tell her? I say, 'Don't give me any ideas.'"

Above Archie's head there was the creak of planks as one of the men reached for another can of beer. It was late in the afternoon, but the air was still hot enough for the green paint on the bleachers at the baseball diamond to go sticky and bubbling in places. Even in the shade underneath them, Archie was suffering. His muscles were sore from the morning's digging, and he needed a drink of water.

"Sounds like you're a real tough guy, Stump," said Bobby's voice. Archie could see one of his brother's legs dangling a few feet from where he stood.

"Well, you can't put up with any crap. So then she starts taking off her clothes, right? And she's all naked, but I'm still not looking up from the rifle –"

"Then how did you know she was naked?"

"Damn it, Harry, I've got peripheral vision, don't I? So she's naked, and she reaches over and –"

"Esther's a real animal, is she?"

"You bet. But I got her tamed."

Archie moved slowly along the shadow lines, searching for things to load into his trailer, sweat running from under his hockey helmet and down his forehead as he listened to the voices of the men above him. No one seemed to notice him; they were too busy. Women in sun hats cheered and booed the players on the field; men in uniforms chewed hot dogs and yelled at the children who ran along the bleachers' uppermost tiers. The seats he was under were taken up by four men who'd spread picnic blankets and baseball equipment around them to discourage neighbours. The schedule in Archie's pocket said the next game for the Good-fellows Club wasn't for another hour, but these four had arrived well in advance. They spoke loudly and spilled beer that dripped on his shoulders. He could hear the voice of Stump Weston, the shopkeeper, who was stupid and talked a lot, and of Solomon DeWitt, the lawyer, who was smart and didn't. Archie liked Solomon for that. Then there was Harry Midgard, the police chief, who drank a lot, and Bobby, the mayor, who drank more but didn't show it.

"– you hunting with us tomorrow morning?" Bobby was saying.

"Not unless we find Fremlin first," replied Harry. Archie could see only the man's face and the beer bottle he kept tilted toward his mouth. "I might need you to help look for him too, so don't get excited about any animal hunt. Murderers who skip bail are more important than tigers."

"Stoddart hasn't skipped bail," said DeWitt, his voice like ice. "He'll turn up soon enough." Archie knew from Solomon's trash can that he was a teetotaller, and according to Bobby he didn't suffer fools gladly.

From the fairgrounds came the merry-go-round calliope, the growl of midway rides. The sun above the baseball diamond was so strong that some things were too bright to see clearly – the uniforms of players on the field, the dazzling white bases. As Archie listened, he peered through a space between the seats and studied the arc of the ball: a gentle lob offered to the sun. It perched for a second on an invisible shelf high above the field before hurtling toward the plate. Then, hopefully, there'd be a smack into leather and not the clank of the bat, which almost never struck cleanly but sent the ball spinning in unforeseeable directions.

Aside from the heat, it was a glorious day to be working. In winter people hoarded like they were hibernating, but summer afternoons made them cast away everything they could. The area under the bleachers blossomed with the produce of Civic Holiday softball tournaments, and he'd already half-filled his trailer with empty bottles, crumpled team lists, abandoned articles of clothing. He'd even forgotten his reason for coming until now, when he stood directly beneath the place where Bobby sat.

"The other day at the town hall I had Bronwen Ferry sniffing after information on Alice Pederson." His brother's voice.

"For Christ's sake, don't talk about that now," said Harry Midgard. "I came here to get away from that mess." But they ignored him.

"She was down at the Veterans Club too," said Stump.

"And you know Danny Barrie is in town? Been here three weeks now – since the funeral."

"I always said he was the smartest boy ever to come out of Sunshine. Now he's proving me wrong by coming back."

"Should have just stayed in England. Nobody was going to bother him there."

"Didn't I hear Daniel was friends with Rocket, Sol?" asked Stump. "Where is that son of yours, anyhow? I thought he was going to pitch for us this time."

No one spoke.

"Terrible day for thirst," said Bobby's voice at last. "Sol, why don't you get us another round?"

"Sure, okay," Solomon said slowly, rising from the bleachers. They put in their orders, and a moment later Archie could see Solomon heading in the direction of the beer garden. When he was gone Bobby spoke again.

"Listen, don't say anything about Rocket around our buddy Mr. DeWitt."

"I don't get it. What's going on? I heard the kid's quit his job, left the province or something."

"It's probably just a little vacation," said Bobby.

"I don't think I follow –"

"Stump, you're a good guy, but you're new and you got to be patient."

"I'm patient already. Here I am drinking beer beside the guy who's charged Esther's father with murder. I had to listen to her yell at me all this morning for not quitting the team. Don't tell me I need patience."

"Harry's got nothing against Frem. It's only a job."

"You tell Esther that. She thinks the whole town's trying to frame him."

"Don't worry, Frem will get what he has coming to him," said Bobby. "Look, half of Sunshine's searching for the man right now. Doesn't that show they care about him?"

"You know damn well they're only out there because he skipped bail and ran away last night. Harry, I can't believe you're even here right now. Don't you think you should –"

"Leave me alone. I don't want to do any thinking today."

"But isn't there someone else who might have done it? Why does it have to be Esther's father? What about somebody like Daniel Barrie?"

"No, Danny's a good boy," said Bobby. "Born and raised here. We have to look out for our own. Although it would serve him right, if he was messing around with a married woman."

"Enough," said Harry. "I told you, it's not something I want to think about." Archie heard each of them take a long slug of beer before Harry spoke again. "I was there when they dragged her out, you know. A few scraps of clothes and a bit of meat, that was all."

"God damn, Harry. God damn."

Archie listened disinterestedly. Gossip was pointless, without a system, just idle talk. He crouched to pick up another bottle, bumping against one of the bleachers' supports as he did so. When he stood up again he came face to face with Stump Weston, hanging upside down, looking straight at him. Then Stump's head snapped out of sight and his voice started up again.

"Did you know your brother is standing underneath us?"

"Don't pay him any notice."

"He looks pretty beat up. Do you think he's okay?"

"Look, I said to drop it, didn't I?"

There was a long silence. Not even Archie moved.

"Christ, the guy's your brother, Bobby. Have a heart."

"Stump," said Harry, "it's none of your business –"

The shadow of Solomon DeWitt returning passed over Archie's head. Then there was a terrifying metallic noise, and a ball torpedoed over the bleachers into the parking lot. Archie bolted out of the shade in pursuit. He sensed someone else behind him, and after he bent down to retrieve the lost thing from under a car there was a man standing there in a red-and-blue uniform, smiling, his eyes hidden behind a pair of sunglasses.

"Thanks," the man said, extending his glove. Archie shook his head and brought the ball to his chest.

"Come on, no jokes. You're making everybody wait." He held out the glove even farther, then shrugged at the people on the diamond.

"Tommy, what's going on?" called the pitcher from his mound.

"This guy won't give up the ball," shouted Tommy. He looked back at Archie with disgust.

The pitcher was jogging across the diamond now, the kind of baseball jog that was slower than a walk. His uniform was too small and his belly showed as he ran. Why couldn't they leave him alone? What had he done? Archie wanted to run away, but by now the Goodfellows Club had noticed what was happening. When the pitcher passed the bleachers, Bobby and Stump stepped off and joined him, one on either side.

"What's the problem?" asked the pitcher. He pointed to the ball in Archie's hand. "That our ball?" He put out his glove and Archie took a step back. "Hey, is there something wrong with this guy?"

"He's okay," said Bobby. "Just a bit of a baseball fanatic. Probably wants a souvenir of the tournament."

"The guy's a retard," said Tommy. "Who the hell wears a hockey helmet in summer?"

"He's not a retard," said Stump. "He's sick. Give him a break."

Archie's feet were determined to take him away, they wouldn't stop moving, but Bobby's hand had clamped on to his shoulder so that he could only step in place and raise dust from the gravel.

145

The pitcher shrugged. "All right, you talk to him. Just don't let him leave with that ball." He glared at Archie one last time before departing for the diamond with Tommy.

Bobby scowled and shook his head.

"Now listen," he said. "You're not going anywhere until you give me that thing." He gave Archie's shoulder a firm squeeze, whether as a warning or as comfort, Archie couldn't tell. Then Bobby released his grip and started toward the bleachers with Stump in tow. "I bet you already have a thousand of them anyhow," he said over his shoulder, and spat into the dust.

EVERY DAY at the end of his research Archie went home and found a place for his discoveries. That evening it took him over an hour to catalogue all of his findings from the baseball diamond, and then he sat very still, remembering the things he'd seen and heard, writing nothing down because he refused to add anything to the world if he could help it.

He thought of his dining room. The walls there were covered in children's artwork: finger paintings, watercolours, pie-plate faces. The best creations of the town's youth, rescued and displayed. One of them was from the 1981 agricultural fair. First place, Daniel Barrie, kindergarten. A picture in primary colours: a figure with a striped shirt being attacked by brown blobs. The caption, in a teacher's handwriting, read: "The goats jumped on me at the outdoor centre." Archie was thinking about that one, trying to fit it together with the name spoken at the baseball diamond, when there was a knock on the door.

Daniel Barrie! cried a voice in his head. Daniel Barrie! Daniel Barrie! Daniel Barrie! He walked to one end of the room, returned to where he'd started, then walked down the passageway again, newspapers stacked head-high on either side. Daniel Barrie! Daniel Barrie! He'd gone back and forth six times when the knocking began once more.

"Archie, it's me," said Bobby's voice. Archie paced six more times. Daniel Barrie, his brain replied, quieter now, fading slowly until it became one with Bobby's voice, self-possessed and reassuring. "I'm going to let myself in now, I hope that's all right." Archie listened for the slide of Bobby's key in the lock. When he finally heard it, Daniel Barrie was gone, replaced by someone else: the dead man in the truck. Archie remembered at last what he'd wanted to tell his brother.

"You really are something, aren't you?" Bobby was already in the kitchen, holding a plastic bag in each hand. "You'd think you could at least answer the damn door." The evening sun was lighting the room through a slit in the window curtains, making Bobby's ears glow. Not for the first time, Archie admired the delta of veins in the bright red flesh. So blue and delicate and peaceful. The only times he thought about shaving off his own scraggly hair and beard were when he found himself envying his brother's smooth head.

"I thought I was going to kill you at the ball park today," Bobby said. He lay the bags on the table and sat down beside it. "That's food from the supermarket. I told Rachel you never eat anything unless you find it, but she keeps insisting."

Bobby hadn't been in Archie's house for more than a year. This time he didn't say anything about cleaning up the place, about moving out. Apparently he'd reached his own private understanding of what all this meant. But Archie knew Bobby hadn't come just to give him food. Although his brother seldom entered the house, there were many nights each year that his sedan pulled into the driveway, always with a question about this person or that. Archie only had to wait for it. He watched now as Bobby talked about the tournament, staring at the room around him. Eventually his brother's eyes came to rest on something in the corner.

"What the hell is that?"

It was the rifle Archie had found earlier in the day. Bobby walked over and picked it up.

"Where did you get this?" Archie didn't say anything. "People just don't throw out rifles, do they?" Bobby took a step closer. "Do they?" He banged the stock of the rifle on the table. "Answer me, for God's sake." He pulled a paper towel from the roll on the counter and mopped his brow with it.

"This rifle's stolen," he said. "From Stump Weston. You know that, I guess. He just realized it was gone about an hour ago. There was a pickup truck taken along with it; have you got that hidden somewhere in here too?" Bobby looked over the gun in his hands. "And this thing's been fired recently, hasn't it? Why the hell has it been fired? No, don't tell me. I'd rather not know."

Archie wanted to answer him, but he was sick with dizziness. It was too much. The house was rocking on its foundations – couldn't Bobby feel it? A tremendous wind had come up and was threatening to sweep both of them, the whole edifice, into the bay.

"You can't keep it here, someone might have seen you. But I'm sure as hell not going to take it. Look at this, I've already got my fingerprints on the thing." Archie could barely hear him over the roar of the wind in his head, but Bobby just took another paper towel and wiped down the stock. "God damn, this is a whole new level of lunacy for you." He went to the window, drew back the curtains, and looked out.

"What a mess," he murmured. "You know, this used to be a nice house. Now even the lawn has gone to hell." He squinted, shading his eyes with his hand. "Hey, have you been digging?" When he turned, he was furious. "What have you been doing out there?"

Archie could only manage a quiet moan against his brother's words and the raging storm. He'd wanted desperately to tell Bobby, but the fever was surfacing again, stopping up his mouth. Don't let him know, it said. Don't let him take it from you.

"God damn," whispered Bobby. He sat down at the table again and held his head in his hands. "God damn." From the expression on his face he seemed to be deep in contemplation, and then his eyes widened, as though something inside him was forcing them apart. "Is it what I think it is, Archie? Am I right?" He stood up, abandoned the rifle on the table. "Because if I am, it doesn't matter what happened or whether you just stumbled upon it; they're going to blame you. I know people leave you alone, but they'll come after you sure enough if they find out. I can't stop them. Some things are too big; I've got a family to think about. You'll be on your own." He reached over and grabbed Archie's hands. "Are you listening? Whatever you've got buried there, go dig it up tonight when that nosy old cow next door is asleep and take it back wherever you found it. You understand?" He let out a deep breath. "Or take him out into the forest, find a good spot and bury him there, cover him in leaves. The rifle too. You'll have to do a good job; there are searches going on for Fremlin."

An electronic beeping interrupted him. Promptly Bobby reached into his pants pocket, withdrew a cellular phone, and snapped it open. He barked a greeting, then listened.

"All right, Harry," he said after a while. "I'm at my brother's house right now. Have someone block off the entrance to the logging road, then drive over here. There are a couple of things that need to go in that truck before you move it." He closed the phone, put it back in his pocket, and stood there thinking. Archie was glad of the respite that the silence provided.

"Don't worry, all right?" said Bobby after a while. "I'll look after you." He got up to leave, and Archie followed him out of the kitchen. The wind was dying now; he'd be alone soon; things were going to be fine. He smiled to himself, knowing he'd never carry out his brother's orders about the body and the gun. It was wrong for Bobby to be concerned. No one would ever come after him. The body was his, only his. That logging road usually yielded nothing more than beer bottles and torn underwear. He'd been so lucky.

But Bobby's warning had triggered something else in him – something that unsettled him even more. As he followed his brother past the piles of newsprint and cardboard in the living room, he remembered his dream of the house's completion. How many times in the past had he been so close to achieving it? The collection spectacular, each room filled and sorted. And each time it had slipped away from him with the rising sun, the new day's waste. If he could only get people to stop their lives for a week, a single day, even. Then he could draw a circle around it all. But what was he to do when a single body left out of the cemetery was enough to cause the fear he'd seen in Bobby's eyes? What did it mean?

Bobby reached the entranceway and opened the door. A girl with a ponytail rode by on a bicycle, followed by a tiny, barking dog. There wasn't a breath of wind.

"You know, Rachel and me, years ago, we used to talk about doctors for you," Bobby said quietly, his eyes on the concrete step. "Did you know that? God, we spent whole nights talking about doctors. But here we are, and this is the first time I mention it now, and I can only say it because somehow, for better or for worse, that possibility got lost along the way. Now I'd have to check myself in too, for being crazy enough to let things go on like they have."

The girl was turning on to a different street now, and the little dog, wary of this new direction, bayed at her from the corner like she'd crossed some wide expanse of water with his most precious possession.

"I was thinking something today," Bobby said, raising his head, staring up into the sun to study the outline of the building. "Archie, I don't know how to put this, but when was the last time you were hugged?" He coughed. "I don't know how I got to wondering about it. I mean, it must be twenty years." Bobby looked at him. "You know what I mean?" Neither of them took a step.

"You're welcome at the house any time," said Bobby. "You know that, don't you?"

Archie nodded. A moment later, Harry Midgard drove up the lane in his police cruiser, but before Archie could run back into the house, his brother told him in a calming voice that it was all right, that he'd called Harry over himself. He said he was going to sort things out.

STEPPING ON SHADOWS

Where did all the monsters come from? There were so many of them – monsters who ate your food and creaked around the apartment and never cleaned up after themselves. Susan always wanted to know who made the messes and broke the broken things, and Zeljka always had the answer: It was monsters. But when Susan asked her who invited all the monsters to live with them, Zeljka could only shake her head. It was a mystery. Did they follow her home from kindergarten? No, no, no. All Zeljka knew was that the place where they'd grown up must have been a place without parents, because they did bad, bad things and they didn't care one bit.

The monsters in the apartment were smaller than the ones in the house where she'd first lived with Susan and Marge. Those had been barn-monsters, enormous ones that jumped from rafter to rafter. On windy nights they roared and played see-saw on the roof, while Zeljka snuggled between Susan and Marge in their bed and they told her how once upon a time, before they fixed it up, the house was the place where cows slept and chickens roosted. Zeljka liked that house. Then the lawyer stole all their money so they moved to the apartment.

"But he did his job," Susan said, hugging her. "Nobody can take you away from us now." Her *majka*'s relatives wanted her to go back to Croatia, where she was born. "But Canada is your home now, isn't it, darling?" said Susan. "It was your *majka*'s home too. She used to come up to Sunshine in the summers, and she wanted you to stay here with us, because we were her friends. She wrote it down when she was sick last year. Do you remember her telling you?"

Zeljka remembered crying a lot. She remembered an apartment in the city with an elevator, the bed she shared with her *majka*, a park full of dog poo. She remembered hospital smells.

"We're both your *majka* now," Susan explained. "But you don't have to call us *majka*. Just call us Susan and Marge like you always did."

Zeljka loved Susan best, then Marge, then Daniel. He was her brother, she told herself. *Brother*, she repeated, over and over, flicking her tongue between her teeth as fast as she could until it stung. She tried to remember what he was in the other language, but she didn't have the word.

Daniel wasn't a very good brother, she thought. If he was, he would have been nicer and played with her more often. Instead he just sat by himself reading books with no pictures in them. Marge said he was studying. Sometimes Zeljka watched him study for a long time until he noticed her standing across the room.

"Why is she always scratching her neck?" he asked Susan, and Susan brushed back Zeljka's hair to show him the hidden, itchy place that Zeljka could see only when Susan did the trick with two mirrors. There was a little red circle back there where the worm lived, but it wasn't really a worm, just an infection, and she was never, ever supposed to scratch it.

"All the kids in her kindergarten class had it," Susan explained to Daniel. "You tell them not to touch each other, but they're too young to know better."

"Even Oliver got it," Zeljka said.

Daniel didn't like it when Zeljka talked about Oliver. Marge said it was because Oliver's mother had died, and Daniel had been friends with her, so he was very sad. When the day came for the funeral, he had a fight with Marge and Susan about whether Zeljka should go. He wanted her to stay at home with him.

"She's too young for funerals," he said. He was turning the pages of a book and frowning. "She won't want to sit there for hours while that man goes on about how much he loved Alice. It will just upset her. And besides, Zeljka never met Alice."

"She knows Mike and Oliver and Nel, though," said Marge.

"But it's not their funeral."

"Funerals aren't for the dead," said Susan. "They're for the people who are left."

"She doesn't even know what a funeral is," said Daniel. But then he went red, as though he'd said something he hadn't meant to say.

"Of course she knows," said Susan, and she came over to put her arms around her. "You remember our conversation, honey? About funerals?"

Zeljka remembered Susan talking about her *majka* and the funeral they'd had for her when Zeljka was almost five. Is that what Susan meant? She couldn't remember anything about that time now, and she didn't know what to say.

"A funeral's for the people who are left," she answered at last.

"You're not really concerned about Zeljka, anyhow," Susan told Daniel. "It's you who doesn't want to go. Well, fine. Nobody says you have to. But what has that got to do with Zeljka? Let her do what she wants." When she said that, Daniel went back to reading his book.

"Why isn't Daniel going to the funeral?" Zeljka asked Susan, and she said that was a question for Daniel to answer. He looked up, still frowning.

"I told you before," he said quietly. "Funerals are for people who really died."

Zeljka felt Susan's arms squeeze a bit tighter around her.

"God, Daniel, don't start into that again. They have proof. At some point you'll have to accept it. They have the dental records, they –"

"But Alice is a dentist, remember?"

"Isn't Oliver's mother really dead?" Zeljka asked.

"Yes, she is, honey. Daniel's just being silly."

Daniel glared at her. "You weren't there at Usher's party, Susan. You didn't hear her talking. She wanted to escape."

Then the telephone rang and Susan went to answer it. When she came back into the room she told him that Oliver wasn't going to the funeral either. His father was bringing him over to play with Zeljka. Now Daniel would have something to do while he stayed at home. Daniel glared at her even harder.

WHEN OLIVER first arrived he was sleeping, but once his father left he woke up and started to cry, and Daniel said, "Why should I be the one to take care of this kid?" Marge told Oliver that if he'd go to the funeral with them they could all play at the park once it was finished. Then Daniel said, "Great, so I have to stay here by myself," and Susan said, "You really don't know what you want, do you?" and finally they all got into the car together, with Zeljka, Oliver, and Daniel in the back seat, and Daniel telling Zeljka to watch her elbows.

At the church they sat far away from the coffin and it was boring. People talked a lot and prayed and sang slow songs that Zeljka didn't know. She wanted to go to the front and see Oliver's mother, but Marge whispered that at some funerals they kept the coffin closed because not everyone wanted to look at a dead person. "Then how do they know if she's in there?" Zeljka asked. She remembered what Daniel had said: Funerals were only for people who'd really died.

When it was finally over they were supposed to play at the park, but Oliver's grandmother took him away and Marge told Zeljka it might be better to leave the playground for another afternoon. They drove home again instead, and once they were inside the apartment, Daniel went straight down the hallway into the bathroom. She followed a little way behind him.

"Zed, leave him alone for a bit," called Susan after her. So Zeljka turned the doorknob very slowly, trying not to make a sound. She wasn't supposed to open the bathroom door when someone was inside, but it wasn't locked. She pushed it open inch by inch. She slid through the crack, her foot first, then her stomach, then her neck. Daniel was sitting on the side of the bath in his suit.

"Daniel, I love you."

She didn't understand why he was still staring at her like that. She wanted him to say "I love you too" and give her a hug. But at least he didn't seem angry with her like he usually did.

"Come here," he said, so she went over and sat down next to him. He stroked her hair with one of his hands; the other one was caught underneath him. "You're a good kid," he said, and then finally he hugged her. It didn't feel like a normal hug, though. It felt like he was dead.

WHEN DANIEL and Susan took her to the wildlife park a week later, it was just as boring as the funeral at first. There were only people and cars and a lineup, and she wanted to go home, but then they got to walk around a path where the animals were locked up in cages. There were llamas and donkeys and seagulls that ate your lunch and foxes and snakes. There were no gorillas, though.

"Why did you promise her gorillas?" Daniel asked Susan.

"How was I supposed to know? I thought all zoos had gorillas."

"It's not a zoo, it's a wildlife park."

Susan said it was confusing because there were animals from across the ocean mixed up with ones you could find on the peninsula. After that, Zeljka always wanted to know which ones belonged where, until Daniel and Susan told her to stop pestering them. Then they came to the turkey with the enormous tail. Daniel pointed and told her they'd be eating one of those tonight. Turkeys were from North America, he said. He asked her if she felt sorry for it, trapped in the wildlife park, when it could have been roaming the forest. He told her that a turkey like the one Marge was cooking spent its whole life in a tiny cage, just eating and eating until it nearly exploded. Then they killed it. This one had scars on its beak and some of its feathers were broken or missing. A metal band was wrapped around one of its horrible, scaly legs. The turkey was ugly, and she didn't feel sorry for it at all. She hated it, and she hated the thought of eating something so disgusting.

They walked along the trail and Zeljka jumped on all the thin, black *sjene* that were stretched out on the ground. The *sjene* were getting longer all the time as the sun went down, so that by the end of the loop they were dancing everywhere. She liked morning and evening best, when hers was tall, taller than the adults. She stepped on Daniel's whenever she got the chance.

"You're not stepping on my shadow, you're stepping into it," said Daniel. Then Zeljka stepped on his head.

At the pavilion Daniel read out a sign that said you could adopt the animals. It didn't mean that you could take them home with you, he explained; you just paid money to buy them food. Daniel said it cost three thousand dollars to adopt the bear for a year.

"How much for a goldfish?" asked Susan. Daniel said there weren't any goldfish. The cheapest animal was a chicken for fifteen dollars. Susan shook her head before Zeljka could even finish asking for fifteen dollars. Then Daniel told them he wanted to be by himself, and he went off toward the parking lot without saying goodbye. Susan said that was very rude of him. She and Daniel never got along, Zeljka thought, although sometimes when Susan didn't know it, Daniel stared at her in a strange way, like he was sad. Zeljka was glad he'd left; Susan never seemed as much fun when he was around.

Susan took Zeljka's hand to lead her around the nature trail, pointing at things and asking Zeljka their names in Croatian, but

Zeljka didn't like that game. No matter how many words she taught Susan and Marge, they always ended up speaking to her in English again as though nothing had changed.

"I have to pee," Zeljka said, and Susan let out a big sigh.

"I asked you before if you had to go," said Susan. "Can you hold it?" Zeljka shook her head. "Come on then, let's duck into the woods." She reached for Zeljka's hands, but Zeljka hid them behind her back.

"I can go on my own," Zeljka said.

"No you can't." Susan reached for her again and Zeljka squealed. "All right, but make sure you crouch down all the way like I showed you."

Zeljka started into the forest. There were bushes tangled together all along the nature trail, but on the other side of them she came to a place full of trees.

"That's far enough," said Susan.

"But I can still see you!"

"Come on, Zed, no one's watching. I'll tell you if anyone comes." Zeljka continued into the forest.

"I'm not going far," she sang.

"You'd better not leave my sight, young lady."

In the forest it didn't smell like animals any more. The ground was black and soft, with patches of flowers everywhere she looked. There were green plants that tickled her knees, dewy spiderwebs that she brushed away whenever they touched her skin, and a gigantic tree that stretched over everything else like an umbrella, making the forest dark. If she went behind it, no one would see her pee.

"Zed, where are you going?"

"Behind this tree." She turned around. Susan was peering in, pushing a branch away from her face. "Don't look!"

"All right, all right, I'm not looking."

She walked behind the tree and took off her shoes. The ground felt nice, so she took off her socks too. The soil was squishy in between her toes. She reached down to touch it, and when she stood up again, she frowned. She'd forgotten what she was supposed to be doing. Then she saw the *mačketina* walking toward her. Its shoulders were as tall as hers, and at first she was frightened, but it didn't look like it wanted to eat her. Instead its head hung low to the ground, as though it were unhappy at being on its own. It slowed down as it approached her, its big, lonely eyes looking right into hers.

This was much better than those stupid cages, where you couldn't even see the animals sometimes. Now she could reach out and stroke the *mačketina*'s velvety orange coat if she wanted. She could throw a stick and it would chase it.

"Hello," she said quietly. The *mačketina* didn't make any noise, even as it stepped through the forest. No matter how hard Zeljka tried she always snapped twigs, but the *mačketina* seemed light as air.

"Are you a ghost?" she whispered. The *mačketina* stopped beside her and sat on its bum like a dog. It turned its face away and looked deeper into the forest as though it was waiting patiently for someone else to arrive. "Where did you come from?" she asked it, reaching out her hand.

"Zed, have you finished yet?" It was Susan's voice, coming from the path.

"Yes," she replied. She picked up her socks and started to put them on. She was going to take the *mačketina* with her. Susan would be frightened at first, so Zeljka would have to show her it was friendly.

"Come on, let's go meet Susan," she said as she slipped back into her shoes, but when she set out the way she'd come the *mačketina* didn't want to follow. Instead it got up silently and walked back into the forest, its tail waving a sad goodbye. She thought about running after it, but then Susan called her name again. When she returned to the path it looked like she was in trouble.

"Darling, you can't spend all day like that."

"But there was a *mačketina* in the forest."

"Wow, a matchka-teena," said Susan, as if she wasn't interested. "What did it look like?"

"It was a boy *mačketina*." She surprised herself by saying this. Until now she hadn't thought of it as a boy or a girl. But now, having said so to Susan, she was sure she was right.

"Really? I didn't know that there were boy matchka-teenas as well as girls. How can you tell the difference?"

"He had a moustache."

Susan laughed. "I didn't realize matchka-teenas had moustaches." It was then that Zeljka realized Susan didn't know what a *mačketina* was. She didn't even know how to say it properly.

"I'm not making it up," Zeljka said. "This one did have a moustache. It had black stripes and a long tail, and it made footprints in the ground. Come see." She took Susan's hand.

"Now you take my hand? A minute ago you weren't going to be caught dead in the forest with me."

"But there was a tiger in there! Just like the one we saw in the cage."

"Oh, so now it's a tiger, is it? This is getting tiresome, Zed."

"But that's what a *mačketina* is! I'll show you where it walked." She began to yank on Susan's hand.

"Zed, if we went in there, do you think we'd really find tiger tracks?" Zeljka nodded. "And if we didn't, do you know I'd be upset with you for lying to me? We'd get Daniel and leave the wildlife park right away, and there'd be no more animals and no television tonight either. Now, are you really sure there was a tiger in the forest?" Zeljka nodded. "Fine. Let's go see. But I warned you, didn't I? What did I say will happen if you're lying?"

"No television," sulked Zeljka. Then Susan squeezed her hand tightly and they went into the forest together.

"I don't see anything, buster," said Susan after they'd circled the trunk of the big umbrella tree. Zeljka pulled free and ran to the place where the *mačketina* had flattened some flowers as it walked. She pointed to a fat mark in the soil. Susan bent to look at it, and then she kneeled beside Zeljka and took her by the shoulders.

"Honey, what did the tiger do? Did it come near you?"

"It sat down beside me."

"And then it went away?" Zeljka nodded. "Okay, honey. I'm sorry I didn't believe you. I think we'd better leave the forest now, very quietly." Susan's eye was starting to wink at her. It was like when they played wink murder at kindergarten, and one person was the killer and they all fell down pretending to be dead. She wanted to wink too, but Marge had said it wasn't polite to copy Susan like that.

Once they were on the trail again, Susan began to walk so fast that she said Zeljka was a dawdler and a piggy-back ride might be better. She bent down to pick her up, and a second later everything was fast and jolting. Zeljka tried to be careful not to strangle her like Susan said she always did. They found Daniel way out in the middle of a field surrounded by a circle of big stones. People were wandering around and taking pictures of each other, and Daniel looked angry with them. Zeljka wanted to climb the stones, but Susan refused to let her off her shoulders.

"You won't believe this," Susan said to Daniel. "Zed said she saw a tiger in the forest, and when we went to look there was a paw print."

"What was she doing in the forest?"

"Never mind that. We'd better find Cam Usher."

But the man who sold the tickets said Cam Usher had gone away, and he wasn't impressed by their story.

"You saw our tiger in the enclosure over there, didn't you?" he asked them. "It's still there. If there's really one on the loose, it's somebody else's." He shook his head when they asked him to look at the paw prints, but he promised to tell Cam what they'd said. On the way home in the car, Susan and Daniel didn't argue like they usually did. They were too busy agreeing that the whole thing was suspicious.

A FEW NIGHTS later she dreamed the tiger could speak. It talked like her *majka* did, in Croatian, and she didn't understand what it was saying. They were in the church with the coffin at the front, and the tiger talked louder and louder until the walls were shaking, but she didn't know how to answer it. *Mačketina* was all she could say. Please, *mačketina*, please. Then a dead person climbed out of the coffin and it was Beatrice from next door. *You goddamn monster*, Beatrice shouted as she walked down the aisle toward her, the tiger still bellowing in her ear. Zeljka woke up crying and tripped over Daniel's mattress on her way to the hallway and hurt her knee. When she got to Susan and Marge's room they rubbed her back and kissed her until she fell asleep.

In the morning she slid out from between them and walked down the hallway to the living room. She went to her easel near the sofa, poured her tub of crayons onto the floor, and found the stubby red one. She was going to make a card for Oliver. It had been a long time since the funeral, but maybe it wasn't too late.

"How do you spell 'sorry'?" she asked when Susan passed through the living room on her way to the kitchen, rubbing her eyes. Susan called the letters to her as she went.

"How do you spell 'dead'?" she asked a minute later. Susan came in wanting to know what she was doing.

Then Daniel appeared in his bathrobe and asked what all the noise was about. When he heard that Zeljka was going to Oliver's house that day, he wasn't very happy.

"She shouldn't spend any more time with that family," he said to Marge and Susan in the kitchen. Zeljka sat on the living room sofa and listened.

"Daniel, what is it with you?" asked Marge.

"Mike thinks a visit will be good for Oliver," said Susan. "And it will be good for Zed too. They've had to go through the same thing, with their mothers . . ."

Susan meant that Oliver's mother had died, Zeljka thought. But then, she remembered what Daniel had said about that, and she remembered the coffin at the funeral. It had been closed so that nobody could see what was inside.

IN THE CAR on the way to Oliver's house, Marge smoked the whole time – she always smoked when Daniel wasn't around – and told her to be careful about what she said to Oliver and Nel.

"Do you remember how you felt after your *majka* passed away?" Marge asked. "They'll feel like that right now."

Marge always said her *majka* had passed away, and Susan said she'd died, but they both meant the same thing. She wasn't here, and she was never coming back. In fact, Zeljka couldn't remember how she'd felt when her *majka* died. Sometimes if she saw a photograph or she smelled a smell, if she surprised herself by saying a word in Croatian that she'd never said out loud before, then the world became a strange place for a second. One time in the mall she brushed up against a woman by mistake and suddenly everything seemed like a dream, as scary as the one with the tiger and the church. Her *majka*'s coat, she thought. But it didn't happen very often. The photo albums were on a very high shelf in Marge and Susan's bedroom, and the two of them hardly ever told her stories about her relatives in Croatia any more.

At Oliver's they built things with his construction blocks while his father sat at the table in the kitchen reading a pile of papers and Nel played by herself upstairs. Oliver built a boat and Zeljka built a house. He didn't seem any different. She wondered if it was like this when her *majka* died – if she'd just played with her toys and her friends like always.

She wanted to tell him what Daniel had said about his mother being alive, but then she remembered Marge's warning. *Be careful what you say.* Maybe Oliver already knew, though; then it would be okay. And it wouldn't be her fault, anyhow. It would be Daniel's.

She moved across the floor on her bum until she was right beside Oliver. He was trying to put as many little plastic men on

162

his boat as he could without any of them falling to the floor. His tongue was sticking out as he worked and he didn't really look at Zeljka when she came close. All at once she had a feeling that she was doing something bad, after all. Then she had an idea. Maybe there was a way to tell him without really saying it.

"*Tvoja majka –*," she began. It was hard to remember the words. "*Tvoja majka zapravo nije . . . mrtva,*" she finished. There. She'd said it, but she'd been careful.

Oliver looked up, annoyed.

"I was talking in Croatian," she whispered. "Do you know what I said?" If he guessed, it wouldn't really be telling.

He didn't answer; instead he threw his boat down between them, and the little men went skittering across the floor. Oliver gave a high, shivery laugh that reminded her of the jungle birds at the wildlife park.

"That isn't funny," she said.

"Yes it is." And he laughed again. It was a hard laugh, sharp, like a chain that he was whirling without caring who was hit by it. His laughter made her very angry, and she'd do anything to make him be quiet.

"You shouldn't be laughing," she said. "Your mother is dead."

The laughter stopped. Oliver's eyes widened. Then he glanced to the kitchen where his father was sitting. Mr. Pederson didn't stir from his papers.

"You're not supposed to say that," Oliver said. "I have to tell my dad when anyone teases me about that."

She shook her head. If Oliver told his father, she wouldn't be allowed to come over any more. Marge and Susan would be angry with her.

"Don't tell," she said.

"I have to tell," he said loudly. "I have to."

"I didn't mean it," she whispered. "Your mother isn't really dead. Daniel said so."

They were close enough together that she couldn't see his face; everything was blurry. She heard the rush of air through his mouth, in and out, she saw his chest slowly filling like a balloon and then going flat again. She wanted them to stay like this forever, with the secret between them. Then he got up and started toward the kitchen.

"No, don't!" she shouted. But he didn't stop.

From her place on the floor, she watched as he leaned over and put his mouth up to his father's ear. Slowly the man's gaze left the papers in front of him and moved across the room until it stopped at her.

Before he could do anything, she hurried to her feet and ran over to them. Oliver took a few steps backwards to stand behind his father's chair as though she were going to attack them both.

"I have to go home now," she said.

"Home?" Oliver's father said, surprised. "You just got here. We haven't even had lunch yet. Are you hungry?"

She didn't say anything. Hadn't he heard her? She wanted to go home.

"All right then," Oliver's father said at last, shrugging. "I'll call and see if someone can pick you up." She watched him go to the telephone on the wall and dial. "Oh, hello, Daniel," he said. He took a big breath. "Is Marge or Susan there? Well, Zeljka wants to go home. Yes, I know she just got here. If they aren't in, I can tell her there's no one to –" He listened for a second. "Yes. If you want. See you soon."

Oliver's father didn't help her to put on her shoes or coat. While she was getting ready he sat at the kitchen table, not speaking. When Nel came down the hallway wanting lunch, he told her it would be another hour and she should go play in her room. Nel didn't reply, she just disappeared upstairs with Oliver following her. Then the doorbell rang and Oliver's father answered. Zeljka stood right behind him, eager for Daniel to take her away.

"Well guess who's here," said Oliver's father.

"Hi, Mike," said Daniel from the porch. He was looking at his feet as though he'd dropped something. "Is she all ready?"

"Sure," said Oliver's father. "You didn't have any trouble finding the place, I suppose."

"What? Oh, no, no trouble." He still hadn't looked up. "Listen, about everything that's happened, I imagine it's been pretty tough –"

"Yes, it has. But I've learned a lot. Quite a few surprising things."

"I guess you would," said Daniel quietly. He didn't sound like he wanted to be here. "Well, if Zeljka's got her shoes on –" He motioned for her to come outside with him, but Oliver's father didn't move and she had to step around him to get through the door.

"You know, Zeljka mentioned something to Olly," said Oliver's father as she and Daniel were going down the stairs. Zeljka froze, and Daniel stopped beside her. "Something about Alice not being dead."

Zeljka looked up at Daniel, expecting him to be angry, but he wasn't paying any attention to her. He was staring across the lawn toward Mooney's Bay.

"You son of a bitch," said Oliver's father.

It was Zeljka who turned around first. Oliver's father was huge and heaving, he was practically filling the doorway. His face, usually so calm, had scrunched up like he was going to cry. At any moment, she thought, he was going to run down and hit Daniel.

"Come on," Daniel told her. He took her hand, led her quickly across the driveway, opened the car door, and buckled her in. Through the windshield she could see Oliver's father still standing on the porch. "Never mind," said Daniel as he got in. "Forget it."

On the way home Daniel drove fast. He passed five cars, and he swore when they had to stop at the stoplight. He didn't say anything to her until they were in the parking lot beside the apartment building and he'd turned off the engine.

"Zeljka, don't mention what happened to Marge or Susan, okay?" he said. His foot was tapping on the pedal like he had someplace else to go and he had to get there fast.

"Why not?" Suddenly she wanted to tell them all about it. It was the most important thing in the world.

"Because they wouldn't be happy that Oliver's father got angry with us. It might mean we couldn't go over there again."

She thought about this for a second.

"I don't want to go back there, anyhow."

He tried to pat her on the head and she leaned away from him. He wasn't her *majka*, he couldn't tell her what to do. It was his fault that Oliver had told on her. It was because of him that Oliver's father was angry. Daniel wasn't her brother. He was a bad man.

"*Mogu* –," she exclaimed. "*Mogu reći* –" But the words she wanted weren't there, not in that language.

"It's no good speaking Croatian to me," he said. "I told you before, I don't understand it." He started to say something else and pointed his finger at her, but then he used it to scratch at the back of his neck. His eyes narrowed as his hand began to move back and forth, harder and faster, against his skin.

"Jesus, there's something back there –" His eyes narrowed even more. He got out of the car, marched around and opened her side, then went into the apartment building ahead of her, not even bothering to shut the car doors. She had to close both of them herself before she ran up the stairs to follow him. When she reached the apartment he was in the bathroom, squirming around in front of the mirror.

"God damn it," he yelled. "Susan, will you look at this?" She came from the kitchen, her hands covered in flour, and he showed her his neck. "It's ringworm, isn't it?" She made him bend over, then nodded, and he turned to glare at Zeljka.

"Thanks, sis," he said, and he walked past them both, down the hallway, and out the front door. Zeljka went to the window and watched his red hair floating down the street. As it turned the corner toward the ball diamond she hoped that he'd never return, that his ringworm would never go away. She knew this was a bad thought, one that only a person like Daniel would think, but she couldn't quite bring herself to take it back.

✦ *I gaze through the chain-link fence and try to act as though the little girl hasn't just run away, as though there were no little girl to be frightened off in the first place. How could I have been so stupid? By now she's telling everyone about the strange man who spoke of Alice Pederson. People will be looking for me. At any moment there'll be the crunch of approaching footsteps, a hand on my shoulder, a threatening voice. I should go after her now, find her among the circles of people in the field and say I meant no harm. But that would just look worse. I can only stand here, waiting for something to happen, listening.*

Guitar strings being plucked. A beer bottle breaking. That's all. Perhaps she's already forgotten me.

We never should have come to this party. I want us to go back to your cottage. For tonight, at least, I'll put aside my petty concerns. I'll apologize. The heating will be turned off when we get there and the bed will be an old, creaky cot, but it will still be better than a field full of snow.

I make my way along the fenceline toward the skating rink. Out of the night a tall, dark-skinned man approaches, one hand dragging over the chain links and raising a faint chime. I say a meek hello. He nods, tucks his chin into his scarf, and continues past me toward the farmhouse.

At the rink, high banks of snow bracket an ice surface as big as a football field and lit around the edges with torches. A few dozen people are gliding in different directions: couples holding hands, a group playing hockey along the far side, and a few solitary figures doing circuits of the perimeter. I wait for each of them to pass, trying to pick you out. Eventually a young man with a gaunt face stops in front of me.

"You want to join us, buddy? There are extra skates over by the bench."

I shake my head.

"Thanks, no. I'm looking for someone."

"Hey, aren't we all?" he says, and winks. "Not too many chicks around here, though."

I should laugh politely, but I'm too busy peering over his shoulder for you. He shrugs and skates off.

I don't know where else you could be – or at least I don't know where I might look for you. The thought of searching the crowd near the farmhouse and encountering the little girl again is hardly appealing, and it would take too long to walk back to the car. The only alternatives are the dead trees and swampland to the west, or the pastures stretching beyond the ice rink. Darkness and desolation; no one could be out there. But then, right now I don't mind the idea of solitude. And there's also the yellow book in my pocket to consider. Perhaps if I could find a private place – behind the snowbank at the far end, away from the skaters' eyes – then I might remove the rubber band encircling it and learn more about Alice Pederson without frightening any other little girls.

I glance to the rink again; no one seems to be watching me. Quickly I walk along the edge until I'm out of the torchlight and hidden from the farmhouse, the bonfire, the henge, everything. There's only the snowbank shielding me from the party and, beyond me, an empty field. The sky overhead is crowded with stars.

My hand has just gone to my pocket for the yellow book when I hear the muffled sound of a voice from the other side of the bank. Your voice. Except that it's not coming from there; it's too loud to be that distant, but too muffled at the same time. When I listen more closely, it seems to issue from the snow itself, as if you've been buried alive. You don't sound panicked, though; your voice is soft and gentle, and after it breaks off, another begins. A man's *voice. From here I can't make out the words, only the tone, deep and placatory.*

Looking down, I see for the first time two holes dug into the bank a few feet apart, both just large enough for someone to crawl through. The kind of thing that children might have done: the entrances to tunnels. I crouch between the two, looking down them in turn. Each leads in a separate direction, then curves slowly inward so that I can't see where it ends. They might join up, they might just peter out, or perhaps there's a whole network of passages running through the piled snow.

I listen more intently, trying to decide which one to choose. I don't like confined spaces, but I want to surprise you and this man, whoever he is. I want to see your reaction when I catch you out. Finally, reluctantly, I crawl forward and enter the tunnel on the right. The floor is packed hard, but the warm weather has left it slippery with meltwater, and immediately my trousers are soaked through at the knees.

After a few feet I stop. Your voice seems to be closer now, down at this level, but I can't tell whether it's coming from the end of the tunnel I've chosen or from another direction. Soon the passageway begins to bend more distinctly, and when I look behind me, the entrance has vanished.

There should be complete darkness here, but the walls have a dark blue iridescence. From the outside it was impossible to appreciate how close to the surface the tunnel lay; now, through the translucence of the ice, I can discern a flickering haze of yellow, and I realize that I'm near the very edge of the snowbank, looking toward the bonfire near the farmhouse. There are smaller patches of light that must be the torches around the rink, and I can even see – if I squint hard, if I allow my eyes to follow my imagination – the inky sky and the pinpricks of stars.

I hear your voice more clearly now too; it appears to be coming from farther down the tunnel. The ground is just as slippery as the walls and seems to propel me forward, as though at any moment it might tilt downwards and I'll be sent careening into the heart of the earth. The passage curves even more sharply, until I wonder why I haven't come back on myself yet. Your voice and the voice of the man grow louder with every shuffle, but by the time I expect to see you ahead of me, there's only a dead end, hollowed out to make a tiny, empty chamber with ceilings high enough for kneeling.

"The band claims it would continue to operate the wildlife park," I hear you say.

"No, that's non-negotiable," replies the other voice. "I won't sell the park." I recognize it now: it belongs to the man with the wide-brimmed hat, the owner of this place.

The two of you must be in the other tunnel. Could it have followed a symmetrical path, slowly turning inward too? Perhaps the passageways were meant to join up here, and the people who'd been digging gave up right on the brink of reaching each other. There can't be more than a foot or two of packed snow between us. I imagine tapping on the wall, getting your attention, or smashing through the barrier and surprising you, demanding to know what's brought you here. But instead of announcing myself, I only breathe quietly and try not to move.

"What about the archeological certificate I arranged?" It's the owner's voice. "You're sure it won't be second-guessed?"

"It's public information," you tell him. "Anyone who checks the records –"

The man snorts with apparent frustration. "Look, why are we talking about business, anyhow? We scheduled the consultation for tomorrow, remember? I didn't even think you'd be at the party."

"You could have told me about tonight," you say. "Instead I hear about it from some hitchhiker –"

"I didn't think you'd want to come all this way alone on a Friday."

"Of course I would. Besides, there are other people here from the city. It looks like you called everyone."

"That was the idea."

"Then why not me? I was here for the first henge party too. You can't just –"

"Christ, it's after eleven. I'm sorry, I have to go, I'm behind schedule."

I turn to leave. It would be safer to stay still, to wait until both of you are gone, but I want there to be no chance that one of you will enter this tunnel and find me here, cornered and cowering. Never mind that you might make it out of your tunnel before I can escape mine, that the three of us might meet in the dark field.

In the end I'm too clumsy. When I try to crawl quietly out of the little room, my hands slip forward on the glassy floor and I land heavily on my chest, the sound of the impact echoing through the chamber. Before I can catch my breath, your voice is in my ears.

"Did you hear that?"

"The other tunnel," says the owner. Then, more loudly, "Who's over there?"

I don't reply. Instead I scramble up and start down the tunnel again, flailing all the way so that it feels like I'm swimming rather than crawling. Behind me, two voices are shouting. A fist begins to beat against the partition between the tunnels, each blow thundering after me. Upon reaching the open air I get to my feet and run, sprinting around the snowbank, past the ice rink, through the field along the snow-packed trail.

What am I fleeing? Why should I be the guilty one? There was nothing said that I should be punished for hearing. It's you who should be running away. You've been to this place before, attending other parties. You're that man's lawyer; you didn't come here this weekend just for me. I don't know why you even brought me.

My lungs are burning by the time I reach the farmhouse, but I slow down only because I don't know where else to run. You have the keys to the car. I'm trapped here. Perhaps I should go inside, call a taxi company, and take a long cab ride back to the city.

Before I can decide, though, I hear footsteps, two sets of them, slow and methodical, approaching from behind. Finally they stop, and when nothing else happens, when the sense of someone close behind me raises the hair on my neck, I'm compelled to turn.

It's the little girl. She's holding the hand of a woman who is lean and about my height, with a sharp nose and pursed lips, an orange toque on her head.

"You're looking for Alice Pederson?" the woman asks.

I nod. Alice Pederson. I'd almost forgotten.

"Let's go into the house," she says, motioning with her free hand.

I follow the woman and the little girl along the path, still trying to catch my breath and unprepared for whatever is to come, but also relieved. Somewhere at my back, you and the man with the wide-brimmed hat are still with each other, and I'm glad to be taken away from you like this. I wouldn't want you here with me now. I feel for the book in my pocket, and the little girl looks over her shoulder, staring at me as she did at the fence. I can't tell whether it's with simple curiosity or some other feeling entirely.

WISHBONE

H e'd fallen in love with Alice on a ladder. It was July, he'd finished university and had turned to painting houses for the summer. Marge and Susan said there must be better jobs for him – he was headed to Cambridge on a scholarship, wasn't he? – but he liked the time outdoors, the sun-bleached mindlessness of the work, the way it proved to him that his body existed and had meaning. His shirt off in the heat, paint splattered all over his skin, shoulders peeling. He peered at her through the windows, watched her move through the rooms, at play with her son and daughter, talking with the husband, and, occasionally, for thrilling, too-brief moments, alone on the far side of the glass, the house a veil between them. Sometimes she waved to him, as though embarrassed to be caught out by herself, and other times she embraced Mike in front of him, oblivious of his presence. Mike noticed, though, and stared back even as he held her. Daniel was conscious of himself then, his sunburnt chest, his arms thin and weak despite the summer's work. He couldn't tell whether Mike was suspicious or amused, and he averted his eyes.

After a few days the family disappeared, and it was only her. Alice Pederson, the dentist, now just a woman alone in her house, smiling back at him from the kitchen, the bedroom, the den. The fumes from the paint making him giddy and daring. That afternoon she invited him inside. There was a quiet reference to Mike and the children, gone for the week on a camping trip. Her blue dress clingy with sweat.

At her table they ate cheese sandwiches and took turns teasing each other. Most of what they knew of one another came from headlines in the Mooney's Dump paper. She called him Geography Genius and wanted to hear how he felt about his Exciting Future Overseas. He laughed and asked her if she was still lobbying against the fall deer hunt. Apparently the town council hadn't liked her arguments, but then half of them were beef farmers. He said it must be difficult caring about animal rights in a place like this one.

"What about you?" she asked him. "What do you care about?"

He thought hard, searching for something that would compare with her career, her family, her compassion for living things. There was nothing like that. At his scholarship interview, hoping to tell the panel what they wanted to hear, he'd made grand statements about local planning and the value of community, but what was he going to be studying at Cambridge? Weather systems and ocean currents.

"I used to care about getting out of Mooney's Dump," he told her at last. "I guess I'll have managed that much."

They talked until sunset, moving from topic to topic as though everything had to be crammed in. She asked him about his studies and how he'd found it living in Toronto, told him about going to dental school there. He was glad she didn't mention her family. It was as though the two of them could talk forever, with nothing and no one to intrude upon them. By the time he went to put away his equipment, the paint in the open buckets had grown a thick, white skin.

"It's a shame you're leaving," she said as he was about to drive off. He didn't know whether she was referring to his departure for England in two months or to the one he was making at that moment.

Just before lunchtime on the second day she asked him to come inside again. A tour of the house this time. He watched her walking in front of him, her bare feet, the way she tossed her head to clear the hair from her eyes. In the bedroom they lingered longer than necessary, chatting, and he tried not to glance at the mattress, its rumpled sheets. The living room was safer ground. They sat on the sofa, his gaze fixed on her until he noticed the framed photograph of Mike on the table behind her. When she said she had to get back to the office, he replied that he was sorry and reached toward the round frame, picked it up, set it back face down.

"That's a dangerous game to play," she said and laughed. He got up, returned to painting, half hoping she'd follow him outside and ask him in again. He'd never been so daring before and worried he'd gone too far, but still, it had been exhilarating. That evening when she got home from work and walked into the house, all of the family pictures were lying face-down. He was waiting for her on the couch.

"I'm not afraid of games," he said.

"Of course you aren't," she replied wryly. "You're not the one breaking any rules."

He kissed her on the cheek and felt the muscle of her jaw clench, but she didn't pull back. Her forehead next, then her long neck with its constellation of three tiny birthmarks. Finally he pressed his lips against hers. She let them rest there a moment before she turned.

"I'm sorry. It's my fault, I know, I invited you inside . . ." Her eyes swept the room around them. "It's only because he's away."

He thought she'd tell him to leave, but instead she lay her head against his shoulder and let him stroke her hair while she spoke of things he didn't want to hear about. Falling in love, moving back to Mooney's Dump. Mike's decision to stay at home and raise the children. His ambition slowly draining away, his life whittled down to family matters, while the dental clinic sapped her time and she barely saw him or the children. The ongoing struggle to make ends meet.

"You don't belong here," Daniel said. "You should pack your bags, get away from this place."

"Haven't you been listening?" she said. "I've been trying to explain why I can't leave. Why they depend on me." She sat up to take his hands. "But you amaze me. You talk about going as though there were nothing to stop you." She was right, he realized. There was nothing. Mooney's Dump had always seemed like a tiny planet, isolated and desolate, but lacking a gravity of its own, easy enough to escape. By the end of September he'd be at Cambridge; in some part of his mind, he'd already left. Even when Alice kissed his ear, he made himself believe that he barely felt the tug of her drawing him back.

The rest of that week they met in her house, after he'd painted all day and she'd seen patients. Mostly they talked, sometimes reaching out tentatively to touch each other and make their desire known. A kiss with lips parted. His hands on her stomach. No more than that. She stood whenever she heard the sound of a car on the road, and she wouldn't let him stay the night.

"If it rains they'll come home," she explained. Afterwards he drove into town studying the sunset and cursing clouds. Thursday, two days before the camping trip was supposed to end, he already felt resentful.

"You want them back," he said, accusing. "You miss them." When she didn't reply, he went to kiss her and felt her cautioning hand on his chest. The week's blurred boundaries were becoming hard and stubborn again, and they were both exhausted from a long evening of not touching.

"Never mind," he said. "We'll see each other tomorrow, at least."

They lay on the couch together, and he'd almost joined her in sleep when he heard the sound of fingers drumming on skin. Thousands of fingers, tapping softly above them, not on skin at all but on the roof. It had begun to rain.

THE GAS STATION, the pharmacy, the bank. Everywhere he went, people were watching him. What could they be thinking, staring like that? *There goes Daniel Barrie, who killed Alice Pederson two years ago.* No, that was impossible. Only he and Rocket had been there that night after the party at Cam Usher's; no one else even knew about him and Alice. But that wasn't quite true, was it? Rocket could have talked to anybody by now, wherever he was, and Marge and Susan knew about the affair too, although Daniel refused to tell them anything more. It had been a mistake to open his mouth at all; Marge wasn't happy with his silence, and she wouldn't let him rest.

"Go to the police," she told him during dinner one evening when Zeljka was at a friend's house and she could talk more freely. "If you know something and you don't feel like sharing your secrets with Susan and me, that's fine. But a man's in jail. He could end up wrongly convicted. Is that what you want?"

He took another mouthful of his spaghetti and reminded himself that it wouldn't come to a trial for Dr. Fremlin. Eventually people would figure out she was still alive. Marge hadn't known her like he did, had never heard her talk about leaving town. Alice was too careful to have been murdered, too smart to have committed suicide when there were other ways of escaping. She could have figured out how to run away without anyone giving chase.

"Whatever you're thinking, she's dead," said Marge. "Don't you see what will happen if you don't go forward and they find out about the two of you? They'll think you did it. They'll put you in jail."

"Marge, stop hectoring him," Susan said. "Let him make his own decision."

"How can you say that? You don't even know what he's hiding."

Daniel shifted uncomfortably in his seat. He'd never expected Susan to defend him against his mother.

"Nobody knows what was between Alice and me," he said quietly. "Or would understand."

"Fine," said Marge. "Go on looking out for yourself, Daniel, you don't need my help. But what about Rocket? If you know where he is, if you're hiding something to protect him, you should come clean. His parents are worried sick. Just think about that. Stop being such a coward and think of someone other than yourself." Then she and Susan took their plates into the kitchen, leaving him to survey the cramped apartment from his chair, hoping futilely to find some place of refuge. Not for the first time he wished they hadn't sold their house.

Daniel had already spoken to the police once. They'd phoned him a few days after the henge party, when he'd just arrived in Cambridge. Alice Pederson has disappeared, Harry Midgard told him. That's terrible, Daniel replied. He didn't say that Rocket had called with the news first, that his own guilt and worry had kept him awake all night. Instead he let Harry explain that they were contacting everyone who'd been at Usher's party. Did you speak with her there? Harry wanted to know. I might have said hello, Daniel told him. There'd been a lot of people, he couldn't be sure. Did you see anything suspicious? Harry asked. Not that he could remember. All right then, good luck over there, said Harry. Don't let the rain get you down.

When Daniel remembered that conversation, how easy it was, he thought he really might be able to step inside the police station now, sit down with Harry, and tell him everything. The interview would be friendly and polite. Harry would nod understandingly and thank him for the information. But maybe Daniel was wrong. Harry might well be furious that he hadn't come forward from the beginning. There could be an interrogation, a trial. People might not believe him; they'd hear what had happened and think he'd killed her. Each morning he shook off his dreams, with their fraught re-creations of his and Alice's last meeting, and began again the process of deciding what to do. He wished he knew where Rocket was – together they could sort out their story, decide on a plan – but Rocket had disappeared. So much for friendship. Didn't he realize that hiding only made him look guilty? After Alice's disappearance,

Daniel had told him not to worry. He'd said that if they both stayed quiet about what had happened at the party, everything would work out. Eventually the police would establish that she'd just run away. But then the body had been found, and Rocket had vanished even before Daniel returned home. Now he had to deal with everything himself, and it was too much. By nightfall, watching television on the couch was the most he could manage.

"DO YOU STILL have sex with him?" They'd been sitting on Alice's patio, both of them facing the lake. It was an evening in August, almost dark; the time was slipping away. "I want to know everything about you."

"No one can know everything about someone else," Alice replied.

"Well, do you?" he insisted. "Have sex with him?"

She picked up the glass of beer beside her and sloshed the contents over the railing.

It was almost impossible for them to see each other now. She was always working or trapped at the house, and when she did find a few hours for him, they had to meet here, in her home, while Mike and the children were at the movies or the Owen Sound library. She told him she couldn't afford to leave her car where it might be seen; one telephone call from anybody in Mooney's Dump, just to see if she was all right, might be enough for Mike to ask questions. So on nights like this one Daniel had to park his mother's car up a dead-end road nearby and walk the rest of the way. Once he arrived, they avoided the bedroom and the possibilities it presented in favour of places like the back patio, where they shared timid caresses and long, desperate hugs.

"The first time we met, you must have been fifteen," she said. "Do you remember? I removed your braces at Stoddart Fremlin's clinic."

"I bet you wanted to jump my bones way back then," he said.

"Sure. You were the sexiest teenager I'd ever seen."

Such statements thrilled him. He liked how she didn't point out that when he was fifteen, she was twenty-seven and already married to Mike. Instead she joined in the game.

"If only we'd found each other earlier," she said. "Then there wouldn't be any of this mess."

But there was an unspoken understanding that these things were expressed frivolously. They were reckless, uncommitted daydreams, and not to be given any weight. At the same time, when he heard her make such statements, he wanted to believe her. He was the one who went too far, who inadvertently brought the game to a halt and ruined everything.

"You never answered me about Mike," he said now. "I can see why you'd marry someone like him. Smart, handsome . . ."

"Really, you have nothing to be jealous of. You're gifted and intelligent –"

"He must be good in bed."

"For God's sake, Daniel."

Mike's skin was smooth and dark, not all pastiness and freckles. He and Alice had been married for ten years. They'd done everything together, tried every position, every trick. Daniel was sure of it. Each night in his room before he fell asleep, he let Alice and Mike make expert and exhilarating love in front of him. They never tired, their minds never strayed. It was better than any sex he'd ever have.

"Were there other lovers before him?" he asked, wanting her to say yes and remove some of Mike's power. It wasn't a game now; there was nothing playful in his thoughts.

"What about you?" she asked in return. "How many lovers have you had?"

"You're avoiding the question." He had no interest in revisiting his hangdog university crushes, the few disastrous flings, or, even farther back, his humiliating experience with Esther Fremlin at the reserve. Alice would only laugh at him.

"This isn't about sex, anyway," she said. "You're not jealous of Mike about that." He smiled at the self-confidence in her assertion, the absurdity of it. "Go ahead and laugh, but I'm right."

"What am I jealous of, then?"

"You're jealous because he wrote a book."

He started to reply, stopped. He searched for some clever rejoinder, but he was too flustered.

"That's crazy. I don't give a damn what he's done."

Mike had been a year younger than Daniel was now when he'd published his novel. Alice hadn't told Daniel that, but he knew it already from the blurb on the dust-jacket. The day after she'd first mentioned the book's existence, he'd gone to the Mooney's Dump library and read it cover to cover, standing the whole time at the back of the building, as though to take the thing home would be some kind of admission. It was about a young couple: a small-town white girl and a black man from the city. He didn't know how Alice had put up with it. As far he could tell, only the names had been changed.

When the librarian assured him there weren't any more books by Michael Pederson, it was both a relief and a disappointment. It meant that nothing more of Mike's could taunt him from the shelves, but then, there were no more character sketches to puzzle out, no more dialogue he could attribute to Alice, no more secret portholes through which to peer into her past.

"You don't need to get upset," she told him. "Mike doesn't sit there at night and gloat over his accomplishments, I can tell you that. It's as though he never wrote the thing." She raised her glass to her eyes, peered at it, set it back down. "I told him not to stop writing. You should have heard him, though. The children first, he said. The dental clinic first. Anything but himself. And now look at him. Look at me. When I finally get home at night I make excuses to be by myself. To be with you." She turned toward him, her face stern. "So don't say you envy Mike, all right? You'll only make me angry."

He nodded, then stared out over the broad, green backyard, the distant bay.

"You're lucky," she said. "In England, there won't be anybody to worry about but yourself."

"I'll worry about you," he told her.

He was thankful in some ways when September came and she agreed to help Cam Usher build his henge. It seemed to make her happy. She got to be near the animals at the wildlife park, spend time with her telescope – a childhood hobby, she explained, something she'd done with her father. During Daniel's visits to the house she spread out the plans for the structure to show him her calculations and diagrams, and they laughed together as she led him slowly through the numbers and angles. He felt like a child beside her, and he loved her even more.

"I don't understand it," he said as she folded up a star chart.

"What do you mean?" she said. "The constellation? It's simple –"

"No, I don't understand why you spend this time with me." She set the chart on the table, cupped his face in her hands. "I don't deserve any of it. If I thought you were just playing –"

"I'm not," she said. "Really, I'm not. I care about you. Even if we can't be lovers."

"But that's the strangest thing. It would make more sense if this were just a joke to you."

The sun went down earlier now. He'd be flying to Cambridge in a couple of weeks. Each time they met she told him both in words and actions not to take things seriously.

A WEEK AFTER her funeral he opened the door to the florist's and Mike Pederson walked out with a bunch of lilies in his hand. Daniel turned the other way, but it was stupid of him. There was no way the man could possibly suspect anything. Mike wouldn't even realize that the two of them shared a kind of bond; they'd both lost her.

Once Daniel had ordered a dozen roses and the clerk had disappeared into the back of the store, he began to think of what he should have said to Mike in the moment they'd passed. He didn't know. Then he realized the woman behind him had just asked him something, and he asked her to repeat it.

"I said, you're Daniel Barrie, aren't you?" Her voice was friendly but low enough not to be overheard.

"Sure," he replied, matching her quietness. She leaned close, spoke in a whisper.

"What do you think Alice Pederson was doing driving thirty miles an hour over the speed limit through Orangeville a couple years ago, on a day when she was supposed to be at her office?"

His head snapped up. He should have expressed bewilderment at the question, but in his panic he managed only irritation.

"Joy-riding? You've got me. Ask her husband."

"Mike doesn't know," said the woman. "Neither does her office. Funny thing is, it was also the day you were supposed to fly to England from Toronto. The same morning you left your ticket behind."

"Look, who are you, anyway?" he said.

She didn't answer him. "Alice told her secretary it was a family crisis and then never talked about it again. Her husband doesn't remember any crisis."

"I don't see what any of this –"

"But as for me," the woman said, interrupting him in a louder voice, "I think maybe the Pedersons had a bit of a family crisis going on after all. You know the type I mean?"

"I don't know anything," he replied. As soon as the clerk brought the roses, he paid and left the store, remembering that Marge had warned him there was an insurance investigator.

Rocket, he thought. Rocket would know what to do. But where had he gone? It was the question he'd been asking himself for days now, but no one seemed to have any inkling as to the answer.

When Daniel reached the car, he realized he no longer felt like visiting the cemetery as he'd planned. The idea of walking public grounds, exposed, made him anxious now. And hadn't there been lilies in Mike Pederson's hands? Daniel didn't want to meet up with that man in such a place. Instead, he drove back to the Sunshine Apartments building, climbed the stairs, and found Marge sitting at her dining table, studying her hands. He set the bouquet of roses on the placemat in front of her.

"I got them for you," he said flatly and started for the bed-room, determined not to turn around. But he couldn't help himself. He wanted to cry when he saw her face and knew he'd made her happy.

THE FIRST TIME he left for Cambridge, he'd got as far as the check-in counter at the Toronto airport before discovering his passport and ticket were still in Mooney's Dump. It had been a hurried departure; he'd spent too long talking covertly with Alice on the phone, saying final goodbyes and trying to persuade both of them that leaving was the right thing to do. Or trying to convince himself, at least. For her part, Alice seemed far too quick to accept the inevitability of his going.

"This is important for my future, you've said so yourself," he'd told her. "It's a prestigious scholarship. The faculty is the best in the world –"

"You'd be a fool to pass it up."

"I'll be back for Christmas."

"I know. I'll miss you."

Sitting in the back seat behind Marge and Susan on the drive to the airport, he'd tried to summon enthusiasm for what was ahead. He told himself he should be excited, not looking back to some-thing he'd never really had in Mooney's Dump. Whole worlds would be opening up to him. By the time he said farewell to Marge and Susan at the terminal, he was even beginning to believe himself. And then he discovered he'd left his ticket and passport behind. They were sitting at home on his bedroom dresser, he real-ized, exactly where he'd put them when he'd picked up the tele-phone to call Alice.

It was almost three o'clock. His plane would take off at half past five. Marge and Susan had already started home, and it would be a three-hour drive for them back to Mooney's Dump. There seemed to be no other choice: he called Alice at her clinic. Reluctantly she agreed to break into his mother's house and try to make the airport in time. Later he'd tell Marge it was Rocket who'd used the backdoor key under the mat and retrieved the documents before driving down, and in fact it would have made more sense if Rocket had been the one he'd called. But Daniel hadn't even thought of him.

He spent two hours wandering the departure lounge, then stood outside on the concourse with his luggage and waited. Alice pulled into the terminal just as his plane sailed overhead. There was a speeding ticket on her dashboard.

"Thanks for trying," he said through the driver's window. He leaned in to kiss her but she drew away.

"You did this on purpose," she said. Then she got out and hugged him.

"Stay here with me tonight," he said. "We can rent a hotel room."

She shook her head. Of course, he thought. He should have known it wasn't going to be like that. Even when he asked her to drive him back to Mooney's Dump she was hesitant.

"There might be another flight –"

It didn't matter, he replied. Cambridge could wait for him a bit longer. Only once they were an hour from home did he tell her the whole truth: while he'd been waiting for her, he'd changed his mind. He'd decided not to go to England.

"Don't be stupid," she said. "You can't give up your scholarship just to stay in Mooney's Dump. That's crazy."

"I'll go in January," he said. "They'll let me defer for a term." He said another degree in geography didn't really interest him, anyhow; it had just been the easy thing to apply for when they offered him the scholarship. He told her that for a long time now he'd been worrying that he always took the easy route like that. It would be good for him to spend a few months doing independent research from home, maybe change his focus to urban planning. These statements sounded unconvincing to his own ears, but Alice didn't argue. Instead she only gripped the steering wheel, kept her gaze levelled straight ahead.

"Just don't say you're doing it for me," she said bitterly. Then, without warning, she pressed on the horn and held it down. They were driving a straight stretch of road with no vehicles approaching and a single van following behind them. The noise was unbearable. The van pulled up beside them, and its driver waved his middle finger in their direction before speeding ahead. Finally she released her hand, the sound died, and she drove on as though nothing had happened. Daniel was amazed: he hadn't thought her capable of such a blatant, public transgression.

"And don't think that staying will put me in your debt somehow," she said. "I won't love you more because of it."

She dropped him off at home, where Susan and Marge weren't any happier to discover he'd returned. When he told them of his decision, they thought he was joking, and he found himself insisting that they believe him.

"When did you have time to ask about deferring?" said Marge suspiciously. "You got back two minutes ago."

He shrugged. The truth was that for weeks he'd been going over the possibility of staying in Mooney's Dump through the fall. He'd called the scholarship trust and the admissions office in Cambridge. He'd even asked Rocket about moving in with him. But if Marge knew these things she'd only accuse him of forgetting his passport intentionally. He hadn't. He really hadn't. Leaving it behind was just the result of the last-minute rush and a preoccupied mind. Still, as he'd waited in the airport for Alice to arrive, he'd concluded that it was a sign: he'd be better off staying, after all.

He didn't bother to unpack his suitcases. The next day he took them out to Rocket's ramshackle place on the edge of town.

"Great, go stay with Rocket," Marge said as he left. "If you want to throw away your education, that's fine."

Rocket had been living by himself ever since he quit hockey to work at the gas station. Daniel felt for him, stuck in that life, alone, after everything that had seemed destined to come his way. When he was a teenager, Rocket's parents and Dr. Fremlin had been set on making him a hockey star, and these days everyone knew that the DeWitts didn't hide their disappointment in him. But then, Rocket had never been a proper jock – he said the only consolation of the long bus rides to and from tournaments was the time they gave him to read – and in high school together it had been Daniel who felt like the stupid one.

Now things were different. It had taken Rocket four years of night classes just to get his high-school degree. People probably saw him and thought he was wasting his life, but Daniel understood why he went on the way he did. He got to do what he wanted. Maybe he was withdrawn sometimes, but at least he didn't spend time fawning over an older woman. Daniel liked being away from everyone, sharing space with an old friend after the years they'd spent apart while Daniel was at university. Rocket made no demands of him and had no expectations. He didn't ask whose calls Daniel always seemed to be waiting for, and if he thought Daniel might have been better off studying at Cambridge than reading old geography textbooks from the Mooney's Dump library, he didn't say so. His house was just four small rooms, with flea-market furniture and posters taped to the walls. Daniel slept on the pullout couch, used his savings to pay his share of the rent. Sometimes not a word passed between them all day. Daniel thought of them as two refugees sticking together, honouring each other's need for solitude. Later, though, in England, he realized that the friendship had been like the light at dusk, creeping away so slowly that they hadn't noticed, even as it vanished before their eyes.

"Did you see the paper?" Rocket had asked him one night in October. "Chief Kahgee is saying that according to the 1854 treaty, the Baushkidauwung band has legal rights to the peninsula's whole shoreline."

"Do they quote your dad?" said Daniel. Rocket was always reading out articles that featured Mr. DeWitt, though Rocket and his father didn't speak much any more and Rocket wasn't involved in local politics.

"No, but there's another story where they interview him about the burial ground he thinks is at the Moonstone Wildlife Park. He says he might bring up an archeological team." Rocket lowered the paper. "Hey, didn't you take archeology courses? Maybe he'd hire you."

Disinterestedly Daniel murmured his assent. Lately Alice had been working on the henge at Cam Usher's practically every evening, and Usher was all she ever talked about. She'd describe the newest animal in the wildlife park, inevitably rescued by Usher from some cruel owner or factory farm, or go on enthusiastically about the man's plans for an organic food co-operative. Daniel didn't want to hear any more about Usher than he already had.

"You don't really care about this, do you?" Rocket said. Daniel looked up, startled.

"Sure I do," he protested lamely. He could have said that Rocket was always talking about land claims or demonstrations and never actually did anything himself, but he didn't want to fight. "It's moot, anyhow," he remarked instead. "Usher will never let archeologists near his place. He doesn't want to lose his land."

That's what Alice had said, at least, the last time he'd spoken with her on the phone. Daniel had listened sullenly, his mind filling with images of her and Usher making their plans together for the park. Afterwards he'd sworn to himself that he'd do something equally important in Mooney's Dump. He'd teach farmers about sustainable agriculture, or organize a public transportation system. Something. But it was pointless, of course. He didn't have the resources, the training, the contacts. In the end, frustrated, he'd simply called Alice and asked to see her again, resentful that she never had time to meet him any more.

The secretiveness was what drained him so much, he decided. He wanted to tell Rocket about her, he was aching to tell someone, but he'd made a promise to Alice.

"Nobody can know about you and me," she'd said. "You whisper anything to one person around here, you might as well tell the whole world."

WHEN SUSAN asked him if he wanted to go to the wildlife park with her and Zeljka, his instinct was to say no. Only two days had passed since his encounters with Mike and the insurance investigator at the florist's, and he had no desire to appear in public again, especially not on Cam Usher's property. He hadn't been there since the henge party, and he felt a slight panic at the idea of returning. The memory of the crowds, the drumbeats, the last moments with Alice still had a vividness that frightened him. But he had to confront them sometime, he told himself. Besides, Marge had already begun her daily harassment of him, and if he didn't get out of the apartment she was going to drive him crazy.

"Bobby Boone just called," she'd told him at breakfast. "He wanted to know if you're still staying with us. He keeps reminding me this is a two-person apartment."

"Should I go somewhere else, then?"

"He was checking up on you, Daniel. People are suspicious. Doesn't that worry you?" Then she'd gone into the kitchen and begun to prepare a turkey for dinner. It was outrageous considering his vegetarianism, the late July heat, the lack of air conditioning. Soon every room smelled of roasting flesh, and he was glad when Susan announced that it was time to go.

As the two of them shepherded Zeljka around the wildlife park he found himself restless, his mind constantly returning to the question of whether Cam Usher might appear, and whether Daniel would say anything if he did. Finally he excused himself and made his way to the circle of stones in the middle of Usher's field, hoping to find some peace there. By summer daylight the henge was tranquil, even benign, and a carpet of dandelions had grown up in the area ringed by the moat. It was nothing like the place he remembered. He should have taken some kind of pleasure from the transformation, but instead it made him queasy, disoriented. Too much had changed. When he was last here he'd never been overseas, had never worried about the police. He looked at the tall stones and thought of Alice. All around him tourists were taking photographs, and he scowled at them. When Zeljka and Susan arrived with the news that there were tigers in the forest, the trip only became more surreal. Impatiently he waited in the car while Susan told Zeljka's story to the parking-lot attendant.

When they returned to the apartment, the odour of cooking turkey was overpowering, and Daniel thought he was going to be sick. He wanted to be alone, but Marge told them dinner was ready so they sat down to eat. On the table next to Zeljka's place Marge had set the wishbone, scraped clean of meat, grey and slick, lying there like an upside-down smile.

"What's that?" Zeljka wanted to know.

"It's from the turkey," Marge said. "Once it's dry, two people each grab an end and pull. Whoever breaks off the biggest piece gets to make a wish."

Daniel examined the wishbone out of the corner of his eye. There was barely half an inch of connection at the joint before the forks began to branch away from one another. It seemed a sad thing, a circle begun but incomplete, soon to be further divided from itself by rival hands. The very thought of such a practice was disturbing, and he decided there was something shameful about bones. They were a stark reminder of what had been sacrificed: the framework of a living body lurking at the end of meals along with flattened peas and smears of cranberry, to be scraped into a trash can promptly, hidden away. The wishbone ritual was wrong, and he hoped they'd be done with the thing soon so that he wouldn't have to look at it much longer.

After dinner Marge told him that she and Susan would wash the dishes, so he sat by himself and read while Zeljka went to play in her room. Eventually Susan emerged from the kitchen and joined him on the couch.

"Marge wanted to finish up by herself," she said. "She's angry with me. She thinks I haven't been hard enough on you for refusing to tell the police about you and Alice."

He tried to conceal his surprise. He wasn't used to being Susan's confidant, especially when it came to matters involving his mother, and he wondered if this was a ploy the two of them had devised.

"Is that what you think too?" he said cautiously. "That you've been too easy on me?"

"No. But you worry me, Daniel. Sometimes I think you even enjoy all this secrecy. You lord it over us –"

He set down his book.

"That's not true," he said too loudly, then lowered his voice. "Maybe I just don't want to complicate things by talking about them. Mom should understand that well enough; that's how she handles all her problems, isn't it?"

Susan nodded sadly, as though this were something she'd already considered.

"You're doing exactly what she'd do in your situation. I think it frightens her."

A moment later Marge walked into the room and they fell silent. The wishbone was in her hand. She stepped up onto the dinner table, fastened the bone to the overhead lamp by a string, then climbed down again and returned to the kitchen without a word.

That night in bed he found himself thinking of what Susan had said. Perhaps she was right; he was too much like his mother. Staying silent had consequences, and not only for him. What about for Rocket, wherever he was? Maybe he was waiting for Daniel to go to the police before he came out of hiding. And what about Dr. Fremlin? The papers seemed so sure of the man's guilt, as though he'd never be let out of jail. Perhaps they just needed someone to blame. But that meant if Daniel told the police what he knew, they might put him in Fremlin's place, and it would take a reappearance from Alice before they'd let him go. Would she do that, he wondered? If she heard he was in jail for her murder? He thought back to the moonlit strip of road near the wildlife park, their last words. She hadn't seemed to care for him at all; she'd only spoken of getting away. No, he couldn't talk to the police directly. But he had an idea.

Early the next morning he borrowed his mother's car and drove half an hour south to the Owen Sound shopping centre. There was a phone booth outside the entrance, and he walked to it slowly, looking around to make sure no one had followed. As he dialled, he held in his hand a dust-cloth he'd taken from Marge and Susan's linen closet. There were two rings before he heard a click.

"Sunshine Police Department," said a man's voice. It sounded like Harry Midgard. Daniel slipped the cloth over the mouthpiece.

"Alice Pederson isn't dead," he said, changing his accent, trying to sound like he was from someplace else – Georgia or Alabama.

"Pardon?" said the voice.

"Alice Pederson isn't dead." Louder this time.

"I'm sorry, I can't understand you. Try talking right into the telephone."

He took away the cloth and exaggerated his accent even more.

"Alice Pederson isn't dead," he shouted, sounding more like Zeljka than a Georgian. "Fremlin is innocent. She's still alive. Do a DNA test and you'll see." He hung up, his heart pounding.

When he got back to the apartment the smell of turkey was everywhere. He checked the oven, ready to reprimand his mother for cooking in the heat again. It was empty. Then he stood by the dining table and the odour was even stronger.

"It's the wishbone," he told Marge. "It's making the whole place stink." But Marge and Susan and the kid said he must be going nuts. They claimed they couldn't smell a thing.

Disgusted, he took a shower, as though he might be able to wash off the deed at the shopping centre and the clinging scent of the dead bird. The curtains held traces of smoke, and he knew Marge had been sneaking cigarettes in here. Surely she realized that every-one knew she was smoking again. Even Zeljka knew. When he'd towelled off, he could still smell the burnt tobacco, strong enough to usurp the odour of the wishbone drying outside, and it was as if he hadn't showered at all.

IN NOVEMBER he'd received a call from Alice, wanting to know why he'd booked an appointment with her at the dental practice.

"I have a cavity," he told her. "What else was I supposed to do?"

"Go to someone in Owen Sound. I don't want you coming here. People might suspect something."

"What, that you're a dentist? Don't worry, I'll sit in the waiting room for an hour like the rest of your patients and no one will think twice about it." He knew Alice would, though. Something had changed. She begrudged his decision to stay in Mooney's Dump, he thought; she wanted to be free of him. When they did see each other, the kisses and stroking felt more and more like the preludes to arguments.

He went to the clinic excited to see her in a different setting, publicly sanctioned, where the novelty would keep them from going over old issues, but in the dentist's chair, with his mouth open under the lamp, it felt like the wrong decision. His teeth were stained and not entirely straight. Saliva threatened to run down his chin at any moment. He swallowed and coughed, nearly upsetting the tray beside him. She examined him without speaking, poked and prodded until the hinge of his jaw ached. One slip and the tool would go sliding off the tooth to impale his cheek. What would she do then? He couldn't look her in the eye. A locking of their gaze now would be a gesture more intimate than sex.

She leaned back from his mouth, and there was an electrical hum as the chair tilted upright.

"There's nothing wrong with your teeth," she said. Her voice had a hostile edge.

"What? That molar has been killing me all week." She didn't reply. "Damn it, I wouldn't fake a cavity." But even as he said it, he realized the pain had disappeared. He slid his tongue around his mouth, trying to find the aching tooth, and was unable to distinguish it from the others.

"Really, Daniel," she said, "what did you think we were going to do in here?"

Then, one evening in the middle of the month, she called him from her home and asked if he could come over right away. It was the first time since the summer that she'd suggested a meeting without planning it well in advance. When he arrived, she said

Mike and the children had gone out for dinner. She'd told them she had a cold. It looked like the truth: her skin was pale, and she was wearing a winter coat despite the heat of the house.

"What is it?" he asked. "What's wrong?"

She kissed him. It wasn't careful like most of her kisses, but hard and needy. Something felt wrong; it was the kind of kiss she'd give if she were acting in a film. But she led him up the stairs to the bedroom, pulled him onto the mattress.

"What's happened?" he asked. "Tell me."

She placed her lips against his neck, and he reached to unbutton her coat. When she sat up to take it off, he sat up with her, felt her hands on his belt buckle.

"Was it something at the henge?" he asked.

His hands fumbled underneath her sweater for her bra strap, still half expecting her to pull away, but instead she arched her back and the clasp came undone miraculously on the first attempt, all her skin suddenly bare to his touch.

"Was it Cam Usher?" he whispered.

Before she could answer, there was the sound of a car in the drive. Both of them stiffened. Then she bolted from the bed and reached to refasten her bra.

"Go down to the basement," she ordered him. "Hurry. There's a door that takes you out under the patio." She was into the hallway before he could reply.

He'd almost made it to the bottom of the basement stairs when he discovered he'd left his jacket behind. Before he could start back up, there was the sound of the front door opening. He pictured the scene: Mike standing on the threshold, the children behind him, staring in at Alice with Daniel's jacket in her hand. But a second later it came tumbling down the stairs. The door at the top slammed shut.

He listened to the voices: Alice's excited greeting, the children talking over one another as they told her about the restaurant being closed, about getting takeout pizza instead. Mike's concerned questions: *How do you feel? Did you get some sleep?*

The door leading outside was in front of him, but he sat down on the bottom step and waited in the darkness. He didn't want to go home and watch game shows until she decided to call; he wanted to see her again. There was something wrong, and he needed to know what it was. After half an hour, though, she still hadn't appeared. There was only the sound of the children's rapid footsteps from above, the slower pacing of Mike and Alice. Pale starlight shone through the small, square window above his head. He stared at the concrete floors, the washer and dryer, the four pairs of skis set neatly in the rafters, wanting to take them down, smash them, destroy the orderliness of the place. But when he finally left some time later, he closed the door gently and stepped in old footprints so as not to leave a mark on the snow.

ONCE HE'D MADE the phone call at the Owen Sound shopping centre, he bought the paper every day, but all that appeared were details of the case against Dr. Fremlin. There were timelines of the man's business partnership with Alice, quotes from patients who claimed to have heard them arguing. Maybe the police were keeping the investigation into the identity of the body a secret, Daniel told himself. Or maybe they'd decided the call was made by a crank. Part of him hoped they had. It was foolhardy to have telephoned them, he appreciated that now. Anyone would think he'd wanted to be found out. Better to lay low and see what happened. He told himself that Rocket and Fremlin were grown men who could take care of themselves, and to avoid Marge's harangues he read in Zeljka's room for hours on end while Zeljka played in the living room. Each meal in the apartment, the wishbone dangled before his eyes. It was white and dry now, and every time Zeljka sat at the table she asked if they could break it, but Marge said no and kept it hanging there inexplicably.

Then, near the end of July, he received a phone call from Solomon DeWitt, who wanted to meet with him at his office. Daniel agreed reluctantly. He felt sorry for the DeWitts, but he didn't know any more than they did where their son had gone, and he wasn't interested in sharing his speculations as to why Rocket might have gone missing. The very thought of sitting alone in a room with Rocket's father made him nervous. It didn't help that the man was Dr. Fremlin's lawyer.

Solomon's office was cool and austere, with dark wood panelling and cream-coloured blinds that filtered the afternoon light. When Daniel entered, he almost believed that he'd find Rocket waiting inside, as though he'd been hiding here all this time, but there was only Rocket's father, who rose from behind a large, file-covered desk and offered his hand. As Daniel shook it, he realized his own palm was damp and cold.

"I would have called you sooner, but I hadn't heard you were back in town," Solomon said. "You know Richard has disappeared?" Daniel said he did, and Solomon motioned for him to sit down. "He left the day Stoddart Fremlin was arrested. My wife and I are distressed, Daniel. We want to know why he went."

As he sank into his chair, Daniel told him he hadn't seen Rocket for a year and a half.

"But surely you spoke to him while you were in England."

"No, I'm sorry. I didn't."

This was a lie, of course. They'd spoken the first day he was in Cambridge when Rocket had called to tell him about Alice. Rocket had said the police were asking the public for information, and he'd wanted to know what to do. Daniel had told him not to worry, not to say anything. She's just run off, he'd reassured him. Then why not talk to the police, Rocket had asked, and Daniel had replied that if the police heard about what had happened at the henge party it would only stir their suspicion. Then who knew where it would end? Alice had run off, that was all; there was no reason both of them should end up in jail until she came back. When Daniel hung up, though, he'd been less sure of himself. It didn't seem like Alice just to leave like that, no matter how upset she'd been. She was too fastidious a planner. But still, she'd talked about escaping, hadn't she?

Solomon DeWitt took a deep breath; Daniel wasn't giving him the answers he wanted.

"What about after the body was found and Stoddart Fremlin was arrested? He didn't contact you then?" Daniel shook his head, even as Solomon's voice rose in pitch. Finally the man sat back and closed his eyes. "You know I'm defending Stoddart, don't you?"

"Sure. It should be an easy case, right?" Daniel said, trying to sound casual. "There's no real evidence against him."

"Stoddart's a good man," Solomon replied. "He spent thousands of hours coaching Rocket and never took a penny from us. I'd testify on his behalf if I could. But people saw his car pick her up. He says he can't remember anything from the henge party. The fact that Alice worked for him before she took over his practice doesn't help."

"There's reasonable doubt, though, isn't there?"

"All I'm saying, Daniel, is you have to imagine yourself as a jury member. If you heard those details presented together as evidence, would you bother with reasonable doubt?" Solomon rested his hand heavily on the desk. "It was foolish of my son to leave when he did. Don't you see? It makes him look guilty too."

Then he leaned across his desk, and his voice dropped to a murmur.

"But you –" Solomon's finger was pointing at him. "You've come home. It's curious timing, isn't it?"

Sweat was collecting on the back of Daniel's neck. He wiped it away with his hand as casually as he could.

"It was time for a visit. I'd been away eighteen months."

"Yes, you had been," said Solomon. "That's quite a coincidence too." When Daniel didn't say anything, Solomon picked up a pen, examined it, set it down. Then he rested his elbows on the desk and rubbed his eyes. "Daniel, please, help me. You lived with Richard, you must know something. His coach is accused of killing a woman in this town. My son's vanished, and God knows why he left. What's going on in his mind?"

"Rocket didn't do anything," Daniel said, but it was a mistake to talk. Solomon's eyes were on him now, scrutinizing him without mercy.

"You were with him at the henge party. He told the police you went home together. Is that right?"

Daniel nodded. His mind was racing.

"Daniel," said Solomon. "If there's something you'd like to get off your chest, you can tell me. Nothing would leave this room. I swear it."

"I don't know what you mean," Daniel said. The light seemed to have dimmed, his head throbbed. "What do you expect me to say?"

Solomon stared at him gravely.

"Son, everyone knows about you and Alice Pederson."

Daniel felt his heart give an enormous thump, like a dead bird hitting the ground. He was ready to run out of the room.

"Look, Mr. DeWitt, I don't know why Rocket left. Maybe he's just gone on a road trip and hasn't told anyone. There's nothing more I can tell you. I'm sorry."

He stood and walked toward the door. When he turned, Solomon was still sitting behind the desk, watching his retreat. Neither of them said goodbye.

BY THE TIME Daniel had arrived at Cam Usher's field the night of the henge party, the festivities were already well underway. He'd come late, not wanting to be there during the opening ceremony and stand anonymously in a crowd while Alice accepted the community's applause for her part in building the henge. He preferred this time, when the revellers had been drinking for a while and were beginning to break off into clusters, when there was a better likelihood that two people could speak in private. He moved from group to group, looking for her.

The next day he'd be flying to England – for real, this time. He'd made up his mind that there was no point in delaying further and pretending any good would come of a life in Mooney's Dump. Alice wasn't reason enough to stay. The night he'd been summoned to her house had been a kind of ending for them, although he hadn't known it at the time. In the month since, she'd only been able to meet with him twice, and on the phone her voice had a discomfiting, harried detachment, as though she were speaking lines whispered to her by someone with a knife at her throat. She didn't even talk about the henge with enthusiasm any more, and she barely mentioned Usher. "What is it?" Daniel asked her repeatedly. "You can tell me." But she never did. Instead she insisted that he couldn't come over, that Mike and the children were home. "I don't care, I'll show up anyhow," he replied, but she only became more upset, and in the end he had to back down from his bravado. "Don't worry about me," she'd said the last time they talked. "I'm not worth it, really."

She felt guilty, he thought. The night she'd called him over, she'd been on the verge of giving her desires free rein for once and she'd frightened herself. It seemed obvious enough. But when he said this to her, she denied it. She claimed she wanted to be alone. Well, he'd leave her alone, then. He'd fly all the way to England, if that's what she preferred.

Everyone at the henge party seemed to know he was going, because most of them made some joke or another: *Don't forget your ticket this time. We won't let you come back if you do it again.* He'd heard such comments before, and he laughed humourlessly at this dredging up of the old humiliation, annoyed with Marge and Susan for having told people what had happened in September. The Yeobright Scholar knocked off his pedestal. Not even smart enough to remember his passport. He'd be glad to leave this town, and the sooner the better; there was no point being here for the holidays, sitting in Rocket's house by himself while Alice spent time with her family and went on ignoring him. He roamed around in a haze, drinking beer and making polite conversation.

Rocket was off on his own near the park fence, far away from the group of hockey players who sat around the fire, while children on snowshoes raced across the field, cheered on by parents holding torches. There was no sign of Alice, and he worried something had happened. After all her preparations for this night, she couldn't have stayed at home.

He'd looked everywhere except the farmhouse. At the foot of the stairs leading to Usher's veranda was a sign declaring the building off-limits to guests, but Daniel had seen people going in and out, so when midnight approached and Alice still hadn't appeared, he went in through a side door that led to the kitchen. The room was deserted, the house silent, and he was about to leave when he noticed clothes hanging from a line by the wood stove. A pair of jeans and a red sweater that looked like hers, and beside them a black bra, matching underwear. Something had happened. He passed through the room with a sense of urgency, then checked the whole of the ground floor before heading up the stairs.

He found her in Usher's bedroom. She was sprawled on the bed, the comforter bunched around her legs, her back exposed. Naked and asleep.

You're wrong, he told himself. You're wrong, you have to be. Don't jump to conclusions. There must be another reason for it. Weren't her clothes hung carefully on the line downstairs? Not scattered on the bedroom floor in a moment of passion. And there were hundreds of people milling about on the property; Alice would never be so brazen. Her clothing must have gotten wet somehow and needed to dry. Maybe she'd been feeling ill and had to lie down. It was a relief just to see she was safe, wasn't it?

He thought of her curled like that in her own bedroom, how it must feel for Mike to lie against her. Did she always sleep unclothed? Maybe not. Maybe this was something new for her, a thrill, exposing herself in someone else's house. The broad bed tempting her to crawl into it with nothing but her skin against the comforter, to lie there, vulnerable, listening to the voices of the partygoers below, wondering who might climb the stairs and discover her there. And now Daniel had been the one to do it. Surely it wasn't just a coincidence. This could be exactly what she'd planned.

He looked at the curve of her back, followed the slow, rhythmic, barely discernible movement of her shoulders as she breathed. She looked so beautiful. Inside him a nervous excitement was building. He shut the door to the room, found himself stepping toward her, quietly, until he was at the side of the bed. He slipped out of his coat, then his shirt and pants. There was no room for thought, only an instinct, determined and confident. He slid under the cover next to her, reached his arm around her waist. She was so warm.

Alice stirred against him. After a moment she turned her head and looked at him. Her body went rigid.

"What are you doing in here?" she cried.

"I thought –," he began, but he couldn't finish. His arm seemed to withdraw of its own accord. He could feel his heartbeat thudding frenetically in his chest, his legs, his fingertips.

"Are you crazy, coming in like this?"

She sat up, taking the covers with her, leaving him exposed in the cool air. He pulled his knees to his chest and tried to think of something he could tell her.

"I fell asleep," she said eventually, sounding calmer. "What time is it anyway?"

"It's almost midnight. Are you okay?"

"I'm all right, I just fainted and needed to rest. It's no big deal. Get up, Daniel. Get dressed."

"Jesus, I looked all over for you. I saw your clothes downstairs, and I got scared. Then when I saw you, I don't know, I didn't really –"

"Did you think I'd just forget that I'm married, that I was lying here exhausted, and make love to you?"

With her voice like that, there was no use trying to reason with her. Hastily he dressed and left the room.

He needed to find Rocket. He wanted a ride home. Once he'd reached the bottom of the veranda stairs he headed into the field, listened to the catcalls again as people saw him rushing through the snow. "Hey, did you lose your passport again?" He glared at them. The field was enormous, and he circled it without success, then walked down the lane and along the road almost a quarter-mile to the place where he and Rocket, arriving late, had been forced to park the pickup. The vehicle was still there, but Rocket was nowhere in sight. Exasperated, he went back to Usher's, unsure of what to do next.

As he passed the farmhouse, the veranda door swung open and Alice stepped out with Cam Usher beside her. She met Daniel's gaze, and after speaking a few words to the man she descended the stairs alone.

"Don't look so tragic," she said to Daniel when she reached him. The anger was back in her voice. His face burned.

"So how's Cam doing, anyway?" he said mordantly.

"Don't. Don't end things like this." She tilted her face away from him. He should have stopped then, but he felt too wounded.

"It's not my fault. I'm not the one who doesn't call, who doesn't –" But before he could finish she started down the lane toward the road. "Where are you going?" he called after her.

"I'm walking home."

"What? You can't do that. It's five miles." He'd gone too far. He had to fix things, quickly, before it was too late. "Wait, let me find Rocket and I'll give you a ride," he called out. She didn't turn around.

When she'd disappeared from sight, he searched the field again for Rocket, desperate for the keys to the pickup. Finally he checked the parking lot, still half-full of cars but deserted of people, and saw him standing on the far side with Stoddart Fremlin next to Fremlin's car. They looked as though they were arguing.

"– ignore me," he heard Fremlin say as they drew closer. "Gave you everything, Richie. Don't forget that." Then the man stumbled and collapsed into Rocket's arms. Rocket dragged Fremlin to the open door of the car and set him on the seat.

"Go on, lie down and sleep it off, you old bastard," he heard Rocket say. But his voice had more pity in it than malice.

"Everything all right?" Daniel called out as he drew near. Rocket started, then turned to face him.

"Christ, you scared me." Rocket looked embarrassed, as though he'd been caught out in something. After a moment he gestured to Fremlin. "He's drunk," he said with disdain. "I'm going to take him back to his place."

"Why not just leave him here?" Daniel said.

Fremlin was crying now, softly, and muttering to himself. He tried to lift himself from the seat, failed, then fell back onto the upholstery.

"I should," said Rocket. "But he'd probably freeze to death or something. Look, can you come along? If I drop you off at the pickup, you can follow me to Frem's place and give me a lift home."

"Fine," Daniel agreed. "But drive slowly. I'm looking for someone."

They started down the lane in Fremlin's car, the moon out in full and everything illuminated: the tops of the cedars, the ditch flowing with meltwater, the frozen, glistening bay. Once they reached the main road it wasn't more than a minute before they saw a solitary figure walking on the shoulder.

"There," Daniel said. "Pull over." He rolled down the window to call out to her. "Hey! You want a ride, lady?"

A bad joke. She didn't laugh. A car drove by them, then another. He could sense Rocket straining against his seat belt, trying to make out who was standing there.

"Hi, Dr. Pederson," Rocket said after a moment. "Are we going your way?"

"Hello, Rocket," she said. "That's very kind of you, but I'll be fine."

She set off again, following the path of the car's headlights, her legs lit up as though they were on fire.

"I'm going to walk with her," Daniel said to Rocket, and opened the door. "I'll swing by Dr. Fremlin's place to drive you home in a little while."

"Never mind then, I'd rather just walk home," Rocket replied. "It's not that far." He reached into his pocket, fished out the keys to the pickup, and handed them over. "You sure you two will be all right?" He sounded as though he finally understood something.

"I don't know," Daniel replied. "We'll see."

From the shoulder he watched the car pull away, then jogged to catch up with Alice. She'd stopped now and was gazing across the lake, her face wan in the moonlight.

"Look, I'm sorry," he said. "I wasn't going to try anything back there. I didn't mean to ruin things." If she took any satisfaction from the admission, she didn't show it. "But you've been hiding something from me. Ever since the night Mike and the kids walked in on us. If you're not sleeping with Cam –"

"Don't talk to me about Cam Usher. Don't talk to me about any of it. His stupid wildlife park, that damn henge . . ."

"Why are you so upset? What's wrong?"

"I need to get out of here," she said, looking toward the shore, toward the road, anywhere but at him. There was the distant slap of waves where the lake-ice met open water. It seemed as though she was about to start away from him again, and he reached out. After a few seconds she stepped closer and they held each other.

"Let's get away together," he said. "I'll take you someplace –"

"Where?" she said. "To England?"

That wasn't fair of her. She couldn't blame him for going. It was Alice who'd never leave her life. Already she was prying herself out of his arms, turning away from him, walking down the road again, back to her family. He watched as she paused for a moment.

"We never promised each other anything," she shouted, her face hidden. "Not once." Then she turned to look at him. "Take care of yourself, Daniel." She raised her hand briefly before continuing on into the night.

"You too," he called out, his voice flat. He thought of following her, but he'd already chased her once and he had nothing left to say, so he held up his hand and waved at her retreating form. All he wanted was to be on the plane, he decided. In England he'd do things. He'd keep himself busy and be successful and never need to think about Mooney's Dump again.

The truck wasn't much farther down the road in the direction Alice had gone. If he got in it, he'd have to pass by her on his way into town, and he wasn't ready for that just yet. He needed to drink more, to lose himself in the crowd, to forget what had happened and prove to himself that it wasn't important. He made his way back along the road toward the henge party. It wasn't until he'd almost reached the lane that he felt a wrench of regret, and he looked back for her. But there was only darkness; it seemed she'd been in a hurry to rid herself of him, after all.

The next day he left the country, and he'd barely arrived in Cambridge when Rocket called to say she'd disappeared. After that, Daniel began to see her everywhere he looked: running down Trumpington Street, punting on the river, leafing through children's books in Waterstone's. She could be anywhere, biding her time, waiting for a chance encounter with him. Never mind the past, she'd say. Let's be together. It didn't matter how implausible this scenario was; he cleaved to it easily, glad to let it fill his thoughts rather than face the worry and fear that lurked around the edges of his mind. Of course she'd just run off. Hadn't she told him at the roadside that she'd desired as much? *I need to get out of here.* She was only following through on what he'd been advocating for her all along.

Still, the thought of her gone from the town was disconcerting. In response he went compulsively to lectures, immersed himself in study and the order it offered, embracing the logical progression of arguments and facts in an attempt to block out thoughts of Mooney's Dump. He couldn't go back there now. During tutorials the other students terrified him with their intelligence, their articulacy, and he worked all the harder, knowing that he had to measure up, had to succeed and make a place for himself here, had to feel a sense of belonging if he was going to keep himself from wanting to go home.

IT WAS EARLY MORNING, well before dawn, and the lights of the Sunshine police station were blazing. Daniel stood outside the building, not quite ready to walk in. He'd been up late, sitting at the kitchen table, watching the wishbone slowly turn on its string in front of him while the radio played in the background, when there'd been a news bulletin that caught his attention: Stoddart Fremlin was on the run from the police. He'd just crashed his plane. The announcer didn't say why it had happened, whether the man was trying to flee the country or kill himself, but as Daniel had listened, he'd realized that either way it was his fault. He'd got up from the table, put on his coat, and reached for Marge's car keys on the hook next to the door. Then, just before he'd left, he'd cut down the wishbone with some scissors and thrown it unbroken into the kitchen trash.

Alice was to blame too, he decided. If not for her, Fremlin wouldn't have been charged with murder. Rocket wouldn't have fled town. And now Daniel wouldn't be standing here outside the police station, indecisive, nearly paralyzed. He'd been about to go inside and tell Harry Midgard how she wasn't really dead, how on the plane back from Cambridge the revelation had come to him: she could have swapped her own dental records with those of a dead patient. She could have planted the body in the lake somehow before she ran away. Ingenious, he'd told himself. But it was too ingenious by half. Harry would never believe him. He could imagine the derision on the man's face, and he saw how outlandish the story was. He didn't even believe it himself.

Well, he'd tell Harry about their relationship at least. He'd confess to being in the car with Rocket, to Fremlin being passed out behind them. Then his conscience would be appeased; there'd be nothing more to hide. It wouldn't be his fault any more. Whatever happened after that, it would be in someone else's hands.

The moment he stepped inside the building, he changed his mind, but the door had already swung shut behind him. He surveyed the room, expecting to find a dozen officers waiting to greet him, and instead there was no one in view, only desks and bulletin boards bathed in a ghoulish yellow glow. They must be searching for Stoddart Fremlin. He was saved.

Then a woman behind the counter shuffled some papers and caught his attention. She had blonde hair spilling from under her police cap, wide eyes with crow's feet, and a mouth that curled up at the edges as though she were smiling at some private joke. He took her in slowly, willing himself to speak.

"I – I just wanted directions," he said at last. "To the fairground. You know where that is?"

She looked at him a moment, and then her upturned mouth stretched into a smile.

"Directions to the fairground?" she said. "You don't need those. You're Daniel Barrie, aren't you? Harry said you'd show up."

"What are you talking about?" he whispered.

"I'm talking about that phone call you made," she said. "The one about Alice Pederson. Really, you should have worked harder on your accent."

His legs wouldn't move. When at last he began to start toward the exit, the woman's cruel, lilting voice brought him up short again, turned his lungs to steel, and even when Harry Midgard emerged from his office to coax him into taking a seat, he still couldn't quite take a proper breath.

"You know, we did the DNA test a long time ago," is what the woman had said. "Sorry, honey, but it turns out she's a goner after all."

TIGER'S EYE

She was the only listener who sat alone, pressing her face against the cool bars while the rest of them huddled close to the flames in the pit. They'd formed their circle out in the field, almost out of sight from the farmhouse but close enough to her cage that she could see and hear them. At first the fire had leapt hungrily from old planks and dead branches, drawing sweat out of skin, smoothing shadows from foreheads, but now that most of the fuel was consumed, it licked at its own ashes with a failing yellow tongue. The bodies of the audience had dimmed too, and were invisible but for the pinpricks of light in their eyes – reflections of flame that wriggled like glow worms in the distance.

They were telling stories. It was a common practice on these nights late in the summer. After dusk someone started the fire, as though to summon them, and soon they were passing through the long, brown grasses toward its light. They sat on benches they'd dragged from around the wildlife park, and although sometimes there were questions and protests, titters and teasing, for the most part they were rapt as each stood in turn to share a tale. There were long stretches in which the only movement she noticed besides the gesticulations of the tellers was the random, reflexive stab of hands at mosquitoes. Occasionally one of the listeners lost interest and turned from the fire to shine a flashlight into her eyes, laughing and calling her name, but she didn't move. She knew they were really afraid, worried that she might have escaped and crept toward them, and they were turning their lights on her to assuage their fear. From somewhere outside the circle came the bark of a predator, the scream of a tropical bird. The world around them was dark, inscrutable, and alive. Someone ran into the bushes and dashed back with more brush for the fire, squealing at the rake of imagined claws – hers, perhaps – across his back. The rest of them laughed and cheered his efforts.

Each storyteller unwound his tale from beneath a wooden mask. The one worn now was carved and painted to resemble the head of a gazelle, with long lashes that curled toward the muzzle, and two corkscrew antlers spiralling into the night. As the woman beneath the mask paced around the fire, she related the legend of a wife and her lover, and the ferryman who refused to carry one to the other, causing the death of both at the hands of the wife's jealous husband. It was a story without a single sympathetic character, the kind that made people shift uneasily on their benches. The narrative ended with a question: Who was most guilty? Each person was left to decide. The gazelle mask was raised, and for the briefest of moments the storyteller looked past the listeners, through the bars, and straight into Tamar's eyes.

No one stood to take the teller's place inside the circle; there was confused murmuring as to whose turn it was. Then a growl broke from the west – flimsy and contrived to her ears, but it caused some members of the audience to gasp. Out of the darkness crept a figure on all fours, his shoulder blades rolling. He wore a mask that was familiar to her. An orange brow, white fangs, black stripes, spaced as evenly as bars in a cage. Eyes like drills. The sinews of her heart twisted closer together at the sight.

"I am the Tiger," said the voice within the mask, and there was the clapping of hands. "For years now I have roamed the world, from my birthplace in the jungle to this parched and far-flung territory. I am one of the last of my kind, for we have tasted the flesh of Man, and he has avenged himself upon us so that now we are nearly extinguished from the earth." She watched as the figure rose slowly from hands and knees into a standing position and became more completely a human being.

"I was brought to this country by a man – a man who sought to help our cause by introducing our story to the people of his place. Here, with him, I have been given a safe home, hearty meals. But by night I escape the bars of my enclosure to prowl the dry tinder-box of the forests near your dwellings. Don't be afraid; I do not wish to consume you. I only seek to peer in your windows and discover more about your race. Of late it has become a dangerous preoccupation. There are some who have learned of my roaming and would hunt me for my skin." Loud hisses and boos from the audience greeted this comment; a sympathetic beam of light shone in her direction. The figure in the tiger mask waited for silence before he continued.

"That is a story for another night. In this hour of visitation I come to you with a different tale." The figure ignored the cedar stump upon which other storytellers had perched. Instead he moved around the fire with a slow, supple gait, as though an inexorable will and raw nerves lurked beneath the mask.

"The animals of this peninsula have their own myths, and often I have stalked them, not to kill, but only so that I might creep close enough to eavesdrop on their stories. If I had faith in my ability to do their tales justice, I would tell them to you, but they are better left to others. Many times I've tried to imitate their voices, and inevitably I only sound like myself. Because of this deficiency, I can never share my own stories with other animals, who fear me and would not stay to listen. Therefore I turn to you instead, with my Tiger face visible to all, so that you might hear my tale and repeat it to them, should any of them befriend you as Man has befriended me."

As he drew breath, there was a shifting on the benches, the adjustment of zippers. Tamar scratched out a place on the dry ground and laid down her head, ready to receive the story.

SHE HAD COME on a ship. At first she did not know it was a ship, because she was confined to a squalid cage in its belly, with a cake of newspapers underfoot to absorb her urine. The place was black and silent. She could hear and smell other animals, but they provided no solace; indeed, she almost went mad trying to escape their odour – the sickly sweetness of the boa constrictor, the family of koalas with one of the babies dead and rotting in its mother's pouch. Twice each day a man came to feed them, taking Tamar's head in his sweaty hands and squeezing milk down her throat until it came back up. Sometimes he cleaned her scat from the cage, sometimes he only wrinkled his nose and kicked her, shouting in his chirpy, incomprehensible language. She'd been constipated for the first part of the trip, and now he seemed to consider her feeble defecations an act of spite. It was exhaustion more than fear that kept her from defending herself.

Death was only a few days away when the captain's wife discovered her. The woman had the cages changed and the meals made regular. A vent was opened to bring in the salt air of the ocean, and each morning Tamar was put on a leash by the cheerful woman or a short-tempered sailor and taken for a walk along the deck. The sea smells were dizzying, with the occasional whiff of land blowing from this direction or that, and only the undulations of dark green water visible on the horizon. Home was lost, a remote assemblage of half-remembered scents. Already the human presence, so fearsome at the moment of her capture, had become ordinary, even comforting. The crewmen seemed to take pity on her; they offered smiles and stroking hands and, sometimes, against the objections of the captain's wife, strips of cured beef. It was too late for the koalas. They'd been taken from the ship's belly to be nursed into health, but one morning while Tamar was on deck she watched as their limp bodies were dragged from an open cage and thrown overboard. Tamar replaced them as occupant of the captain's quarters, and the wife seemed to take a special pleasure in coaxing Tamar to excrete in a box one of the sailors had constructed. She paced up and down the cabin, watching, until Tamar satisfied her hopes, and then she rewarded her with scraps of meat. Later, Tamar's habit of passing scat in a corner drew noises of praise from Cam when he first witnessed it. At that time she didn't know he was called Cam, hadn't yet heard the repeated utterances of his name by other humans, but she was already eager to please him, for after a month caged in a dark seaside building she'd entered his care and received generous meals, a home where movement was possible, if constrained. The new place was confusing. The sounds and smells of other animals filled the air, some of them familiar, others unidentifiable, and none ever visible. The meat he brought her was always fresh and rich, but where it came from was a mystery.

By the time Masa arrived at the wildlife park to take up residence with her, Tamar was well ensconced in her life with Cam and unprepared for sharing. She knew no other tigers save for the elusive phantom of her mother, which still slunk from tree to tree in the back of her mind, carrying the other cubs by their scruffs. There could have been no preparation for Masa. He was bigger than Tamar, the hair around his face longer and coarser. Until then she'd never considered her own appearance but had simply assumed that she must resemble Cam. She realized now that she'd been wrong. Her kinship was with Masa, who walked with an uneven gait, and whose left eye was framed by a bright pink scar the shape of a crescent moon. It was a hook on which he hung his indifference to her and every other living thing.

During the day the two of them were separate, as Tamar lazed before the visitors in a small, bare enclosure that was girded by a water-filled moat and a low metal fence adjacent to the field. At night Cam led her to a larger pen at the back where Masa always stayed. This one was distant from the paths of the wildlife park and surrounded by a dense wall of trees so that Masa was hidden from view. Despite his size, Masa deferred to Tamar in all things, and they kept mostly to themselves. Between the rock-pile and the old drainpipe was an invisible line, redolent of both their traces, which divided their territories. They crossed this boundary only for food or shelter – and not always for those. Even in the harshest weather, Masa preferred to sleep outside rather than share the thatched hut with her. At night they stared across the concrete ground at one another. She was mesmerized by the fierce red-yellow of his eyes, the dots and lines on his face.

Humans did things differently. Cam often appeared together with a brown-haired woman, and they didn't seem to fear each other's proximity. They kept close to one another, ill-prepared for self-defence, in a way that alarmed her. The woman offered herself to Tamar in the same manner, not seeming to realize there might be an impulse to break skin, snap bone. She draped her fragile body across Tamar's back or laid a hand under her chin. Tamar had saved the woman's life many times – saved it from her own lurking instincts, which were suppressed only with great difficulty. Sometimes it was nearly unbearable. During teeth-cleanings the woman would reach a hand inside her mouth and was kept from harm only by the metal rod that Cam lodged between Tamar's teeth. After these sessions, Masa kept an even greater distance from Tamar than usual, as though to emphasize his scorn at her surrender to human hands.

Masa's life expressed itself to her gradually, in the intimations of his movements, his mealtime habits, his reactions to Cam. She came to believe that when Masa was a cub he'd been kept by a man who trained him to fight. The crescent moon was only one of many scars on his body, the rewards of staged combat with dogs, bears, men. Masa had lived from battle to battle without any vision of another life, until Cam and a group of others took him away by stealth. When they came, Masa treated them as yet another wave in an endless succession of attackers, and he managed to tear flesh before they could slip a noose around his neck. He wasn't ashamed of this now, but proud to have fought so bravely. He refused to see their act as a liberation; instead it was only a transfer from a stronger to a weaker master. In the monotonous ease of life at the wildlife park he treated Cam with contempt, and Cam responded in kind; one of his own fingers had been taken in the guerrilla act, consumed in the furnace of Masa's body.

At first Masa growled whenever Cam was near. His teeth flashed, his body shrank and stiffened, ready to pounce, and Cam kept a careful distance between them. Then, one day after her shift in front of the visitors, Tamar returned to find the air laden with an acrid smell. Masa gave no indication of what had happened, but the fur on his back and around his head was singed, and he lay unmoving in his corner, his face hidden from her. She didn't cross the boundary. The next evening, after their meal, Cam entered the enclosure. He was armoured in heavy padding, and a metal wand rose from one gloved hand. Masa sprang to his feet. He began to pace in the corner as the gate closed, and Tamar sensed that she was about to witness something she did not want to see; something that had happened once before.

The wand seemed familiar to Masa; he kept it at a distance as best he could. Cam looked over to Tamar where she stood on her side of the pen and said a few reassuring words. It wasn't meal-time; it wasn't time to train. He told her to lie down. When he seemed satisfied that she wasn't going to approach, he turned his attention to Masa once more. The wand brushed against a tree stump. It crackled and smoked at the touch.

As Cam drew closer, she waited for Masa to strike, but he only cowered in the corner, tried to make himself dissolve into the cement wall. The wand moved outwards, reached toward him slowly, as though Cam were reluctant to touch him with it. When at last it nudged his neck, it did so tenderly, and another time she might have thought Cam was stroking him with it. But Masa jumped and yelped, so quickly and loudly that Tamar did too, and felt every hair on her body straighten with panic. The smell of burning hair returned.

The wand drew back. Cam's face, stoic and resolved, terrified her almost as much as the wand itself. It was only a stick, no matter what twitch and spark it had within it. With Cam's expression like that, though, anything might happen. She could be next. The muscles in her legs fired and sent her spinning in a circle as the wand began to creep forward again. Even as she turned, she followed its movements. This time Masa cried out before it even touched him. His eyes had rolled skywards, as though understanding this was the only direction of escape, as though he might will his body to float away. When the wand tapped him on his shoulder blade he flailed into the high cement wall, stretching flat against it for a split second and then falling like a rag to the ground, heaving and simpering.

Each time Cam drew close to Masa he touched him with the stick and Masa cried out. Cam seemed distraught now, as well, and Tamar began to bawl, but it didn't make a difference. Masa gave up his attempts at evasion and only flinched involuntarily each time the thing struck. There was a rhythm to the touches, so that if one came just a second too late, it caught him in the middle of the flinch and his cries doubled.

The next day it happened again, and for the next six days after that. On one occasion the woman was there, watching, and afterwards there were loud words between the two humans. Then, one evening, Cam entered the enclosure without the wand. Masa no longer growled but only cringed and kept to his corner. If there were still aggressiveness and self-possession within him, they'd been driven deep within his fear.

The woman never entered with a wand. Instead she spoke to Masa from the other side of the fence, coddling, praising and offering treats. She always failed to entice him, and Tamar could smell her disappointment. Afterwards the woman liked to move to a place near Tamar's side of the enclosure where they could be close, where she could trace circles in the fur between Tamar's ears. Sometimes they would lie together until the sun went down with only the bars between them, dozing, feeling the expansion and ebb of the other's lungs against the steel.

TAMAR HAD BEEN IN HEAT twice before Masa took up residence with her, and each time she'd spent days in agony, writhing and screaming with unfulfilled desire. The good fortune of his arrival became evident to her as her estrus approached again. He understood it too. When it came they were ready, and for the first time Masa crossed the territorial line boldly, without an invitation. But her whole body was an invitation – they could both smell her. It was the first time he'd been so close, his body heavier and more dangerous than she'd thought it before, his eyes desperate. As he circled her, she growled quietly and turned to keep her head toward him. She touched him first, her nose against his front leg, then all of her side against his. Finally he was behind her, his body pressing. Her neck tingled with a sense of exposure. When he finished, his paws closed on the skin of her neck and held it tightly. He gave a piercing, high-pitched cry. All of the impetus for union vanished, and her body tensed. She was dimly aware of a human presence on the periphery of the enclosure, the sound of whispers. When Masa withdrew from her, she hissed as though he'd been thieving a kill, and he had to be quick to avoid the swipe of her unsheathed claws. She paced, as though something were to be done, then collapsed in the morning heat and lay on her back.

It wasn't long before he appeared at the dividing line again, making impatient grunts. A lazy roll on to her front was all he needed to cross. There was an underlying confidence in his stride now, though he still moved cautiously, wary of her claws. This time they both made noises. Afterwards she napped and emerged from sleep with renewed desire. The woman and Cam were watching her from the other side of the bars, but she ignored them and trotted over to where Masa lay sprawled on the dusty ground. He started out of his doze when she mounted him. This wasn't what he expected. Tamar rocked forward, pressing herself into him, just as he had done. At first he didn't move, but then he rose, leaving Tamar to slide off him, and swung behind her in a swift arc. He forgot his prior caution and moved too close, so that when she cuffed him across the haunch he took her claws hard, yowled in surprise, and backed away. After a time he began to creep forward again, a supplicant. She let him nuzzle her, rub against her, until she sat on all fours. Slowly he slid over her, and her gaze moved beyond the enclosure, locked on the woman's face until it was over.

The border between her and Masa remained open like that for days before the estrus passed. Then, with no further sign than the smell of her body, the reverie ended. Masa made one tentative foray into her territory, but she hissed and showed her claws, and after that they returned to their mutual aloofness.

A few days later, Masa vanished. A tree fell across the fence during a storm, and its branches dangled far enough into the enclosure for him to scramble up them and escape. The next morning a group of men arrived at the park, meeting briefly before departing as quickly as they'd come. She knew they were there to search for him, but he returned of his own accord a few hours later, alive with smells: lilac, strawberry, the mud of creeks. The foreignness of his body, which had so recently been saturated by her own scent, dazzled and unnerved her. The new odours were known to her and suggested that Masa hadn't wandered far, but while once the smells had been distant and ephemeral, now they had a distressing vividness. He wore these smells proudly and didn't clean himself of them for days. Toward Tamar he directed unprecedented spite – the condescension of a wild thing to the tame.

His next chance came in winter. It was the quietest of the seasons, snowbound and bereft of visitors, when Tamar divided her time between the fragrant straw bed of her shelter and the paths she trod around the pen. In the daytime enclosure she paced the edge nearest the field, watching as Cam and the woman worked with others to place enormous stones upright with loud machines that groaned like elephants. Tamar waited anxiously for the sun to set, for the work to finish, for the woman to come and spend a few minutes with her, stroking and praising her through the bars of the night-enclosure while Masa made petulant movements in his corner. Each day there was more activity, until one morning vehicles seemed to go back and forth along the lane from the road without end. That day there was no sign of the woman, but at last after dark she visited for a short while, once Cam had fed them. When the woman departed in turn, Masa ambled to the gate and watched her go. It was then he discovered that Cam had forgotten to fasten the latch that night. Within minutes Masa was gone.

It never entered Tamar's mind to follow him. Neither of them was interested in the other's companionship, and with the woman's scent so close, with Tamar's stomach distended from eating, the world beyond the enclosure's walls was more an irrelevance than a temptation. Here were known borders, as snug as the captain's quarters on the ship long ago, with bulwarks against disorder. So she remained alone in the darkness, listening to the distant sounds of many human beings in the field. Then, just before Cam arrived with the morning's meat, she realized that Masa had come back. He lay near the open gate, his coat thickly matted with frost. When Cam saw him, he shouted angrily and marshalled him into his corner. For the next few days there were many more people around the wildlife park and in the field, as though to look for Masa, even though he had returned.

On one of those nights Cam entered the enclosure with familiar padding once more covering his body. The wand was in his hand, and he strode purposefully to the far side of the pen. Masa curled up immediately and would not move. When the yelps and screams began, Tamar hid inside her shelter and watched. She thought they were never going to stop. There was no hesitation on Cam's part this time, and he didn't relent with the smoking, crackling touch of the wand, not even when the air was poisoned by the stench of burnt hair and Masa's claws bled from their futile tearing at concrete. The next day, Cam went to work adding height to the fences and stringing wire along the top. He also began to examine Masa's scat with a stick. Sometimes, when he was finished, he sat by Tamar and stroked her head, weeping. But while once he'd spent hours playing with her each day, now she saw him only when he arrived to replenish food and water or to move her between the hidden pen and the public enclosure. As for the woman, she never appeared again.

MANY SEASONS LATER, when Masa's escape was only a vague memory, there was a period of drought. Although the water troughs were always full, the air was itchy and dry, and it fostered a restlessness in Tamar that she hadn't experienced before. She spent more time awake during the day, pacing the edges of the enclosure, eliciting the laughter and gasps of the people who came to watch her. The movement felt preparatory for an action she didn't comprehend, but one evening, when the visitors had gone home and she was waiting for Cam to transfer her back to the night enclosure with Masa, she realized what it was. There was no reason to hesitate: the moat around the enclosure hadn't been filled for weeks, and it was bone dry. From the place where she'd been sitting, she hopped into the moat, leapt up to the far side, then scaled the low fence. The looping path was next, the end of which she'd never before seen. After the aardvark, the bear, and the cockatoos, everything was new. When the row of cages ended, she lost herself in forest.

So this was freedom. This was what it meant to take many, many steps without a corner or a moat to block you. Here was the shade promised by the lush green leaves she'd only known as a distant waving mass; and all around, there were scents in full, seeping from their sources, not simply vapours clinging faintly to fur or clothing. Where the birds went, she could follow. It was clear to her now why Masa had been so willing to leave. She went deeper into forest, passing between giant jagged rocks, the moss on them thick and clogged with grey soil after the season's drought. She moved without bothering to disguise her presence, and familiar squirrels made unfamiliar noises, accustomed to teasing her from the top of the cement wall before fleeing into territory free of tigers, now outraged that the ground beneath them had suddenly become unsafe. There were the scents and sounds of other animals she'd never encountered before, but these creatures gave her a wide berth. Her old world was out of hearing distance and almost a dream. Even the sun seemed small and alien above the shimmering canopy of leaves.

Eventually she came to a tract of grass and low stones where there were human smells. She followed them to the summit of a hill, and the scents congregated in a place of disturbed earth, so she settled there to take the summer breeze on her face and look out over the islands crouched in the bay. Something about them was enticing – their isolation, their sure boundaries. Even this green area, with its stone walls and its ordered slabs, comforted her in its desire to contain space.

Feeling hunger, she had a compulsion to return to Cam, but then she saw that a murder of crows had settled on the grass below her. She stirred herself and crept toward the forest, remembering that she had stalked birds before. They were always gathering around the enclosure, hoping to pick at the bones left by her and Masa. Cam shouted at the things and threw pebbles at them, praising Tamar and even Masa on the occasions when they were able to pounce on a lazy one that lingered too long at a carcass. Now she wound her way through the trees until she was only a few strides away from the place where the crows were preening themselves. She was so intent on them that she barely registered the human presence. As she charged past the man, she balked for the slightest instant. There was something familiar about his smell. Then she saw the crows reacting, and she barely reached the last straggler with a claw. Tamar took it in her mouth and carried it quickly from the scene. She could never share a kill, not with Cam nor with Masa. But as she stole away, she remembered how she knew the man's scent. The woman had carried it, on her clothing and sometimes on her skin. Tamar crept onwards toward the hills with a pang of memory.

As she expected, the crow was poor eating. In obedience to her hunger she tracked other prey, but the animals in the forest were wary of predators and too quick for her. Chipmunks always seemed to have a hole nearby; skittish deer flashed their tails from a distance. In desperation she tried a porcupine, which showed no fear and only rolled into an indolent ball when she attacked it. For her effort she received a face full of quills, and she was reduced to humiliating whines as she retreated. She left urine traces to warn other tigers off her territory, but she felt a hollow certainty that none would ever arrive to smell them, just as she could detect no evidence of predecessors, not even Masa.

Despairing, she made her way home by following her own tracks, two days old and already faded. Then, at the edge of the wildlife park, before she'd decided to show herself to Cam, she perceived a human girl a few paces from the edge of the forest, and Tamar remembered what was imminent if she continued in the direction she was headed: the maddening, inaccessible odours of caged animals, the threat of Cam's wand, the path she'd worn along the fence in walking it without end. Perhaps she didn't want to go back quite so soon, after all.

Returning to the highlands above the bay, she travelled along the top of the escarpment toward the setting sun. Not a single cloud hung over the peninsula, and that night there were no lights except for a sliver of moon and the occasional eyes of a creature hurrying to get out of her way. By morning she'd reached a space of open fields, with wire fences that were easily scaled. She was tired and needed to sleep, but then she heard the lowing forms in the middle of the meadow before her.

No tiger could have been more clumsy in its stalking. She moved downwind and crept as best she could, knowing that she was obvious and in want of training. There'd been none as a cub except for scuffles with her brothers and sisters, barely memorable. But then, the cattle acted as though they'd never been hunted. And in the golden early-morning light, with the long, ragged grass of the meadow against her body, her fur felt less like a beacon than it had among the cedars in the forest.

The cattle were roused out of their docility only when open field lay between her and them, and she had no choice but to break into her charge. The alarm calls began to sound, and a mother bellowed for her calf. It was the young one that Tamar had targeted. With her legs churning under her, she caught it from behind. Fluidly, as though she had been practising, she took a hop-step-jump that sent her barrelling into the shoulder of the calf, and she knocked it to the ground with her momentum. Her front claws reached for the neck and strangled it as the creature bucked and kicked, while her back paws raked the stomach and wrestled for a purchase in the soft flesh. Under the pressure of her grip the calf's breathing was choked, the limbs failed, the wide single eye that watched her began to dull. When all motions stopped, Tamar sat up, alert to her surroundings. The rest of the cattle had moved across the meadow. They stood in a circle and watched her, troubled.

She felt a compulsion to drag the body away to a more secluded place, but the calf was no crow, and she wouldn't be able to scale a fence with the carcass in her mouth, so she ignored the indignant cries of the cattle and in full range of their vision began to eat. She tore open the body at the tail and pulled the hair from the haunches with her incisors, rubbing off the skin with her tongue. Once the flesh was exposed she pressed her face to the side of it and jerked upwards with her teeth. She proceeded like that along the length of the body, taking half an hour to dress it. When she was done, she ate, devouring the intestines, the kidneys, the heart and liver and lungs in turn, taking care to avoid tearing the rumen and releasing its foul contents.

She alternated gorging and lying on her side, idly watching the herd. They were hiding another calf that stayed near its mother at the back, but Tamar wasn't interested. When she finished, only the skeleton and the head were left.

The next few days were spent in an ambling, sated lethargy, meandering farther and farther away from home. Already the memory of Cam had been eclipsed by the preoccupations of stalking, watering, sleeping. There were other herds of cattle along the way, all of them helpless and stupid. It was too easy, and she ate with a sense of her life's new simplicity, its happy loneliness.

It ended too soon. She was preparing for the ambush of a calf in a field, far from the site of her first success, when there was an ear-splitting thunder, as loud as the one that had taken her mother years before. Her first instinct was to freeze. Then she looked in the direction from which the sound had come and saw a group of men walking toward her across the field, each carrying a rifle like the one Cam used to bring down crows. She made for the safety of the forest, reaching the trees at the same moment that farther thunder filled the air.

There was shouting from the field, the lunatic barking of dogs. Tamar bounded breathlessly through bushes, over rocks. Birds and smaller creatures scattered. This was new geography to her, and there was no design save to escape. If she'd been more careful, she might have anticipated that there were other men ahead of her. Instead she ran right among them, and suddenly she was surrounded by humans, the air frantic with their voices, their arms all in motion like the branches of saplings in a storm. It was Cam, she was sure, who brought her down. He alone was calm and still, with the rifle in his hand and his eyes upon her. There was no boom this time, only a stab of pain in her neck and then a deadness spreading from the wound. Before she fell asleep she heard his voice and felt his fingers on her forehead. She knew that in his eyes she'd be the same as Masa now. The next day when she awoke back in the enclosure she found no respect in Masa's eyes, either – no camaraderie with a fellow escapee, but only a well-practised posture of disdain.

THE MAN IN THE TIGER MASK still stood by the fire. It was down to embers once again, the audience nearly invisible, the fireflies in the field beyond them drifting like stars that had fallen from the heavens. On another night, as warm and still as this one, the modulations of his voice might have drawn her toward sleep, but now she listened, listened, as though it were the only thing left for her to do. When he finally fell silent and settled on the stump between the fire and his audience, the gesture seemed to peel away the first layer of a spell.

It was almost completely dark, but her eyesight was keen enough to perceive that the storyteller had taken off his mask. She had long ago recognized the voice and movements as those of Cam. Now she gazed upon his ruddy, smoke-streaked face. Flashlights were flaring into service; the people on the benches began to move away across the field in groups of two or three.

She'd understood virtually nothing of what Cam had said; she didn't speak his language. The only words she recognized were ones that had come to her over and over: her own name, as well as *crow*, and the double-syllable used about her by visitors to the wildlife park. *Tiger*. A short, easy word, as though there were a stubborn human tendency to make large things small. She'd tried to follow the course of Cam's tale, but in the absence of comprehension, all night she'd been telling her own story to herself alongside his. Now in her mind the two narrative were like vines, curled and knotted around each other until they were indistinguishable. But then, she liked to think that the tale he'd told was not so different from her own. They'd been together many years, and although they did not speak, there was a certain common space of understanding.

PLATO'S CAVE

For five hours he circled the peninsula, not quite prepared to end his life. He was hoping for some moment of revelation, a descending peace that would notify him when he was ready, but every time he pushed the wheel of the Cherokee forward to dip the wings, his hands began to shake and his eyes misted over. Long after the sun had set and he'd emptied the whisky bottle beside him in the cockpit, he still couldn't choose between crashing into the forest north of town and plunging into the lake. The idea came to him of a kamikaze dive toward the Sunshine police station, but he quickly pushed away the thought. He didn't really want Harry Midgard dead; he just didn't wish to live with the fear that someday the man might appear at his door with more questions. In the end he decided to land, write Richie a note, and leave it at the airfield for someone to find. Then he would take off again and jump out of the plane from a thousand feet, experience the sensation of unassisted flight, and let the aircraft go where it would. He was approaching the runway when he realized that in the course of his procrastination the fuel had run out. It seemed his decision was being made for him.

With the engines silent and the runway lights coming upon him fast, he found himself clutching the wheel, pulling back with all his strength, fighting to keep the wings stable. It was a surprise, a secret shame and pleasure, to find a will to live still thrashing within him. But the plane came in too steeply, the landing gear crumpled, and the propeller flew off like a popped cork. Breaking glass showered all around him. There was a screeching and sparking, and the terrible whine of the fuselage as it rocketed along the tarmac.

When he finally came to a stop, the first shock was that the plane had held together. The second was that he was still alive. The choice had been made after all, but it wasn't the one he'd expected.

He felt terribly light, as though he didn't even need to use his legs when he unstrapped himself and stepped out of the plane. But that was an illusion; they gave way upon contact with the ground and he fell. Fighting nausea on the dark, dry grass, he tried to think clearly. If anyone saw the crash they'd call the police. Surely under the conditions of his bail he wasn't allowed to fly, and he'd mortgaged the house to pay for his release. They'd take his home from him now; they'd put him back in prison. It was late, the airfield deserted. Perhaps no one had noticed. He began to slide around the meadow on his belly, gathering up pieces of the plane. The lightness had reached his head, keeping his own actions a cloudy distance from him, and it took Bronwen Ferry's hand on his shoulder to return him to a world beyond the grass. Then he realized it would be more sensible to flee. When she went to greet an approaching car, he got to his feet and made his way clumsily across the meadow, hampered by the soreness in his arms and legs. On the far side there was a wire fence to climb and a concession road beyond.

"Where the hell am I heading?" he muttered as he began to walk in the direction of Sunshine. A voice in his head answered confidently: he was going to Esther's, to hide there. He needed time to rest and collect himself.

The route from the airfield to the place where she lived was three miles long, mostly downhill but far too exposed for his comfort. Anxiously he walked along the ditch, his heart galloping, his eyes alert for headlights drawing near. The voice in his head sang in time with the painful rhythm of his legs – gloating, over and over: *You are alive, you are alive, you are alive.* The thought was amazing and perverse. Perhaps he'd been wrong to want death. The crash could have been a sign – to live, to carry on. He hadn't been to church for fifteen years, not since hockey tournaments had begun to occupy his Sundays, and in all that time God had been absent from his life. Now it seemed as though a voice had spoken. Why not believe it was a divine hand that had guided the plane on its final descent, sheltering him from flame and carnage? No other explanation seemed more plausible. It had been a miracle. Perhaps that same hand was urging him to Esther now.

The driveway was empty when he got there, the windows dark. Of course. Someone would have called her about the crash. She'd be out among the searchers and might not return for hours. He went to the side of the house and lay on his back beneath a hedge, listening to each car that drove by on Manitou Street, trying to guess which one would bring her. The passing of the motors, the starry sky, and his exhaustion from the journey lulled him into sleep and fretful dreams of being hunted, until he was awakened by the sound of an engine dying in the driveway.

It was both of them, her and the idiot boyfriend. Stoddart watched them disappear into the house and considered how he might speak with her alone. The boyfriend couldn't be trusted to stay quiet. For that matter, it wasn't certain that Esther could be trusted either.

A window at the back of the house allowed him to see into the dimly lit living room. They were quarrelling about something. The boyfriend stayed several paces from her, hands on hips, until eventually he walked out of the room and a door slammed. Stoddart went around the house to the front window and peered in. Esther was laid out across an old, shaggy sofa now, smoking a cigarette.

He tapped on the glass, so gently that at first he couldn't even hear the sound himself. When he knocked with greater force, she noticed the noise and came to investigate slowly, cautiously, then ran to the door.

"Jesus. How the hell did you get here? We were just at the airfield –"

He put his fingers to his lips. "I need to stay with you tonight."

She shook her head, grimacing, and closed the door between them. He listened to her move deeper into the house, and then a few seconds later she returned.

"Stump's asleep," she said. "Come inside."

So this was where she lived. A tiny living room that doubled as the dining area, with the table he'd given her for the old apartment almost touching the sofa. The kitchen was adjoining, and a stack of dirty dishes had been left in the sink. None of the plates or mugs matched. When he stopped staring and faced her, he discovered she'd been inspecting him in turn. Other than the soreness in his limbs, there was only the heat of a bruise on his forehead.

"I'm fine, really," he said. "I'm not hurt."

"You've been drinking," she said. "Drinking in the plane – what were you trying to do? I saw Harry Midgard at the airfield. He says you've broken bail by flying. The police are searching for you."

"I need to stay here," he said.

She shook her head. "They'll come looking."

"Just one night."

They argued in whispers. Finally she relented and said he could sleep in the cellar, where he wouldn't be seen when Stump left in a few hours to open his store. Then she led him down the hallway.

"You shouldn't be hiding," she said as they went. "It makes you look guilty."

"They think I'm guilty already," he replied. "You probably do too." She opened her mouth as though to protest, but she didn't say anything. "Or else why did you stop coming to visit me in jail?"

"I've . . . been busy," she said. "Besides, don't pretend you missed me." Her voice became hard. "The way you were talking before, it sounded like you were just waiting for Rocket to show up and rescue you, anyhow. Well, where is he now? They're saying he ran away as soon as you were arrested."

He stood at the top of the basement stairs and watched her go down. The same old Esther. She'd always been jealous of Richie and the attention he'd received, didn't understand how special the boy was, how seldom such a talent came along. Well, she had nothing to envy any more. She was right: Richie had abandoned him. This latest disappearance was only part of it; for the last three years the boy had refused even to answer Stoddart's phone calls. If Richie appeared now, chances were it wouldn't be to help; instead he'd be making accusations, giving testimony against him.

Stoddart wanted to tell Esther how close he'd come tonight to ending things. Perhaps she'd already guessed; perhaps Harry Midgard had raised the possibility with her himself. To make her understand, that was the difficult part. The only way would be to tell her about Richie, and the very thought filled him with horror. He'd made the wrong decision to come here. He wasn't looking for her help. It was forgiveness he wanted – but not from her. No, not from her at all, if he was honest with himself.

In a rush of panic, he started to breathe harder. By the time he reached the bottom of the basement stairs there was an iron band around his chest, squeezing the life out of him.

"What's wrong?" said Esther's voice. He lay back against the steps, pressing his hand over his heart. He couldn't detect a beat. Was that possible? Could you feel your own death? Esther was leaning over him, loosening his collar. The basement was bright and dark by turns as though an electrical storm were passing through. Ah, he thought. Here it is. After the failure of nerve in the plane, the futile procrastination, and God's jesting, momentary reprieve, the old sod was calling him to order after all.

A second later he felt a thump, sickening and strong. For the second time that day there was exhilaration coupled with despair. His hand rose to cover Esther's mouth.

"Don't scream," he said. "It was just a dizzy spell."

"You were so white –"

"I'm fine. Look." He stood up, not knowing any more than she did what would happen, but it turned out to be true. He was fine. He was immortal after all. Perhaps death was always to be just beyond his grasp. Struck by the sudden conviction that Esther could see these thoughts in him, he turned his eyes to the basement. It was nothing more than grey walls and a ceiling of pink insulation bulging from between the beams.

"No mattress down here," she said, taking some sheets from the ironing board in the corner and laying them on the floor. "The sofa upstairs –"

He shook his head. It would be too great a chance.

"I don't understand why you're doing this," she said. "You said there was nothing to worry about. No evidence, no motive." She walked by him to the stairs and started up them. "You've got no chance now. Not unless you go to Harry right away, tell him some story . . ."

She was going to betray him, he thought. As soon as she was out of sight she'd pick up the telephone, call Harry Midgard herself.

"Esther, wait," he said. There was more urgency in his voice than he intended, and she stopped in midstep.

"I didn't kill Alice," he said.

She stared at him as though she didn't comprehend this information, as though he'd said it in some foreign language.

"But people think you did," she said. "Haven't you seen the newspaper lately?"

"Yes," he murmured. "But you, at least –"

Esther didn't speak.

"You're a thankless child," he said grimly. "And I'm a weak, despised old man, isn't that right? Well, grant me one request, at least. There's something I need to say to Richie. If you know where he is –"

"Damn it, we're not talking about Rocket," said Esther. "Besides, I don't know where he's gone. Why are you so desperate to see him?"

"It doesn't concern you," he said sharply. He knew that Esther always thought it concerned her, though, whenever Richie was involved. She thought his relationship to her father was meant as a judgment of her. She didn't understand that it had never been about her at all.

"You don't have any idea, do you?" she said. "You think I haven't heard people talk? You think that with you in jail and Rocket disappearing right after you were arrested, no one's said anything about you two spending so much time together all those years?"

His skin prickled.

"What have they been saying?" he asked, trying not to reveal his alarm.

"You honestly haven't heard?"

He shook his head. She hadn't answered his question, he thought, but he was glad.

"Maybe that's why they want to lock me up then," he said. "So they can punish me for – for whatever they think I've done." He was thinking of change rooms, years of them. The smell of old sweat in hockey equipment, the steam from the showers. The boys cursing and telling jokes.

"It's not true, what people are saying. Is it, Dad?"

Her question brought him back to the present. So she'd asked, after all. For years he'd wondered how he would react to such a moment.

"I don't know what they're saying," he replied. "How can I tell you whether it's true or not?"

"God damn it," she said. "I knew it was true." Then she leaned over the staircase railing as though there were a physical object lodged inside her that she was struggling to disgorge. When she finally raised her head and spoke, he almost couldn't hear the words.

"I've been thinking about something," she said. "You remember the time we went to the reserve with Rocket and Daniel? We were going to find morels."

"Yes."

"You said you wanted Rocket and me to go off together."

"Did I?"

"I always thought it was because you wanted me and him to spend time together. But it wasn't for us, was it? You were thinking of him and you. You were trying to stop yourself, for once." She didn't say it accusingly; instead her voice seemed filled with pity.

"Don't feel sorry for me," he said.

Esther had lifted herself from the railing and stood straight up.

"I wasn't feeling sorry for you, Dad. I was feeling sorry for Rocket."

"Esther –"

But she was already running up the stairs.

THE FIRST DAY that Richie practised with the peewee team, Stoddart understood at last why he'd volunteered to coach hockey. Until then his own motivations had been obscure to him, a crude, cobbled-together psychological gloss about filling the gap left by Judith's departure, about needing to escape Esther's scrutiny at the house. These reasons seemed valid enough, but they never quite explained to him the pleasure he took from coaching a group of unfamiliar boys in a sport he'd never played, the rules of which he hadn't even known at first. Then he saw Richie's lithe body wheeling and darting, and, afterwards in the change room, the tanned shoulders and silky black hair. Suddenly it made sense; all other justifications became hollow and false. At eleven years old, Richie was almost a head higher than the rest of them, but not spindly like most tall boys. The muscles in his back twitched and subsided with the smooth grace of an ocean wave. On ice he was unstoppable. He skated faster, shot more powerfully, and body-checked harder than anyone else. In the change room he was cheerful enough, but too introverted to be a natural leader. Already the other players had begun to notice. In a few years, if he didn't change, if he didn't swear like them and go to parties and brag about blow jobs, they would pounce. But for now, that beautiful, angular body and the feats it could accomplish were enough to garner their respect. By the end of the season the boy had scored more than a hundred goals and won the team half a dozen cups in tournaments. His teammates were the ones to give him the nickname Rocket. Stoddart never called him that; it was too childish.

After the last game in March he decided that the boy needed further, private coaching. Assiduously he went over the possible concerns in his mind. Some parents would say it was unfair, but there was no denying Richie's talent or the need to nurture it. The extra ice time would be expensive, but Solomon DeWitt was a lawyer; he could afford the cost. With a frightening ease, Stoddart found an answer to every objection. When at last he approached the boy's parents, they nodded and smiled all the time he spoke. They'd always been worried by Richie's lack of confidence and were ecstatic at his success in sports, ambitious on his behalf. They called Stoddart a miracle worker.

He began to drive Richie to the rink three times a week, spending an hour with him on the ice and then in the change room, scrawling positions and tactics on the blackboard while the boy undressed. He tried not to anticipate the moment when Richie would walk to the shower with a towel wrapped around him, his hand clutching the place where the corners met. At night Stoddart meditated on that fist, wondering what kind of reticence it might suggest. He writhed and tangled himself in his bedsheets, certain he was insane. If the boy had any kind of affection for him, it was that of an athlete for a coach, nothing more. They shouldn't be spending so much time together on their own. People would notice. No, he didn't want it. He'd refuse to coach the team next season. He'd make himself stop thinking about Richie DeWitt.

But it was useless. The boy had too many charms. The way he flung himself into corners after pucks. His guilty smile after a goal, betraying a desperate effort to remain humble, to stay ordinary despite the delight of his gift. The joyful shock so evident on his face, as though his talent were a real, physical thing, a box he had just opened for the first time.

One day that spring, Stoddart asked him if he'd like to see something special. Richie looked sceptical. A solution cave on the reserve, explained Stoddart. What's a solution cave? Richie asked, and Stoddart told him he'd have to come and find out. It was the only one of its kind along the entire cave-pocked length of the peninsula's escarpment, and practically unknown: there were no campfire rings, no walls covered in graffiti. They could drive up on Monday, a school holiday. Stoddart had arranged to take the day off from the clinic. Richie said he'd check with his parents.

"You've never been to this cave before, right?" Stoddart asked him when Richie confirmed he could go.

Richie shook his head. "How could I? You just told me about it."

"I thought, since it's on the reserve –"

"We hardly ever drive there," said Rocket. "Only to visit my grandparents."

Stoddart smiled. He was glad the cave would be something new.

The morning they set out was warm and sunny, with only a thin strip of dark cloud to the south. Ruth DeWitt waved goodbye to them from the living-room window and Richie waved back to his mother, while silently Stoddart denounced the woman for her foolishness. He'd never let Esther go away by herself with a virtual stranger. And where was the father? Solomon DeWitt seemed too busy practising law to know what was going on in his own son's life. When did he ever take Richie fishing or play baseball with him? It was no wonder that Stoddart had felt drawn to Richie from the first; he was needed.

It wasn't true, though. He knew that. Ruth DeWitt was no fool, and Solomon DeWitt did spend time with his son, despite the workload. Perhaps not fishing and playing baseball, but talking, at least, and reading with him. Richie always seemed to have finished another book.

He looked over at the boy, who was staring out the window, and had a stirring of envy for Solomon DeWitt. The man didn't know what he possessed.

"Esther wanted to come too, but she's at a friend's house," Stoddart said. Richie nodded indifferently, and Stoddart wondered why he'd felt compelled to make such a remark. He hadn't even mentioned the trip to Esther.

As he drove, he talked about all the training he and Richie would do together before the hockey season, hoping to spark the boy's enthusiasm, but Richie only sat leaning against the door, responding to questions with one-word answers in a flat, passive voice. He doesn't want to be here, Stoddart thought despondently. When they arrived at the reserve, he pulled into the general store and with a show of counterfeit high spirits asked Richie if he'd like to go in for a treat. To Stoddart's relief the boy grinned and nodded.

Once they were inside, it felt like a mistake. He could sense the eyes of the young woman at the till on them, the disapproval of the man near the ice-cream freezer. A white man and a native boy, they were thinking. He tried not to look at them and browsed the aisles instead, the shelves close together, stocked full in anticipation of the tourist season: hamburger buns, fireworks, pickles, orange candles shaped like Indian maidens. Richie drifted toward the fridges at the back, past the staring man. Stoddart could barely breathe.

"That's a fine-looking boy," said the woman at the till, smiling, and he nodded. Richie had the bright, sharp eyes of his mother, her elegant neck. The cheekbones and nose were from his father, prominent enough to signal – to those who were concerned with such things, at least – where his ancestry lay.

"Is he your son?" asked the woman. Her face gave no hint of the intention behind the question. Despite himself, he nodded slowly.

"Yes, I suppose he is."

The man near the ice-cream freezer started toward him, glowering.

"That isn't his son," he said to the woman at the till. "That's Solomon DeWitt's boy."

"Of course he is," said Stoddart quickly. "We're just visiting the place together. Solomon has to work." He sounded like an idiot. The man was standing right beside him now, too close, his eyes even with Stoddart's and his broad chest taking in air like a bellows, as though he were drawing it out of Stoddart's very mouth.

"Why are you saying he's your son, then?" the man muttered. He leaned past Stoddart to set a tub of frozen yogourt on the counter.

"Son? What I meant was – I thought you were asking if he was with me. If he was my boy. Not my son. I'm his hockey coach. We're just visiting."

But the man didn't seem interested any more. The woman's smile had vanished. The man uttered a few unintelligible words to her, all soft consonants and closely guarded vowels – Ojibwa, it must be – and she replied tersely in the same language. Stoddart told Richie to hurry up and choose his treat.

In the car Richie sat in silence, sipping ginger ale through a straw.

"Why did you pretend I was your son?" he asked after a time. Stoddart was surprised – he thought Richie hadn't heard – but by then he'd been thinking about the encounter in the store long enough to have a ready answer.

"I thought she said 'boy,'" he replied. It didn't sound any more likely the second time. "I think of everybody on the team as my boys. Why? Did it bother you that I said yes?" He let a teasing note slip into his voice. "Wouldn't I make a good father?"

Richie looked at him for a second as though measuring him out for a suit. He reached over and gently brushed off a small twig that had been clinging to Stoddart's sleeve.

"You'd be all right," he said. He withdrew his hand and went back to sipping his ginger ale.

For a long time afterwards, Stoddart's arm continued to tingle. It was as though his cotton shirt didn't even cover him and Richie had placed his palm directly on skin. It had been a gentle, light touch – because Richie was trapped within his seat belt and couldn't reach very far, perhaps. Or maybe he was being tender. Stoddart felt his throat constrict. It was wrong to ascribe such things to the boy. Completely wrong.

He drove until they came to a shore road that terminated several miles later at a trailhead. When they were parked, Richie pulled on the windbreaker his mother had handed him at the door, while Stoddart retrieved a pack and a checkered hunter's jacket from the back seat. To arrive at the solution cave they had to hike the Devil's Backbone, a difficult trail over a series of ridges, once upon a time a coral reef, now limestone covered in moss and stunted cedars with white blazes periodically to mark the way. Stoddart had travelled the route many times and knew the location of dozens of fossils embedded in the rock – shellfish and other invertebrates from times of flood and inland seas – but today he had no interest in stopping. He walked briskly, breathing in short, shallow gulps, and Richie struggled to keep up.

"We still have a long way to go before the cave," Stoddart said sternly when Richie stopped to examine a jack-in-the-pulpit he'd spotted beside the trail. "I told your mother we'd be back by three."

"I thought you said it wasn't much farther."

"It's not if we get moving."

"I don't even care about the cave, you know. I'd rather look for things around here."

Stoddart reached over and pulled at Richie's windbreaker.

"We can stop on the way back if there's time. How about that? Come on, let's go."

The solution cave wasn't on most maps. Only a few that he'd seen showed a single dot and the words in small print: *Plato's Cave*. That kind of name wasn't unusual on the peninsula. Apparently the area's early cartographers had been well read, because the local topography included places such as Treasure Island, Birnam Wood, River Styx. These names were repeated by most residents of Mooney's Dump without any awareness of their literary origins, a fact that Judith had loved to point out when she took to mocking the place, before it got to be too much for her.

Judith had been the one to show him Plato's Cave. It lay at the end of a path that branched from the main trail, the fork marked only by a single slash of orange paint on the side of a tree. Most hikers were busy following the white blazes and walked right by it. On a weekday like this one, before the beginning of summer, the cave was almost sure to be deserted.

He told Richie what to look for. When they came to the place where Stoddart expected to find the tree with the orange marker, though, there was nothing to be seen.

"Maybe the tree was knocked down," Richie said. "Maybe the paint wore off." Stoddart grunted. If that was the case, there'd be no hope for them. There were dozens of side-trails to inspect, most of them dead-ending at the escarpment face, high above Georgian Bay. It could take hours. Then he let the thought slide away. For weeks he'd been anticipating this trip. It didn't matter what time they were supposed to return. They'd find it even if they ended up searching until dark, sleeping in the forest, huddled together for warmth. He didn't care.

After a few minutes he heard Richie's footsteps fall off behind him.

"I don't want to go any farther," said the boy. "I'm tired, Frem."

He felt a flutter of alarm. No, they couldn't stop now. He couldn't say why, exactly, but they had to reach the cave.

"Look, this is good training for hockey," he said. "Imagine you're in the third period. Your legs are tired, you're down by two goals. You going to be a quitter?" He gave a little laugh.

"I'm not a quitter," said Richie fiercely.

"All right then."

Ahead, through the dark woods, he thought he saw something move – a slim, tall shape that was radiant and white. A moment later another joined it, then another, until all at once the cedar branches on either side of him had been replaced by something else: a stand of birches, stunted by the rocky ground and not much more than head-height, their branches still bare from a long, cold winter. The trail passed directly through the centre of the grove, and the trees stretched gnarled fingers across the path like hungry, pale phantoms straining from the gates of a cemetery. For the first time, the thoughts in Stoddart's head stopped their hurly-burly and he became aware of the stillness all around them. There were so few noises that he could identify each one in turn: the scuff of Richie's shoe on rock, a chickadee singing, his own heart. As they passed through the grove, they came upon a place where the path diverged, and at the centre of the fork was a single birch with a large orange eye staring from its trunk. The blaze he had been looking for. Of course. How could he have forgotten the birches? That was why the paint was orange here. It had paled during the years but still stood out in strong contrast with the bone-white bark. The cave was close now, and he had to focus on the ground, the trees, the morning sun – anything to avoid thinking ahead and losing his calm.

From the fork, the path to the cave ran directly to the edge of the escarpment, then dropped through a diagonal cleft in the rock. The way was steep, and long ago someone had tied a thick brown rope from a tree at the top to aid with the descent. Stoddart insisted on going down first.

"If the rope holds me, it will hold you," he explained. "And I can help you better from the bottom."

"I can do it on my own," countered the boy, who hadn't uttered a word since his last complaint. "I'm not scared."

"Nobody said you were," he said. "Just wait."

The rock was slick from the last night's rain and there was nowhere for his boots to gain a purchase. He had to trust his hands as they slid down from knot to knot. When he reached the bottom, he shouted up for Richie to follow slowly, but the boy was too confident. He wasn't even going to use the rope until Stoddart yelled at him to grab it. Even then, Richie held the thing perfunctorily and continued on his way. He was laughing when he caught his toe on an exposed root and went twisting through the air.

There was no time to react, beyond a wild, futile groping toward empty space. Then the boy struck him on the chest, knocking him off his feet. The ground below the cleft was soft with mud and pine needles. A single rock jabbed into his right buttock and left it in spasm underneath him.

The boy's back pressed into him as they lay there. From somewhere behind them came the sound of gurgling water.

"Sure, you don't need my help," said Stoddart once he'd caught his breath. He waited for a response, began to panic when none came.

"Thanks, Frem," Richie said at last. A leg twitched; the boy's body heaved within his arms. They stood up and brushed themselves off.

"You all right?" he asked. Richie nodded, still stunned. "Hey, give me a hug." Stoddart put his arms around him, felt Richie go tense. That was to be expected, he thought. At that age they were embarrassed about showing affection.

"Hey, look over there," said Richie, and tore free from the embrace. He'd seen the mouth of the cave. It was a few steps away, barely tall enough for a man to pass through without ducking, and round as though a giant fist had punched the cliff. Richie hadn't learned his lesson: he ran over the rocks without pause before poking his head in.

"Most of the caves around here were made when the lake was higher and bashed at the cliff-face," explained Stoddart, following. "But this one's been formed by an underground stream." He pointed to the trickle of water that ran past their feet. "It runs under half the peninsula before surfacing here. Then it dissolves the rock, turns it into a solution, and carries it away. That's why it's called a solution cave."

"I know that already," replied Richie matter-of-factly. "I looked it up." Stoddart felt annoyed and proud at the same time. Richie was a clever boy.

With the heat of hiking, Stoddart had tied his jacket around his waist, but it was cool inside the cave, which faced north and didn't catch the sun. He stayed at the entrance and let Richie explore on his own for a while, knowing that the cave wasn't much larger than the examining rooms in his office and that the boy couldn't get lost. When he entered, it was just as he remembered it. The soothing drip-drip from hidden places, the play of light across stone. And now a trace of Richie's warmth in the air, even from here, providing a hint of life. Standing there was like returning to a once-familiar dream that had not been dreamed for months. Almost light-headed with the joy of it, Stoddart retrieved his flashlight from his pack and called Richie over. He pointed out stalactites dangling from the ceiling, the place where the underground stream emerged. It fed a small pool that dominated the cave floor near the back, the water so clear that his flashlight's beam cut straight down to the smooth rock bottom. A school of minnows shimmered through the light like a ribbon and was gone.

"How deep do you think it is?" asked Richie.

"High as your head. Cold, too." Richie crouched to put a hand in the water. Stoddart laid a few fingers lightly on the boy's hair. They fell off when Richie stood up again.

"It's freezing!" Richie exclaimed.

"I'll bet you wouldn't swim in it," said Stoddart.

"Sure I would. How much you betting?"

Stoddart looked him in the eye.

"Fifty dollars."

"Fifty? You're kidding, right?"

Stoddart shook his head.

"I don't even have fifty dollars," said Richie.

"You will if you take the bet." He said it nonchalantly, as though he made such wagers every day.

Richie wanted to know how long he had to stay in.

"Just as long as it takes to go all the way under," Stoddart replied. He rummaged through his pack. "Look, I even have a towel."

"Except I didn't bring a swimsuit," said Richie.

"You don't need one," said Stoddart. "There aren't any girls around, are there?"

"What if somebody comes?" Richie looked apprehensively toward the cave mouth.

"Don't be a sissy," said Stoddart, and Richie made a face. Stoddart had said that to other boys in the change room between periods at hockey games, urging them to go into the corners, hit more, hit back. He'd never said it to Richie.

The boy started to take off his clothes, and Stoddart made motions of rifling through his pack again.

"Did you hear that?" said Richie as he was unzipping his jeans. They both stood still. There was the passage of the stream, a breeze in the treetops, the distant slap of Georgian Bay on rock.

"It wasn't anything," said Stoddart. "You're imagining things."

Richie stripped down to his white underwear. He noticed Stoddart looking at him.

"I'm not taking these off," he said.

Stoddart knew that underwear was a sticking point for the boy. After games and practices Rocket was always the last one on the team to shower. He was probably shy.

"Doesn't matter to me," Stoddart said. "You'll be cold later, though."

Looking unhappy, Richie hooked his thumbs under the elastic of his underwear and slid them down. He tried to step out, but they caught around his ankles and he almost fell over. "You want help?" Stoddart asked, his voice striving for sarcasm but cracking despite itself. His lungs had turned to solid blocks, his hands were clammy, as though it was he who was jumping into the cave's dark waters. Richie extricated himself from the underwear and crouched low at the side of the pool.

"It really is freezing," he said. He glanced back at Stoddart, and then there was a splash and a shriek. He was in up to his waist; a second later he'd immersed himself. He came back up with another scream and immediately began to scramble out of the pool. The cave was filled with the soft kisses of his feet on rock as he ran to where Stoddart stood holding the towel open, waiting to fold the fabric and his arms around him.

"That's my boy," whispered Stoddart, rubbing Richie's back vigorously. Once in a while one of his hands slipped farther down. With the other he pressed Richie's face into his chest. "There, there," he said, grasping one of the boy's hands and pulling it to him. "There, there." Richie's body didn't move.

"Now look at that," Stoddart said eventually. "There's nothing to be ashamed of."

A FEW MINUTES LATER it was Stoddart who thought he heard something. He paused, heard it again. Unmistakable: a female voice, the clatter of stones outside. Richie still hadn't moved, but now without a word he began to dress. At the last moment, the boy bent toward the pool and took water in his cupped hands. He splashed it on the ground near Stoddart's feet and wiped and wiped his fingers against the stone.

Stoddart had just slipped on his pack when a shadow enveloped him. A woman with curly grey hair and a green hiking suit was standing in the mouth of the cave.

"Why hello!" she said, then turned back toward the cleft in the escarpment. "Bill, there are people down here." A man appeared a few seconds later, in identical attire except for his baseball cap.

"Good afternoon," the man said. "I suppose that was your car we saw in the parking lot at the north end?" Stoddart nodded. "We wondered why there weren't any spiderwebs across the trail at this time of morning. You're the first ones we've seen today. We're with the trail association, repainting the blazes."

"Great day for it," said Stoddart, smiling. He looked back at the boy. "Come on, Richie, we should get going." Then he gave a small, theatrical bow to the man and woman. "We'll give you some privacy."

"It's a neat little cave, isn't it?" said the man. Stoddart nodded, while Richie managed to escape into the sunshine and out of view.

The man spoke again before Stoddart could follow. "Where are you from, anyhow?"

"Mooney's Dump."

"Oh, a local boy, eh?" said the woman. "We just moved up here ourselves. We have a place at Chippewa Lake – you heard of it?"

"Sure," said Stoddart. He didn't want to be talking.

"At least, we have it for now," said the man. "Who knows, with all these land claims going to court, the wagon-burners might take it back any day, right?" He gave a too-loud chuckle, as though daring Stoddart to say something. Stoddart nodded slowly, grimly. This wasn't the time for an argument. He needed to catch up to Richie.

"Don't mind him," the woman said good-naturedly. "He's more open-minded than he makes out."

"I'm sure he must be," said Stoddart, and he bid them goodbye.

When he emerged from the cave, there was no sign of Richie. At the bottom of the climb up the escarpment, there was no sign of the rope either.

"Richie," he called. "Hey, you forgot something." He had to crane his neck to see the top. No one appeared. "Richie! Are you up there?" He tried to imagine the boy dragging up the rope without thinking, then marching on, forgetting that Stoddart needed it too. Richie would continue for a few minutes, wonder why Stoddart hadn't caught up, then realize his mistake and run back. But Stoddart couldn't make himself believe that story. The boy was too clever. Too clever by half. What was he thinking?

"Richie!" he called. "Rocket!" Nothing.

He considered trying to make it on his own. An unassisted climb was not impossible. He'd done it years ago, before the rope was installed, when he was in his thirties, his prime. Judith had done it too. It had been a dry day with no slippery stones to negotiate. They'd had each other to help.

After pulling the shoulder straps tight on his pack, he leaned close to the cliff, raised both hands, and let his fingers crawl over rock. When they found an outcropping that felt sturdy enough to grab, he took hold of it and began to feel with his boots. He planted his feet carefully, slowly easing his weight onto them, making sure he was secure, groping with all his strength. His next handhold was a cedar root that snaked across the cliff. The stone was warm, and beads of water ran into the spaces between his fingers.

When he finally looked down, he discovered he'd climbed only seven or eight feet. He was less than halfway, the most difficult section was still ahead, and he was labouring for every little gain. In places only one handhold and a foothold were possible. His breath whistled and hummed crazily into the stone. His buttock was still throbbing from when the boy had fallen on him.

At some point he felt the top, and even then he wasn't done: he had to gather his legs under him for leverage before giving a final jerk and delivering himself in a heap to flat ground. He made it on the first attempt, then lay on his back and looked up into the branches of the birches above him. Against the blue sky they looked frail and thin now, more skeletons than ghosts.

He rolled over to find two paint buckets beside him. They'd been upended, and the brushes lay in spreading pools of white that were beginning to spill over the edge of the cliff. He threw the rope back down and broke into a sprint along the path in the direction of the car. Running felt easy after the finger-bruising creep up the rock face, despite the pain in his buttock, but he couldn't enjoy the movement. He didn't even know that the boy had gone toward the car; if he'd headed in the other direction, he could be halfway around the cape by now, ready to be found by that man from the general store, to tell a story about what had happened. How dare he? He'd never said no, never protested. It had been wonderful. And now he was going to turn traitor. No one else would understand. Why had Stoddart ever thought of bringing Richie to the reserve? It was abominable. He'd never let it happen again.

He was so lost in his own outrage and fright that he didn't realize he'd caught up with Richie until he was almost even with him. The boy hadn't sensed his approach either; he was walking with his hands out as though he were traversing a tightrope. When

Stoddart's footsteps eventually roused him from wherever he'd been, he turned and gave a surprised cry.

"What the hell were you thinking?" Stoddart shouted. "You knew it wasn't just me down there. How did you think those people were going to get out?" He was trying hard to let only his rage and not his fear manifest itself.

"You got out," Richie said incredulously.

"I climbed."

"On your own?"

"Sure, on my own." Richie's eyes widened, and Stoddart felt as though something had been proven. "You thought you were pretty smart, didn't you? Well you were stupid."

"I'm sorry." It came in a whisper.

They began to walk together without speaking, and he wondered about the object of Richie's contemplation. He tried to remember him in the cave – the boy's words, gestures, reluctance – and couldn't. There were only the echoes of his own sensations, the building euphoria and the wild release. He couldn't discern any images of the thing itself, the contact and the intimacy. It was too bright and dazzling to look at. He'd lost Richie even as he gained him.

"Someone might have cracked their head open, climbing up there," Stoddart snapped. Richie stopped and tilted his head, as though he'd only heard a faraway roar and not a voice right behind him. "Then how would you have felt?"

Richie didn't say anything. Something had changed between them, perhaps permanently. It was inevitable, Stoddart knew that, but still he felt a stab of regret. No harm had been intended. He wanted there to be some way to go back to the old trust, the familiar flirting and the quiet jokes. It had only been one thing, one little, new thing between them.

He studied the boy and was suddenly disgusted with himself. An eleven-year old. How could he have let himself go so far?

"Listen," he said. "About the paint buckets you knocked over."

Richie looked frightened. It was more than that – he was petrified, as though it had been another person hauling rope, spilling paint, but Richie was going to be punished for it all the same. They were both in a dream now, with a companion who was not quite the same as the one they were used to in the waking world. Stoddart longed to return them both to their old reality.

"I told those people we're from Mooney's Dump, you know," he said. "They heard me call you by your name."

He let that information sink in before he continued.

"If they ever follow it up, I'll tell them I stumbled at the top and bumped into the cans. You see what I'm saying? I'll tell them I didn't mention anything because I was angry about the things being left there right at the edge for someone to trip over. You'll be off the hook."

Richie's face lost its frown of worry and took on some other, more impenetrable expression.

"Thanks," he said quietly.

"Yes, well. Partners in crime, eh?" Stoddart replied. Then they fell into silence again, following the thin path that wasn't even a path in places, relying on the fresh white blazes to provide direction. Stoddart felt the sun heating his skin, smelled the crisp air heavy with cedar musk. There were gulls sailing on the thermal winds off the cliffs, crying to one another. Perhaps it would work out in the end. After all the planning and worry and giddy frustration, perhaps the two of them were entering a new season with this day between them, as fragile and dangerous as it was. To dare, to get away with it, to embark on adventures together and succeed, to make the veins and vessels pulse red and blue under the skin, more vital than ever before.

Passing one of the freshly painted blazes, Richie threw out his hand and smacked it against the paint. He came away with his palm turned white and his print left on the tree. It was a stupid gesture, arbitrary and incomprehensible. Richie bared his teeth and grinned.

"Hey, the paint's wet," Richie said. "Don't touch it." Then he slid his fingers along his own cheek, leaving pale streaks across the skin, and gave a stuttering laugh. Stoddart laughed too, uneasily at first, but then deciding that it was all right, it was the old Richie again: a clever boy, making jokes, loveable once more.

Just before they got back to the car, he decided the rope had been a test, and he had passed. He was still the stronger one.

HE SWORE it would be kept to Plato's Cave. One day he might return and remove the imaginary seal he'd placed across the opening, but until then, the cave would stay as it had always been – comforting darkness and smooth bare rock – and what had happened there would never be repeated. All men needed such a place, a hidden cavity for themselves alone. Some caves had ceilings of glass, others were paved with linoleum; either way, what mattered was maintaining a boundary between the world they encompassed and the world of daily life. He told himself it would be fine. If he could manage to keep certain memories within the cave, then perhaps he might also retain some semblance of his prior self and of the Richie he had loved before. And he was right.

But the cave grew.

There were no doubt whispers in the Mooney's Dump hockey community that the boy got special treatment, although no one protested publicly when Stoddart insisted on coaching each new team Richie joined. They understood that something magical was going on. Rocket DeWitt was a player unlike any other the town would ever see, someone to put Mooney's Dump on the map, and it was expected that he'd need individual guidance if he was going to do it. So Richie spent extra time at the rink. During hockey tournaments out of town he got a room to himself in the hotel, a privilege that he seemed to accept more out of obligation than with gratitude. In the off-season he and Stoddart went on expeditions together, and soon enough Richie could tell a cumulus cloud from a cumulonimbus, a Jack pine from a white pine. He knew the peninsula's trails and hiding places as well as anyone.

At sixteen he scored almost two hundred goals. He also failed Grade Ten math, but his parents weren't as upset as Stoddart thought they would be. They blamed the stressful travel schedule, and they nodded when Stoddart said things would improve at the end of the season. He vowed to keep a closer eye on the boy, and he brought him over to his house for tutoring. As time went on, Richie arrived late with greater frequency, claiming that he'd forgotten what day it was or that his bicycle had broken down, and occasionally he didn't show up at all. There were taunting claims from the boy that he'd found a girlfriend, that he was too busy to bother spending time with an old man. Even those evenings when he did appear at the appointed hour, Stoddart never quite sensed the eagerness he desired in the boy, only a dogged compliance, as though an unfortunate debt were being paid. But together in the darkness, it didn't seem like so great a matter.

Things went on like that until Richie left Mooney's Dump at seventeen. Then, playing for a junior team on the other side of the province, the boy wilted as Stoddart suspected he would. Secretly Stoddart was relieved: it proved he'd been needed. But once Richie returned to Mooney's Dump at twenty without even a high-school diploma to his name, he said he didn't want to see Stoddart any more. He rented a tiny shack of a house on the other side of town, let his answering machine take messages that he never returned. When Stoddart stopped to fill up his car at the gas station, Richie greeted him as he might any old man.

Every day as Stoddart had sat in the Owen Sound jail there'd been two memories that came back to him. The first was of an evening outside Richie's shack, a few hours before the solstice party at Cam Usher's. Stoddart had driven there without even putting on a jacket. He'd stood at the door in the cold, banging on it with both fists, demanding that his phone calls be answered, his invitations accepted. He'd begged Richie to return to hockey, shouted reassurances that at twenty-three it was not impossible.

There was a half-empty bottle of whisky in his car, and he didn't care what was heard by the neighbours. Then he remembered that Daniel Barrie was living there too.

"Daniel," he yelled. "Are you in there? Send Richie out. Make him talk to me."

"Daniel's at the library," replied a voice from deep within the building. "Go home, Frem. It's too late for you now."

He didn't want this memory, tried to rid himself of it, but it was lodged in place, reproaching him with its clarity, even as all recollection of the party later that night remained lost to him.

The second memory was of the time at Plato's Cave – the sun brighter in his mind than any since, the hike never-ending, the walls cool and real. This memory he hoarded with a guilty satisfaction, and every day he brought it forth, in private moments, to polish it like a trophy.

HE WOKE UP in darkness to the sound of a man whistling off-key and wondered where he was. Then he felt the hard cellar floor beneath him and remembered.

The whistling was cut short by the slam of a door. The boyfriend off to work. Soon after, there was the pad of Esther's feet moving around the house, eventually ceasing. He was exhausted by the struggle of sleeping with only a blanket between him and concrete, wary of morning and wishing he could escape back into a semblance of rest, but his body was too stiff and aching, too filled with adrenalin at the prospect of what was to come.

Carefully he climbed the stairs, trying to avoid making a sound in case someone was at the top. He pushed open the door to stillness, then looked across the room and saw a set of car keys lying on the table. From where he stood there didn't seem to be a note, but he felt certain that Esther had placed the keys there for him after the boyfriend had left. She must have convinced the man that he should walk to work.

Stoddart crept along the hallway to the door of the bedroom and peeked through the crack. She was lying under the sheets, her shoulders bare, her brown hair radiating across the pillow. She could have been fifteen again. His eyes began to well up, but an ugly thought stopped them. This was a contrived scene. It wasn't possible for her to be asleep now. She'd be too disgusted with him, too full of loathing. If this sight of her at peace was her last gift to him, it was one he couldn't accept. It felt more like an evasion, a snub. A refusal even to say goodbye. Well, he deserved nothing better.

He went back to the living room and took the keys, moved swiftly to the driveway, got in the boyfriend's pickup. As he was about to drive off, his foot touched something hard under the seat, and he reached down. It was the stock of a rifle. He brought the gun to his knees, discovered it was loaded. Had the boyfriend simply left it in the truck? he wondered. Surely it couldn't be from Esther. She'd know better than to imagine it would help him in escaping the police.

But perhaps she was offering him something else entirely.

He needed a place to think for a while where he wouldn't be seen, so he started the truck and followed residential streets north toward the edge of the town. The sun had just risen, everyone was still asleep, and he didn't expect to see the man bicycling toward him. When he did, it was too late to drive out of sight. They came to a four-way stop at the same time, and their eyes met. Archie Boone. Stoddart nodded a cautious greeting and let the man cross before he stepped on the accelerator. It didn't matter, he told himself, his heart still pounding. Boone was one person who kept things to himself.

A few blocks later he turned on to an old logging road that ran between two houses and into the bush. It was a track he'd once walked with Judith, originally part of the old Aboriginal portage route that led to the marshlands in the middle of the peninsula. He'd made it; no one would follow him here. Even now, things were going in his favour. He'd been delivered from prison. He'd been spared in the plane crash, pulled back from beyond the brink of cardiac arrest. The very implement of self-destruction he'd desired had been given to him. And all these years – after all the nights he swore it wouldn't happen any more, and it did – he'd got away with it, time and time again.

As he drove up the narrow road he thought, I am not being spared out of divine charity. I am being kept alive to await judgment. For surely that was God's intended justice, the way to explain such apparent miracles of survival. He was forever to live in anticipation of a reckoning, not knowing when it was to come, recriminating without atoning, remembering without testifying. Harry Midgard was always to lurk behind him, while Richie would remain out there somewhere, watching him, planning someday to come forward, torturing him with the wait. It was horrific to imagine, but perhaps, after all he'd done, it was only fair.

The trees were beginning to encroach now, so that every so often a branch poked through the open window. When a large one slapped him on the face, he braked and stopped the engine. He'd come far enough.

He picked up the rifle from the seat beside him and set the barrel squarely under his chin. Ahead he saw the distant gleam of the wetlands, and he heard the drone of deer flies as they began to explore the truck. The peninsula was alive. It seemed a good enough place. Slowly, slowly, he slid his hand down until he'd reached the trigger. It was cold and smooth and ready for his thumb.

✦ *There seem to be even more people at the party than before. I follow the little girl and the woman in the orange toque past dozens of groups, up the steps of the farmhouse porch and into a large kitchen. There's no one inside, but the heat from a wood stove fills the room, and the woman removes her coat. She gestures for me to sit across from her at a long table in the middle of the room, while the girl lingers at the entrance.*

"Can I go back to the tiger now?" she asks in an accent that I can't quite place.

"Get Mike for me first," the woman replies. The girl nods and leaves.

"Is she Russian?" I ask. The woman shakes her head. It's clear she doesn't want to talk about the girl. I don't either. I'm wondering who Mike is, and why he has been summoned.

"You said you wanted to speak with Alice Pederson," she says. "Is that right?" I nod. "About what?"

"I have something for her. From a friend." I pause at this last word, not knowing whether it's accurate to call the hitchhiker a friend either to Alice Pederson or me. I remember his smile as he said farewell and wonder if perhaps he knew that my inquiries would lead to an interrogation like this one. "A hitchhiker I met on the highway tonight," I amend.

"What do you have to give her?" the woman before me asks.

"I'm not sure," I reply, not sure either that it's any of her business. I take a deep breath. "Listen, I'm in the dark as much as you are. If you could just point me toward Alice Pederson –"

"I'm Alice Pederson."

"Oh." For a moment I'm embarrassed, but then I realize I should be angry. "Why didn't you say so?"

She doesn't take any notice of my question. Instead she focuses on the movement of my hand as I reach into my pocket and draw out the stained yellow notebook, set it on the table, and slide it across to her. She runs her finger along the spine tentatively.

"I picked up the guy who gave it to me just north of Owen Sound," I say, even though it was you, not me, who offered him the ride. I never would have done that. But I don't want to explain anything about you to this woman now.

"And this hitchhiker, what did he look like?" she asks, examining the book.

"Tall, broad shoulders, long black hair," I reply, remembering too well the figure in the back seat of your car and your interest in him. I try, and fail, to see any sign of recognition in the woman's eyes. "Someone you know, maybe?"

Alice shrugs.

"You weren't expecting anything?" I persist, and she shrugs again. It seems as though I'm not asking the right questions. "Well, I think that's all I can tell you," I say, annoyed. "If you don't mind –"

I'm about to get up when two men enter the kitchen. The first takes off his wide-brimmed hat to reveal a head of curly blond hair. The owner of the place. Cam – that's what you called him in the tunnel. He looks at me with suspicion, and I can't tell if he's remembering our first meeting by the fence or if he's just seen me fleeing across the field. The other man has a shaved head and dark skin: the figure who passed me on my way to the skating rink. He must be Mike. Once he's through the door, he and Cam stand apart, not looking at one another, as though to make clear that they're not friends but are sharing space together now for some other, mutually distasteful reason.

"What's going on?" the man asks Alice.

"This fellow brought something for me."

"For you?" he says, surprised. "You mean – for Alice?" She nods, and he walks behind her, lays a hand on her shoulder, stares down at the book.

"Wait a minute," I say to the woman. "Aren't you Alice Pederson?"

She glances up at Mike. The owner of the place goes to the counter and fills a kettle with water.

"What are you playing at?" Mike demands of me. "Who put you up to this?"

"He says it was some man on the highway –," the woman begins.

"You'd better be honest with us."

"Mike, look, the guy's confused," she says, and he lets out a deep breath.

"I knew none of this would work," he tells her. "It's too difficult. Nothing's the same. Nobody remembers anything."

What is he talking about? My eyes dart to the book. I want to snatch it, run back to the car, find a police station. But I don't think I'd make it. It's the silence of the owner at the counter as much as the bald man's hostility that frightens me. I'm sweating, the fire in the nearby stove crackles and roars, but I can't bring myself to move away, to take off my jacket, to do anything.

"Let me ask you a question," the owner says to me. "I asked it before when I met you, but I don't think I got a proper answer: Do you know what's going on tonight?"

"It doesn't seem that I do," I reply irritably. "So why don't you tell me?" But the man turns to the woman and Mike.

"Someone's just been playing a little game with him," he says.

"It doesn't matter," the woman replies. "I think I know who this is from." She looks at Mike as though expecting him to realize too, and after a moment he nods.

The woman presses her hands against the side of the book. I want it back, but it's too late. I want you here with me now, but it's too late for that, as well. I can't bring myself to ask the owner where you are.

"What's inside it?" Mike asks.

"I don't know," the woman replies. "I haven't read it yet."

"Well, why not? It could be important."

"It could be," she agrees, but then instead of opening the note-book she looks at her watch. "It's almost midnight, though. Cam and I need to leave soon. There's still the meeting with Daniel and the walk down the road to get through. If we don't keep on sched-ule, the whole night will have been pointless."

"I don't understand any of this," I say. "Can you please tell me what's going on?"

"Look, I'm sorry," she says. "You've just walked into the middle of something we're doing. It's kind of complex. We thought for a while you might be playing along with the act. But Cam's right, you don't know anything about us, do you? Do you know what my real name is?"

I shrug, annoyed.

"You told me you were Alice Pederson."

"I am," she says. "But just for today."

"That doesn't make things any clearer."

"Mike will explain things to you. But listen, you might have brought us something important here. Thanks. Maybe the night won't be a waste of time after all."

She looks down at the book. She's almost caressing it now.

"You know that murder-mystery board game?" she asks. "You must have played it as a kid. At the end, there's this moment when someone reaches to open the envelope, and after all your logical deductions and guesswork, you're finally going to find out who did it. God, I hated that moment, the tension of it."

"Come on, Bronwen, open it," says the owner. "What are you waiting for? We don't have much time."

"All right." She slides a finger under the rubber band encircling the book and removes it, then lifts the front cover, only halfway at first, as though she's afraid to see what might be written inside. "Here we go."

THE COMPANY
OF OTHER SOULS

As she walked up the steps to the clinic, Alice made her decision. For days she'd been mulling it over, and this morning
the thought of it had woken her at five. In the shower, during
breakfast with Nel and Oliver, in the face of Mike's concern, she'd
been thinking about it without end. "No, I'm just tired," she'd told
Mike when he asked her if something was on her mind. Now she
knew the answer: she wasn't going to run away. With a grim satisfaction she removed her overshoes on the damp carpet and
entered the reception area of the clinic where Esther waited.

"Hey, what's wrong?" Esther asked as she approached. "You
look pale. Did you eat breakfast this morning?"

"I'm all right," said Alice, trying to smile. "Who's up first?"

"Ruth DeWitt," Esther replied, and handed her the file.

Alice hesitated a moment before she took it. She didn't want to
see Ruth DeWitt, of all people. Not this morning, when the henge
party was nearly upon them and she hadn't slept properly for days.

"Tell Ruth I'll be a minute," she said. Then she made her way
down the hall to an empty room, picked up the telephone inside,
and banged out a familiar number on the keypad. As it rang, she
found herself already beginning to doubt her decision. It would be

so much easier to leave, right now, before the celebration began. No need to face anyone. No need to return that evening to Cam Usher's field and the circle of stones at the centre of it.

When Daniel answered the telephone she asked him if he'd be at the party.

"I already said I would be," he replied. "Why? Won't you be there?"

"Of course," she told him, but her voice broke as she spoke.

"I've finished packing," he said. "I thought you might be calling to say goodbye."

"Don't be ridiculous. I wouldn't do that on the phone."

"The way things have been lately –"

"I told you, I've been busy. Look, I'm at work. I have to go."

"You sound upset –," she heard him say, but she hung up and leaned against the sink in the corner. There'd been too much arguing in the last few weeks, too much secrecy and guilt, and it was her fault. Daniel didn't deserve to have things end like this.

She tried to gather herself, but as she made her way reluctantly to the room where Ruth DeWitt waited, she found her mind returning to the possibility of leaving. She wanted to pick up and get out of here. Get a rest for once in her life. Sort things out. She needed some distraction, something else to occupy her mind besides the story she'd been carrying with her for the last few weeks, the one she'd been telling herself again and again, despite the fact that it wasn't a story she particularly wished to remember. It only made her want to flee Mooney's Dump, never to return, and the prospect of staring at Ruth's face brought it back to her with even greater and more painful clarity than before.

THIS WAS A STORY about a woman who crouched at the bottom of a hole in a field, digging, with a string and a measuring tape stuffed into her pocket. It was the middle of November, a month before the solstice celebration, and the ground had yet to freeze; the year's freakish cold weather would arrive a few days later. For now the field lay rutted from the tires of heavy machines. All week they'd been boring into the earth, hauling long slabs of stone from the nearby quarry and setting them in a circle around the hole where the woman now stooped, gouging the soil in front of her with a trowel.

The woman in this story wasn't very smart. For one thing, she hadn't questioned the owner of the field when he told her that, contrary to the claims made in the local newspaper, there was no Aboriginal burial ground anywhere on his property, and no chance that the land would be taken away from him. He knew this, he said, because an archeologist buddy of his had done a survey. The owner of the field relied on many such friends to assist him in his various projects. He was ambitious beyond his means, so when he started a wildlife park without any background in zoology, and when he envisioned a henge of standing stones without knowing precisely how to design one, he had to recruit other people, the woman in the hole among them. She was a dentist by trade, but as a child she'd learned about astronomy, and because of this training the owner, whose name was Cam Usher, sought her out to help him. He told her he wanted to make the henge a working calendar of the seasons and a device for tracking stars. She knew it would be a substantial project to take on, when she already saw too little of her husband and children, but Cam, who'd heard of her campaign against the autumn deer hunt, offered to let her spend time with the animals at his park, and he emphasized that there'd be chances to work on her own. It was as though, before she recognized it herself, he'd seen a desire in her for solitude.

Through October the two of them had designed the henge, and then Cam had brought in half a dozen of his friends – some of them farmers like Hamish Ferry, the rest artists, craftspeople, and professionals from Owen Sound – to help with the physical labour. They'd spent a weekend lowering the stones into exactly the right positions, but now the woman was crouched in the hole and digging alone because she was stupid. Her measurements had been incorrect, and the pointer stone stood too far west, slightly out of alignment. Embarrassed, she'd asked Cam if they could pull it out in order to make the necessary adjustment. The next morning the pointer stone had been drawn from the ground by a hydraulic lift, and now it hung above the hole, suspended by chains and dangling like a talisman, smooth as slate. Her task was a matter of shaving a few inches from one side of the cavity to bring the henge back into order.

She crouched and dug and thought of tigers. When they entered her thoughts these days, they were often accompanied by a young man named Daniel, who knew nothing about the animals but who was in some ways responsible for her acquaintance with them. After all, the woman's agreement to help Cam had been partly an attempt to distance herself from Daniel, and it was in the wake of this agreement that Cam had taken her into his confidence about the tigers. If Daniel were ever to become aware of this particular motivation for the woman to work on the henge, no doubt he'd be even more bothered by the time she spent at the park than he already was.

There were two tigers, in fact, although only one was ever seen by the public. That one, Tamar, was the most tender and affectionate animal this woman had ever known. The other was more difficult to love. Masa kept to himself, slinking along the far corner of his pen. He'd been freed by stealth from a sadistic owner in the city, and because of his presence the woman could never forget her obligation to the secret network of sympathizers who'd been involved in his liberation. They were mostly local people, she knew that much – she suspected there might even be a few of them among the ones who'd helped to build the henge – but their membership wasn't divulged to her. Cam said if they were found out, he'd lose more than the park; there was a prison cell waiting for him and anyone else in on the scheme. She herself had been brought into the penumbra of this group because of a tooth infection that had left Masa refusing to eat. She'd agreed to treat it and keep the secret, thinking of the good that might be done and not of other consequences.

"If the reserve gets this land, I don't know what will happen to the animals," he'd told her. "Most of them are rescued from somewhere or other. A few of them took years to become accustomed to their habitats. They couldn't be moved again."

The day before, the woman had come upon Cam administering electric shocks to Masa. Cam was gentle and compassionate; he cared about animals more than anyone she knew. Such an act was almost beyond belief.

"It's the best way to condition him into fear," Cam had said when she'd protested. "Zoos use the same technique with predators. He's too dangerous. Or have you forgotten?" And he'd held up his left hand with its missing ring finger. The public story was that it had been crushed while Cam was moving boulders in the field.

Cam and secrets. Even she herself, who made surreptitious phone calls to the young man in her life and plotted meetings with him, was no match for Cam. His secrets weren't the kind that kept to themselves. They burrowed into the woman's skin, contaminated her with their exigencies and their implications, so that she had to preserve them not just for Cam's sake but for the sake of the tigers, for the sake of the nameless men who showed up at the farm without being introduced and went about unnamed business before vanishing again. She had a responsibility to all of them now.

Cam's secrets were worthy ones, she told herself. He was working for a better world, and she admired his dedication. It was partly in an effort to be so steadfast herself that she found herself returning to the wildlife park day after day. But that only made things harder. Cam was too focused on his various projects to be a confidant, and she dared not discuss the tigers with her husband. She didn't even invite him and their children to the henge, lest they be infected with Cam's secrets too. As a result her husband grew suspicious. He resented her time away, and he seemed unable to believe her when she told him the harmless truth about her friendship with Cam. He nodded and said he didn't worry, then disappeared upstairs to fume in private. As for the children, they never protested, never asked her to come home sooner. It was as though they'd learned not to have any expectations of her.

She'd almost finished digging. The only sound other than the scrape of her trowel against stones was the occasional rumble of a blast from the nearby quarry. A layer of sweat made her shirt cling to her back, and she shivered in the cold air, eager to be indoors. It was only when she had an inch or two left to shear away that she saw it: a grey protrusion from the earth near her ankles. She crouched farther down to look more closely, place a finger on the object's edge. It was smooth and dry to touch. An animal bone, the woman thought. Too small for a cow; perhaps a deer. She yanked and it slid easily from the soil, as long as her forearm, darkened by the years, with bits of fabric clinging to it. She scraped farther into the earth and found another like it close behind, then another. Another. Slowly a shape began to emerge.

AS SHE WALKED into the examining room, Alice wondered what Ruth DeWitt would say if she heard such a tale. She'd been with Solomon for thirty years – the only white woman and Native man in local memory to marry and live in Mooney's Dump – and although busy with a real-estate agency of her own she was intimately involved in her husband's legal work, so she had strong opinions about stories like Alice's.

Ruth was sitting in the chair with her hands on her stomach, her eyes closed. She spoke without opening them, as though she'd been reading Alice's mind.

"Did you hear? The decision about the quarry was handed down yesterday. We won. They're giving the land to the reserve."

Alice moved behind the chair and tilted it back until Ruth's face was fully under the examining lights. The hygienist had done the cleaning; all that remained was for Alice to make her inspection.

"Congratulations," she replied. "I bet Bobby Boone is furious."

"Oh, that old rat of a mayor knew he was taking a gamble when he opened the quarry on disputed land. It was an act of provocation from the start."

Alice smiled. She could imagine Solomon DeWitt saying the same words, an octave deeper but with identical cadences, a similar confidence. Perhaps Daniel had the DeWitts in mind when he talked about how people were halves trying to become whole again.

"Open wide," Alice said.

What was it like, Ruth? she wanted to ask. Sticking together through the university years, with people staring and your friends warning you about Indian men and your parents refusing to speak to you? And then the first child, and everyone saying how beautiful mixed-blood babies are. You and Solomon trying to build your careers and still be good parents. At some point you must have wondered if Mike and I went through the same thing, but you've never mentioned it, have you? Neither have I. We'd have a lot to talk about, if we could ever get beyond the local news.

When Alice had finished the examination, Ruth stood up and started toward the door.

"Are you coming to the party at the henge tonight?" Alice asked her. She could guess what the reply would be, but she'd feel better about the evening ahead if she knew there'd be no chance of running into the DeWitts and having to talk with them in that place while the story of the woman and the bones replayed in her mind.

"We'd like to go," Ruth replied hesitantly. "People say you've put a lot of work into the whole thing."

"But –?"

Ruth looked uncomfortable.

"Alice, you must have heard. The band has a claim on Cam Usher's land." Alice nodded, trying not to let her expression change. "It wouldn't be proper for us to be seen there right now."

"Cam's done checks," Alice said quietly, not wanting to seem too insistent. "Didn't you read the *Beacon* last week? He says there's no evidence of a burial ground."

"But he won't let the band on the property to confirm it," Ruth replied. "I know he's your friend, Alice, but I'm afraid it's going to end up in the courts. He hasn't been very forthcoming with us. It makes you wonder what's going on at that place. You'll be careful, won't you?"

Alice said she would, although she didn't know why. Whatever gossip was circulating about the goings-on at Cam's – more rumours of witchcraft and depravity, no doubt – she hadn't thought the DeWitts would be ones to believe it. But perhaps it wasn't a coincidence that Ruth had arranged her checkup for this particular morning, before the official opening of the henge and the celebration to come. Maybe she knew about the woman in Alice's story, the one who'd pulled bones from a hole, who'd walked into the middle of a swamp. I'm sorry, Alice thought. I'm sorry for what that woman did. She didn't mean to do it. She was trapped. It wasn't her fault.

WHEN THE WOMAN crouching in the field realized that the skeleton next to her was human, she should have stopped digging. *They say the burial ground was somewhere around here in the eighteenth century*, Cam had told her. *There's no written corroboration, though, just oral history.* She should have returned to the farmhouse, even though Cam had gone on one of his day trips to Toronto and the building was empty. She should have made phone calls. But she was livid.

Cam had lied to her. There'd been no survey after all.

If the bones were reported, the henge would be uprooted. Cam would lose his property. Not just this field, but the house, the wildlife park. She didn't know how land claims worked, but it seemed plausible. As she continued to scoop away earth, she told herself she was doing it for Cam, for the men who helped him, for Tamar and Masa. Not because she was afraid of becoming involved in a controversy or because she wanted selfishly to preserve the henge. She tried not to think of how long it had taken to perfect the structure, the hours just to make this last little correction, but still she could feel her own conviction rising: once the pointer stone was back into alignment with the stars, something would be locked into place, and you couldn't possibly change it, any more than you could alter the slow rotation of the night sky.

Quickly she worked with the trowel, levering out the bones, setting them on the ground outside the hole. Each time she stood to add another to the pile she surveyed the field, afraid that someone might appear. When she came to the skull, she hesitated for a moment. Skinless, toothless, and soiled with earth. It went on top of the pile and glared at her.

There was a square of tarp nearby in which she wrapped the bones. Then, tucking the roll under her arm, she made her way slowly across the muddy field, the pull of the deep sludge so strong in places that she thought it might swallow her rubber boots. The swamp came next, and she followed the thin lines of green where shrubs and other plants clung between dark pools, picking her way along a fallen tree, sloshing through a channel where water purled gently from one place to another. There was a sudden rush of wings in her ears and she froze, terrified. A great blue heron tracked away from her across the wetland, wings beating. It should have migrated long ago. Perhaps it was a former inhabitant of the wildlife park, escaped and forgotten but still hunting close by.

She couldn't go any farther. In the distance she saw the rise of the escarpment, but between there and here was only a great plain of flat water and dead, black trees. Standing on the edge of the expanse, next to a sumac covered in bunches of shrivelled red berries, she leaned forward with the roll in her hands and shook it out as though trying to purge a picnic blanket of sand.

The bones splashed and sank unceremoniously. The water was perfectly clear; she could see the stirring of the silt at the bottom as they settled. Then all her calm dissolved, and the swamp seemed ready to rise up and consume her. She ran back to the field, tripping and stumbling and scratching herself on branches. She packed dirt into the places where the bones had been, finished her measurements, and went to the farmhouse to wait for Cam. But as she stepped through the kitchen door, she realized that if he heard what was buried under his land, he might decide to sacrifice the henge after all. What's more, he might tell other people what she'd done. Then everyone would know about her cowardice, her selfishness. So once he'd returned and stood behind her chair at the kitchen table, rubbing her shoulders and thanking her for all the work she'd done, she said nothing. She only shook inwardly, outraged at his lie about the survey.

When she returned home she couldn't tell her husband either. Instead she claimed to be ill and stayed in the house while he took the children out for dinner, then called the young man in her life and asked him over. Another mistake. She hadn't been thinking clearly. She'd only needed to feel close to someone for once, and after what she'd done it no longer seemed to matter what other transgressions she committed. But when her family returned early it seemed like a justified rebuke, and she accepted it. The young man hadn't been so understanding. He thought her coldness since that time had been meant to punish him and not herself.

She wondered who it had been in the hole. Someone small, judging by the bones. A teenager, perhaps. A woman. Struck down by smallpox, old age, a wild animal. Someone who had been cared for, or at least respected enough to be interred.

She tried to believe in what Cam had said. There was no burial ground. Perhaps it had just been the body of some wayward pioneer. After all, what were the odds of building the henge on the exact same site when there were hundreds of acres from which to choose? But then, the fields tended to flood, the ground was marshy, and the henge had been positioned at the highest, driest point in the area – just the sort of place to bury the dead.

SECRETS HAD A WAY of growing inside you. It became difficult to breathe sometimes, a struggle in the company of other people to pretend that all was well. Mike would never forgive her if he knew what she'd done; she was convinced of that. He'd think it cowardly not to tell anyone about the bones, to treat human remains in such a way. Racist, even. And perhaps it was. Hadn't she agreed with Cam when he said that the Ojibwas on the reserve were too indiscriminate in their demands for land? That they shouldn't go after property-owners like him who sympathized with their cause? Even if she was unsure, she'd still nodded along with him. Remembering that conversation now, she realized she'd been wrong to think that if he knew about the bones he might let the band take the henge from him. With regard to most subjects he maintained a wall around his true opinions, so that in many respects he was still a stranger to her, but one thing was clear enough: he'd fight to save his land no matter what. With regard to the wildlife park he had a tenaciousness and a ferocity of purpose that frightened her sometimes. Because of her fear she didn't reveal what she'd found to him or anyone else. Later, she thought, after the henge party, she'd find a way to tell people what she knew.

It was easy enough to stay silent. She'd worried that everyone would sense her guilt, but they only said she looked tired, needed a vacation. No one except Daniel seemed to suspect anything was wrong.

"It's Mike, isn't it?" he'd wanted to know last week on the phone, full of concern. "He can't keep you hostage in this place."

"I'm here willingly, Daniel," she said. "Just like you are." She had to remind him of this sometimes, since he never admitted that putting off his studies at Cambridge had been his own decision and mistake. Often he seemed on the edge of blaming her for everything instead.

"You're unhappy and you won't tell me what's wrong," he said. "You're pushing me away."

"I'm not pushing you anywhere, Daniel."

"Maybe it's because you don't trust yourself around me," he said.

"Of course I trust myself," she replied. But she wasn't sure. Too often lately she'd felt an inclination to lose herself in his energy. Sometimes it was hard to pull back, to stay guarded from Daniel and his knowledge of her, his uncanny understanding of who she was.

No, that wasn't true, she told herself. The simple fact of Mike was enough to stop her. There was an old arrangement to be honoured. She was the one who'd promised to support them both in Mooney's Dump. A quiet country life, she'd said, perfect for writing books and raising children, as though it would be easy for him to do both himself. Had she been the only naive one, or had Mike understood the consequences of the bargain even then, letting her go off to the clinic for twelve hours a day? He might have recognized in her a certain contentment with the deal, a gladness not to take an equal role in parenting, an ambition to establish her own career. And now, for the sake of filled cavities, caps and crowns, a few thousand teeth, he was a stranger to her. She should love Mike more for his sacrifices, not less. She should spend more time thinking about how to recuperate his loss, not simply turn to another man in snatches of stolen time. She shouldn't let Daniel lie against her breast, his cheek where his hand was not permitted, listening.

"Darling," she called him once as he did it, placing her hand on his red hair. It was a term she also used with Mike. She was startled by the way the word had slipped out, and she worried about what else might follow.

BY THE TIME she left the clinic, the sun was setting and she'd almost managed to forget the morning's encounter with Ruth DeWitt, but when she stopped at the gas station Rocket was on duty, and the sight of him brought back the story about the woman in the hole. To keep it at bay, she studied him as he cleaned the windshield of the Jeep in front of her. He was tall and handsome, with a broad chest and careful hands. The kind of man who might be a good politician or a good lover with equal ease. Unbelievable that he should end up in this job, when once he'd been the pride of the town. A wasted life, people would say. But then, how was Daniel any different? How was she?

"Good afternoon, Dr. Pederson," Rocket said to her amiably. "What can I do for you?"

She tried to detect some note of conspiracy in his voice, wondering if Daniel had told him about his relationship with her, but if Rocket knew anything he didn't show it. She asked him to fill the tank, then settled in her seat and listened to the droning of the pumps. On the other side of the concrete island a car pulled in. It took a double-take for her to realize that the man at the wheel was her father.

It was always shocking to see him, although it happened often enough. The town was too small for them to avoid one another. There'd been a decade of these silent, unacknowledged encounters, and on every occasion, just when she thought the wound had healed, it was ripped wide open once again.

The first time she'd brought Mike home to Mooney's Dump from university, her mother's determined attempts to keep the peace had come to nothing. The words that issued from her father's mouth were outrageous, and she and Mike left within an hour of arriving.

"Why didn't you warn me?" Mike asked on the bus ride back to the city. "Didn't you tell him about us?"

"I thought that when it came down to being face to face with an actual person –" She broke off and pressed her cheek against the window. "He's my father. I didn't think we could be so different."

She'd been wrong. Dreadfully wrong.

I don't have anything against you people, but –

Almost eight years had passed before her mother left him, and then when she called Alice to announce her move to Walkerton, her tone was triumphant. "I finally said to myself, Enough is enough." There was a long, insistent pause. Alice knew she was supposed to congratulate her now, to accept the divorce as an act of solidarity with her and Mike, as though there weren't a hundred other reasons to have ended things. But if that was really the case, if her mother was siding with them now, whose side had she been on until then?

A few weeks later when Alice had run into her father on the street again, she'd feared his gaze, thinking that it would be accusing and hateful, as if to say, *It was because of you she left*. But he stared right through her, looking lost and lonely. Now when Alice saw him she noticed the deeper wrinkles, the extra pounds. As she watched him at this moment between the pumps, she realized that he'd stopped sweeping his few remaining strands of hair across his scalp. For the first time in her life, she saw the pink skin on the top of his head.

She imagined getting out of the car, stepping over hoses, and whispering in his ear: There's a white boy who wants to sleep with me, Dad. Does that make you happy? I've violated a pagan grave too. Aren't you thrilled?

A moment later he drove away.

AS SHE ARRIVED HOME and got out of the car, she decided to tell Mike about the bones. Not tonight – there was already too much to worry about – but soon. She should have told him at the start. What she'd done was bad enough; to keep it secret from him was only another crime. It didn't matter whether he'd forgive her; there'd been too much silence between them, not just about the remains, but about Cam and the tigers, about her and Daniel. About her fluctuating, irresolute desire to leave.

When she entered the house, she found Mike waiting for her in the kitchen.

"Your mother called," he said curtly without looking up from his newspaper. She knew what he thought about her mother. "I told her you're working late this week and it's not a good time."

"Is she still planning on driving here Christmas Eve?"

"Yes." Even that had been a cause for battle. The problem extended beyond the cost of their telephone conversations, although that was all Mike ever allowed himself to argue about. It went back to that first meeting ten years ago. If Alice mentioned that she'd seen her father at the gas station, they'd start into it once more, but there was no time now. The henge party would begin in less than an hour.

"Where are Oliver and Nel?" she asked, removing her coat and draping it over a chair.

"Upstairs. They're waiting for you to read them a story."

"I can't. I have to go soon. You know that. Judy Sutter's coming to give me a ride."

She leaned down to kiss him, but he didn't look up from his paper.

"You got home ten seconds ago and you're just going to leave again?"

"I'm sorry," she began, but then she decided there was no reason to apologize. Mike had known about the party for more than a month. He'd already told her he was happy to stay home with Nel and Oliver while she went alone. He was always like this, ready to play the martyr, denying any resentfulness, but storing it up inside himself until it erupted at the worst moments.

"So will this be the last time you go off to Usher's," he said now, "or will he have you building something else next?"

"Listen, why don't you come with me?" she said, ignoring the question. "We could take the kids."

He shook his head, still not meeting her eyes. "I'm just saying, damn it, you haven't planned it very well if you can't even spend five minutes with your children."

"Don't yell at me."

"I'm not yelling!"

There was the sound of the children's feet running along the hallway above them, the slam of a bedroom door. Heading for cover. She wanted to do the same thing: run away, be gone from here. Behind Mike a red glass ball fell from the Christmas tree in the living room and rolled across the carpet.

"Listen, I wanted to talk to you about something," he said, his tone calmer but still angry. "I checked the savings account today. There's five hundred dollars gone. What happened to it?"

She hadn't expected him to find out so quickly. The money had been given to Cam in order to help pay for the henge, but she couldn't tell Mike that, not now. There was too much antagonism in his eyes.

"I – I don't have to account for every nickel I spend," she said.

"No, you're the breadwinner. It's your money. I'm just the house husband."

"Stop it. I didn't say that at all." She took a deep breath. They'd been reduced to this, then. If she didn't say something now, she'd seem callous, but the problem was exactly the opposite: when these arguments arose, she felt too rubbed raw to bear them. "Look, I have to get ready. I'll go up and change, and then I'll say goodbye to the kids."

"Never mind them," he said. "Don't bother playing the perfect mother all of a sudden. Just go." He started toward the stairs.

Stupid. A stupid fight. But it could have been worse. She didn't want to imagine his reaction if she'd told him about the bones.

By the time she heard him knocking on Nel's door she already wanted to apologize, and she had to stop herself from calling out. It was too soon. Later tonight she'd come home and have a long, hot shower. The children would be in bed, Mike would be breathing heavily. She'd ease in beside him and wake him up, and they'd make love and fall asleep together and everything would be good again, at least for a few hours, before they had to rise in the dark and prepare for another day.

In their bedroom she undressed and found her favourite pair of jeans, a T-shirt, and her red wool sweater. She thought of going downstairs without saying goodbye to Mike or the kids, but she didn't want to leave the house that way, so she followed the sound of his voice to Nel's room and peeked inside. The children were sitting on the bed with Mike between them, and in his hands there was a book with a picture of Peter Pan on the cover. Alice leaned against the door frame and watched Nel and Oliver's faces as he read to them about the pirates searching for the Lost Boys, the Native Canadians searching for the pirates, and the wild animals searching for the Native Canadians, all of them chasing each other endlessly around their island. She frowned, not remembering any Native Canadians in the story, until she realized: the original Neverland had "redskins" in it. She smiled at the change Mike had made, and she wished he would look up at that moment to see her, but he was too enraptured by the story. They all were.

Her foot crossed over the threshold. She was about to join them on the bed, take Oliver in her lap and stroke Nel's hair, when a car horn sounded from the lane. She turned from the doorway quickly and went down the stairs, grabbed her jacket and left the house.

IF JUDY SUTTER was disturbed by Alice's silence during the drive to Cam's, she said nothing to indicate it, but then, of Alice's hygienists Judy was by far the meekest. She lived by herself and never accepted dinner invitations from the Pedersons or, as far as Alice knew, from anyone else, so it surprised Alice that she'd volunteered to help with the final preparations for the henge party. Another night Alice would have tried to strike up a conversation with her, but on this evening she felt too withdrawn herself to overcome another person's social awkwardness as well. After Judy had turned down Cam's lane and brought the car to a stop in the parking lot, she and Alice went their separate ways with what seemed like mutual relief, Alice pointing her toward the farmhouse where the others were supposed to meet, while Alice started in the other direction toward the wildlife park, which had closed after the Thanksgiving weekend and would remain off-limits to party-goers tonight. Beyond the locked gate only a narrow pathway had been dug out of the snow, and there was no one in sight. The promise of solitude. From her jacket pocket Alice drew the long silver key that would admit her.

The path was lit by old-fashioned lamps on wrought-iron posts. They gave off a pale light, shining like one full moon after another against the cedars. Many of the cages they illuminated were empty, the occupants having been moved indoors until spring. Other creatures padded about in the snow – the deer, the llama – more active now than when enduring the shouts of summer visitors. Small, shining eyes followed her as she walked toward the tigers' secret night enclosure, making her self-conscious. It was wrong to be here. She wasn't really needed until the opening ceremony, so there was no good reason why she should have got a ride with Judy. She could have spent more time at home before driving to Cam's herself. But she'd chosen to come early because she wanted to be alone, to steal time away from Mike, from Nel and Oliver, from Daniel, even, and not least of all from Cam. She could be in the farmhouse now, helping him, she thought. Then she chastised herself. How had it come to pass that she felt so indebted to someone who never seemed to feel obligated in return, despite all the efforts people made on his behalf? Why should she be the one to feel guilty? She wasn't the person who'd lied about the survey. It wasn't her fault that she'd found the bones.

When she reached the tigers' enclosure Masa lay dozing in his corner, while Tamar had stretched out along the fence, the two of them mutually aloof as always, even though Cam claimed they were social animals and needed to be kept in the same pen. They must have just eaten, because there was a dark stain on the snow and a heavy scent of blood, as though the air itself were drenched with it. Alice's stomach turned, and for the first time she realized that she hadn't had dinner herself. Now all desire for food left her. She went over to the place where Tamar lay and reached through to place a hand on the creature's forehead.

"Hello, sweetie," she said. "Have you missed me?" Then she sat down with her back against the bars, feeling Tamar's warm body on the other side, the gentle heave of her breathing. For months now Alice had been coming to this place, simply to stroke fur and show affection, to be with someone who didn't speak and asked nothing of her. How much easier it was to be kind when kindness was not demanded of her.

In the distance came the familiar thunder of a detonation from the quarry. She remembered what Ruth DeWitt had said: as of yesterday it was reserve territory. Tamar's breathing became quicker and shallower, as though she were listening to the explosions too, and Alice realized her own heartbeat was racing. Strange that the quarry should still be operating after dark. Perhaps they weren't simply excavating rock; perhaps the band had taken over already, and they were tunnelling toward the henge in search of bones. It was a ridiculous thought, but she couldn't bring herself to laugh. Instead she imagined being at the opening ceremony an hour from now and standing before all those people, every one of them but her ignorant of what was buried underneath their feet.

For Daniel it was so easy: he could just hop on a plane and leave the country. Perhaps Alice had been wrong the whole time about the two of them; it was she who was jealous, and not of some woman in Daniel's life but of his freedom. That was why she'd been so eager to see him tonight, she realized. After all her evasions, she might finally be ready to make her jealousy known. It was because she could admit now that she wasn't here willingly as she'd told him. Once, a long time, ago, she'd chosen to return, yes, but these days there was no real possibility of leaving, regardless of what she'd been telling herself. All the frantic contemplation had just been a charade to deceive herself into thinking she was free. In the same way, her reluctance to talk to him this past month wasn't self-punishment for the bones or for her impetuousness that night in asking him to the house, not entirely; she was really punishing him for his freedom. He didn't have tigers to protect, money to repay, henges to defend, children to raise. He hadn't wronged the dead. If he had, he'd be struggling like she was now to think of some way of making amends, struggling in vain because she was too ashamed even to tell anyone what she'd done.

Maybe there was something she could do, though. One tiny thing, at least, if it wasn't too late. In the month since she'd travelled through the swamp it had frozen solid, and now the bones would be buried in mud and ice. All the summer markers would be gone. But she remembered there'd been a sumac tree, at least. Perhaps that would be enough to find what she was looking for.

She stood and patted Tamar, then walked quickly from the tigers' enclosure and back along the path. This was crazy. She'd end up missing the opening ceremony. And how would she find her way in the dark? In the shed near the farmhouse, though, she discovered a flashlight and an axe, and with them in hand she set out across the field. Today was the first time in weeks that the temperature wasn't well below freezing, and there was a scrim of fog over the field that came up to her knees, the stones of the henge looming out of it like sentinels, the flashlight's beam burning a halo into the mist. In the distance a group of people had begun to pile wood for a bonfire. The flashlight would attract attention to her, she realized, but she needed the comfort its beam provided.

She crossed the field and entered the frozen swamp to find a layer of water covering the ice. The difficult, sodden journey of the previous month had become slick and perilous, the axe more of a hazard in her hands than the bones had been. She shuffled along like a child wearing skates for the first time, remembering from the autumn the dark pools in this place. Now nothing but ice separated her from their depths. A foot of it, perhaps. An inch.

The sumac tree, when she found it, was half-buried by snow. Its berries had hardened and fallen off, and the few ones remaining had started to bleed from the thaw. Ice had closed in around the tree's base, but standing beside it she felt reassured at least that there was solid ground underfoot. Somewhere close by, obscured by ice, there was a bank where the earth vanished and the vast plain of water from her memory began.

Reluctantly she stepped forward in the direction where she guessed the bones would be. The ice felt sturdy enough, but she might have the wrong place; the footing around her might cave in. Don't worry, she told herself. The water can't be more than a few feet deep. She lifted the axe above her head and brought it down with as much force as she could manage. The ease with which the blade cleft the surface was fearful and exhilarating. She smashed and smashed until there was a space of open water in front of her.

It was no good. The swamp here was shallow as she remembered it, but the axe had stirred the bottom so that she saw only a dark slurry of mud. Without thinking she found herself taking off her jacket, pushing up the sleeves of her sweater. She didn't want to reach into freezing water and search the darkness with the hope of touching bone. She'd cut herself on the ice; she'd get hypothermia. It was as though her body had made its own, separate decision when her hand first slipped beneath the surface. She lay on her front across the ice, water seeping through to her skin, and stretched until her entire arm was submerged.

There was nothing. The swamp had been known to swallow whole automobiles; it wouldn't spare a few meagre human remains.

A full moon rose on the horizon – the brightest in a century, if the newspaper was to be believed. She stood, shivering, and put her jacket back on, looked out across the swamp's blank face. Some act of atonement was called for – some rite to consecrate this secret, sacred ground. Such a gesture was beyond her, but there'd be no one else to make it. The words to the hymn that Mike and the children had been practising came to her, and she began to utter them tonelessly, then stopped after a few lines. It was foolishness to be reciting a Christian hymn for Native bones. A blasphemy even. Soaked to the skin in the darkness, with the eye of the flashlight already beginning to wane, she dropped the axe and turned to follow her footprints in reverse through the swamp, thinking that when she got to the farmhouse she'd call Mike and ask him to pick her up. She had no cause to celebrate tonight, nor did she have the energy any longer to deal with Daniel. She wondered if she even had enough to make it out of the swamp.

When she reached the field, there was only a moment of respite before she saw the crowd of people gathered by the henge and realized what time it was. The opening ceremony had begun. Cam would be speaking to them all, welcoming them, apologizing for her absence. She couldn't go there now. She couldn't tell them how glad she was that they were there, how thrilled she was about the henge. No, it would be too much.

Turning off the flashlight, she began to circle the field, keeping as far away as possible from the centre, her legs stiff and weak. Cam's voice was shouting in the distance. It took a few seconds before she realized it was getting louder. He was calling her name, running toward her.

"Where are you going?" he cried as he reached her. "I was worried about you. Come on, everybody's waiting." He held out his hand, and she let him lead her across the field. She was conscious of her wet clothes, a growing dizziness, but apparently it was too dark for anyone to notice; they all seemed pleased that she'd arrived. "Here she is, our architect," Cam announced cheerfully, and they clapped and smiled. She saw rows of teeth glinting in the firelight. What would they have said if she'd appeared with the bones? Had that been her intention in searching the swamp? To bring back what she found and make her confession? *We're standing on graves.* No one would admire such a gesture. They'd feel betrayed, coerced into complicity with what she'd done. ". . . and as a dentist she stands at the forefront of our community," Cam was saying. She leaned over to him – it felt like she was falling, she had to put a hand on his shoulder – and whispered in his ear.

"Don't make me say anything to them."

He frowned. "I thought we agreed . . ."

"Please." She almost added, *You wouldn't like what I'd tell them*, but before she could, he nodded and continued with his address as though everything was fine. At first she didn't recognize anyone among the listeners. Then she made out Bobby Boone under the bill of a baseball cap, his hands shoved into his pockets, and across the circle Stoddart Fremlin. Where was Daniel? She twisted around to search the ring of faces and couldn't find him. Cam's voice faded in and out: ". . . what people can do when they come together . . ." The crowd was too close to her; it was impossible to breathe. She needed to eat something, she knew that, but even the feeling of hunger had passed away. Lifting her head, she saw only blackness. Where were the stars? The moonlight must be blocking them out. Then she dropped her chin. What a spectacle you're making of yourself, she thought.

The crowd gave one last round of applause and began to disperse. Before anyone could come up to her, pat her on the back and congratulate her, she started toward the farmhouse, shivering as she went. The vibration of electrical generators throbbed in her ears, and the smell of diesel was overpowering. By the time she reached the veranda Cam had caught up to her, and he opened the door into the kitchen.

"Your clothes are soaked," he said. Once she was sitting at the table he went to the clothesline strung above the wood stove, removed a towel, and handed it to Alice. "What happened to you? What were you doing out there?"

"It was your fault," she blurted. "I was in that swamp because of you." She wondered why she was telling him now. What would it accomplish tonight, of all nights? But it was too late. "You said your archeologist friend surveyed the field."

"What are you talking about?"

"Remember a month ago? When I had to realign the pointer stone?"

"Sure."

"While I was digging I came across some bones." She pronounced the words carefully, watching for his reaction. He let out a deep breath.

"What did you do with them?" he asked.

"I threw them in the swamp."

"Jesus." For a moment his gaze flashed beyond her, toward the kitchen door. She turned, but no one had come in. "Have you told anybody else?"

When she shook her head, he looked relieved, although his brow was still furrowed.

"Listen, Alice. Forget about it. They were from a cow, probably, or a horse –"

"There was a skull."

"Fine, so it wasn't an animal. It was probably an old hermit or somebody who got lost in a blizzard." He wasn't looking her in the eye any more.

"You don't really have an archeologist friend, do you?" she said.

"Of course I do," he replied, his tone indignant. But that wouldn't do the trick tonight. She wasn't going to be bullied into silence.

"And this friend of yours, he searched the site?"

Cam studied the floor as though weighing his response.

"I described the property to him," he said, more quietly now. "He didn't think they'd bury people so close to a swamp."

"But he didn't actually do any digging?"

He mumbled a reply and she had to ask him to repeat it. "I said, they don't dig nowadays. They use radar equipment. It's expensive, and you need people who know what they're doing. I didn't want to attract attention."

"Oh Cam –"

He waved his hand dismissively. Cam was never interested in going over his own mistakes. "Alice, you can't say anything about this to people, all right? I don't know what you're thinking, but there's no reason to do something we'd both –" He paused, scrutinized her face. "This is my whole life we're talking about. This is years of hard work at risk."

As he spoke, the image came to her out of nowhere: Cam in the tigers' enclosure a month ago, dressed in protective padding and wielding that horrible prod. The look in his eyes: so cold and confident. She didn't want to remember it now.

There was a crack as a knot exploded in the wood stove. She stood, glanced down, and realized her hands still clutched the towel he'd given her.

"You're trembling," Cam said. "You need to get out of those clothes. I'll find some dry ones for you –"

"I don't feel very well," she said. Standing had been a bad idea. The wood stove felt like a furnace, her legs were failing; the world was on a tilt. "I should go home . . ."

She couldn't tell whether or not he caught her before she hit the floor. When she woke up, she lay in his arms and he was labouring to climb the stairs.

"Put me down," she whispered. "I'm fine." But she could barely feel her own body. It's hypothermia, she thought. The swamp. The lack of sleep, of food. How could she have made so many mistakes?

He carried her into his room and set her down on the edge of the bed, then went over to a bureau and rummaged through it.

"Here," he said after a moment, carrying a pair of jeans, a shirt, and socks. "They'll be too big, but they're dry. You need to rest a while."

The air was cold. After he'd left, she stripped off her wet clothes and left them in a pile on the floor, too tired to do anything else, then crawled in under the bed's thick quilt and fell asleep.

She awoke once, briefly, and in a stupor looked around the room. The curtains were drawn and her clothes had disappeared, while the things he'd left her sat in a neat pile in their place. She was alone.

Impossible to know how long she'd been lying there. Could be night or day. The whole henge party might be over. Daniel could be headed for England, everyone might be looking for her. It didn't matter. Arms and legs were dead, she couldn't move. Might have been a tranquilizer slipped into her glass, except she hadn't drunk a thing. Get up, get up, she told herself, but instead she slid back into sleep.

IN HER DREAMS she rode on the back of a tiger. They climbed cliffs together, mountains without summits. Stones tumbled past them, an unending rush of rocks, rolling, smashing into each other and

281

showering pieces of rubble. Some of the fragments were smaller than a finger and others were as big as churches, ploughing through the earth like ships through the ocean. Below her were the lights of the town, the people asleep, unsuspecting. The tiger bounded higher and higher, never stopping, bounded toward the stars.

She felt the body lying behind her before she was fully awake. Reflexively she curled against it, reached her hand back in search of Mike's hip. As she stirred into consciousness and opened her eyes, she realized her error. It wasn't him. Looking down, she saw a slender arm, white and freckled, encircling her waist as though it might hold her and not be noticed. Even before she turned, she knew it was Daniel's.

"What are you doing in here?" she demanded. The arm became heavy and limp around her.

"I thought –," he began.

"Are you crazy, coming in like this?" She sat up and tried to think. How long had he been lying there? Then she turned to him. He was wearing a pair of boxer shorts and nothing else. It was too much.

She asked him for the time, told him she was all right, that she felt better now. But her head was aching. She could smell the beer on him. She didn't want to be here.

"I looked all over for you," he was saying, a hint of sullenness entering his voice. "I saw your clothes downstairs, and I got scared. Then when I saw you, I don't know, I didn't really –"

"Did you think I'd just forget that I'm married, that I was lying here exhausted, and make love to you?"

He dressed and left without a word. A sulk, she thought, but she was glad he'd gone. There was nothing to be gained from one night together, not after all the effort she'd made to maintain distance for so long. Surely Daniel would understand that; no doubt he was already feeling sorry about what he'd done.

For several minutes she sat on the edge of the bed, until finally a growl from her stomach roused her and she dressed in Cam's clothing, rolling up the shirt sleeves and the legs of the jeans several inches, still almost tripping on them as she made her way downstairs. She was hungry. There'd be food outdoors, but she wasn't ready to go out there yet, so instead she opened cupboards and drawers until she found a bag of cookies, then ate half a dozen with barely a breath drawn between them. Her clothes were hanging over the wood stove, already dry, and she took them into the bathroom to change. When she emerged, she saw Cam starting up the stairs.

"There you are," he said, and came back down. "Did you –"

"It's all right, I just woke up, I feel better now," she said. He nodded, as though relieved, but when he began to speak again, it didn't seem to be her welfare that concerned him.

"You have to understand about the henge," he said. "About what you found. They'll take everything if they know."

"I understand," she replied. But to herself she thought, I understand where your priorities lie.

"So I can trust you not to say anything," he said.

She nodded slowly.

"All right then," he said. "Good." He smiled as though there was no more to be said between them.

They walked out of the house together, and as soon as she stepped on to the porch she saw Daniel in the distance, his eyes already upon her.

"Isn't that Daniel Barrie?" she asked Cam, trying to sound unsure and uncaring. "Maybe I should go and say hello." She looked at her watch. "Listen, if you see Judy Sutter, can you tell her I'll find a ride with someone else? She's probably itching to get home." Cam nodded, and Alice stepped off the porch.

"We still need to talk," said Cam.

"Yes," she replied. "But not right now."

WALKING ALONG the roadside, away from the wildlife park, away from Daniel, she remembered Cam's words. Perhaps it would be better if she returned to the farmhouse and had it out with him tonight. Another confrontation couldn't make things any worse. But she didn't want to turn around, not with Daniel already heading back to the party. Besides, there was a certain tranquility in being out here alone. She splashed along the shoulder, watching the moonlight ripple in the disturbed puddles.

She hadn't been fair to Daniel. As angry as she'd felt, she could have been more patient. Daniel was young and immature, that much was obvious from his behaviour in Cam's bedroom, but for her part she should have known better than to end things in the way she had. At the same time, it seemed almost easier that the night had finished like that, with Daniel's jealousy and her own exasperation colliding in a fury of spiteful, ruinous words. He wouldn't second-guess himself now about leaving. There'd no longer be any secret relationship for her to nurture. If she chose, she could go on with her endless hours of work and solitude, avoiding her family, maintaining her guilty secrets, safe in the knowledge that there was no connection between her and Daniel any more, no chance of following him to England. She'd been right: they'd never promised each other anything. That meant there was no obligation they had to fulfill.

It was different with Cam. She'd given him her loyalty, and now she had the power to reveal his secrets, to betray him. He'd never forgive her if she did, but then, hadn't Cam already turned traitor himself? He'd exploited her friendship and trust – hers and that of everyone who'd helped to build the henge – and now her only duty should be to the truth. She didn't want such a duty, though, not with all the consequences it might entail. They were too frightening.

Home was almost five miles away, but she didn't mind the idea of a long walk. Not a single vehicle had been on the road since Rocket had passed by in Stoddart Fremlin's car, and the pavement shone like a river running parallel to the lakeshore. She'd be at the house in an hour and a half, and she could already imagine the creak of floorboards as she walked up the stairs to Mike, but for now the only noise was the grating of her footsteps on the slushy gravel. And something else.

She stopped, listened, heard the crack of breaking ice coming from the bay where open water began. Not just the sift of waves against the floes or the snap of shifting fault-lines. It sounded like a person struggling.

"Is someone out there?" she cried. There was no answer, but the noises continued.

She looked up and down the road. Not a single house here, only the swamp on one side and the bay on the other. A quarter-mile back to the beginning of Cam's lane, and no headlights to be seen along the entire strip. It would be foolish to go out there alone in the dark. Another mindless risk.

She stepped off the road into wet, deep snow and started toward the shoreline. It was hard to be certain, but she felt sure there couldn't be more than a hundred yards of ice before the waves began. She placed a tentative foot on the edge of its glassy surface, polished into radiance by the warm weather, then carefully made her way toward the noises, straining to make out the figure in the water.

ALCATRAZ

*Every man is a piece of the puzzle, a part of something bigger.
But to be at the heart of it – is that what I'm trying to do? No.
Stay on the outside. Close your eyes and lips. Try again.*

The worst part was the border at Niagara Falls. In the past he'd
left the country on trips to hockey tournaments, but never by
himself. He didn't have a passport, and he'd barely remembered to
bring his birth certificate. As he idled the pickup in line for the
inspection booths, he began to fabricate answers. New York City.
Vacation. Back by July twentieth. He didn't know what would
happen if they searched the vehicle and found the thousand dollars
in the duffle bag beside him. Or, worse, if they said there were
orders to keep him on this side of the border, if there were police
with questions for him. A murder charge, even. A cell at the
Sunshine police station: the same one in which they'd put the old
man that morning.

In the end it turned out as though he'd scripted it himself. *New
York. Vacation. Back in a week.* Lying through his teeth, and still
they waved him through. Maybe no one had noticed that he'd left.
Or no one cared. At the first rest stop he pulled over and flopped
down on a shaded patch of grass, panting from the heat of the

journey, remembering his father's voice on the telephone a few hours before. *Stoddart just called me from jail. They've charged him with killing Alice Pederson.* He'd listened to his father's precise, impassive lawyerly phrasings, and then he'd begun to pack. Now here he was, two hundred miles away. He hadn't told anyone he was going and knew that his parents would worry, but there'd been no way to say goodbye. They wouldn't have let him leave without demanding to know the reason for his departure, and he couldn't tell them that. It went further back than the stupid decision to stay quiet on Daniel's say-so, further even than the night at Cam Usher's. Inevitably it would lead to the old man, to his house, a thousand hockey practices. To the cave.

Forget all of it, he told himself. No more Daniel, no more Frem. They'd have to look after themselves now, and he refused to feel remorse. He was moving on. From his wallet he produced his credit card, then pulled out a jackknife and cut the flimsy square to shreds. It would have been tempting to use it, but there'd be too great a risk of being traced. The cash in the duffle bag, until today hidden on his bookshelf between the pages of *Bartlett's Familiar Quotations*, would have to be enough. He gathered up the pieces of silver plastic and, struck by a sudden resolve, removed the birth certificate from his pocket. The knife blade didn't waver as it sliced the laminated card in two, but when he went to quarter the thing he hesitated. It was the last proof of his identity that he possessed. Uncertain, he set one half on top of the other and slid them into his wallet.

HE MADE THE TRIP across the continent in long, exhausting draughts, as though there was someone in pursuit. At first he hugged the shoreline, driving along Lake Erie to Cleveland, but the sight of water was too familiar and heartbreaking, so he took parallel roads farther south that were less reminiscent of home. There were ten-hour stretches in which the only stops were for gas and takeout hamburgers. At night the windows stayed rolled down, the radio blasted any clear station he could find, and he sang along, making up the words to songs he didn't know.

> *It all comes back to me now –*
> *Where you headed, anyhow?*
> *Little Rock, Los Angeles;*
> *Reservations, if you please.*
> *It all comes back to me now –*

The highways were crammed with station wagons and camper vans, the shoulders littered with the victims of steaming radiators, flat tires, parched fuel tanks. When his eyes became too heavy for the moving world, he pulled over and lay down to sleep stretched out on the upholstery, plagued by dreams of Sunshine in which he was sixteen again and at Frem's house once more, the old man snivelling, cajoling, and in the next moment rancorous, wrathful. He awoke with a fear that Frem was lurking close by, just out of view, then started the engine and drove off as though, if he were quick enough, he might leave the night's dreams on the roadside behind him.

Through Nebraska a red sedan followed him for more than an hour, accelerating when he accelerated, turning when he turned, but at a dusty crossroads it disappeared. Only as the foothills began to emerge out of the purple fields did he feel safe enough to slow down. After Denver he meandered up to Mount Rushmore and the Black Hills, as far as Little Bighorn before he realized he was approaching the border again. Preferring to resist its tug, he went no farther north and steered for the Utah salt flats. Las Vegas from a distance at night was too brilliant and startling to be believed, and he passed through it without stopping, the rush of people on the streets more than he could handle after the loneliness of the desert. At the city limits his mind offered up a phrase. *The one landscape we constantly hunger for.* Who'd written that? Had anyone? He couldn't remember. His father would, he thought, and he felt a tightness in his chest. With regard to things like quotations and matters of fact, his father almost always knew.

When he reached California he'd been on the road three weeks. It was the beginning of August, and in Sunshine they'd be getting ready for the Civic Holiday, but it didn't seem to be celebrated in these parts; none of the gas-station attendants and waitresses had even heard of it. Aching and stiff from his nights in the truck, he decided to mark the day by checking into a motel outside of Barstow. The shower in the room couldn't be made hot enough to loosen his muscles, but it left his skin steaming long after he'd finished. That night as he sprawled in the bed he could almost taste the Pacific, and the next morning he turned north to delay the coast, followed the Sacramento Valley until he came to San Francisco. On the first gut-dropping climb up one of the city's more terrifying streets the pickup's engine kicked and died, confirming that he'd come to the end of the line, and there was nowhere else to go.

THE WOMAN APPEARED at the beginning of September. By then he was working nights, bouncing for a bar that hadn't asked to see a work permit, staying above the place in a mouldy yellow room with a camp-bed and a sink. On rainy days he lay beneath an old stained comforter and read paperback editions of Browning, Faulkner, Conrad, preferring stories about places that were distant and safe. The rest of the time he explored the city, convinced that if he became acquainted with every street, every building, he might be able to keep Sunshine at bay. He hiked the burnt hills to the east, drank coffee at sidewalk cafés, and stared with covert amazement at the passersby. Men kissing each other in public. Of course places like this existed, he'd always known it – places where there were no boundaries, where everything was acknowledged – but still it unsettled him.

He was navigating the zigzag of Lombard Street when he felt eyes upon him. Squinting into the sun, he saw the silhouette of a woman at the top of the hill, her head bowed, seeming to track his descent. Suddenly he felt certain that she'd been following him, and he quickened his pace. At each switchback he glanced up and she was still there, motionless, until he wondered if she might be some statue that he'd overlooked.

It shouldn't have bothered him. People were often watching him now, men and women both, at restaurants and on the streets, their stares insisting on something he couldn't quite be sure of, expecting a response. He looked in another direction every time, embarrassed and baffled by their bald desire, angry, even, because it felt like a challenge as well as anything else, meant to disable him.

He would have forgotten the Lombard Street incident, but an hour later as he waited in line for the cable car he noticed a woman with the same profile as the first watching him. She was wearing a grey skirt, her hair in a bun and horn-rimmed sunglasses over her eyes, and she stood observing him from across a busy intersection. He thought of running to confront her, but his heart was going crazy, so instead he jumped the line and hopped aboard the departing car, wrapping his hand around a pole to steady himself. As the vehicle began to grind its way toward the sea, a man sitting behind him asked if he was all right.

"Take my seat, mister," the man said. "You look dizzy."

Until then he'd been plagued by other visions – sightings of figures in the street who resembled people from home. They always turned out to be some stranger, and often, upon closer scrutiny, he realized they didn't look at all like the person he'd taken them to be. *Is it my conscience that makes up these impostors?* he'd wondered. *Or is it something else, something higher up?* The woman was different: he didn't know her and didn't want to. That night outside the bar he watched every face that entered, expecting her at any moment.

The next morning he decided to spend the day reading in his room, but he found himself scanning the same sentences over and over, unable to concentrate, only listening for footsteps on the stairs and smoking one cigarette after another. The pencil in his hand scribbled nervously in the margins of the pages, almost of its own accord. He flipped back through the chapters to see what he'd written and was confused by what was there. Sentences that carried over from one page to the next, that filled every cranny of white space. *Really, universally, relations stop nowhere . . . Every act of intimacy a potential violation . . . The need to catch hold of a single word, an idea blown from mind to mind.* Was that actually his handwriting? The words seemed indecipherable, meaningless.

How to get it all down, bridge the gap? How can you even begin? . . . If you're going to do it right, you'll have to learn to forget. You must become an ignorant man again.

He'd had enough. The room was too hot and stuffy, he couldn't stay here any longer. Never mind the woman in grey.

Once he'd dressed and ventured into the streets, he made his way down to the pier where the ferry to Alcatraz departed. It was Labor Day, and wherever he looked people were working: the hot-dog vendors bellowing their pitch, the ticket agents counting money, the dockhands jumping nimbly from bow to pier and slipping ropes through heavy iron rings, shackling the boat to land.

"Rocket!" someone shouted from the crowd.

No. They couldn't have said that. He looked frantically for the source of the cry and saw nothing.

At the island there was a sign that read FEDERAL PENITENTIARY, and underneath it, in faded red spray paint, INDIAN LAND. He'd heard about this; it was partly why he'd come.

Avoiding the offer of a guided tour, he made his way toward the prison house at the top, following an old concrete road that had tufts of grass in its cracks. Outside the entrance a young woman standing on a wooden stool was speaking to a crowd. She wore a green tank top, and her shorts gave way to solid, tanned legs. A vicious wind swept from the direction of the Golden Gate, so strong that a man nearby was struggling to keep hold of the baby stroller in front of him. The woman had to shout at the top of her lungs for her words not to be blown into the bay. Every so often a gust caught her whole body and she threw out her arms, rocked on the stool like a gymnast making a landing, and came to rest again.

"We've stolen Native lands," she shouted. A sympathetic cry went up from the people standing nearest to her. "Thirty years ago Indians made a symbolic stand here at Alcatraz and tried to claim back their territory, but the government wouldn't listen –"

He hadn't expected this. He didn't want to deal with it now.

"Go home," he muttered. The wind played a trick and amplified his voice. Heads turned. The woman looked his way and paused, just for a moment, as though to register his position in the crowd. Then she shifted her gaze and continued.

"We have to give back self-determination to Indians by returning their territories. Not just a pocket of rock here and there. That's just another form of abuse. We have to look with new eyes at the claims in the courts."

He didn't know why exactly he was becoming so upset. At first he'd suspected it was her use of the word *Indian*. There was something else, though, some aspect of her manner that made it seem as though she'd jerked a rope holding him in place. Don't speak, he thought. There's nothing worth saying that you can tell these people. But he couldn't stop himself.

"It will never work," he said. This time he knew he wasn't muttering. More heads turned. "If you're the one who's demanding the land, you're practically starting the reservations all over again."

A short, thin man with a goatee stepped between him and the woman on the stool.

"I don't get it, buddy. She's here to help. What's your problem?"

The wind picked up. Almost imperceptibly, people around the one with the goatee were starting to move his way. He didn't reply. Why should he?

There is much music in this little organ, yet you cannot make it speak.

"Hey, can't you see?" shouted someone in the crowd. "The guy's an Indian." There was a hush; it seemed no one else had noticed. People usually didn't. The woman looked embarrassed, then horrified. His stomach was churning. Nothing would be worked out this way, not through talking, not through an argument here.

Then he saw the woman from the cable car and Lombard Street standing at the edge of the crowd in another grey outfit, this one darker than the clothing she'd been wearing previously. She must have followed him across on the boat. This time it seemed someone else had joined her: a tall, bald African-American man, standing beside her and glaring at him. The glare of someone he knew. He turned away, unwilling to look back and see for certain if it was Mike Pederson. The crowd was waiting for him to say something, but he only walked by the woman on the stool and then through the prison doors.

Mike Pederson in San Francisco. It couldn't be a coincidence, not when he was next to the woman in grey. They'd travelled here to find him.

He made his way down a corridor until he came to a room with long, barred windows. A sign told him he was in the prison library, but the walls were bare, unadorned even by shelves. There was nowhere to hide. The sound of footsteps moving toward him echoed through the corridor, and he glanced down it. At the far end was the woman in grey, approaching determinedly. As he ducked behind the corner, he thought of making his way out the prison doors and back to the ferry, but he didn't want to return to the entrance, where the young woman on the stool and her crowd of followers would no doubt still be gathered, and where Mike Pederson might be waiting. He started in the other direction, trying not to run, and was halfway down the corridor when he saw the man ahead, peering into isolation rooms one by one.

He darted into a wider passage, turned a corner, made his way along another hallway. Finally, unsure of his next move, he stepped into an open cell and sat down on the thin, hard bed. Why was he even hiding? Whoever the woman was, surely she had no authority here. He should be challenging the two of them, declaring that he had nothing to hide, demanding they leave him alone.

There were more footsteps now, heavier and slower. Sitting there on the bed with his hands under him and his knees together, he watched through the bars, trying to control the involuntary shaking of his arms. The sounds grew closer, became so loud that he wondered if someone was already in front of him, invisible, peering through the bars.

Then the man was there for real, passing so slowly that he might have been a film projection. There could be no doubt: it was Mike Pederson.

"Richard," he said. The sound of his name sent one last enormous shudder through him that quashed all the rest.

"What do you want?" he said. A moment later the woman in grey was there too. She stepped inside the cell, moving to the front corner with the bars against her back, while Mike remained at the door, watching over his shoulder as though the two of them had been followed here in turn.

"You know who I am?" the woman asked.

He waved a hand in Mike's direction. "No. I only know him." The truth was, though, that he could have guessed her identity. In June he'd heard about the investigator that Mike had hired. Even back then, before the old man had been arrested, when no one had any reason to connect Richard with Alice Pederson, he'd made a point of staying well away from this woman. He'd crossed the continent partly to avoid this very situation.

"I'm Bronwen Ferry," she said, and he nodded.

"I know your folks." And he knew more than that, now that he looked at her closely. He knew her eyes: dazzling electric swirls of blue that were characteristic of certain families in Sunshine. He knew the accent, the vowels stretched and rounded, the peninsula way of speaking. Six weeks since he'd heard a voice like that one. It wasn't something he'd thought he would miss.

"How did you find me here?" he said.

"Parking tickets," she replied. "Your licence plate turned up in the police database. They've impounded your truck."

He grunted. He'd left the pickup sitting in the place where it had died.

"You've been shadowing me," he said. "Why didn't you approach me until now?"

She glanced over at Mike, but the man only stood there, staring at the cell across the corridor.

"There was no need to surprise you with a confrontation," she said finally. "We wanted to give you some time to think about things."

"You wanted to see if I'd run."

"No." Her voice was firm. "We aren't chasing you. Nobody is."

"Then why come all this way?" he said, speaking directly to Mike, irritated and perplexed by the man's silence.

"To let you know that you have the chance to go home," Mike replied. His tone was peaceable, but the last word hit Richard like something cold and wet.

"What do you mean?"

"He means you don't need to be afraid, Richard," said Bronwen. "No one in Sunshine thinks you had anything to do with Alice's death." In his mind there was a flash of a woman lit by headlights, a dark lakeshore. Despite himself, Richard glanced at Mike, but the man didn't show any reaction. "Daniel Barrie's in town again," Bronwen went on. "Did you know that? He returned just after you left."

He considered this information. It should signify something that Daniel had gone back, but what? The past had been pushed too far down to spring unfettered now into his brain. He had to repeat the information to himself: Daniel was back. He could have stayed in England, but he hadn't. It sounded like a comforting thing, yet at the same time it outraged him. Daniel Barrie was in Sunshine, while he was here, hiding, as a reward for his loyalty.

Bronwen began to say something else, stopped. She seemed so circumspect in talking to him. Why? Did he really appear that fragile?

"Richard, I should tell you," she said at last. "I'm fairly certain that Daniel didn't kill her."

It took him a moment to find a reply.

"I never said he did."

"No. But perhaps the possibility might have crossed your mind." He shrugged. "I talked with him almost a month ago," Bronwen said. "He told me what happened the night Alice disappeared. How you agreed to stay silent for him."

Richard flinched. It had taken so much travel to shut away the memories, and now here they were returning. Daniel and Alice on the icy road. The old man's drunken pleading in the parking lot. *Don't abandon me. Don't. I need you.* The terror in him began to rise.

"It would make sense for you to imagine the worst," Bronwen was saying. "Daniel was the last one to see her. He asked you not to say anything to the police. Did he tell you about the affair?"

There was still no reaction from Mike. He just looked at them both intently as though this were a drama under his direction, one he was following to make sure it went exactly as rehearsed.

"Daniel didn't tell me anything," Richard replied, unable to keep the bitterness from his voice.

"It's all right, Richard. If I were in your position, living in Sunshine with a police investigation going on and Daniel out of the country, I'd have started to wonder too. When the body turned up, you must have suspected that he'd been lying when he said she'd just run away."

He shrugged again. "I couldn't be sure."

"What about after they arrested Stoddart Fremlin?" said Mike.

Richard tried to breathe deeply. Of course there'd be no avoiding that name, not now. Outside the bars a tour group passed by, each person staring in as though the three of them were part of an exhibit.

"They charged Stoddart around the time you left," Bronwen said when the group had disappeared, her voice lower than before. "Did you know that?" He nodded, and then, strangely, she nodded too.

"The same day, even?" She'd realized then. She knew what it had meant for him to flee Sunshine when he did. The options had been clear enough: tell the truth about what had happened after the henge party and save Frem, or stay silent to save Daniel – and to save himself, as well, because the police would suspect him too, wouldn't they? Daniel had said as much. In the end Richard had decided simply to leave, and it was the right decision, he was sure of it. The heft of each shirt, each book, each balled-together pair of socks into his duffle bag had brought a solid, guiltless pleasure. It was only on the road south that he'd thought of the old man in his prison cell and felt a brief flare of regret. A moment later he'd reached for the radio dial and changed stations, turned up the volume.

"You think I should have stayed," he said now. "Should have come forward, told the truth. So that he'd be let free and they'd arrest Daniel instead."

"I didn't say that."

"You're thinking it. You both are. Anyone would." And maybe they were right. But none of it mattered now if Daniel had talked to the police. "Have they let the old man out of jail, then?" he asked. Bronwen paused, looked to Mike. What was passing between them? What did they know? Could it be that Frem had come here with them? Was he down the corridor, waiting for his moment to appear and make his accusations? *You betrayed me, Richie.* No, I won't stand for it, Richard thought. I'd do violence to them all before I let that happen.

"Richard," said Bronwen. "Stoddart's dead."

"What?" he cried. The anger fled from him and something else, heavier and disorienting, took its place.

Dead. The word flickered on and off like a bulb in a thunderstorm. *Dead, dead.*

"He shot himself a month ago," said Bronwen. "While he was out on bail. The police found his body in a truck down an old logging road."

He'd shot himself. The thought struck like a blow aimed straight at Richard and thrown by the old man himself. *This is what you get for deserting me.* It didn't seem possible. Frem was someone from whom you escaped. He wasn't someone who would ever die.

"It's my fault," Richard murmured. "I should have told the police the truth. They must be looking for me after all." He almost felt relief. "Have they arrested Daniel yet?" he asked, looking up at Mike. The man shook his head.

"The police decided Stoddart's suicide was proof that he killed Alice," Mike replied. "They've closed the file on her death. But some of us aren't so convinced by their story." His voice had been calm until he hit upon his wife's name, then it had quivered very slightly before continuing. Even as Richard took in what the man had said, he felt an urge to comfort him. There was concern on Bronwen's face too; she seemed to be restraining herself from going over to him.

"I don't understand," Richard said after a while. "If Daniel told the police what happened, they'd know that Frem couldn't have –"

"Daniel hasn't really told the police anything," Bronwen said. "Only that he and Alice had some kind of relationship. Or, at least, that's all Harry Midgard will admit to knowing."

"What? I thought you said –"

"I think Daniel tried to explain to Harry, once, about what happened after Usher's party, but my guess is that Harry didn't want to listen. If I were him, I wouldn't like to hear about it. Why ruin an open-and-shut case? Besides, Harry watched Daniel grow up with the other kids in town; he knows he isn't a murderer."

"So that's the end of it?" Richard said incredulously.

"No," Bronwen replied. "Because Daniel decided to come to me. He felt guilty, apparently. I guess you'd understand that feeling well enough." She said it with compassion, not with spite. He imagined Daniel in Sunshine, his burden weighing him down until finally he'd cracked and sought out this woman. Her eyes: they were the eyes of someone in whom you could confide. He wondered if things might have been different if he'd crossed her path in June.

"I wanted to tell someone," he murmured. "All that time, I was desperate to tell somebody." Nobody could live their life like that, in one place, dragging their secrets behind them. Then he pictured Daniel again, and a darker thought came to him. "He might have killed her, you know. That night by the lake, after I drove away. Why are you so certain he didn't?"

"I guess I shouldn't be," Bronwen replied. "But with some people, I think, you can see into their hearts just by talking with them." She said this as though not quite sure of it herself, and he shook his head.

"It isn't like that. People fool you. Most of them, down deep" – he tried to breathe – "there are things that would make you sick." With one hand he clenched the thin mattress beneath him. "What about me? Do I seem like someone who could leave a man in prison, who could run away to California?"

"Maybe you were doing what you believed was right," Bronwen replied. "Perhaps some part of you figured it was justice. You thought Fremlin deserved to be in jail." One of her shoes slid forward, then back, as if she was scraping something from the sole.

"I don't know what you're talking about," he said, and stared at the sliding shoe, the floor, taking refuge in its rough, grey patterns. Please, stop talking, he thought. Don't go any further.

"Richard, I think I understand why you came out here. Why you didn't want to end up testifying in a courtroom. Why you wouldn't want anyone looking into your life."

He wanted to run now, was almost willing to try. *You would play upon me, you would seem to know my stops.*

"I talked with Esther Fremlin last week," Bronwen said. "She met with her father just before he died. He told her something . . ."

She knew then. It was appalling, how open his mind had become. *Didn't I leave Sunshine just to preserve its fragile sanctity? To prevent the secrets from escaping?* And now this woman offered them in her hand as though she didn't realize what she held.

"Richard, it's safe to come back," she said, her voice soft.

"You don't know anything," Richard replied. "Don't pretend you do."

"I know he hurt you," she said after a time.

He nodded. But Frem hadn't hurt him, he thought. Not physically. Frem never hit him, barely even touched him, except for those times when they were alone together in the darkness.

"Richard, whatever he did to you" – she looked toward Mike as though for support – "it's nothing to be ashamed of."

"I don't want to talk about it," he said quickly. "It's in the past. The past isn't important. You can't do anything to change it." Strange how easily these words came out of him. *Without fear of infamy I answer thee.* "Look at me," he said. "I'm fine."

Bronwen took him in with a long sweep of her eyes. The black denims, the white T-shirt. His hair almost to his shoulders and three days of growth on his chin. What did she see to put that expression on her face? They didn't even know each other. She seemed like she was going to say something, but her mouth closed and her bright blue eyes shut tight. With her fingers she pressed against her forehead, kneading the skin.

She didn't deserve his hostility, not now, but he felt a pressure from below, a suspicion forming, tugging at him, strong and horrible and frightening.

"Who else knows?" he demanded. "Who have you talked to? My mother and father? Have you told them?"

He imagined his parents greeting him outside the house in Sunshine, full of the new knowledge, their words conscientiously chosen in advance. They'd say wise and caring things, but their shame would be obvious enough. He remembered the day he'd told them he was quitting hockey, his father nodding grimly, the man's stunned, self-searching disappointment unspoken but clear, while in Richard's mind the speeches and lessons had all come back, the ones about making the most of talents, never giving up. It would be a thousand times worse than that now. What could he possibly say to them?

"We haven't told anyone, Richard," Bronwen insisted. "Nobody knows."

He saw Mike nodding in agreement and felt thankful, but it wasn't enough. Richard understood how things were in Sunshine. Once a secret was released, it ran quickly through hidden crevices and inevitably resurfaced in a thousand places.

"I don't know if I can believe that," he said. He was thinking how once people had greeted him on the streets. They'd smacked him on the back, wished him good luck in the next game, called him a hero. And always he'd thought: *If you only knew, you'd despise me, every one of you.*

"I can never go home," he said. He hadn't meant to say it aloud. What was going on? There didn't seem to be any inside to him now. It all spilled out the second it came into being.

"Does not going home matter to you?" Bronwen said. "Do you want to go back?"

That brought him up short. "No," he replied hastily. "No, I'm happy here."

"What about your parents?"

"What about them?" he snapped.

"I didn't tell them about Stoddart, but I talked to them last week when I discovered your truck was down here. They're worried about you, Richard. They wanted us to find you and ask you to come back. They're the ones who're paying for this trip."

It was a dirty trick, he thought, to talk of parents. He was a grown man now.

"I guess they were too busy to come themselves, right?" he said dully.

"They wanted to, but I couldn't guarantee that we'd find you," Bronwen replied.

"So you brought him instead," he said, pointing to Mike, and then turned to him, irate. "Why are you here? You get a kick from this sort of thing?"

Mike took a long breath.

"It's my wife who died. That's why I'm here."

Richard should have nodded, but the words felt too much like an accusation.

"It wasn't my fault," he said.

"Nobody says it was," replied Bronwen. "But you were there that night. You have a story to tell. Richard, in a couple of months it will have been two years since the henge party. People might start to remember. We need to open the case again. Daniel Barrie's too frightened to talk in public; now that the police have let him off the hook, he's decided it's better to keep quiet. But if you went public with what happened, people would believe you. It's in your hands."

"Why?" he said. "Why bother? It won't bring her back." Once he'd said it, though, he turned his face from Mike, ashamed.

"What about the truth?" Bronwen said. "What about Alice? Don't you think she deserves to have justice served? Her killer could still be out there."

"Who? Daniel?" He shook his head. "No, the police have their man, and right now Daniel's in the clear, you said so yourself. Going public would only force them to arrest him."

"Don't you want to settle in your own mind whether he killed her?" she asked.

"Don't play on my conscience. You said yourself, you don't think he did it. Do you really think the truth is going to come out after so many months?"

The two of them stood there for a few seconds, apparently unable to answer, before Mike spoke.

"All right. Bronwen won't say it, but I will. You're afraid to go back, Richard. You're afraid that if you testify about Alice, other things will come out. I understand that. It's your right to protect yourself. But don't pretend to be indifferent about things like justice. We came to this island on the same boat as you did. We heard you outside the entrance with that girl. Don't tell me there's nothing inside you that wants to speak."

"Maybe there is," he replied quietly. "But what would it be worth? What would be the point?"

Mike shrugged. "For one thing, you'd be able to go home."

He heard the dying off of the man's voice echo through the cell block. Even the architecture was willing their words into public life. He rose from the mattress, needing to escape.

"Richard," said Bronwen gently. "Mike and I fly back tomorrow night. There are seats available on the plane. Come with us. Tell your story. Let us help you."

"Not everyone –" He fought for control of himself. "Not everyone there would be as careful around me as you're being." As he stood there she stepped toward him and reached out.

"Don't –," he said, pulling back.

"I'm sorry," she said quickly. "I just –" Mike walked over and slid an arm around her shoulders.

"Come on," he said to her. "It's up to him now." He turned to Richard. "We're staying at the Union Square if you want to call us tonight." His voice was measured but severe; it seemed he'd had enough. Richard watched the man's hand slip down Bronwen's back and suddenly felt betrayed.

"Sure, the Union Square," he said caustically. "Do I ask for Mr. and Mrs. Pederson?"

"What's that supposed to mean?" Mike demanded.

"Nothing," he said. He didn't want to be talking like this, but there was nothing to be done. "I'm glad you two got this chance to go away together. It must be hard, staying so dedicated to your wife."

As though something had bitten it, Mike's hand dropped sharply from Bronwen's back.

"Listen," he said, almost in a whisper. "I know you've had a hard time –"

"Don't," said Bronwen. She sounded exhausted. "You're right, Mike. Let's go."

But Richard went first, moving quickly out the door and down the corridor to the prison entrance, noticing with a certain sense of release that the crowd and the woman on the stool had disappeared. Then, without slowing or looking back, he continued to the dock. It was an important gesture to have walked out before they did, he decided later, a necessary show of self-reliance, even if it was undercut somewhat by their arrival at the shore a few minutes later and his realization that the three of them would have to share the last boat back to the city.

THE NEXT NIGHT he didn't go to work. Instead he walked the streets, most of them familiar to him now, and thought of the old man.

As a teenager there'd been a time when he lay in bed at night wishing for Frem to die. He'd never been clever enough to hope for suicide. Instead he'd imagined a heart attack, a slip down stairs, a lightning strike, even though he told himself these things would never come to pass. He'd have to murder Frem in order for death to visit the old man, and that was something he could never do. It was too frightening to imagine the look of rage that would cross Frem's face when he felt the switchblade at his breast, the hands on his neck. Too distressing to imagine the swell of public sympathy afterwards at the loss of a dentist, a father, a mentor to the boys of Mooney's Dump. No one would believe Richard if he told them why he'd done it, even if he could bring himself to make such a confession. They'd all be against him. *Did he ever force you? You were a big strong boy. You could have stopped him, beat him, dragged him to the police. Why didn't you tell anybody? Didn't you know it was wrong? Or were you enjoying yourself too much?*

He remembered Frem jeering, sulking, demanding to be comforted. The condescension and contempt if his wishes weren't fulfilled. From this distance the old man almost seemed pathetic. Why had it never felt like that at the time? Or perhaps it had. Hadn't there always been a sense of shameful obligation? Near the end he'd thought of their encounters as an unfortunate debt being paid off, not his own, but one undertaken by some earlier, inscrutable self, the eleven-year-old who in fear and self-loathing hadn't spoken out. Payments were made on those Thursday evening walks to the old man's house, running into friends along the way who asked him where he was headed. All those chances to have said something, gone. Vanished like the old man.

He searched himself for traces of sadness, but there were only guilty surges of relief. Never again would the telephone ring and that voice beseech him. No manic knocking at his door. There'd be no danger of their history becoming public knowledge. Except that now Bronwen Ferry knew. *It's safe to come back*, she'd had told him, but he didn't believe her. He tried to see himself in Sunshine, taking a job at the quarry, digging for the rest of his life with everyone talking, pointing. People who'd only ever cared about what happened at the rink, how many goals he'd scored. And he'd believed them. He'd thought hockey was what mattered most. Only when his last game was over had he realized that the game had never really mattered to him, and that if he could be free of it, he could be free of the old man too.

But there'll never be freedom for me, he thought, not in Sunshine. Better to remain here, anonymous and safe. No matter that he still hadn't had a proper conversation with another person in this place, not unless he counted the previous day's meeting at Alcatraz.

This morning he'd taken a bus to Mike and Bronwen's hotel, his forehead throbbing from lack of sleep, the sunlight diminishing as clouds moved in from the ocean and the blue sky retreated east. In the lobby he'd asked the concierge to ring their room, and a few minutes later the two of them had emerged from an elevator.

"We're glad to see you," Bronwen had said slowly.

It had been hard for him to breathe – the lobby was too dark, the walls too close – so he'd led them out to the sidewalk. The air was growing heavy, as though it was about to rain – not just a shower, but a real late-summer storm. Any second the palm branches would begin to whip and thrash. Bronwen and Mike could sense it too. They seemed anxious for him to speak and release them.

"I'm not going back with you," he told them. "I guess you've figured that out by now."

Perhaps he could find work on a boat, he thought, as he watched their mouths set into frowns. There were no allegiances out there; he could end up anywhere he wanted. But even the ocean had codes and conventions. He'd have to go farther, into outer space, to be really and truly free. He could almost imagine himself taking off from where he stood, flying away from them, off the earth.

"I guess that's it then," said Bronwen. "Thanks for coming here to tell us at least."

In the cracks between buildings he could see dark clouds moving swiftly across the sky. When he started to talk, he almost didn't recognize the speaking voice as his own.

"It would take everyone to set things right again," he was saying. "Every cog working together. But that's beyond me."

He had more to tell them; he felt on the edge of something profound, something that could redeem the time and satisfy whatever need Mike and Bronwen felt.

"I don't want to become a symbol –," he began. But people were running for cover and it was too difficult to think. Whatever it was that pressed at him, it stayed just beyond the point of articulation. A flash of limestone cliffs went through his mind. Bronwen glanced pointedly at the sky; she seemed to have given up on him.

This wasn't how he had wanted things to end. Somehow he'd hoped to convince them that his decision was right. But they looked annoyed now, as though all the time at Alcatraz the three of them had been speaking past each other.

"Wait," he said. "You don't understand –"

Bronwen was talking. Talking loudly, insistently, and he wasn't even listening to her. What was she saying? Richard's head whirled. It was like the prison and the woman on the stool all over again. More polemics, more argumentation, leading nowhere. A vicious circle of words, forever demanding more speech, impossible to break. Bronwen had stopped speaking now and was waiting for him to respond, but there was nothing he could tell her.

"Goodbye then," she said. "Take care of yourself." This time she didn't try to give him a hug.

Bronwen didn't really care about what happened to him, he thought now as he walked the streets. She was just doing a job. In a few hours she and Mike would be back in Sunshine reporting to his parents, and that would be the end of it for her. Eventually word would spread that Rocket DeWitt was living in San Francisco. For a few years his name would come up whenever conversations turned to the fortunes of the town's young people. Then he'd be swept out of the community altogether, existing only in the pauses and gaps, just as the reserve was always treated with silence, just as Alice Pederson was no doubt being relegated to the shadow-world of the unspeakable. That's how people went on there; that's how you survived.

It was almost midnight. A few blocks from Golden Gate Park, he entered a used bookstore that was still open. With tourists around him whispering in Italian, he sifted through bins until he found a hardbound book with blank pages, its yellow cover marked by a stain, the pages so old and discoloured that it was almost impossible to imagine they'd ever been white. He bought it with the intention of writing something. Not just his own story, though; no, in order to tell that one he'd have to squeeze the whole town onto paper. But how? He wasn't like Bronwen: he didn't believe that people's hearts were so open that he might reproduce them on the page. There wasn't room enough in a thousand volumes for that, even if he could guess rightly what was there. As he weighed the book in his hand he was glad of its lightness, its finite pages, promising an ending. Otherwise he might never be able to stop.

Chase the dreams on to paper, out of mind. Relinquish all of them, even the one about belonging. Especially that one. There are more important things.

When he left the bookstore he realized he could suddenly remember Bronwen's last words to him, the ones he'd been unable to answer. She'd asked him a question: "If you're so convinced that you're finished with Sunshine," she'd said, "why does it seem like you miss it so much?"

"I don't miss it," he replied to himself now as he started down the street, wishing she was there to hear. *I don't miss it*, he thought, panting in the cool, damp San Francisco air. "I don't. I don't miss it at all."

WANDERING ROCKS

They travelled slowly through the woods under the full moon, having left the groomed tracks some time earlier. They'd been going for an hour, up and down unfamiliar hills, trying to find the trail again and return to Cam Usher's party. It was Marge who'd proposed an excursion – a little jaunt into the forest, she had said. Now she'd lost her sense of direction entirely, so she focused on the ground and followed Susan's shadow as it flickered across the snow. She wanted to rest and look around, make some sense of where they were heading, but Susan doggedly broke trail and Marge was obligated to follow, until her limbs seemed separate from her, struggling and suffering by themselves. The world swam in a sickly pale light.

"We're lost, aren't we?" she cried at last. "Wait, stop. I'm too tired to go any farther."

"The wildlife park's just over the next rise, don't worry," Susan replied. She'd made the same claim three times before. Marge threw off her poles and sank until she lay on the snow, her skis smacking together and crossing so that her legs tangled.

"It's going to be over by the time we get back, isn't it?" she said.

"At this rate the century will be over." Susan helped her up, then gently brushed the snow from her clothing. "Listen, don't worry, he won't go without saying goodbye." In twelve hours Daniel would be leaving for England.

She reached out her arms, and Marge stepped into them, felt the pleasure of her nearness. If they held each other like this long enough, perhaps they'd begin to merge into one another. They'd pass back and forth not just the heat from their bodies but feelings, thoughts, until nothing was private any more. She pulled away a few inches to look Susan in the eyes, as though they were the point of entry, and noticed the steam rising from her head – like mist off the bay, Marge thought, early on a cold morning.

"NICE TO MEET YOU!" said Stump, walking away and grinning over his shoulder. "Hope to see you at the store!"

He hated parties. There were too many people to meet and half of them were scumbags. All the smug, anonymous faces stayed in their little groups and acted like best buddies, drinking and smoking and doing illegal drugs, probably, staring at him like he was going to steal their wallets when he approached. Too much guesswork about the whole thing, trying to figure out whether they were local or just jerks from Toronto up here for the night. It seemed like Usher had invited half the country.

He went to the barbecue pit near the farmhouse and ordered another hot dog. While the girl tending the grill reached with her tongs he snuck a look at the packages of buns stacked beside her and saw they were the brand sold by the other convenience store in town.

"You know, you could get those buns a nickel cheaper at the Mooney's Dump Variety," he told her.

"Sure," the girl replied casually as she flipped a burger, not bothering to look at him. "But they say the new guy who runs the place –" Her voice stopped abruptly, her body stiffened, she stayed facing the grill.

"What about the guy?" Stump asked.

"I was just going to say, I haven't met him," she replied. "It's better to do business with people you know." She turned slowly and wrapped the hot dog in a napkin. "Here you go, mister. I hope you don't mind, the bun's a little burnt."

She had nice eyes, with long lashes, set in a face that was round and shining. Young, but not as young as he'd thought. Not a girl at all.

"Your cheeks are red," he told her. "Must be the heat from the coals."

"Yeah, and the smoke and ashes too," she agreed quickly. "It's disgusting back here. I feel like what's-his-name, from the comics –"

Stump shrugged. He didn't read the comics. Normally he'd say this out loud, insist that the business section was all he had time for, but now it seemed like the wrong thing to tell her. He wanted to make some connection, and there was a question about to burst through his lips, whether or not it was ready to be spoken.

"What's your name?" he asked her.

Esther told him without hesitating, eager to make up for her slip, reprimanding herself for not recognizing him from the start as the variety store's new owner. When he replied that his name was Stanley Weston, she didn't flinch, didn't pretend suddenly to recognize the name. All she said was: "It's nice to meet you, Stanley."

So this was the guy from Owen Sound everyone had been talking about. "Have you been schmoozed by the schmoozer yet?" was the question people were asking tonight. The hand-shaker, the price-beater, your new best friend. He didn't seem so bad. His voice was high and uneven, as though he couldn't breathe very deeply, and his Adam's apple bobbed up and down like a fist being shaken when he talked, but his smile seemed honest enough.

"You know, it's not always true," he said.

"What isn't?" she asked.

"What you said, about doing business with people you know. It's not always better."

"Why not?"

"Well for one thing, you never meet anyone new," he replied. "I mean, imagine if you only ever got to talk with the people in town you grew up with."

"Welcome to my life," she said, and he laughed. It wasn't the laugh people had told her about, the hyena's bray that outlasted everyone else's. It was deeper and warmer than that.

She looked beyond him to the groups of people scattered across Cam Usher's field, the strangers and the friends, the familiar faces she couldn't quite name most of the time. To spend the rest of the night among them would be frustrating. You never saw enough of the people you liked best. You said hello, you moved on, maybe you said hi to them again in a different group, and that was it. And then there was her father, somewhere out there, probably drinking too much again and keen to run into her so he could berate her one more time for choosing to come back and live in this place.

"Listen, are you stuck selling hot dogs all night?" Stanley Weston asked her. "Because I could spell you off for a while –"

"Nah, I'm just here until Sherry Easterbrook shows up for her shift," she replied. "In five minutes I'll be over at the rink." She met his eyes for a second. "You play hockey?"

He shook his head.

"I don't even own skates."

"Well, Stanley, if you're going to make any money selling things in this town you'll have to get some soon, because all the important stuff around here is settled in stinky old change rooms."

Then she realized what she'd just admitted by saying this, after all this time pretending not to know who he was. He looked at her for a long time, silent, before taking a bite of his hot dog and beginning to chew. She wondered if he'd bother mentioning now that he owned the Variety, and if he did, whether she could possibly act surprised, whether she could pretend to remember how they'd started talking, and laugh, and say, "You should have told me right then who you were." Maybe he'd say it was his fault, and afterwards they could go on with that patched-together lie between them, both of them knowing it was a lie, but happy at least that it was one they'd made up together.

WHEN THE PROTESTERS began to circle around him with their skeleton faces, Solomon slouched and hid himself in the crowd. He hadn't expected this. Snatching glimpses through the cracks between bodies, he saw their eyes lodged in hollow painted caverns, looking for him. Or if not looking, on the verge of finding him, at least, which would be the same thing in the end. One of the elders fixed upon his face, and he waited for her cry of angry recognition, but she passed by him and he was spared. Ruth was right: he should have stayed at home.

How dare they not tell him about the protest? he thought as the group departed. They could ruin everything with such carnival shows if they forced the government's hand too early. He'd told them that before, but it seemed he'd lost all claim to authority a long time ago when he moved off the reserve. Now he was just Solomon DeWitt the lawyer, the man who mingled with white people at white gatherings on sacred ground.

He made his way to the henge and stared bleakly at the structure, then wove around the standing stones, inspecting each in turn. There was a spotlight positioned in the centre so that their shadows slashed outwards like hour marks on a giant clock.

These stones belong to us, just like the land, he thought. They're from the quarry – ripped from the bowels of the earth. How much stolen treasure like this scattered across the peninsula? And yet we're the ones seen as the outsiders, not part of the community but barbarians waiting to invade.

Out of the corner of his eye he noticed Bobby Boone approaching. Boone must have seen him too, but he was making a show of examining the henge.

"Hey, DeWitt, what do you know?" Boone bellowed at last, when they were too close together for him to keep up the pretence any longer. He wore a snowmobile jacket and a baseball cap that read *Vote Sunshine*, and in each hand he held a tall brown bottle. "You want one?" he asked. "No, of course, you don't imbibe, do you? Too bad, you deserve a beer after your big courtroom victory yesterday."

"It's all right," Solomon said carefully. Boone had drunk too much, it was obvious, but that was no reason to let his guard down.

"You know what?" Boone said. "I want to shake your hand."

"Really, Boone, it doesn't matter –"

"I want to shake the hand of the man who convinced a judge to take my quarry and give it to those Indians who so richly deserve it. Here, hold this so I can shake your hand, will you? Thanks. Christ, would you look at that, now you can't shake either." Boone took back the beer.

I'm standing on graves with this man, thought Solomon.

"I'll tell you something, DeWitt. Maybe you and I were on different sides in the case, but that's no reason for us to be enemies."

"I didn't say we were," Solomon replied. Boone wasn't listening.

"No sir, I don't hold grudges. No time for them. You see this cap on my head? In two months we're going to have a brand-new name for the town that will change the economy completely, and I want all you Indians in on the deal. Listen, what do you think about holding a Sunshine Dance out on the reserve?"

Solomon shook his head slowly.

"It's not something our Nation does –"

"And let me ask you something else," Bobby went on. "Do you play hockey?"

Solomon looked around for a distraction, but there was no one approaching. The two of them were alone, surrounded by the circle of stones, and Bobby Boone stood with his back to the spotlight so that his features were in shadow.

"No, not hockey," Solomon replied. "You're thinking of my son –"

"I know about the boy," Bobby said irritably. "I mean you. We have an old-timers team that could use a big wiry fellow."

"I'm sorry," Solomon said.

Boone looked at him for a moment, his gaze piercing as though the drunkenness had vanished.

"Well that's too bad," he said at last. "Maybe we'll sign you up for softball in the summer."

Solomon nodded noncommittally. Boone had got him thinking about Richard. The boy was here now, no doubt, perhaps in the farmhouse or elsewhere in the field. The boy, he repeated. Not a very accurate term for someone taller and stronger than himself. The young man then; the one who wouldn't accept that his parents still loved him. The one who thought he was only a disappointment, who couldn't show his face at his own home now that he was finished with hockey and hadn't gone to university. Solomon had seen the look in his eyes the last time they talked, the embarrassment at having to admit that he was still working at the Mooney's Dump gas station.

"You know, it's funny, you coming here," Bobby Boone was saying. "I mean, with the band so sure there's an Indian cemetery on the property and everything."

Solomon frowned. Boone should mind his own business. Solomon was here to see his son as much as anything else. He had a whole speech to deliver, although every time he thought it might be Richard in the distance his words seemed false and empty. To tell the boy about the jobs opening up at the quarry was the wrong approach. But the most important things; how to broach them in a conversation? No words should be necessary. He wanted to find him now and grab him, shake him into seeing all of this, but Boone had reached across and taken hold of his arm, was leaning in far too close, his beer-stinking breath filling the air. He looked at Solomon with frightening, glassy eyes and spoke as though whatever he had to say was the most important thing in the world.

"I'm surprised at you, really," Boone exclaimed. "Don't suppose I'm the only one, either. Awful risk, isn't it? There's probably some that would call you a traitor."

"What?" Solomon muttered. "What are you talking about?"

"Oh, I'm rambling, DeWitt. Don't mind me. It's just that when I mentioned to one of those protesters tonight – Kahgee, was that her name? You know, the one on the council – anyhow, when I told her you were here, you should have seen the look on her face."

It was intolerable. Solomon tried to tear himself from Boone's grasp, but he realized the man had already let go. One of the beer bottles he'd held lay between their feet, its contents spilled and darkening the snow. Boone turned and walked toward the farmhouse, sipping from the remaining bottle as he went.

"Good night, DeWitt," he called over his shoulder. "See you around town."

HAMISH FERRY was one of those residents of Mooney's Dump whom Eudora had heard about but almost never saw: the farmer who invented things, who seldom came to town and was glimpsed only in the middle of his visits to the barbershop and the feed store. But there he was now, sitting alone on one of the benches right in front of her, the others around the fire taken up by parents and children roasting marshmallows. Eudora had approached him thinking he was someone else, having noticed only his scruffy beard, but never mind that. Never mind Archimedes Boone. She was glad it wasn't him. After so many years of not speaking to the man, it was good to be relieved of the decision she'd been confronting: whether to speak kindly or allow the old enmity to continue.

"Do you mind if I join you?" she asked, and Hamish murmured a reply that she couldn't quite hear.

When she sat down, she saw that he looked nothing like Archie at all. There was a beard, yes, but short, straight, and brown. Whereas Archie's eyes had a warm, dull glow, this man's were full of spit and spark.

"You're Eudora Northey, right?" he asked in a rough voice, and she nodded, pleased that he knew her. "I heard your husband died." She froze, then nodded again, slowly. "I was sorry to hear that," he said.

"Well, it was a long time ago now," she said. "You must have been a child back then."

He stared at her.

"I guess," he said. "I don't remember exactly. How old are you now? Sixty? Sixty-five?"

"A lady never tells," she replied coldly. He'd been gazing into the fire, but now he turned to her and studied her face intently. She was sorry she'd sat down.

"I'd guess about sixty-three," he said after a while. "Am I close?" She didn't reply. "Hell, secrets are a waste of time. Look, I'm thirty-seven and I don't mind telling you."

"Perhaps I don't wish to know," she said. "I just left the ice rink to get away from all the gossips over there. If I wanted information they'd be the first to tell me."

"You shouldn't have left," he said. "They'll start talking about you now that you're gone." She wondered if another show of indignation was necessary, but he spoke so matter-of-factly that she decided it would be a waste of time.

"Oh, I'm not a very interesting topic of conversation," she replied instead. "Besides, if I didn't give them a chance to say nasty things behind my back, they'd say them to my face."

Hamish chuckled, and she felt as though she'd won some small victory, but then they both fell into silence.

"I'm sixty-six," she said at last. "Tell a soul and I'll kill you."

"Three years off!" he cried and stamped his foot. "Well, you don't look a day over sixty-four."

He asked her if she'd seen the henge, and she had to admit that she hadn't, so they got up and walked a short distance across the field along a path lit by torches. He didn't speak, and idly she tried to guess what he was thinking. Finally they reached an icy wooden bridge over the moat that surrounded the stones. He held her hand as they crossed.

My fingers aren't the kind she'll like, he thought. They're too stubby and callused from work. But she was wearing mittens, and if she noticed that the wool rasped against the coarse surface of his skin, she didn't say anything. Once they'd reached the other side, he turned to the henge and smiled.

"I helped to build this thing," he told her. "I've been here a hundred times, probably, and I never get tired of it." He ran a hand along the smooth inner exposure of the southeastern stone. "Did you ever build anything? Make something out of nothing?" He looked over at her and she was just a silhouette against the fire. "Do you know what it feels like to have a thing of yours in the world? Something that will last?" He leaned against the stone, threw all his weight at it, dug his heels in, and pushed until his face was red. When his boots slid out and his strength failed him, he stood straight again and swallowed air in great gulps.

"I had a friend," said Eudora Northey. "He collects things. For posterity. Maybe he would know what you're talking about."

"Nobody I ever met collects anything but junk," he said, still gasping. "I'm not talking about junk. I mean something new."

Just then there were screams from the bonfire circle. Two children were running around the perimeter, a boy chasing a girl, both of them holding branches in their hands from the nearby pile of cedar brush. It seemed that sometime during the chase, the one in the boy's hand had caught fire. Around and around they went, the girl looking back in terror, the boy screaming along with her, aware of the flames an arm's-length away but apparently unable to stop himself or let go of the bough.

"Where are the adults?" Eudora Northey was saying. Her voice seemed very far away, though. Hamish was transfixed by the sight of the two branches moving in unison, never varying in distance from one another, spinning around the fire. It had given him an idea.

"Oh God," he said. "Oh God, I think it will work." He leaned against the stone again and thought for a second, then felt in his pockets. Nothing. "Eudora, do you have a pen and paper? It's important."

"I think the children are all right," she said after a moment, still staring in the direction of the fire. "Yes, there's a woman over there who's got them under control. It's all right now."

If he waited another minute it would be gone. Quickly he darted between the stones and crossed the bridge in one long skid, then tried to cut across the field, but the snow was too soft and he sank up to his knees. Cursing and staggering, he made his way back to the path that led to the parking lot, knocking over a torch along the way. It sizzled and winked out, but he didn't stop. A spectre had risen on the horizon behind the farmhouse, over the bay, and it shone more brightly than the moon. He was in pursuit, heading toward the central spoke that appeared to impale the farmhouse like an enormous sewing needle. A paper and pen were all he needed to set down its design and, with the same few strokes, his own immortality. An enormous metal roaster had been erected in the sky, and it spun slowly through the air, spears of broccoli bigger than oaks passing through the clouds and beginning to bake in the warm winter's night, beckoning him onwards.

"HONESTLY, I'M not Daniel Barrie," Quentin protested. "I've never even met the guy."

He tried to move the stranger's hand from his shoulder, but the grip was as solid and stiff as a corpse's, and with thick fingers the man pulled Quentin closer to him, squinting, before he finally let go.

"It's that red hair of yours. Listen, you see Daniel, tell him that Stoddart Fremlin is looking for Richie."

It was the third time in an hour that someone had made the mistake. Quentin had never heard of Daniel Barrie until tonight, but it seemed he was some sort of local celebrity. How similar to each other were the two of them? he wondered. Probably it was just the colour of their hair, maybe the same leanness. But what about the eyes? The nose, hands, shoulders? Quentin imagined asking his parents if he had a twin brother, as a joke, and watching their eyes glaze over, their mouths open and close silently like the jaws of fish, a secret cracked open on their faces. Some impossible story about a crazed nurse fleeing the city with the babe in her arms, ending up in this tiny, backwater town. Another night he would have liked to meet his double and decide for himself if the resemblance was real. Not now. He was too busy looking for Cam.

Quentin walked in the direction of the henge, hoping that from the slight rise in the centre of it he might better survey the field, but even from that vantage point there was no sign of him. The only person to be seen was an old woman in a brown mackintosh pacing between the stones. Quentin checked the hockey rink next, then followed the chain-link fence that divided the cleared land from the wildlife park, wondering if he'd made a mistake in coming here. There were better things a lawyer could do with his evening than drive three hours to stand in a snowy field.

As he stared out over the landscape, he decided it must have been something about this place that had hardened Cam. The isolation, perhaps; the barrenness. It had been different in Toronto. When they'd met at the party a few months ago, Cam had been carefree, charming, the man everyone was talking about, both men and women, the one they all seemed to want. But he's chaste as a priest, they complained. Never takes anybody home, or if he does, he won't kiss and tell. For all they knew, he only slept with the animals up in his little game reserve.

Still, it didn't matter. Once Quentin had been introduced to him properly, it took less than half an hour of Cam's company to render him helpless. He didn't even consider turning down the man's invitation to visit Mooney's Dump, such were his hopes and fantasies. The next Friday he'd driven up, arriving in time for dinner, and was given a tour of the wildlife park. A beautiful dozing tiger was the final stop. Then Cam had poured drinks in the farmhouse, asked him questions. Everything seemed perfect. It was true that Cam barely talked about himself, but everyone had said he was a bit of an enigma.

When the change happened, it came all at once, late that night in the living room, with the occasional howl of a caged animal the only sound other than their voices.

"You know there's a Native reserve with a claim on the quarry next door?" Cam had asked him.

"Oh God," he'd replied. "Let's not talk law right now. I'm so tired."

But Cam hadn't relented. He'd wanted to hear if Quentin ever handled land claims, if he knew about Aboriginal issues, until in the end Quentin had looked him in the eye, tried to sound as if he was joking.

"Cam, if I didn't know you any better, I'd say you got me up here to get free legal advice."

He barely knew Cam at all. If he had, he wouldn't have said that. Or he wouldn't have come in the first place. But instead Cam had stood abruptly and in a cold voice said he thought it was time to say good night.

"Look, I was kidding," Quentin had protested. "I already work at the firm sixty hours a week, I guess I'm sensitive about it overlapping with –"

It didn't help. Shortly afterwards Cam had shown him to the guest bedroom, and the next morning Quentin had left before breakfast.

But I was right, wasn't I? he thought. I've talked with others in the city now, I've heard the stories. *Usher's always on the lookout for fresh blood to help build Arcadia up there. I'd bet it's the only reason he ever visits Toronto. Why, did you get conscripted into his little army? Did he make you think there was some special connection between him and you? Oh Quentin, that's how he makes everybody feel.*

At first he'd told himself he should be happy about how things had turned out, as though by the strength of his own cunning he'd avoided a trap. But Cam didn't get in touch to apologize, didn't try to woo him back. Until tonight, Quentin had thought he'd never speak with him again. Then, unexpectedly, he'd answered the telephone and found Cam inviting him to a celebration on his property. A party that had already started. When Quentin said it was too short notice, Cam insisted. There was no mention of what had passed between them before.

Come on, you'll enjoy it. Besides, there's something important I need to talk about with you.

He shouldn't have caved in. No one in his right mind would travel three hours on a weeknight at the whim of someone who hadn't spoken to him in months. Yet here he was, searching the darkness for the very man who'd asked him here. Well, he wouldn't play this game any longer. This was the last time he'd ever drive to Mooney's Dump.

Where are you, Cam? he wondered. What's going on under those curly locks of yours? Have you been thinking about me? Or is there something else going on?

The field seemed to have grown, the fenceline was never going to end, the farmhouse that was Cam's last possible hiding place drew no closer. From a place far beyond the barrier beside him came noises: a flurry through the snow, the cry of a jungle cat. Quentin stopped, his chest tightening, his breath coming short and shallow. Somewhere in there was the tiger, pacing.

ONE, TWO, THREE, four, five, six, seven, eight, nine, ten, eleven. One, two, three, four, five –

"Come back here, Zeljka," said her *majka*.

"I'm counting!" Zeljka said. She took big, long steps across the field to the fire and counted them as she went. Her *majka* was behind her and shouted "Be careful!" and Zeljka nodded without looking back. She was going to eat marshmallows soon. When she got to the fire a man with the bag came up with marshmallows for her and she held out her hand but then her *majka* said, "No marshmallows right now, thank you" and he went away.

"We can have marshmallows once we find my friends," her *majka* told her. "Do you see them anywhere?"

Zeljka still wanted marshmallows so she spun in a circle and looked around. Her *majka* had said they were going to meet two ladies, and there were two ladies sitting by the fire.

"*Majka*, I see them!"

Her *majka* shook her head. "Those aren't the ladies we're looking for, my darling." Zeljka wanted a hug, so she ran up with her arms wide and let her *majka* scoop her up, pull her close.

Jelena squeezed her daughter tight and worried that she'd made a mistake. She'd wanted it to be a surprise, but now it seemed the surprise was to be hers. No sign of Marge or Susan, although it was almost ten o'clock. It was silly to have come without warning them. She was exhausted, and so was Zeljka, although she'd napped in the car; Jelena could feel her already falling asleep against her shoulder. She was heavy, too heavy to lift after such a long day of driving, so Jelena sat down on a bench and lay Zeljka on it beside her, cradling her head in her lap, dreading the walk back through the snow. Such a cold country should not be inhabited. Sometimes she wished that she'd raised her daughter in Croatia as she'd planned, before the news from the doctors had brought her to this place again.

That morning in Toronto while Zeljka was at the church playgroup, Jelena had driven to Mount Pleasant Cemetery. Deep within its sanctuary, she'd idled the car at a quiet intersection and not for the first time marvelled at the presence of such tranquility in the middle of the city: the pristine snow, the cardinals and starlings flittering under pines. Dozens of people were out in the sun, walking along the lanes. She wanted to join them but she knew it would be too taxing. Instead she drove to the familiar knoll in the northeast corner and parked at the bottom.

The climb to the plot required all the energy she'd been hoarding. It always felt worse here, as though her body knew the place already and was succumbing in advance. It took her five minutes of stopping and starting to make the top of the hill and the familiar rectangle of earth. She stared at it for a long time and wondered whether she'd shiver if she stepped there.

The names on the nearby headstones were mostly Chinese, with the odd intrusion of a Russian or Pole. The Scots and English had clustered on the western side of the cemetery, as though the place was an enormous map of the world laid out over this part of

Toronto. She thought it strange that it should matter to people, that they should be so concerned to lie among their own kind – indeed, that there were cities of the dead at all. Immense stretches of farmland lay to the north of the city, but no one wanted to be buried in lonely places, it seemed; even in death, they wanted company.

Fireworks exploded in the distance, doubling on the surface of Mooney's Bay. Jelena looked down at Zeljka, asleep on the cold bench, and knew there was no more time for looking. They had to be back in the city by noon tomorrow if she was going to make her appointment with the radiologist, and she needed to rest. She'd have to find a motel. Or perhaps Marge and Susan had returned to their house already, and if she drove there now she and Zeljka would find them sitting by the fireplace, sipping tea, surprised and welcoming. Zeljka wouldn't remember them. Before she'd been born, Jelena had spent her summer holidays in Mooney's Dump at a friend's cottage and become close to Susan and Marge, but this year she hadn't made it up to see them, and Zeljka had been in her play-group the last time they'd stopped by to visit in Toronto. A sad thing. Something that would have to change. She thought of the meeting with the lawyer scheduled for next week, the question she was eager to put to Susan and Marge tonight. It was such an enormous thing to ask of them, but she'd already broached the subject obliquely with Susan on the telephone, and obliquely Susan had indicated that the two of them might be willing.

"Come along, my darling," she said, reaching to stroke Zeljka's cheek. "Back to the car." Zeljka's eyes blinked open. Then she sat up straight in one motion as though she'd been pinched, slid off the bench, and began to walk toward the parking lot, not even looking behind her to see if Jelena was following.

THE SOUNDS of splashing and breaking ice continued as Alice made her way from the shore across the frozen lake. The moon hung above her like a bright stone.

In the darkness she could see a figure clamouring at the edge where the open water began. She shouted toward the wildlife park, called Daniel's name, called Cam's, called for anyone, but it was pointless. Nobody could possibly hear her: midnight had come and gone, the road was bereft of traffic. She'd have to run half a mile back to the party for help. By then it might be too late. She returned to the shore and searched the bushes for a branch, finally finding one as long as herself, thin and covered with dead leaves. It would have to do. Whoever was out there, they'd already gone silent.

The ice was slippery after the day's sunshine, and she took short, slow steps, like someone counting in a new language. Eventually she shifted to her belly, felt freezing water begin to seep through her clothes for the second time that night. There was nothing else to be done, so she crawled along, shouting words of support. She was close, terribly close, when she realized she'd been yelling to one of the tigers.

The animal was pawing at the ice, claws extended and scrabbling. Each time it pressed on the surface, the ledge shattered. The tiger had already begun to break its way through toward land, but there were dozens of yards left and it swam as though exhausted, paddling back and forth compulsively along the edge. With no landmarks to provide perspective, Alice couldn't distinguish its size to tell whether it was Masa or Tamar. Hadn't she just seen both of them in their enclosure a few hours ago? But surely there weren't any other tigers at large on the peninsula. One of the two must have escaped.

She watched as the animal made another futile lurch for safety and smashed through the ice again, submerging completely. When it didn't resurface, Alice crawled closer to the edge, and she imagined its limp body sinking into darkness, then a surge of energy carrying it forward until it was under her and broke through, its open mouth and the frigid lake waiting to consume her. But suddenly the tiger was there again to end the vision, gasping for air like a newborn baby. It must be Tamar, Alice thought. She knew there was no reason for this intuition, except that somehow it made what she was about to attempt seem a little less foolish to her.

With her fist she smacked the ice in front of her, testing its thickness, and when it held she wriggled until she was a few feet from open water, extending the branch the rest of the way.

"Tamar, look what I have for you," she said. "That's it, get the stick. The ice is thicker here. Come on, Tamar, don't be afraid."

She coaxed and entreated until the animal paddled toward her, timid as a child told many times not to accept the offerings of strangers. At the last minute it turned from her and began to swim out toward the middle of the lake, then made a wide arc and returned. It didn't hesitate as it reached the ice but charged up like a locomotive, with a determination that suggested a last effort. Alice was tired too, from the running and the crawling, but she gripped the branch as tightly as she could, both hands fisted around the bark. When the tiger struck the other end, her body was jolted from her fingers to her frozen feet. The animal scrambled over the leaves, ice cracking all around it, and in a moonlit instant as it lifted into air she could see the telltale scars that revealed the animal's identity.

As though in slow motion she felt the weight of his body on hers, pressing over her to safety, sensed the surrender of the ice. She splayed her arms in pointless resistance to the plunge below the surface. Her head went first, smacked against something, her boots filled with water. She thrashed her arms in an attempt at orientation with the lake enveloping her. All for a tiger, she thought, even as she flailed. The foolish dignity of it. When she looked in the direction she thought was up, she saw a round white beacon that could have been the moon or the face of a curious animal.

At first Masa was too exhausted and terrified to move. He lay flat on the ice, frightened that it might break again beneath his weight. The lake had stolen all his heat; he'd never felt so cold. He needed to run now, to gain the shore and feel the fire rekindle in his muscles, but there was no energy for that. The ice was slippery, and when at last he began to edge back toward land, his paws kept sliding out from under him. He wanted to be on solid earth again. In a corner of his mind the enclosure beckoned with its promise of warm straw, if Tamar would share. But now that he'd emerged from the deadly waters, it seemed distant and unappealing. He had the whole horizon before him to explore, the wide earth rolling beneath his claws. There were no sounds except the lap of waves on ice. In a few hours he would be hungry, and then it would be time to hunt.

DANIEL REMEMBERED a day when she'd laid across his chest, listening. *You have a busy heart*, she'd said to him. Now he leaned against a stone at Usher's henge with one hand holding a cup of cider and the other at his neck, feeling his pulse. It was slow and even, and he let it count out the time until she returned. She'd be back soon. She'd have to be. No one was crazy enough to walk five miles home at night in winter. She couldn't stay so angry with him. By now she must have realized that he was sorry for what had happened in Usher's bedroom; she must regret the things she'd said at the roadside. He wanted her to be here beside him. He found himself hoping to see Marge and Susan, even, but it was late and almost time to go if he was going to finish packing tonight. Besides, he'd arrived hours ago and those two hadn't bothered to find him yet, so why should he want to say goodbye? In the distance, the ice on the bay was an indistinct swath of reflected light. Brightest full moon in a hundred years, Alice had told him. The last one of the millennium. A whorl of cloud hung over the town in the west, low enough for the lights from homes and streetlamps to turn it a mustard-gas yellow.

When the music started, the notes were so quiet that he imagined they were from Mooney's Dump itself. Then he saw the people coming toward him, the glint of metal instruments in front. He wouldn't have expected much order from a group that, until a few minutes ago, had been drinking and milling about in the field, but there was a melody growing, a disciplined rhythm, precise harmonies. Behind the musicians trailed a chain of revellers, no more than two abreast, some of them singing, the words unintelligible from this distance, their bodies moving in place even as the line stalled, sped up, turned back on itself, approached the henge. It had meandered all the way across the field and still he couldn't see the end of it.

Others had heard or seen the line of people too, and they were running from all over the field to join in, dozens of them, residents of Mooney's Dump and visitors alike. The head of the train reached the moat and circled around it, then crossed over the bridge with the musicians in the lead. They were single file now, their hands around the waist or shoulders of the person in front of them, moving in a slow forward dance. He appeared to be the only person who hadn't joined, and as he stood by the North Star stone he felt hundreds of eyes upon him. Someone grabbed his jacket, pulled him in, and he found himself moving with his hands on a stranger's hips, rocking from side to side. Thunder sounded under the music, but no one else seemed to notice.

There were other rings of partygoers on both sides of him now, and he wondered if they were they all connected in one long spiral. It seemed that all of Mooney's Dump was here. No, he thought, that was impossible. Where was Mike Pederson, whose face he'd been dreading all night? Where were the hundreds from the reserve? Where were Susan and his mother?

Then he noticed someone. The woman a few people up. He glimpsed the back of her head in the firelight and stumbled for a moment. Alice. The jacket, the jeans looked the same. With the shadows and the flickering light from the bonfire he wasn't sure, but it could be her. When they stopped, he decided – when they reached wherever they were going – then he would work his way along the chain to look.

They twisted like a dropped rope dragging in a lake, uncoiling and drawn in at the same time. The person behind him was yelling something, but he didn't answer. His heart was busy.

"LOOK," MARGE SAID. They were holding each other in the forest, lost, and it felt good and Susan didn't want to look, but she turned her head until their cheeks pressed together, and she saw what Marge had spotted through the trees. A lustre on the horizon: the waters of Mooney's Bay, several miles distant. They'd nearly found their way back to the party after all.

"We were moving parallel to the shore the whole time," Susan murmured. It was her fault, she realized. She'd been the one to suggest leaving the trail in the first place; she'd been the one who was frustrated by Marge's pace and had gone faster because of it, so that she hadn't noticed the land sloping down to the neat square fields below them. From here they could see the grey pit of the rock quarry to the east and, to the west, the darkness of the icebound swamp. Straight on, toward the bay, glowed the lights of Cam Usher's farmhouse. From here it was an easy downhill ski to warmth and safety.

"Only a few more minutes," she whispered into Marge's ear, and kissed it. She meant they'd be there soon, but Marge took it to mean that Susan wanted to stay here a bit longer, the two of them alone in the night, and without speaking she moved her head down until her lips were against Susan's neck. Susan tilted her head to feel the full pressure of Marge's mouth on her throat.

Far below them, beyond the range of their eyes and ears, people were dancing, the pipes and percussion beginning to swell through the open field. They were all holding hands: Bobby Boone and Solomon DeWitt had linked fingers like two old friends, Quentin gazed along the line to Cam Usher, whose missing ring-finger left a cold space on the palm of Hamish Ferry, while farther along, Beatrice and Gabe Wheeler clutched one another's sleeves, remembering a day when they'd stood outside the church and the sun was glorious.

One by one they pass over the moat, steadying each other, trying to maintain the rhythm of the dance, some singing and shouting and some pulling their partners under the arms of people elsewhere in the train so that the line tangles and there's no one direction any more. Haverford Ferry is lifting his boots in time with the music as though they weigh fifty pounds each, Eudora Northey is laughing as Harry Midgard stuffs marsh-mallows into his mouth. Somewhere in that long, long line, Esther Fremlin pulls Stump Weston to his feet, while Daniel Barrie, although he doesn't know why the empty feeling inside him should be any more profound than before, has already begun to mourn, even as he struggles against the ragged tiredness that has been slowly overtaking him all night. Jelena is driving, and beside her Zeljka sleeps as they pass the house where Mike Pederson sings to himself while Oliver rolls over in bed and Nel rises to go to the bathroom. Tamar is pacing in her cage, Phil Whitehead is drinking another beer, Dr. Easterbrook is strum-ming his guitar and Alice is drowning and Bronwen is watching a late-night film in Toronto, Susan is touching Marge and Masa is creeping past the farmhouse trailing steam behind him like a phantom, Mr. Aligarry takes his antacid pills and Archie dreams of people speaking to him in French and Tamar turns another corner and Rocket DeWitt puts Stoddart Fremlin into bed and Marge is coming and Judy Sutter pulls into the driveway now, glad to see that her husband has left the lights on for her, hoping he is still awake, happy to be home.

✦ All of it has been a game, then. Deadly serious, but a game nevertheless. A re-enactment of another night, a gathering two years ago. This evening hundreds of people have been retracing their steps, and dozens of others are playing the roles of those who didn't return. One last bid to discover the truth about a woman's death: this is how Mike Pederson describes it to me from across the table in Cam Usher's kitchen while Bronwen Ferry sits next to him, poring over the hitchhiker's yellow notebook, and Usher drinks coffee in the corner, silent. The two men have yet to speak to one another.

Mike tells me that Bronwen has been working hard. The librarian who claimed to witness Stoddart Fremlin pick up Alice Pederson at the roadside two years ago now admits that she didn't see Alice actually get in the car. The residents of Sunshine have started asking questions again. The police still haven't re-opened the case, but the chief, Harry Midgard, is here off-duty, watching the way things unfold. Since Mike wasn't here at the first celebration, he's had a similar role, wandering among those assembled, waiting for secrets to reveal themselves, hoping for some sudden recollection – that someone left the party early, perhaps, or was seen talking with Alice at a crucial moment. But so far, it seems, the night has been a failure. There are too many movements to reiterate, too much difficulty in re-creating the original night. Mike doesn't seem happy that I've disturbed the proceedings even further, and I wonder if you've been causing similar disruptions, *wherever you are. Then I realize that Cam Usher must have explained what was going on while the two of you were together in the tunnel.*

The townspeople replaying the henge party, two years after it happened. It's such a large undertaking for so slim a chance, when they don't even know how she died, never mind who was responsible. Astonishing, almost heartbreaking, that so many people would agree to return. What new clue could surface from reproducing the night, what memory could be triggered, what story could emerge two years after the fact? But I don't speak these questions aloud.

"What about the First Nations protest?" I ask instead. "Was it real? Or were those white people under the makeup?"

"No, the band agreed to participate when I explained what we were attempting," Mike replies. "Besides, the case is still in the courts. The land is still Cam's. It's not a dead issue for them."

Eventually Bronwen rises from the yellow notebook to confer with Usher and Mike. While they speak I reach for the book myself and begin to flip through the pages.

"There's no great revelation in it, from what I've read," I hear Bronwen say. "Only a few parts mention Alice."

"What were you expecting?" asks Usher.

"I don't know. In San Francisco I thought he might be holding something back, something he saw that night." She shakes her head. "But it looks like he's in Sunshine again, at least. Maybe it's a good sign." She begins to say something else when Usher interrupts her.

"Come on, we'd better get going," he tells her. "We have to meet Daniel."

As Bronwen puts on her coat, I wonder if the clothes she's wearing – the jeans, the mittens, the orange toque – are Alice Pederson's, if these people have been fastidious to that degree in their restaging of the night. I can't decide. Already I've seen Alice's name several times in the notebook, but nowhere is there a description of her so intimate as to reveal the colour of her garments.

"What I don't understand," says Usher as they start toward the door, "is why he asked Robert here to give the book to Alice Pederson." I cringe inwardly at the sound of my name, and I wish I hadn't given it to him at our first meeting. I feel exposed among these strangers. It would be easier if you were with me now, and I want to ask Usher where you've gone.

Bronwen shrugs in response to the man's question. "I don't even know how Richard found out about the re-enactment," she says. Then a voice speaks from across the room.

"I told him. When he called me from San Francisco."

There's a man standing in the doorway. It's you, I think, and I feel a thrill of relief, but then I realize that the figure's red hair has fooled me. This man is thinner than you, shorter. He looks unhappy. The others seem unsurprised by his appearance.

"You two were supposed to meet me on the veranda," the man says to Bronwen and Usher, but the woman ignores the comment.

"You talked to Richard?" she exclaims. "Why didn't you tell me?" She labours to get her arm through the sleeve of her coat as she heads toward the door. Before I can hear the man's answer, the two of them step outside with Usher close behind.

"That was Daniel Barrie," Mike tells me, sitting down across the table. He points to the notebook between us. "You've probably read about him in that thing, how he didn't want to help publicly with the investigation." I nod, encouraging him to continue, even though so far I've read no such thing. "Well, he's agreed to go along with us tonight, at least. An act of goodwill." There's an irony in Mike's voice; his distaste for Daniel Barrie is as clear as it was for Cam Usher.

For a time we just sit there. I read the pages of the yellow notebook while Mike stares at it as though it might jump off the table at him. Then I flip to the beginning and read the first line again. I don't know whether you know Sunshine . . . A tiny, cramped hand, straining to get all of it in. Two hundred pages abandoned to my care. It's not a confession, not a memoir. Instead, it reads like a dry community history. There are details of pioneers, lumber mills,

and land treaties. Some sketches about life on the reserve, speculation about the success of the stone quarry nearby. At the end,
incongruously, a section about the wildlife park written from the
perspective of Cam Usher. On the last page someone has scrawled
in large black letters: DON'T GO BACK.

"What do you think he means?" I ask Mike, holding up the
page for him to see.

"A reminder to himself about the town, or the past," Mike
replies. "Or maybe it's a message to Bronwen: Daniel might have
told him that she's moving to Sunshine." Mike says this quietly, as
though embarrassed by the fact. "It's where she grew up," he
adds. He begins to reach for the notebook, then pulls back. "I
wouldn't place too much value in that thing. I saw your hitchhiker
friend a couple of months ago in California. He's a confused kid.
God knows why he wrote that stuff, never mind why he wanted
to deliver it here. It's a strange way of making peace with a place."
His voice grows deeper, almost angry. "Asking you to give the
book to Alice – who does he think he is?"

I remember again the hitchhiker's smile as he handed me the
notebook. It strikes me now as his final expression of disdain for
you and me, for your pat stories in the car about the ignorance of
rural life, for my complicity in them. A couple of tourists, that's
how we must have appeared to him. City people, arrogant and
gullible, deserving to be exposed as fools.

"I think he wanted to teach me a lesson," I tell Mike. "To
humiliate me."

Mike waves his hand dismissively. "He should have given it to
Bronwen himself, but he's still too afraid of what would happen."
He frowns. "It's like that with half the town. There are dozens
who refused to come tonight. People want to forget."

He drums his fingers on the table, then looks at his watch.
Right now, he says, Bronwen will be walking along the road
toward Mooney's Dump – he uses the old name without self-
consciousness – waiting for Daniel Barrie to pull up beside her in
Stoddart Fremlin's car. A few minutes later the trail of known

334

events will end and there will be nothing left but further specula-
tion. Mike seems impatient for it to be over.

"Usher should be back here by now," he says, out of the blue.
"He's already disappeared a couple of times tonight." I close the
notebook and study Mike's face.

"You don't trust him, do you?" I say, feeling courageous in
phrasing it so boldly, but it seems like a safe guess. He shakes his
head.

"He's not telling us everything." Mike pauses, apparently
unsure whether he should say anything more, but after a moment
he continues. "He claims he only spoke with Alice at the opening
ceremony and then in the kitchen just before she left. But Daniel
Barrie –" He stops again and gathers himself. "Daniel claims to
have found her asleep upstairs in Usher's bed."

I don't know how to respond.

"I'm sorry," I say, before falling silent. Eventually he begins to
whistle the opening notes to a Christmas carol before breaking off
and leaning across the table toward me.

"What about you?" he says. "If you didn't know about the re-
enactment, what are you doing here, anyhow?"

"A friend brought me," I reply. "Maybe you know him. He's the
mayor's lawyer."

Mike nods.

"Sure. Quentin Myles, right? He's Usher's lawyer now too." He
pauses when he sees the grimace on my face at the mention of your
name together with Usher's. "Well, he should have told you what
was going on."

"I don't think he knew about it himself."

It's a few minutes after midnight, past the time when you and I
agreed to meet by the farmhouse. I tell Mike that I have to step
outside, and I leave him to look over the yellow book by himself.

There's no sign of you on the porch. Groups of people still
linger in the snowy field and in the parking lot, their voices a low
murmur for long stretches and then erupting into raucous laugh-
ter. It seems no one wants to leave. A rumble comes from the east,

like an old man complaining that no one will listen to him, and I think it must be blasting from the quarry nearby, the one mentioned so often in the notebook, but then a low hiss rises from the snow and, soon afterwards, streams of water begin to flow from the roof of the porch. Rain. There are squeals and curses from the revellers, pleas for it to stop, but the downpour only grows heavier.

People begin to climb the steps and file past me into the house, a trickle of them at first, then an unending flow, ascending in twos and threes, none of them acknowledging my presence even as I hold the door open for them. I think of the piles of boots inside, the melting slush, the accumulating odours of alcohol and damp clothing. There'll be no room to move in there – everyone standing back to back, narrow corridors between bodies opening briefly, then closing, squeezing people along like involuntary muscle. Hurry, I think. Hurry back to me. But even the rain doesn't conjure you. I don't know where to look next. An infinite number of things could have happened to you by now; you might be headed anywhere.

A man comes up the stairs and pauses beside me. It's Cam Usher.

"Is Mike still in there?" he asks me, gesturing toward the farmhouse door. When I say that he is, Usher leans against the porch railing as though reluctant to enter. With this man beside me I feel anxious, eager to be elsewhere. I remember your conversation with him in the icy tunnel. Was that during one of the disappearances that's worrying Mike? Where else might Usher have disappeared with you?

"I came with a man named Quentin tonight," I say after a time. "Do you know where he is?" Usher stares at me, apparently surprised, and I think that now he must realize I'm the one who overheard you and him, who ran away across the field.

"Quentin?" he replies. "Last I saw him, he said he was going to look for somebody." He continues to watch me. "I suppose he must have meant you." Right now, I think, he'll be wondering *how much of his conversation with you I took in. He'll be trying to decide whether the discussion might have revealed something about him that he wanted to keep private. Selling the wildlife park. Procuring archeological certificates. He sounded like a man under siege, and now he looks it too. But if he has suspicions about me, he doesn't share them.*

I decide not to enter the house again, not to say goodbye to Mike. Instead I mutter a farewell to Usher and go down the stairs, past faces I will never meet, checking each in turn, looking for you. There are people whose eyes seem expectant, as though they've been watching me on the porch and are waiting to be introduced, whose gaze is so insistent that I'm sure they're about to shout out my name, but I pass by them without a word.

As I walk down the long lane from the parking lot to the road, the rain goes on, a steady shower, not torrents to flood the world, but enough to wash away the snow, to cleanse the sidewalks and clear the frozen bay of footprints, so that tomorrow, after the sun has risen, everything will sparkle. Perhaps in Sunshine the sky is already clear. But the downfall has obscured the head of the bay and the town's lights have vanished from view.

Upon reaching the main road I see a figure waving in the distance. It's Daniel Barrie, not you, I tell myself. At first I wonder if I'm the one he's trying to signal, but he's too far away for me even to be sure that he's facing my direction. By the time I reach him, he's walking toward me, and he passes without even a nod of acknowledgement. There are tears in his eyes. I watch him turn down the lane and disappear. Then I continue on toward the place where I remember you parking, not quite sure that I'm going in the right direction. How could I have forgotten? I could be heading toward the reserve, for all I know. A part of me hopes to see Bronwen Ferry along the way, a familiar face to reassure and orient me, but there's only the lake on one side and on the other a great stretch of swampy bush: cedars and sumac and red scrub willow.

In the place where I expect your car to be, there's an empty space. You couldn't have left, I tell myself – perhaps it was farther ahead – and I keep walking. A few minutes later I come to a single vehicle on the shoulder, a door partly open. It's not your car. The engine is silent but the overhead light is on. Through the static of a radio, Bing Crosby sings "White Christmas." The windows are fogged as though someone is inside. I pass it and go on, heading, I imagine, toward the invisible town in the darkness.

ACKNOWLEDGEMENTS

For their attention to technical matters I'm grateful to Harold Baker, Robert Juričević, Tamsin Kostzrewa, Cam Loucks, David McGill, Hrvoje Mihanović, Matthew Peros, Jim Van Wyck, and Joy Ward. Dawn and Bill Loney hosted me graciously, as did Derek Caveney and Amelia Glaser. Oliver Emanuel, Sara Heitlinger, Andrew Motion, Siobhan Phillips, W.G. Sebald, Natasha Soobramanien, and Luke Williams were generous readers. Marcy and Bruce McGill, Laura Robinson, and Carolyn Smart gave good advice. Sara Salih's contribution is immeasurable. My thanks to Dan Franklin, Jennifer Lambert, Ellen Seligman, and Euan Thorneycroft for their enthusiasm and commitment.